The
Golden Lady

by

Roberta C. M. DeCaprio

The Golden Lady

Cover Art by *Nicola Martinez*

The Wild Rose Press
PO Box 708
Adams Basin, NY 14410-0706
Visit us at www.thewildrosepress.com

Publishing History
First Cactus Rose Edition, 2009
Print ISBN 1-60154-593-2

Published in the United States of America

Amanda swallowed the despair in her throat and looked up at the night sky, holding her tears in check. The chill of the night whipped against her. She pulled the collar of her robe higher on her neck and thought how nice the warmth of a fire would feel.

Again he read her thoughts. "I would build a fire, but that could draw the enemy near."

She edged closer to Proud Eagle, covering him with the blanket, and scanned her surroundings. "Do you think they still might be on our trail?"

"Chiricahua are cunning trackers and fierce fighters. None of them can be *zonta*, trusted."

She sighed. "If that's true, then what do we do?"

"We wait till the first morning light."

She tucked her feet beneath her to keep them warm. "What good can that do if they are as fierce as you say?"

"I think by that time they will make their way back to their camp to eat their *yuta*, and I will take you home."

She glanced down at the clothes she wore, now all she owned. "My home and barn are by now burnt to the ground. I pray my horse and cow didn't burn with them." She sighed. "And only God knows what happened to my poor old dog."

"I did not mean your home, Golden Lady."

She frowned. "Then whose?"

He responded matter-of-factly. "Mine."

Praise for *The Golden Lady*

"The Golden Lady is a story about a strong woman who follows her heart across cultures. Richly flavored with authentic language, this tale has all the elements of romance and adventure that make it a great read."

~Deb Tompkins, The Wild Rose Press Author of Mike the Molly and Me

Acknowledgements and Dedication

The Golden Lady was originally written in 1983, after my friend Sue Maloney brought me my first romance novel to read. It was titled "A Rose In Winter" by the Queen of Romance, the late Kathleen E. Woodiwiss. I was so inspired by her story, I decided to write a novel of my own....and so my journey began.

There are several others who took the journey with me that deserve a note of thanks:

To my parents, Carmela and Anthony DeCaprio for their constant support.

To my children, William Jr. and Tammy, who were small when this all began. I was so intent on writing this novel I didn't notice them throwing a frisbee in the house. To their spouses Keith and Laurie, and my granddaughters, Fiona and Mia.

To my dear friends Linda Shaulis Shannon, for typing the first draft many years ago, Sandra Duval Hart, for her constant belief that one day I'd be published, Sara Mann, who devours everything I write, Laurel Ostrander Straight, Linda Andrews Beckering, Sandra Baxter, Gregg Millett and Carilyn Covey Clarke for their continuing encouragement.

For family members who buy all my books; Kathy Doyle Marx, Amy Barone Cannizzo, Peg DeNofio Wos, Debra Jean DeNofio, Judi Doyle Downey and Joan Doyle Duprey.

To my first advocate and editor, James W. Stanco and the late Irene Carr.

To fellow authors Diana Gabaldon, who showed me where to find good research information, Elaine Raco-Chase, who put me onto Romance Writers Of America and the workshops the group offered, Sherrilyn Kenyon and Dianna Love Snell, for their informative conference talks and for purchasing one of my books.

Thanks to these critique partners for their sharp eye and writing skills: Author/friends, Mariah LeGrand, Deb Tompkins, Elaine Stock and Jackie Kearney.

For my sisters: Helena and Cynthia DeCaprio.

For Robert Francis Mace, a 9/11/01 World Trade Center victim, who dreamed of being a writer.

In memory of my beloved Dachshund, Penny O'Scarlet, who died at the age of 18 on November 22, 2008 and my Bengal Cat, Simba Lady who died nearing the age of 19 on December 17th, 2008. They always sat at my feet as I wrote; now they're looking down on me from heaven.

To my husband James C. Lemke, who urged me to take the manuscript out of the file cabinet after 25 years and try again.

And lastly, to my editor Patricia Tanner at The Wild Rose Press for her help and patience and for being an advocate, making it possible for me to share a love story so close to my heart.

Author's Note:

All historical research was obtained through information written by Donald E. Worcester, from his book *The Apaches, Eagles of the Southwest.*

All cultural research was obtained through information written by Thomas E. Mails, from his book, *The People Called Apache.*

All Apache language research was obtained through information written by Madeline Baker, from her online list of Lakota/Sioux and Apache words and meanings.

Chapter One

Willow Creek, Arizona
September, 1864

Amanda looked down at the front of her dress, arms, and hands. All stained with Ethan Gregory's blood, her father's blood. Crimson caked and sticky, her knuckles whitened as fingers tightened around the saddle horn. Paralyzed with fear, she wondered how she managed to stand, walk, leave his faceless body. The fearful images replaying in her mind numbed her with grief and confused her. When did she saddle the horse, straddle his back, and ride away?

The pungent odor of death clung to her nostrils. Her stomach lurched, and she swallowed hard, fighting the nausea rising to gag her. The bitter taste of vomit stung the back of her throat, panic squeezed her lungs.

Please, Dear God, just let me make it to town.

Her racing heart thundered in her ears as she glanced with hawk-like vigilance into the trees lining the side of the road. She knew she couldn't trust the silence surrounding her. There could be more of them hiding in the woods.

Digging her heels into her mount's side, she urged him to go faster. "Hurry, Todd," she choked out, the chilly night cooling the tears slipping down her cheeks.

The old horse picked up his pace, not needing guidance. She had ridden him hundreds of times down the same path. But tonight the road into town was longer and more frightening. Her head swimming through a haze of emotions made her all the more thankful Todd knew the way.

Around the bend, the tiny white clapboard house came into view. Dizziness blurred her actions. She pulled her horse to a stop and pried terror-stiffened fingers from the reins before sliding to the ground.

With legs weaker than thin blades of grass, she climbed the steps to the parsonage. With what little strength remained, she reached for the door-knocker and waited an eternity for the thick oak portal to open.

Reverend Joshua Holmes surveyed her appearance; his large blue eyes mirrored her terror and a flicker of sorrow passed over his face.

"My God, Amanda," he whispered, helping her into the house and slamming the door shut with a booted foot.

She moved toward him on unsteady legs, placing a trembling hand upon his chest. The words stuck in her throat.

He drew her close. "You're safe now."

His heart raced in the same fast pace as her own.

"You're safe now," he repeated, gathering her into his strong embrace just before her knees buckled beneath her.

"Please, Reverend, come help me bury my father," she whispered.

"Grace!" The reverend's voice trembled with emotion when calling out for his housekeeper.

The Widow Thomas hastened to the foyer, her eyes sweeping over Amanda in horror. "Mercy me. The blood!"

"I don't think it's all hers, but I can't be sure." He headed down the narrow hall, to his room, his strong arms holding her close to him.

"I'll get a basin of water and some cloths," Grace

announced and headed for the kitchen.

Numbed by grief, Amanda didn't protest when he laid her on the bed, his eyes searched her face before checking her for wounds.

Her gaze broke from his, to glance around the sparsely furnished room where he took his slumber. Surely he meant well, but—

To her relief Grace hurried through the doorway. "'Tain't fittin' for ya to be doin' that, Reverend."

The reverend ignored Grace, fumbling with the buttons on Amanda's blouse. Still she couldn't speak, couldn't stop him.

A chubby hand stilled his. His cheeks flushed, and he stepped aside. "I only mean to help her."

"I'm here for that." Grace pointed to the door. "Ya get now. Go on," she insisted, "and let me get doin' what I need to for this poor child."

He threaded his fingers through his hair and looked down into her eyes.

He knows the war of emotions wracking my soul, wrenching my heart. My pain is also his.

"Go on, get now," Grace urged.

He hesitated and searched her face with deeper empathy, waiting for her to speak. But still the words stuck in her throat.

Then he stepped farther away from the bed and cleared his throat. "Perhaps I should take care of your horse."

"Good idea. Wouldn't want the critter wanderin' away," Grace agreed. She dipped a cloth in the basin and pushed aside a flaxen curl from Amanda's forehead before washing her face. "You're so fond of the beast, and all, aren't ya child?"

All she could muster was a nod.

"Aye, that you are," he said, resigning to her silence with a sigh. "I would appreciate when you're able to speak—"

3

She nodded again.

"I'll call ya," Grace interjected.

It was his turn to nod now, making his way out of the room and shutting the door behind him.

"Now, child," Grace whispered. "Let's get ya cleaned up."

****

Amanda put her lips to the white china cup and sipped the herbal tea Grace brought her. The hot brew settled her stomach, but did nothing to comfort her mind. She stared ahead, entrenched in thought. How could she ever wipe from her mind the horror she witnessed? The sorrow that followed left her entire body aching for rest. Yet her mind wouldn't allow such peace. Her shattered nerves reacted to an unexpected knock at the door, and she jumped out of her skin, spilling a bit of tea down her chest.

Reverend Holmes peered into the room. "Amanda, may I come in?"

"Yes," she whispered, placing the cup on the bedside table. Modestly, she arranged the stained, oversized nightgown Grace had loaned her.

He moved to the foot of the bed and gave her a timid smile. "Are you feeling up to talking?"

She drew a deep breath, giving him a nod.

The reverend pulled the rocker nearer to the bed and sat, folding his hands in his lap. Patiently he waited for her words.

The way he taught, preached, listened; all of it was done with a patient calm. She marveled over this about him.

She cleared her throat of the large, thick lump of grief that settled there.

He reached for the cup of tea and offered her a drink.

She took a sip and handed the cup back to him, resting her head on the pillow.

"Take your time, Amanda."

A deep, unaccustomed pain filled her breast. "Papa and Duke left early this morning to go hunting. Never—never would Duke leave a hunt without my father." She swallowed the sob rising to choke her. "So when he returned home alone I knew something wasn't right." She closed her eyes, remembering how the dog barked and whined, demanding she follow him. Tears slipped down her cheeks, and the reverend stuffed a handkerchief in her hand.

She opened her eyes, tears clouding her vision. She dabbed them away, the crisp white handkerchief filled with his citrus scent. "I followed Duke to where the creek forks, and that's—" She gulped, fortifying herself to continue. "That's where I found Papa's body. He had been attacked by Indians and there was—" She closed her eyes but the scene was vivid in her mind. "There was so much blood." She cringed, knotting the quilt beneath her chin. "We need to bury him."

"It would be unwise to attempt such a task in the dark." He reached over, helping her to release the grip on the quilt and straightening it over her shoulders. "Tomorrow I will go."

"We will go," she corrected.

He stood. "Rest now."

She reached out a hand to stop him. "Please, don't leave." Again tears trembled on her lashes. "In my mind I see him still—staring, the twinkle gone from his eyes."

He sat now at the edge of the bed, his tone soft, sympathetic. "I'm so sorry."

"And his hands. They were lying there so still. Papa's hands were never idle. If he wasn't chopping wood or hammering nails, he was stoking the fire or playing the violin." She wavered, comprehending the fact her father's hands would never move again.

Amanda stiffened when he pulled her to him,

cradling her in his arms and stroking her hair. "My heart aches for your loss, Amanda."

She hesitated only for a second before his kindness overwhelmed her, and she relaxed, wrapping her arms around his neck and burying her face in his collar. "I'm sorry to intrude on your home like this, but I didn't know where else to go."

"You're not an intrusion. You never could be." He tightened his embrace. "You did right by coming here."

"I'm alone now, Reverend. All alone."

"Nay, Amanda, that's not true," he whispered, placing a tiny kiss atop her head. "You still have me."

****

Josh stared out the open window of his den. Stars graced the night sky; a cool breeze filled the room with the aroma of the late summer blooms from the parsonage's garden. He shivered and closed the window, staring down at his hands upon the sill. For a moment he was carried to another place and time—to his homeland. He remembered now the flowers he and his sister, Marietta, picked for their mother.

She'd smile and say, "Ah, these blooms give me a cheerful heart." Then she'd quote Proverbs. "And a cheerful heart is good medicine."

If only he could give the people of Willow Creek a dose of such medicine. There was anything but cheerful hearts in this town, in spite of the long, hard prayers for the Indian attacks to cease. Right now all he had—all any of them had—was their faith, a hope their petitions didn't fall on deaf ears. With each uprising he felt forsaken and could only imagine the spirit of those with lesser convictions.

A knock at the door brought him from his thoughts, and Grace walked into the room without waiting to be invited.

"Just wantin' to let ya know Amanda's finally asleep."

Josh rubbed his hands over his eyes and turned from the window. "That's good; it's been an exhausting night. I'm glad she's finally able to rest."

"Well, a bit of my sleepin' herbs mixed with the tea helped." Grace plopped her matronly form on a nearby chair. "Poor child, she's been through hell and back." She dabbed at her eyes with the edge of the apron she wore. "Thank God she's got ya."

Josh sat wearily in the desk chair, his thoughts traveling back to when he first arrived in the Arizona territory. A young man of twenty, he felt the Lord had led him from his home in London to this land once governed by Mexico, and to the newly formed settlement of Willow Creek.

"It's the least I can do for her." He sat back in his chair. "When I came here six years ago, Amanda's mother took me under her wing. She introduced me to all the families in town and brought me homemade cornbread after Sunday services. Her efforts made me feel at home in a new place."

"Ah, I remember Amelia Gregory." Grace smoothed back the gray tendrils escaping her bun. "My recollection is she sounded just like ya...came from yer homeland."

"Aye, but she was from Brighton, England, I believe."

Grace sighed. "It was a sad day when the fever took her." She clicked her tongue. "She was so young, so beautiful and full of life, with a lovin' husband and a child to rear." Shaking her head, she sighed again. "Ah, Amelia's passin' sorrowed us all."

"Ethan and Amanda were beside themselves with grief," he remembered.

"But ya comforted them, Reverend. And it was remarkable the way ya took over Amanda's

7

education." Grace smiled. "Ya were just a saplin' yerself, yet ya handled everythin' real fine. Look what a wonderful young lady Amanda has become."

Josh returned the smile. "There's no denying that. She's far from the twelve year old girl I first met. Tall, gangly, long golden braids falling past her shoulders, and a spray of freckles dotting her nose."

Grace giggled. "I remember her bein' a headstrong youngin'. Why, I recall Ethan threatenin' her constantly with takin' a switch to her bottom."

Josh chuckled. "And those threats didn't faze her in the least."

Grace folded her arms across her chest. "That's cuz she knew he wouldn't do it." She frowned. "He should have, a time or two. Children need to be disciplined or else they run amok."

Josh mused. "She followed me everywhere, asking all sorts of questions. To look at her then, no one would have ever believed she'd blossom into the beauty she is now."

"Yup, the caterpillar has certainly turned into the butterfly."

He leaned forward in his seat. "Do you remember when the first three children orphaned by Indian attacks arrived at my door?"

Grace's eyes saddened. "Sure do, poor babies, seein' such horror."

"Amanda was there to help. She was only fifteen years old at the time, yet she fell easily into the nurturer's role, cuddling the children when they cried or singing them a lullaby."

"And helpin' me bathe and feed the tykes," Grace added. "Don't know what I would've done without her."

Josh pinched the bridge of his nose with a thumb and forefinger. "Well, she needs me now, more than ever, and I won't let her down."

Grace stood, untying the apron string around

8

her thick middle. "Ya gonna rebuild her world again, Reverend?"

Josh sighed. "I'm sure going to try."

Grace nodded. "Thought ya might." She shook her head. "That poor child."

There was nothing adolescent about the beautiful, young woman now in his bed. She had come to him in need...but in truth, it was he who needed her. When he held her close and touched her hair, torrents of feelings unleashed from deep within. He hoped with all his heart Amanda would turn, in the days to come, to him for comfort...and love.

Aye, for love, too.

Tonight he'd come to the realization he kept at bay for a very long time. He was falling in love with Amanda Gregory.

Grace made her way to the desk and arranged a few papers into a neat stack. "I fixed up a cot in the sittin' room for ya."

"I'm going to sit with her a while; I think she's frightened to be alone."

"It's understandable, after what she's been through," Grace sympathized. "But she won't be wakin' anytime soon."

Josh arched a brow. "How much of the sleeping powder did you give her?"

"Enough to keep her restin' till late mornin'." Grace reached forward, giving his arm a pat. "Getcha self some shut eye. Ya ain't gonna be no good to her if'n yer not fit to wear ya boots."

Josh shook his head. "Grace, what would I do without you?"

She gave him a playful wink. "Ain't gonna let ya find that one out, Reverend."

****

Amanda blinked her blurry eyes into focus and looked over at the empty rocker. Was it all a dream, or had she seen the reverend sitting there, head slumped forward, a Bible clasped between his hands? She sat up, rubbing her throbbing temples, and gazed over at the open window. The birds sang, the sun shone bright in the sky. Everything was the same as the day before, and yet, it was all so wrong. Papa would never again come through the door, hungry and dirty after a day's work. He wouldn't talk to her or see another day begin. How then, did life go on? Shouldn't there be an unbalance somewhere? Shouldn't things be different?

Her thoughts were interrupted when Grace barged into the room carrying a tray. "Brought ya some chicken soup, child." She handed Amanda the bowl and a spoon. "Now that ya had a long rest, I think ya should be takin' some nourishment."

Amanda grasped the white pottery with both hands. "Just how long have I been asleep?"

Grace sat on the rocker. "Quite a spell, it's nearin' noon."

"Noon... I've slept half the day away!"

"And now ya need to eat."

"No, now I need to bury my father." She placed the bowl on the bedside table and pushed aside the quilt, sweeping her legs off the bed. The sudden movement caused her head to spin. She reached for the bedpost to steady herself.

Grace stood. "Sleepin' herbs sometimes does that to a body." She helped her back into the bed and beneath the coverlet.

She laid her head against the pillow and closed her eyes. "Why did you give me sleeping herbs?"

"It was the only way to get ya to take a rest, child."

She bit her bottom lip, forcing herself to stay calm, before she opened her eyes and looked up at Grace. "At this moment, I am more distraught to think I've waited this long to bury my father. Wild animals could be..." She broke off, not wanting to imagine the possibility.

Grace sat at the edge of the bed. "The good reverend's already taken care of everythin'." She gave Amanda's leg a motherly pat. "Ethan's at peace with the Lord now."

She covered her eyes with her hands. "No. No, this is all wrong," she protested. "The reverend knew I wanted us to go together."

"He wanted to spare ya seein' it all over again, child."

She folded her hands across her heart, staring at the ceiling. "But I'm his only kin, Grace. I should have been there to bid him my love, to say my goodbyes."

"You can still do that."

Her attention spun to the door where the reverend stood. "How can I?" She sat forward in the bed. "It's too late."

Grace stood to leave. "I'll let the two of ya work this out."

The reverend took a seat on the rocker. "It's not too late. Speak to your father's spirit through the leverage of prayer. Bid him farewell through God."

She plopped against the pillow again, staring up at the ceiling. "How can I live without my father?"

Reverend Holmes leaned forward. "Look at me, Amanda."

She stayed silent, continuing to stare at the rafters.

"Listen carefully to what I have to say." He rose from the rocker to sit at the edge of the bed. "Weeping for our losses is good, but we should not weep like those who have no hope. There are three certainties of death for us to rely on. The first being, our soul doesn't die, it sleeps with Jesus. Second, Jesus will one day come for every believer. And third, we will all meet again. I pray you keep these

11

certainties foremost in your mind in the days to come. Relying on them will keep your grief from swallowing you up as it has for many in this house."

He spoke of the children she helped care for, their grief robbing them of their senses. There were five of them now at the parsonage, three boys and two girls. Jenny and Paul still sat and stared, as she did now. She understood the comfort being lost from the world allowed. Within your own thoughts you could relive the days you spent with the loved ones that were gone. She could close her eyes right now and be back at the farm, listening to Papa play songs on the violin, sharing a meal with him, hearing his laughter.

"I knew you'd want this."

She turned to see the band of gold he held. "Papa's wedding ring," she whispered, taking it with a trembling hand. She stared at it hanging on the tip of her finger. "I don't believe I ever saw Papa without it, even after Mama died."

"And that surprises me; men aren't known to wear wedding rings."

Amanda smiled. "Mama insisted...Said if she was expected to announce to all she was taken, he should, too."

The reverend chuckled. "That sounds like your mother."

"He also always carried his father's pocket knife." She frowned. "You didn't happen to find it, did you?"

"Nay, I found nothing other than the ring."

"Are you sure?"

He nodded.

"The handle was made of silver," she went on to explain, "with tiny inlaid abalone chips along the side."

The reverend shook his head. "Sorry, Amanda, the ring was all I found."

She sighed. "Hopefully Papa left it in his armoire. Otherwise the Indians must have taken it." She fingered the band. "Wonder why they didn't steal the ring?"

"It's weapons they want, knives and guns."

Amanda sat forward again and pulled a gold chain from beneath the neckline of the nightgown. "I'm glad they left it." She opened the clasp; sliding the ring onto the chain. It clicked against a smaller one. "Now it can join Mama's. I have to believe they're joined, too. In heaven."

"I believe that as well."

"Papa couldn't bear it without Mama."

"He grieved just as you are now. But all the tears he shed couldn't change what happened. And Ethan knew, for your sake, he had to rise above the pain and carry on."

A tear escaped the corner of her eye. "He had me to carry on for; I have no one."

The reverend wiped it away with a gentle brush of his thumb. "I'll take care of you."

She looked deep into his kind blue eyes. "You have so much responsibility with the children, your congregation. I can't ask you to—"

"You didn't ask," he interjected. "I offered. A man cannot find happiness when he lives only for himself, and I would be honored."

"Why?"

He smiled. "Because I have... I have—"

Grace bounded into the room. "Brought ya some clothes, child."

Amanda fingered the lace of the nightgown. "Guess I can't stay in this."

Grace looked over at the bowl of soup. "Why, you haven't touched a drop."

The reverend stood. "Now you need to eat." He made his way to the door.

"Wait. Did you bury Papa beside my mother?"

"Aye, Amanda, I did."

She nodded and reached for the bowl of soup, swallowing past the lump of grief growing in her throat.

****

In the days following her father's death, she threw herself into the tasks at the parsonage, caring for the children with greater empathy. She moved from the Reverend's room to share one with the girls. Jenny, catatonic since her home had been attacked by Indians, slept right beside Amanda. Being so close to Jenny prompted her decision to become more involved with the girl's recovery.

While brushing Jenny's hair, she noticed the child's eyes focusing on the reflection in the mirror. She watched Amanda pull the brush through the long black curls. A lone tear escaped Jenny's mental prison and cascaded down her cheek.

"What is it, Jenny?"

The child's voice was toneless. "They killed my mama." She shivered. "Next they will kill me."

"No. That's not going to happen." She wrapped her arms around Jenny's shoulders and rocked her back and forth.

In the months Jenny had been at the tiny refuge, she never responded to their kind words or gestures. All she did was sit and stare with blank eyes, needing to be fed and washed, her mind unable to cope with the horror she'd witnessed.

Amanda, getting down on one knee, stroked Jenny's cheek. "Everything is all right now. You're at the parsonage and you're safe."

The child blinked, opening the gates to her sorrow. "Mama brushed my hair."

She smiled through her own tears. "She loved you very much."

Jenny nodded. "That's the truth; she did, because she helped me to get away."

She looped a long dark curl behind Jenny's ear. "She wanted you safe."

The girl clenched her hands in her lap. "But I shouldn't have run. I should have helped her."

She placed her hand over Jenny's, giving it an affectionate squeeze. "There was nothing you could do."

The child frowned. "What can I do now?"

She looked deep into Jenny's dark eyes. "You can continue on with your life, as your mama wished for you to do. And one day you will grow to be a beautiful woman, birthing babies of your own. That will make your mama very happy."

The episode with Jenny took a toll on Amanda. She could empathize with the child now and prayed tonight would be a new beginning for Jenny. Wondering what new beginning lay ahead of her without Papa, she made her way to the kitchen and poured herself a cup of tea from the kettle.

Sitting at the tiny table, she glanced around the tidy kitchen. Grace Thomas certainly did her best to make the place cozy. She reached out and fingered the yellow-checked curtains at the window. They were worn, but clean, as was everything at the parsonage.

The vase of wildflowers in the center of the table brought a joyous burst of color. She leaned forward and inhaled their scent. Of all the rooms in the vicarage, she loved this one the best, especially at mealtime. The aroma of Grace's cooking filled the place, making everyone's mouth water in anticipation of what was soon to be served.

She took another sip of tea, her thoughts expanding on how nice it would be to stay here forever. But how would it look to the folks in town? Reverend Holmes was an unmarried man, and her residing in his home just wasn't decent, even with the Widow Thomas around to act as a chaperone.

Besides, she'd imposed on him long enough with the daily trips he took to feed and milk the cow. It was her farm now, and she had to work it.

"Or at least try to," she said aloud.

"At least try to do what, Amanda?"

The reverend had entered the kitchen and now poured himself a cup of tea.

"I need to go home, take care of the farm."

He took a seat beside her. "That's nonsense."

She frowned. "How is that nonsense? It is my home, it's where I belong."

"Nay, you belong here."

She blinked with bafflement. "I don't understand how I could. It would be most inappropriate, don't you agree?"

He stood and paced. "Oh, I'm making such a shambles of this."

"Of what?"

He moved to the window and gazed out. "It wouldn't be inappropriate if you were my wife."

The heat rose to her cheeks. "Your wife!"

"Aye, my wife." He cleared his throat, turning to look at her. "Your kindness and love for the children here go far beyond your duties. It's obvious you belong here."

"Well, being an efficient helper is hardly a reason for you to marry me, Reverend."

He combed his fingers through his unruly hair. "I didn't mean to imply that would be the reason I'd want to wed you."

She folded her arms in front of her. "I'm listening."

She studied him as he strode about the kitchen again. He was honest and gentle, and no doubt he'd be a caring and loyal husband for some woman. But not for her. Mercy, he was—well, he was like family.

He halted his pacing a second time and stood looking down at her; his large blue eyes gazed deep into hers. "In watching you, I'm awed and amazed at the woman you've become." His square jaw tensed. "You ask what other reason there could be to wed you."

She nodded.

"It's the only thing one can do when he's fallen in love."

The blood raced through her veins, heating her face. "Are you saying you've fallen in love with me?"

A wide grin broke over his face. "Aye, Amanda, I am."

Her head spun. "Oh, mercy."

He knelt down on one knee beside her chair. "I'm sorry, Amanda, for being so selfish."

She was astonished by his apology. "You've been nothing but giving and caring."

He shook his head. "You're still in a state of shock over your father's death. Now is not the time for me to ask for your hand in marriage."

Trembling, she reached for the tea, taking a sip. It would be so convenient to be able to stay here, help with the children, and be spared the agony of returning to an empty farm house. But she couldn't marry him for just that reason alone. He deserved a woman who would answer his proposal without hesitation. She couldn't do that.

"I don't know what would have become of me if you weren't around. When Mama died, you were the rock Papa and I leaned on. You got us through a difficult time, and to say you are not etched deep in my heart would be a lie. But I—I can't..."

"Accept my proposal," he finished her sentence and stood, making his way again to the window.

"I'm sorry, I just can't think about such things now."

"I understand." He turned to her and forced a smile. "Could you think about using my first name?"

His attempt to put her at ease forced a smile in

17

return. "I believe I can manage that." She sighed. "And you understand I need to return to the farm?"

He arched a brow. "Going back to the farm is out of the question. It would be better for you to take a room at the boarding house."

Her spine stiffened. "I will not."

His brows drew together. "Can't you see how unwise it would be for you to be so far from town? What defense would you have if your property were to be raided by Indians?"

She struggled to maintain a calm tone. "About as much as the other farms and cabins that have fallen prey to their destruction. It matters little if a place is occupied by a man. He is murdered right along with his wife."

"You can't seriously believe you could live on the farm alone."

She pushed back the chair and stood. "Joshua Holmes, not only do I believe I can be alone, but that I can handle the farm just fine to boot." She picked up her cup and placed it in the dish basin. "And tomorrow I will begin proving it to you."

He moved to stand beside her. "What are you saying?"

She placed hands on hips. "I'm going home tomorrow."

"Nay, it's way too soon," he argued.

She raised a defiant chin. "I think not."

The reverend combed his fingers through his hair. "Listen, you needn't feel I'd press you into marriage if you remained living in town."

"That thought never entered my mind," she reassured him. "I just need to go home. It's the only way I will ever be able to make peace with all that's happened." She softened her tone. "Don't you see?"

He let out a long audible breath. "Very well, then. I'll ride back with you to make sure you're settled in safely."

She gave him a taut nod. "I thank you, Josh," she added.

His gaze caught and held hers. "Your spirit and determination make you a remarkable woman. Any other in your place wouldn't stand the test." He sighed. "I've watched the way you've healed the children's wounds, even after you've suffered your own. That makes you a wounded healer."

"And do wounded healers ever heal?"

"Aye, they do, Amanda, with the healing of others."

****

Amanda wiped the perspiration from her brow with the back of a hand and helped Grace strip the last bed. The intense heat made the smallest of tasks unbearable, and the tiny second floor bedroom felt like an inferno.

Grace Thomas, walking to the open window, used the hem of her apron to blot the beads of perspiration forming on her plump face. "Not even the slightest breeze is stirrin'. I'm a tad bothered by the crazy dang weather we have in these here parts, hot durin' the day, cold at night." She sighed. "Reckon I'm gettin' older than I figured. Arizona's climate never bothered me before."

She came to stand beside Grace. From the advantage point of the upper floor, she could see most of the town's main street. Together, she and the elder woman watched the usual hustle and bustle taking place below.

The parsonage stood on one side of the church, the graveyard on the other. Across the street she could see Miller's General store. "Jonas Miller is setting out fresh vegetables this morning."

"Humph! Only because he's tryin' to impress that new woman who owns the boardin' house," Grace griped.

She giggled. "Guess you're right, here comes

Abby Freeman now."

Grace clicked her tongue. "My, my, she's sure expressive when she talks."

A dust devil frightened a traveler's horse in front of the livery stable, which was beside the hotel and saloon.

Grace frowned. "That stranger better calm that critter. There's nothin' more dangerous than a spooked horse," she mumbled. "That horse is mighty bothered." She turned to Amanda. "We're all bothered. It's the dang heat."

She placed a gentle hand on Grace's arm. "I think something more than the heat is bothering you."

"Yer right, child, somethin' else is botherin' me."

"What is it, Grace?"

"Ya leavin' here, and takin' yerself back to that there farm." She wagged a chubby finger. "Yer gonna be a sittin' duck out there all by yer lonesome, with them Injuns runnin' around."

She sighed, exasperated. "It's foolish to believe I could stay in town, Grace, when I have a farm to tend."

Grace's gray eyes widened. "What's foolish is ya askin' for trouble, and the reverend's allowin' ya to go without puttin' up a fuss to stop ya!"

She grew annoyed. "He has nothing to say about the matter; it's my decision and my life."

"Oh fiddle-faddle! The two of ya ain't got a lick of sense between ya." She placed hands on her large hips. "And if I could, I'd put the both of ya over my knee and knock the sense into ya." With that she stormed out of the room.

At first, she was astonished at Grace's outburst. Then, picturing herself and Josh rubbing their bottoms after a spanking made her giggle.

"Something amuses you?"

She turned with a start to find the reverend

leaning against the door frame, arms crossed over his chest.

"Just something Grace said that struck a funny note."

His eyes twinkled. "Do tell. I could do with a little humor myself."

Amanda hesitated, not knowing if he'd find the situation as funny. "Grace believes a good spanking would bring some people around here back to their senses."

Smiling, he boldly focused his gaze on her backside.

She blushed, covering her bottom with her hands.

Josh chuckled. "Now, why didn't I think of that?"

****

Amanda placed the basket of food and fresh-cut wildflowers Grace gave her on the seat while Reverend Holmes tied her horse to the back of the carriage. Casting a glance to the back of the wagon, she spotted her saddle, clean now of the blood staining the horn. She knew he had washed it for her, not wanting her to relive that night of terror.

It bothered her he hadn't spoken to anyone during the afternoon meal. She knew his silence was the result of her decision to leave.

He climbed into the wagon beside her, taking the reins. The carriage moved forward, and she concerned herself with the scenery along the way, but the silence grew awkward. At this rate, the few miles' ride to her farm would seem like an eternity.

Unable to bear another moment of silence, she faced him. "You say you understand my feelings about returning to the farm, but you really don't."

He kept his eyes ahead, jaw muscles throbbed. "I can understand your reasons without liking them, can't I?" He frowned, looking her way. "I'm concerned for your safety. Can you understand that?"

She clasped her hands together in her lap. "I can take care of myself."

"Ah, I keep forgetting."

"Well, I can!" she said. "Besides, I'm the only one who will suffer the consequences."

"You're wrong, Amanda," he snapped. "I too shall suffer the outcome."

"Well, there is no need for you to."

He laughed sardonically. "Are you daft, woman? Undoubtedly you must realize when someone cares for another, they also pay the price for their actions."

She shifted in her seat, kept her eyes ahead. "I'm far from daft, Josh. Confused, perhaps, but not daft."

"What confuses you?"

She weighed her words. "I've spent hours lying awake in bed these past few nights, trying to make sense of all that's happened. I've asked myself over and over, what's crazier...the injustice of the tragedy or trying to live with it afterward? I believe my life will never be the same again." She shook her head in frustration. "What possible reason is there for any of this?"

"Man was given a free will, Amanda, and with that free will, man will destroy himself."

"My father was a healthy, vibrant man who had a lot of life left to live. And he never hurt a soul. Why him?"

"You may never know the answer to why your father was taken from you, but sometimes from tragedy comes victory."

"In what way can any of what's happened be victorious?"

"The reason is not for us to know, but in time all things fall into place. There is a season, a time for all things. And this is a time of mourning. But after the grief comes a time for laughter, as well—a new life, new plans."

She frowned. "What kind of new plans?"

He shrugged. "I can't say for sure. We're small players in the grand scheme of things, but when it all unfolds, we'll all be in our rightful place and understand our part."

"You certainly haven't missed your calling. You're right where you should be, and I bet God is downright proud you're on His side."

He smiled. "Nay, I'm the proud one, Amanda, to be on His side."

The carriage came to a halt in front of the farmhouse. Duke came running from the woods. He was glad to see her, looking like he survived on probably a diet of wild rabbit and squirrel. He was a resourceful old dog and never failed in his search to track down small game whenever he'd gone hunting with Amanda and her father.

Josh untied Todd from the back of the carriage, checked the barn and the surrounding field while she made her way to the fresh dug grave.

"I love you, Papa. I'm so sorry I lost you so soon," she whispered, placing wildflowers on the mound of dark dirt. She bowed her head and prayed for a sign Papa heard her.

An eagle's call echoed in the sky. She raised her eyes to see him soar. In spite of the tears slipping down her cheeks, she smiled.

Eagle folklore was something Ethan Gregory had known well. He was amazed and awed by the great bird. As a hunter, her father admired the eagle's ability to glide slow and silent down to catch its prey, always an accurate strike.

"So good are they at getting food," he'd tell her, "they spend the least of the time hunting and most of the time soaring to vast heights in the sky. Not really in the world, but of it."

Her mother had taught her early Christians believed the eagle was the symbol for resurrection. In Egyptian hieroglyphics the eagle was the symbol for the warmth of life.

"An eagle's energy heals and aids creativity," her mother would say. "Their spirit awakens a new birth, a powerful new dimension to life and the force within the world."

Amanda wiped the tears away with the backs of her hands, her own spirit renewed. In spite of all her sorrow, she felt the new dimension in her life beginning. Even the reverend said new plans were on the horizon. Fueled with hope, she bid her father a final goodbye, took a deep breath, squared her shoulders, and made her way to the house.

Though she had been away only a few days, there was much to do. The kitchen, sitting room floors, and the modest wood furnishings were covered with dust. But she was almost thankful for the chores. Keeping busy would keep her sane.

Josh cleaned and loaded the rifle, placed it beside the door, and filled the water barrels on the back porch. When dusk approached, he gazed out the window, looking torn. "I hate leaving you."

Apprehension seized her chest, making her second guess her decision. It was easy to say she could be alone when she was at the parsonage, but now—

"I'm fine," she lied, and gestured around the room. "I've a big day tomorrow with all the cleaning."

He took both her hands in his. "Then eat the meal Grace prepared and get some rest."

She nodded. "After I put fresh coverlets on the bed, that's what I intend to do."

At the door, he hesitated. "You needn't worry yourself about helping out at the parsonage in the morning. You'll need several days to straighten things out here. Grace and I can manage, and some of the older children can help as well. I'll stop by tomorrow to see how you're doing."

She raised her eyes to meet his. "Give me at least a week."

He frowned. "I'm not comfortable with that, Amanda. There's so much going on in these parts right now."

"A few days, then?"

"Very well. A few days it is."

She smiled. "Thank you for everything."

Josh gave her a taut nod. "God bless, Amanda."

A wave of icy fear clenched her heart as she watched him drive the carriage down the path and disappear around the bend.

Duke nudged her hand.

She bent down and scratched him behind his ears. "Oh, Duke."

He wagged his tail at the sound of his name.

She looked around the room. "Papa's gone." She went down on one knee beside the old hound. "We're all that's left."

He licked the tears slipping down her cheeks.

She hugged him. "We're going to be fine, aren't we, boy?"

Duke barked in response.

She stood and reached for the rifle by the door, rechecking it for ammunition. "But it never hurts to be prepared."

****

She woke to the Arizona heat and more work to be done. The heavy chores strained her back and blistered her hands. She winced as she rubbed the honey-based salve into them. The sweet-smelling balm relieved the burning of her rough, cracked flesh. Now she understood why Papa had been so tired each evening, wanting nothing more than to eat a meal and go to bed.

There was no ointment to relieve her aching heart, though, and each day the emptiness at being alone ate at her insides. Thoughts of Papa led her to look through his armoire for the missing pocket knife. When it was nowhere to be found, she sat down amongst the clothes she had scattered about in her search and wept. The emotional strain was just too much to bear.

She decided not to replace Papa's things in the armoire. Instead, she folded them together and bound them with cord. The reverend, when he returned in a few days, could take them to the folks he knew who would make good use of them.

Amanda looked at her father's things in a bundle on the bench by the door. What a small legacy. Papa had one good suit. He'd worn it for Sunday services, the harvest dance, and funerals with his work boots. Mama had hated that. She believed a man needed a pair of shoes, minus the farm muck. But Papa couldn't see wasting money on something he'd wear only a handful of times. A few work shirts, overhauls, a pair or two of long johns, and an old coat made up the rest of the bundle. Then there was the violin, stashed away now in its carrying case. She had no intentions of parting with the instrument. Papa had taught her how to play, and the songs would remind her always of him.

After gathering Papa's belongings, she took an inventory of her own. Not much in itself, just a Sunday dress and bonnet, a few skirts, blouses, robe, nightgown, and undergarments. What she cherished most was her mother's Bible, wedding dress, and a quilt Amelia had brought with her from England. It was handmade by Amanda's maternal great-grandmother, passed down from generation to generation. These few heirlooms meant nothing to anyone but her, and she couldn't bear to think of them being destroyed if an Indian attack should befall the farm.

Before packing the treasured objects together in a knapsack, she took the Bible over to her mother's writing table, and turning to the family's births, deaths, and marriages page, read the names of her ancestors.

Wilson Bentley still lived, but his wife, Cornelia Hastings Bentley, was deceased, passed on a few years before Amanda was born. Her mother's younger sister, Kaylena, also still resided in Brighton. She remembered her mother telling stories about Kaylena, and now Amanda wondered if her aunt looked like Amelia. The Bible entry stated Kaylena's age to be ten years older than Amanda. At the time Amanda's mother left England, Kaylena was just a young girl. Would she be married now? Did she have children of her own? Was Wilson Bentley a crotchety old man, or did he have a sense of humor? To think, in England, she had family. A grandfather, an aunt, perhaps even an uncle and cousins. But with the miles of vast ocean separating them, she would never have the opportunity to meet her only next of kin.

She dipped a quill into the inkwell and entered with a careful script, the day and year of her father's death. Then, placing the Bible with the other items, she secured the top of the knapsack and set it down on a bench by the door, alongside the violin. Should she have to make a quick escape, everything would be handy to grab.

That is, if I'm still capable of grabbing anything.

She shivered.

****

Another day passed, and Amanda was pleased with her efforts. Each night she dropped into bed from total exhaustion, but her labors bore fruit. The farm had begun to take on the warmth of home once again, in spite of the loneliness. Her solitude was interrupted at midnight when she was awakened by pounding at the door. She threw a robe over her nightgown, lit a lantern, and hurried to the front room. Sara Driscoll, hysterical with fright, held her baby daughter Katie in her trembling arms.

She didn't have to ask what happened. An alarm of terror sounded deep within her as she pulled Sara into the house and secured the door.

"That won't keep them out," Sara screeched. She hoisted a crying Katie farther upon her hip. "The filthy savages won't stop at a door!"

Katie screamed louder in her mother's arms, a mixture of tears and snot running down her face.

Amanda took Sara by the hand and led her over to a chair beside the fireplace. "Sit," she said, taking the crying baby. "You need to calm yourself for Katie's sake."

Sara ran trembling hands down the front of her skirt. "Yes. Yes, for Katie's sake."

She patted the child's back and searched her neighbor's face. Sara, only in her mid-twenties, looked much older. Lines of fear were etched deep upon her thin, delicate visage, the soft gray eyes filled with terror. Long strands of brown hair, pulled loose from the braid that hung to her waist, clung to her neck. She was cut and bleeding, and her dress was dusty with sand.

"Did you run through the woods to get here?"

Sara nodded, crossing her hands over her chest. "Katie's hungry. I was just about to feed her when..." She looked away, into the fire.

Amanda swayed her hips back and forth to sooth the child. "Sara," she said, afraid herself of the answer. "Where is Charlie?"

The other woman looked at her with trembling lips. "I don't know. I-I think they killed him." Sara's fingers squeezed her temple. "He saw the barn burning and ran out with his gun...told me to grab

28

Katie and head over here."

"Oh, dear Lord," Amanda whispered.

"Heard about your Pa." Sara's voice was toneless, eyes stared straight ahead. "Planned on coming over on the morrow to pay my respects." She shook her head "Good Lord, what's to become of us?" The tears left wet streaks down her sullied face. "My poor, dear Charlie."

"I'm so sorry, Sara."

Sara cast another glance her way and pointed to Katie. "She's hungry. Has a soiled diaper too." She rose from the chair with an unnatural stiffness, making her way to Amanda. "I gotta get her cleaned up, or else she'll get a rash."

"I'll get something for you to put on her." She handed the baby to Sara and went to the cupboard for clean cloths. "One of these can be used for a diaper." She took a large pitcher from the shelf, grabbed the rifle, and headed for the back door.

Sara's voice rose. "What are you doing?"

"I need to fill the pitcher from the water barrel on the porch."

"No! Don't open the door," Sara pleaded.

She held up the rifle. "I'm armed."

"That won't stop them. Especially if there's more than one."

A chill ran down her spine, and she leaned against the door. "We need the water, Sara."

Sara's gaze darted around the room. "No, what we need is to get in the carriage right now and away from here. Go into town"

"That would be worse."

Sara shook her head from side to side. "No, what's worse is to stay here and wait for them Injuns to attack. We need to get to town. Then, you see," she babbled on, "Reverend Holmes can take me to my sister's house in Tucker's Corners. Away from this place. Away from them."

She pronounced her words slow and stern. "Listen… to… me."

Sara snapped her mouth shut and stared at her.

"It would be more dangerous for us to be on the road," she continued in a softer tone. "Best we stay here, ride out the night. Tomorrow the Reverend's due to come by, and he'll take you and Katie with him back to town."

Sara frowned, casting a quick glance at the pitcher in Amanda's hand. "And why haven't you enough water? What kind of housekeeper is it that doesn't have the household jugs filled at all times?"

She sighed. "A very tired one, who didn't think she'd need water until morning."

Sara clutched Katie to her chest. "The Injuns can come by day or night."

"That's true, Sara, but—"

"They attack at any time," Sara interjected. "It matters not to them. They're savages."

Katie started crying again.

"Sara, please calm down, you're upsetting Katie."

"Heathens, murderers, the devil's spawn," Sara rattled on, her voice rising.

"Enough!" Amanda shouted.

Again, Sara clipped her mouth shut, staring with wide eyes.

"All you say is true, but right now we need water," she reasoned.

Sara bit her bottom lip. "Very well. Get the water. But be quick about it." She paced back and forth. "Yes, yes, be quick. They could be near. They could be very, very near."

It had taken several hours to calm Sara, and Amanda could help her wash and care for Katie. The frightened guests finally fell asleep on her bed, leaving her to take refuge in her father's room. Lying wide awake, she gazed at the window. An open shutter slat had allowed the moon to cast its light across the floor, and she ran a hand over burning eyes, listening to the night sounds.

She yawned, but dared not take her own rest. Sara and Charlie Driscoll's farm was only a stone's throw away. Would the Indians attack again tonight? And if they did, would her farm be next? She swallowed the lump of fear lodged in her throat. What could she do with only one rifle and two others to protect? The fear-filled thoughts running through her head fueled the decision to go with Sara into town when Josh came again to the farm. In fact, she wished Josh were here now to take them.

As a child, she'd played the wishing magic game, whereby she thought up strange and far-fetched scenarios, wishing them to come true. Such things came to mind as a flying carriage, able to take people to places miles and miles away in very little time. Another was the magic letter, which could be sent to someone far away in a blink of an eye. She wished she could send a magic letter to the reverend, asking him to come for her and Sara, and him being able to fly to their aid.

She wouldn't be in this fearful predicament if she had stayed at the parsonage.

The reverend's words echoed in her thoughts.

There is a reason...a purpose for all things.

If she'd stayed at the parsonage, there would have been no one to help Sara tonight. What would the poor woman have done?

She rose from the bed and went to the window, searching the night for shadows.

Duke was restless too. She heard him fussing at the back door, wanting to get out. If he continued to scratch and whine, he'd wake Sara and Katie.

She reached for her robe and lit a lantern, making her way to the kitchen. "I'm praying you just smell a rabbit, boy," she whispered, setting the lantern on the table and opening the door just enough for Duke to squeeze out.

She locked it behind him and peered through the window. The old hound marched back and forth beside a form on the ground. Her hand went to her throat. Could it be?

"Oh, my heavens, Charlie... Charlie Driscoll?"

She reached for the lantern and rifle before opening the door.

Duke ran to her, wagging his tail. When he threw back his head and howled, she cringed. "Quiet, you'll wake everyone." The last thing she needed was Sara and Katie awake and hysterical again.

Duke's ears flattened to his head, and he returned to the shadowed bulge. Back and forth he stalked, growling deep within his throat.

She walked out onto the back porch and hung the lantern on a hook, positioned the rifle, and aimed. "Charlie? Charlie, is that you?"

The bulge groaned.

She made a quick sweep of the area before moving closer. "Oh, God, please let this be Charlie."

The lantern cast enough light for her to see just who did lie groaning at her back door.

It wasn't Charlie Driscoll.

Chapter Two

Even in the dark, Proud Eagle could see the insurmountable fear and horror on the young woman's face. With trembling hands, she raised the rifle, bringing the barrel to rest against his temple.

"I wish you could understand my words, you seething son of the devil," she hissed. "So I could tell you how much I hate you and your kind before I pierce your skull with a bullet."

His flesh burned, his throat was parched, but with his last bit of strength he forced the words to come. "I understand your tongue."

Her eyes widened. She stepped back, stunned.

He coughed. "I will not hurt you. Please, do not shoot." He licked his dry lips. "*Guesa*. I need water."

"You need to die, you stinking Indian," she snarled. "Retribution for the lives you've taken—my father's, Charlie Driscoll's, and many more."

He coughed again. "I beg now for your mercy. I will not harm you."

"You're right on that account, because I'm not giving you the chance." She cocked the trigger. "You'll never be able to harm anyone ever again. And as far as mercy goes, you'll get from me as much as you've given."

He thought of grabbing the gun. One yank and he'd be able to wrench it from her. But he was too weak to raise his left arm, and the gaping wound in his right shoulder rendered that arm useless. "Please, do not shoot. I speak the truth. I have not killed any of your people."

He watched the play of emotions cross her face.

She wrestled with whether she should pull the trigger or not. He swallowed hard, a fleeting ray of hope washing through him. If she was having second thoughts, it meant she had never killed before. The right words might spare his life. For now, at least.

"Another Apache tribe has done the killings you speak of."

She laughed sardonically. "You think I believe what you say?"

The little strength he had was leaving him. "I have no way to prove my words." His eyes blurred, and he blinked to clear them. "But what if I speak the truth?"

She set her chin in a stubborn line. "Either way, it matters not to me."

He arched his brow. "No? You would *zas'tee*, kill an innocent man?"

She glared down at him, her golden hair framing her beautiful face.

The throbbing pain of his right shoulder ripped through him. He pleadedd with her one more time. "Please... help me."

Amanda squeezed her eyes shut, his last agonized plea for help stilling her finger on the trigger. What if he was right? What if he was an innocent man?

Right now he was an unconscious man. Maybe it would make it easier to kill an unconscious person.

Oh, sweet mother of God, how does one kill a person at all? A mixture of confusion and fear gripped her heart like a vise.

Her eyes lingered for a moment on the ugly wound on his shoulder, his tunic soaked with blood. The memory of her father's bloodied body filled her thoughts, and again she cocked the trigger. As horrible as this was to do, it must be done.

"But not by me," she whispered. "Let the authorities deal with you."

When Josh arrived he could summon the law, and all of it—the farm, the wounded Indian, would be out of her hands.

For now, though, she had to get him out of sight, for Sara's sake.

She ran to the side rail of the porch and grabbed the rope hanging on a hook. With trembling hands, she tied his wrists and ankles, grabbed the rifle, and ran down the darkened path to get Todd.

Adrenaline coursed through her body. She'd bound him like a pig on its way to be slaughtered. After tying the rope to the horse, she dragged the Indian, groaning each time his head struck against a rock, to the barn. She secured the door and sat for a moment on a large rock to catch her breath. Her heart raced with the exertion.

All she could manage to carry, while guiding Todd, was the rifle. She had to leave the lantern back at the farmhouse. Only a sliver of light from the crescent moon lit her surroundings. Her gaze darted to the dark woods, and she feared more of his kind would come looking for him.

Panic pushed her to run back to the farmhouse. Her foot caught on something in the vicinity of where she'd found the Indian. She scurried to her feet and discovered a spear...his weapon. Was it the one he used to—

Her stomach lurched. Her vision spun.

"Not now. Not now," she whispered, willing herself to be calm. This wasn't the time to collapse. Hesitating, she picked up the spear and shoved it under the back porch. She grabbed the lantern, held it high, and whistled for Duke. The hound bolted from the woods.

She locked the door behind her and leaned against it, gasping for breath. "You caught yourself a good one this time, boy."

Duke wagged his tail, pleased with himself.

She scowled at the dog. "Don't look so happy. This catch is trouble with a capital T."

Amanda placed the rifle by the door and noticed the blood staining her hands. She shuddered with revulsion and went to the basin. The water ran red as she washed. Her captive's wound was deep. If she left him unattended all night, he'd probably die.

So what if he did? *When the authorities get him they'll only hang him anyway. Better to die this way.*

She scrubbed her hands with the cake of lye soap. If the Indian man died in the night, it would spare Josh the trouble and Sara the trauma. The poor woman had been through enough already.

The thought of leaving him to bleed to death in her barn disturbed her.

As much as I hate his kind, I can't be the one to let him die.

She had to help him. No matter if he told the truth or not, whether he was innocent or guilty, it wasn't up to her to judge.

She cleaned the mess and emptied the basin out the back door, then looked around to make sure no signs of blood remained anywhere. The last thing she needed was more questions from Sara. Next, she filled a canteen with water, ripped cloths for bandages, and stuffed them in her robe's pocket, along with a jar of the sticky, healing salve and a knife. On tip-toe she went to find the bottle of whiskey Papa kept for medicinal purposes and an old blanket. Making sure Sara and Katie were still sound asleep, she grabbed the lantern, and the rifle.

When she pried open the barn door, moaning assailed her. She hung the lantern on a nearby hook and aimed the gun at him. "I have decided not to deny you my help."

He gave a weak nod, his eyes red-rimmed and filled with agony.

"But you're staying tied, and if you make a

move, even just one small motion to make me feel threatened, I will leave you here to die. Do you understand me?"

His response was weak. "Yes."

She placed the rifle within quick reach, and pulling the cork from the whiskey, brought the bottle to his lips. "Here, drink this."

He lifted his head and drank.

She pulled the knife from her pocket and slit the V-necked tunic apart. It was made of buckskin, like the breeches tied at his waist with a rope.

Heart racing, she cut away the bloody material from the wound. After washing her own hands with the whiskey, she poured a little on his shoulder.

He clamped his mouth shut, the muscles at his jaw throbbing.

"Sorry, I know it stings, but it will help to keep the wound from becoming infected."

From the canteen, she poured water onto a cloth and washed his torso and arms. Bronzed and void of any hair, his chest was muscular and hard.

His large dark eyes watched her every move.

Her hands trembled as she applied the ointment and bandaged the wound.

He winced and coughed.

She gave him another swig of the whiskey.

He coughed again.

This time she moistened another cloth and washed his face. With each stroke, the dark blue paint from the center of his forehead to his chin faded. The geometric design extending downward and to the end of his nose, once gone, revealed a face with perfect features.

"I'm sorry I can't do more."

He relaxed and closed his eyes. "You are doing fine."

She removed the headpiece of three hawk feathers adorning the crown of the thick black hair that hung to his broad shoulders and covered him, wrapping the blanket around his moccasin-clad feet to keep him warm. The footwear, curved upward at the toe, was decorated sparingly with painted designs and beadwork.

She gathered the bloody rags and threw them into an empty barrel nearby, daring not to bring them back into the house to be washed with Sara around. She stashed the clean rags, the knife, salve, and whiskey on a shelf for the same reason. In the morning, she'd need to redress and clean the wound again, before Josh arrived.

She reached for the gun, canteen, and lantern, then made her way out of the barn, satisfied she had done her Christian duty.

Now, the rest was in God's hands.

****

Katie's cries snapped her awake. She rose from the bed, feeling like she hadn't slept at all.

In truth, she hadn't.

She dressed and made her way to the kitchen, where she found Sara feeding Katie. The baby sucked at her mother's bosom while Sara rocked back and forth, eyes staring ahead.

"Let me make you something to eat as well, Sara," she offered.

Sara rocked faster. "Charlie. We need to find Charlie."

"Reverend Holmes is expected today. He'll take care of everything and get you back to town."

He'll take us all back to town.

Sara switched Katie to the other breast and continued rocking.

Amanda sighed and went about making biscuits and a beef broth.

When Sara and Katie lay down for a nap, she returned to the barn. With her rifle in tow, she brought the Indian a jar of broth and a canteen of fresh water. While raising his head to bring the water to his lips, her fingers brushed his flesh. He was burning with fever. She listened to his delirious babble as she swabbed his forehead, neck, and chest with a damp cloth.

"Oh, God, you're so sick," she whispered. She cleaned and redressed his wound, realizing by all rights the man needed a doctor. But that wasn't about to happen.

No. She was just saving his neck for the noose.

A sudden chill ran down her spine at the thought. What confused her more was why his demise bothered her. The man was an Indian and deserved to die.

He opened his eyes. "Please. *Guesa*."

She raised his head again and helped him drink a few sips from the canteen, searching his face. A handsome face at that. His eyes, red-rimmed and pain-filled, tugged at her heart. She knew she couldn't stand aside and watch him be taken away. But if she helped him, it meant she'd have to stay back, too.

"*Ashoge*. Thank you," he whispered.

She offered him the soup. "I've brought you something to eat. It's just a beef broth, but it will help you to regain your strength."

What am I doing? If he gets his strength back he might do me serious harm.

But after drinking the broth, he again lapsed into a feverish sleep.

She rubbed her tired eyes and stood. Every bone and muscle in her body cried out for sleep. She sighed and reached for the rifle, securing the barn door.

Sara stood waiting for her in the kitchen, wringing her hands in front of her. "Where have you been?"

She placed the rifle down by the door. "I was in

the barn, doing chores."

"How could you just leave me here? Alone!" Sara's gaze darted to the window and then the door. "They could have come back, and what would I have done with a baby in my arms and no rifle?"

"I'm sorry, Sara. Truly I am." She moved beside Sara, touching her arm. "Would you like a cup of tea?"

"Not right now," Sara said.

She glanced at Sara's untouched plate of biscuits sitting on the table." You haven't eaten a thing. How will you take care of Katie if you don't keep up your strength?" She pried Katie from Sara's arms and led the woman to the table. "If you're not fit to travel, Reverend Holmes won't be able to take you all the way to Tucker's Corners."

Sara popped a biscuit in her mouth. "He has to take me," she said, her mouth full. "I need to get to my sister's place, and away from here."

That's not all Josh needs to do.

After he learns about the Driscoll's farm, he'll have to return to find Charlie's body for burial. She sighed. "Josh is a good man who is severely overworked. That's why I want to serve him a warm lunch. Perhaps you could help me peel potatoes for the stew?"

Sara nodded in agreement and stuffed another biscuit in her mouth.

****

She ran to the door when she heard Josh's carriage, flung it open, and stepped out onto the porch. "Am I ever glad to see you."

He climbed down from the carriage and made his way up the porch steps. "Then am I to believe you've had enough time alone and will accompany me back to town?" He gestured to the wagon. "I drove the carriage instead of riding my horse, in the hopes you would."

She leaned against the porch rail. "Well, at this point I'm not alone. Sara Driscoll is here with her baby." She went on to explain about the Indian raid on the Driscoll farm and the probability Charlie had been murdered.

Josh sat beside her during lunch, and she did her best to bring a bit of normalcy to the mid-day meal. But there was nothing normal about living in Willow Creek anymore.

She forced a smile and spooned stew into a bowl for him. "How are Grace and the children?"

"All are well. In fact, Grace has made apple cobbler and a stuffed goose for supper." He searched her face. "Please, Amanda, accompany Sara and me back to town."

She stood, ignoring the request, and poured them each a cup of tea.

Josh cleared his throat. "The Driscoll farm wasn't the only homestead attacked. I received word as I was leaving to come here. The Callahan farm was also destroyed."

Her breath solidified in her throat. "Did anyone survive?"

Josh shook his head. "I'm afraid not. I'm sure you can imagine how worried Grace and I have been for you, after learning about the Callahans." He glanced over at Sara, sitting opposite him at the table. "And now the Driscoll's..." His voice trailed off.

She grabbed the biscuit bowl before taking a seat. "I understand your concern, really I do. Both farms are so close to mine, but I can't leave right now."

Josh frowned. "Why can't you leave, Amanda?"

She bit her bottom lip. "I just can't, but soon—soon I will."

"When it's too late? When I am called to bury your body?"

She ignored his question, offering him the plate

of rolls. "Would you like a biscuit, Reverend?"

His frown deepened. "No thank you, Amanda, I can barely swallow the tea."

"You should listen to him," Sara snapped.

She turned to face Sara. "I appreciate your concern, but I'm fine."

Sara's voice rose. "You won't be for long. Nope, you'll be murdered in your bed, the house burning down around you."

She wiped her sweaty palms down the side of her skirt. "Don't say such things, Sara."

"Well, its true, that's what will happen, just like poor Paul and Ida Callahan, and all those sweet-faced youngins... and my Charlie," Sara added, tears streaking her cheeks. "Haven't we all been through enough?"

She stood and went to the grieving woman, draping an arm around her shoulders. "Everything will be fine, Sara, once you're with your sister in Tucker's Corners."

Josh arched a brow. "Her sister lives in Tucker's Corners?"

Both women nodded.

"That's a two-day ride out and back." He combed his fingers through his hair. "By the time I lay Charlie and the Callahan family to rest, and drive Sara to her sister's home, God only knows how long it will be before I can return."

Sara motioned to Amanda's room, where Katie slept. "I'd say more like three days out with a baby in tow."

His voice was rough with anxiety. "I'm afraid it's out of the question you remain here alone for so long, Amanda."

She squared her shoulders. "There is no question here, Reverend, only fact. I cannot—" She clipped her tongue. "I mean, I am not leaving," she corrected. "Do I make myself clear?" she snapped, storming out onto the front porch.

Why didn't he just leave her alone?

Her frustration rose to the roots of her hair. If she hadn't found the wounded Indian, she would have jumped at Josh's offer to leave. She could stay at the boarding house. But how could she manage that now?

She glanced out at the barn and bit her bottom lip. If she told Josh about the wounded man, the authorities would execute him. If, in truth, he were innocent of any wrong doing, turning him in would be morally wrong. On the other hand, he could just be biding his time until he was well again. Then once he regained his strength—

She frowned. With that in mind, how could she *not* tell Josh?

"Amanda?"

She turned to find him standing behind her.

"I'm sorry. I had no right to be so—so—"

"Bossy," she finished his sentence.

"Aye. But if I'm bossy it's because you're stubborn." He folded his arms across his chest. "I've never met a woman so bent on having her own way."

"It's a trait admired in a man," she retorted.

"And we suffer the consequences for it as well."

"I'm willing to face my consequences. I've told you that before." She walked down the steps and sat on the bench by the tree.

He followed. "It doesn't have to be this way."

She looked up at him. "Yes, it does."

He sat beside her, his tone softening. "Why, Amanda? Why does it have to be like this?"

If I could only tell you the truth.

She covered her face with her hands. "I'm tired, Josh. Too tired to go into this again with you." She raised her gaze to his. "Please, just take Sara Driscoll to town before I go mad."

He broke out in hearty laughter. "She's that

43

bad?"

She rolled her eyes heavenward. "You have no idea."

He arched a brow. "How marvelous, and I have the wonderful opportunity of her exclusive company on a carriage ride for three days, with a baby."

She giggled. "I don't envy you in the least."

He looked around the farm. "I'd say in comparison, Indian raids aside of course, staying here alone is paradise."

She nodded. "I believe so as well."

His gaze rested on Duke, whining and scratching at the barn door. "What's ailing that hound?"

"He probably just saw a rabbit sneak through a hole," she lied, and stood, making her way up the stairs, hoping he'd follow.

Instead, he walked to the carriage. "Nay, I think there's more to it than a rabbit." He pulled a rifle from beneath the seat. "Maybe I should have a look." He hesitated, looking at the weapon in his hand.

Would he even be able to pull the trigger if need be? Being a man of God and taking vows to uphold peace and forgiveness, he'd find it hard to end a life. But, even if that were true, the authorities would be notified and they wouldn't think twice.

She was down the stairs and to his side in seconds, taking the rifle from his hand. "No. That's not necessary."

He was surprised by her reaction. "Amanda, what is it?"

She forced a smile. "It's nothing, really. I just don't want to get Sara all riled up again." She laughed. "You don't want to go through that, trust me."

He shot a worried glance at the barn. "But I should take a look in the barn, just in case."

"I was just in there a few moments before you

arrived," she lied. "All clear."

He pulled his watch from his vest pocket and made a note of the time. "I've been visiting for over an hour. Anything, wild animal or intruder, could have entered during that time."

"A larger, more dangerous animal couldn't get into the barn. Papa made sure of that when he had his prize chickens housed there." She replaced the rifle beneath the carriage seat. "And if it were Indians or another type of intruder wanting to do malice, do you really think we'd still be standing here talking?"

"Nay, you have a point." He sounded relieved.

"Come with me now," she said, taking his arm and walking with him back to the house. "And finish your tea before it grows too late."

"Aye, I suppose I shouldn't travel at night with Sara and her baby along."

"It wouldn't be a wise move, Reverend." She cast a quick look at the barn. "Not a wise move at all."

****

Amanda helped Josh get Sara and Katie situated in the carriage before handing him her father's belongings. "I know you can find someone who can use these things."

Josh hesitated to take the bundle. "Are you sure it's not too soon for you to give them away?"

"I'm sure." She forced a smile. "Papa would find it wasteful for his things to just sit in the armoire when someone could benefit from having them."

"Aye, that is the way Ethan was." He inclined his head. "I thank you, then, for your generosity."

She waited for the carriage to round the bend before she dashed into the house to fill the canteen and prepare a bowl of potato stew. She grabbed a spoon, the rifle, and headed for the barn.

Duke met her on the way, wagging his tail and sniffing the aroma of the stew. "You almost caused a catastrophe this afternoon, you crazy old hound."

He twirled in a circle.

She laughed. "Your darling antics aren't getting you any of this potato stew."

He sniffed in the other direction and spotted a squirrel. In an instant, he was off and running after his lunch.

The only light in the barn was from a side window, so it took a moment for her vision to adjust. She placed the bowl on a crate and found the cloths and salve she had stashed, and then knelt down beside him.

His breathing was labored as he slept.

She wet a cloth and swabbed his face and neck.

He opened his eyes. "I am glad to see you."

She brought the canteen up to his lips. "I'm sorry I couldn't come sooner."

He remained silent while she cleaned and redressed the shoulder wound.

"Are you hungry?"

He nodded, raising himself to a sitting position.

She reached for the bowl and spoon and fed him. "It's not much, just potato stew."

"I could feed myself, if you would just cut the rope."

She looked down at his bound wrists.

"I gave you my word I would not harm you."

She raised her gaze. "Tell me your name."

He smiled. "I am called Proud Eagle."

The sound of his name seeped in to disturb her. *Eagle, his name is eagle.* Is his coming another sign? But a sign of what?

She placed the bowl and spoon on the crate, controlling waves of confusion. "Well, Proud Eagle, if I cut your hands loose, what's to stop you from…"

He arched a brow. "When I give my word, I keep it."

She frowned. "But you see, I have no prior proof

of that."

His lips twisted into a lopsided grin. "If I can trust the *woyute*, food, is not poisoned, then you can trust I will not harm you."

"Well, it's not that simple. Besides, you have no choice but to trust me."

He chuckled. "*Nzhoo*, very good point, but here is one you should keep in mind. With your care I will grow stronger each day. Soon, these ropes will not hold me." He searched her face. "Is it not wiser to declare a truce now?"

She glared at him. "Do you really believe I could call a truce with you?"

Amusement left his eyes. "Tell me this, then, do you have no bad men among your people?"

She remembered the stories she heard of cattle rustlers and bank robbers, as well as the outlaws holding up the stagecoaches, killing innocent travelers. Her thoughts clouded with unease. "We've had our share."

"And if one white man is bad, does he make all *indah's* bad?"

The fact he'd spoken the truth annoyed her. "No."

His voice was low and smooth. "It is the same with my *nuhdee*, people, there are those who are *inju*, good, and those who are bad. Do not hold against me what I did not do."

She hesitated, mulling over his words. Then she reached for his hands and untied the rope, doing the same to those tied around his ankles. "There, you are free."

He smiled, and looked over at the bowl of stew. "Free to feed myself."

She handed him the food, reached for the rifle, and stood.

He inclined his head with polite thanks and ate the stew. "Please, sit."

Reluctantly she obliged, keeping the gun across her lap.

His large black eyes searched her face. "What are you called?"

The tenderness in his expression amazed her. "I am Amanda. Amanda Gregory."

His bold gaze observed her hair, roamed to her eyes and lips, then he smiled. "Golden Lady fits you better."

****

The temperature dropped, as the nights did in Arizona. Without a shirt and only a blanket to keep him warm, she worried for Proud Eagle, but even more at the alternative of bringing him into the house.

In the end she decided to let him warm himself by the fire. "If you lean on me, do you think you could walk?"

He sat forward, bringing a hand to his forehead. "Everything spins."

She looked around the barn. "There isn't a way I can start a fire without burning the whole place down, and it's way too cold to leave you here tonight."

He shivered. "It would *gunjule*, be good, to sit by a fire."

She set the rifle aside, moved closer to him, and helped him to stand by inching a shoulder beneath his arm to steady him.

"*Ashoge*, thank you, for not aiming the *petiltow* at me."

In her urgency to help him, she'd left herself unarmed. She glanced over at the rifle and then up at him. "I imagine I will now see how true to your word you are."

His eyes froze on her lips.

She felt her cheeks grow hot, and the pit of her stomach tingled. The strange urge of affection she felt for him frightened her to the very core.

She cleared her throat and focused her thoughts on the reason she was this close to him in the first place. "Let's get you by the fire." Her knees trembled bearing his weight. He was a big man and could knock her to the ground if she wasn't careful. "Are you ready to walk?"

"I do not want to crush you." His face contorted with pain, while doing his best not to lean on her.

Together they took the laborious steps to the house, his breathing strained, his hot flesh burning through her clothes. "We're almost there," she reassured him. Or was she appeasing herself? Apprehensive now that she'd invited him into her home.

She brought him to her father's bed, covered him, and gave him water to drink. Then she added wood to the fire. In no time, the heat of the blaze warmed the room. She watched him snuggle beneath the blanket and fall asleep.

Throughout the night, Proud Eagle's fever raged. For several days, he drifted in and out of consciousness. She never left his side, exhaustion seeping into every fiber of her being. She worried for him, more than she knew she had a right to. All her concern, culminated with lack of sleep, took its toll.

****

Days and nights lost distinction for Proud Eagle. His only reality was the pain throbbing through his shoulder, his burning eyes, and the beautiful golden-haired woman.

Her smile was filled with compassion, her voice soft and comforting, her touch gentle and mindful of his suffering when washing and redressing his wound.

She fed him, gave him water to drink, and covered him with a blanket. Her long golden hair fell in curls around her shoulders. Her cool fingers caressed his brow, the wild-flowered scent of her skin filling his nostrils.

Her beautiful face was etched with concern. Concern over him. How he wished to reassure her all would be fine. He was too weak to make the words come. All he could do was watch, feel her touch.

In the dark of night she sat vigil, gazing out the window and unaware of his eyes upon her. The glow from the lantern's light made her nightclothes transparent. He smiled to himself. Her form, silhouetted beneath the material, pleased his eyes. Trim waist, rounded hips, and shapely legs filled him with hunger. He closed his eyes to still the desire growing deep within him. His body yearned to touch all he was privileged to see.

****

Proud Eagle thrashed about. Amanda rose from the chair beside the bed and felt his forehead. Hot flesh scalded her fingers.

She covered him with the blanket, and he kicked it off. Again she draped it over him, and again he flung it off. She looked down at him and frowned. If he was to sweat out the fever, he needed to stay warm.

This time, after covering him again, she climbed on top. With her full weight upon him, he was unable to shed the blanket. She reached for his hands and entwined her fingers with his, talking to him in a soft tone. It wasn't long before he relaxed and settled down to sleep.

His body, so close to hers, set her heart pounding. With each breath he took, his hard, muscular chest rose to meet her breasts. She rested her head upon his good shoulder, feeling the beat of his heart against her cheek, and closed her eyes. Her body relaxed. The rhythm of his breathing lulled her to sleep.

****

Proud Eagle opened his eyes to find the white woman, a leg resting over his thigh and her head nestled on his shoulder, sleeping. Her arm rested across his chest, her long tresses falling in disarray around her face.

Pain forgotten for a moment, he pushed aside a lock of hair from her cheek. It was soft to the touch. Entwining the silky strand around a finger, he inspected the pale threads. Catching the day's light peering through the shutters, it was as golden as the sun itself.

Her features were delicate, like a fragile flower, more beautiful than any woman's he'd ever seen. And her lips, lush and parted, were ripe for kissing. He longed to taste them, feel their warmth on his. The word *mine* came to his thoughts.

Ah, yes, I would have her.

He moved a hand down her back, drawing her closer, his gaze sliding downward to the creamy expanse of her neck. Being this close to her, his heart thundered with desire. Her full breasts, pressed against him, made the blood course through his veins like an awakening river.

Again he studied her lips, tracing their fullness with the tip of a finger. Then, lifting her chin ever-so-slightly, he brought his mouth down upon hers. He let the sweetness of her lips feed him, exploring with his tongue the tender walls of her mouth. His longing mounted with each feathery flick.

Her intake of breath alerted him she was awake. Consuming her mouth, Proud Eagle was lost in ecstasy, his senses playing havoc with his control.

She moved a hand to the back of his neck, fingers playing with the hair at his nape. Chills spiked down his spine, his manhood thickened against her thigh.

She broke away, scurrying off the bed. "How dare you!"

"How dare I what?" he repeated. "I am the one who woke to find you in my bed."

"I was trying to keep you from shedding the blanket," she clarified. "And fell asleep only to wake to your advances."

He arched a brow. "And you, you did nothing?"

She rearranged the collar of her nightgown, cheeks flushed. "I'm going to the kitchen to fix breakfast."

He chuckled. "Ah, I see you are not going to answer me that one."

"There's nothing to answer."

He reached for her hand. "But there is, Golden Lady." He moved his thumb across her knuckles. "*Hat'ugha*, why did you stop?"

She pulled her hand away. "Because, it was inappropriate for us to—"

"Could you not feel the fire between us?" he broke in. She shook him to his very core.

She moved to stand at the foot of the bed. "I'm going to fix you something to eat."

A slow smile curved his lips. "I am not hungry now for *woyuta*." He sat forward in the bed. "I am hungry for your lips, to hold you in my arms again." He loved how the taste lingered long after the kiss. He cast a bold glance at her breasts, arching a brow. "And to see what is so round and full beneath the nightdress."

She raised her chin in a defiant manner. "Well, food is the only thing being served here this morning, Mr. Proud Eagle." She stormed out of the room, yelling over her shoulder. "And don't you forget it."

He reclined against the pillow with a smirk upon his face. He always did admire a woman with much spirit.

****

Proud Eagle's fever had broken, but he was still

very weak. He slept most of the time, only waking to eat and wash. Amanda prayed he'd be well enough to be on his way before Josh arrived again.

After bringing old Todd out to graze with the cow, she fixed a cup of tea and thought again about her family in England. She sipped the hot brew, stories her mother told of Brighton's social life coming to mind. She could almost picture the women all dressed in fancy gowns, the men in expensive suits, attending the opera or ballet. Her mother had been quite an equestrienne, smart and beautiful, invited to all the gatherings. The estate Amelia's family owned was called Bentwood Manor. The mansion sounded so grand with its bay window seats and expansive gardens. Whatever possessed Amelia to leave such a life to teach school on the frontier?

She thought back now to the time she questioned her mother.

"But we have such a simple way of life here," she'd said. "I would love to live in such a grand home. We would have so much more than anyone in Willow Creek, Mama, if we went to England. We'd be rich."

"You're only rich, my dear daughter, when you are satisfied with the things you have." Amelia had looked fondly around the small farm house. "I like it here, and I'm satisfied to stay. We've done the best we can with what we have to work with." She smiled. "Don't compare yourself to others, Amanda. Your joy should be found in being the best you can be, not in being better than others."

Amanda sighed now.

There's a reason and a purpose for all things.

If Amelia hadn't come to Arizona territory, she'd never have met Ethan Gregory, fallen in love, and given birth to her.

And I wouldn't be sitting here without the two of them.

In truth, had Mama stayed in England there's a chance she'd still be alive today. Maybe Papa would be too. Without Amelia, Ethan would have gone out to sea. A life he often talked about. And it's a fact; there are no Indians on the ocean.

A sudden storm picked up later in the afternoon. The wind and rain were so fierce, she couldn't make her way through it to milk the cow. Her concern must have shown on her face, because when she brought Proud Eagle his afternoon meal, he questioned her.

"I am sure the cow can wait," he said, trying to quiet her worries.

She bit her bottom lip. "But it isn't good to let Betsy go too long without being milked." She sighed. "I should have milked her this morning." She remembered the effort Josh made, coming in from town daily to care for Betsy while she recuperated at the parsonage.

Proud Eagle pushed aside the blanket and stood. "What are you doing?"

"I will go to milk your cow."

She moved to his side. "You will not. Besides, have you ever milked a cow before?"

He squared his shoulders. "I am a *nagonlkadi*, a warrior, I will learn as I do."

She stood with hands on hips. "I forbid you."

He narrowed his eyes. "A woman does not tell a warrior what to do."

"I don't care if you're Santa Claus. You're way too weak to leave this bed."

He frowned, one brow lower than the other. "Who is this Santa Claus?"

His quirky expression made her burst out laughing.

His frown deepened. "Is he one of your *nagonlkadi's*?"

"Oh, goodness, no," she managed to say through

her laughter. "He brings children presents on Christmas Eve."

His thick dark brows shot up in surprise. "And for this he is greater than a warrior?"

She pointed to the bed. "I'll tell you all about him if you get back in bed."

He hesitated.

"The cow can wait." She pulled aside the blanket. "Now, if you want to know more about Santa Claus, get back in bed."

****

Long after the white woman went to bed, he lay awake. The story she'd told about Santa Claus kept circling in his thoughts. In his greatest imagination, he could not envision the fat jolly man in a red suit and a white beard, sitting in a sleigh pulled across the sky by eight flying deer called reindeer that had crazy names. Dasher was one, Dancer another. How was it possible for this man to be able to fit down the chimney, as fat as he was, without burning his backside? Yet she swore by the tale, said all the children waited each year for his arrival. And she rhymed the story; called the saga, *A Visit From St. Nicholas*, which the man was also known by. This great legend he must learn for himself, if he ever wished to tell the children of his tribe.

His musings kept him awake, as well as the old hound's whining and scratching at the back door. He rose from the bed, slipped on his moccasins and made his way to the kitchen.

"Enough, boy," he whispered. "Golden Lady is tired, let her sleep."

The dog cocked his head sideways and perked up his ears.

Proud Eagle chuckled. "You are *zenogolache*, the crazy one."

Duke moved with caution toward him.

Proud Eagle knelt on one knee and extended his

hand. "I will not harm you either."

The hound smelt his fingers before licking them.

He scratched the dog behind the ears. "So, now we can be friends."

Duke wagged his tail.

"Good." He stood. "Now, go to sleep."

Duke ran back to the door, again scratching and whining.

He followed the dog. "Ah, such a hunter you are." He reached for the latch and opened the door.

Duke ran out, heading for the barn.

Proud Eagle sniffed the air.

Fire!

He made his way to the porch, crouching beside a water barrel, and peered out in the direction of the barn. It was ablaze.

Chiricahua.

He returned to the house and latched the door behind him, making his way to where she slept.

Amanda woke to a calloused hand covering her mouth, the chill black silence of the room surrounding her.

He spoke in a precise, yet gentle tone. "Do not be afraid, I have not come to harm you." He moved his lips inches from her ear. "Listen to my words very carefully before you speak."

She nodded, swallowing the fear that now ran rampant through every fiber of her being.

He removed his hand and moved away from the bed to let her rise. "You must get up quietly and come with me. We must leave quickly."

Her heart raced. "Indians?" she whispered.

"Yes. They have already set fire to the barn."

She flung the quilt aside. "I've got to save my horse and cow."

"There is no time."

She started to protest. "I just can't leave them to die."

Proud Eagle's voice was stern. "It is too late, they will have taken them." He tossed her the robe that lay across the foot of her bed. "We go. Now! In very little *nkeez*, time, they will be here."

She scurried to find her shoes. "Are they Chiricahua?"

"Yes. Many *nagonlkadi's* from that tribe are wild. They not only raid the *indah*, but other tribes as well." He ripped the blanket from the bed and draped it around his naked shoulders. "We must leave. Now."

She reached for the lantern on the bedside table.

He stilled her hand. "No light, they might see." He took her by the arm. "Come."

She ran with him to the kitchen, her terror mounting. "What are we going to do?"

"We must get to the woods and hide."

Thankful she'd listened to Sara Driscoll about having water jugs filled at all times, she watched Proud Eagle fill the canteen and sling the strap across his chest. "But won't they see us? Find us?"

He turned and held her by the shoulders. "You must trust me, Golden Lady. I know where to take cover." His brows knit together. "But, I would feel better if I had a weapon."

She pointed to the firearms by the door. "The rifle. Take the rifle."

"*Petiltows* make too much noise, will draw attention to where we are if we have to use it. What I need is my spear."

"I shoved it under the back porch."

Proud Eagle took her by the hand and opened the door.

"Wait," she said, breaking away and reaching for the knapsack she had packed for just such an escape. She slung it across her back, and grabbed the violin. "Now, let's go."

"Crouch low," he instructed.

Together they crept onto the porch and off the steps.

"Where is the spear?"

She pointed to the area left of the stairs.

Proud Eagle knelt down, sought his weapon, and in one fluid motion, stood, aiming the spear into the darkness.

Something hit the ground with a *thump*.

Proud Eagle ran to his target with her close by. She sucked in her breath when she saw the dead Indian, Proud Eagle's spear piercing his chest. "How did you know he was there?"

"A *nagonlkadi* is *giannahtah*, always ready and aware of his surroundings," he explained, pulling the spear from the dead man's torso.

Her stomach lurched, and she swallowed hard the bile rising to her throat. Silent with fear, she watched Proud Eagle strip the enemy of his knife, bow, and arrows.

They only want weapons, she remembered the reverend saying.

She backed away to collect her thoughts. Granted, Proud Eagle kept them from getting killed, but to see him in action confused and frightened her.

He looked up at her, reading her thoughts. "I only take what I need to keep us alive."

Still in shock, all she could manage was a nod.

He stood to face her, loading the weapon and aiming it over her head.

She witnessed pain carved in merciless lines on his face as he pulled back the string and released the arrow.

There was another *thud*.

She turned to find a second Indian lying dead.

He even has the eyes and the ears of an eagle.

Proud Eagle stripped that enemy of his knife and arrows, handing her a dagger. "Come, follow me."

She hesitated, staring down at the large blade. It felt heavy and foreign in her hand.

"Come," he repeated in a sharper tone.

She clutched the violin to her chest and ran, not knowing where he was taking her, or how far into the dark woods they would go. She couldn't lose sight of him. She forced her legs to move, her lungs to breathe, her mind to stay alert, and followed him deeper and deeper into the forest.

They ran a great distance before Proud Eagle pulled her behind a clump of bushes and collapsed, gasping for air.

She huddled down beside him and removed the canteen from across his shoulder. "Take a sip."

Proud Eagle reached for the water and sat forward.

She ripped the knapsack off her shoulders and placed it behind him. With a gentle hand upon his chest, she guided him to lie back. His flesh was damp and clammy with sweat; his heart raced. "How were you able to do this?"

"Do what?" he choked out hoarsely.

"Act so swift and precise, and run so quickly after being ill?"

He continued to struggle for air. "There was no choice."

She grabbed the hem of the blanket slung around his shoulders and wiped his face and chest. "Just take deep breaths."

He coughed, then cleared his throat. "Chiricahua can be *yudastcin*, bastards. They *zas'tee*, kill, ruthlessly. Quick is the only way to act when you are face to face with one."

She pushed aside a thick strand of black hair that clung to his neck. "Were you attacked by a Chiricahua before I found you at my back door?"

He nodded. "I was hunting when I was challenged by one called *Nahdaste*, Fire Star. I sent his spirit to *O'zho*, but not before one of his arrows found my shoulder."

She frowned. "What is *O'zho*?"

He pointed to the heavens.

She swallowed the despair in her throat and looked up at the night sky. The chill of the night whipped against her. She pulled the collar of her robe higher on her neck, wishing for the warmth of a fire.

Again he read her thoughts. "I would build a fire, but that could draw the enemy near."

She edged closer to Proud Eagle, covering him with the blanket, and scanned her surroundings. "Do you think they still might be on our trail?"

"Chiricahua are cunning trackers and fierce fighters. None of them can be *zonta*, trusted."

"If that's true, then what do we do?"

"We wait till the first morning light."

She tucked her feet beneath her to keep them warm. "What good can that do if they are as fierce as you say?"

"I think by that time they will make their way back to their camp to eat their *yuta*, and I can take you home."

She glanced down at the clothes she wore, now all she owned. "My home and barn are by now burnt to the ground. I pray my horse and cow didn't burn with them." She sighed. "And only God knows what happened to my poor old dog."

"I did not mean your home, Golden Lady."

She frowned. "Then whose?"

He responded matter-of-factly. "Mine."

Chapter Three

"Yours!" she shrieked.

He reached out, placing a hand over her mouth. "Lower your voice."

She spoke in a suffocated whisper. "I can't go home with you."

"You have no choice."

"Of course, of course I have a choice," she stammered.

He sat up on his elbows, catching a second wind. "Tell me, then, of your choice."

She spoke with quiet, but desperate, firmness. "I choose to go to the parsonage."

"What is a parsonage?"

She looped a stand of hair behind an ear. "It's where the reverend lives."

"And what is a reverend?"

She paused for the right words. "He is—he is—well, a holy man."

"Ah, like a *diyi*, Apache medicine man."

"No, our medicine men are called doctors. A holy man is someone who tends to the spirit."

"Then he is a shaman," Proud Eagle concluded.

She frowned. "What does a shaman do?"

"A shaman can talk with spirits, heal, and find things that have been lost. For many days he does not eat, and then the powers show themselves to him through visions or dreams. In the eyes of the tribe he is the favored one."

"In a way Josh is a healer with his kind words."

He arched a brow. "Josh?"

"The holy man. That's his name, Joshua

Holmes."

"And you like this Joshua Holmes?"

She nodded. "He is a good, kind man and has been like family."

His eyes caught and held hers. "Is he your man?"

She remembered the morning Josh proposed and an unwelcome blush heated her cheeks at the possibility of marrying him. "I believe he has hopes to be."

Proud Eagle's voice held a grudging tone. "And you. You hope for this as well?"

She folded her arms across her chest. "That's none of your business."

He sat up, hugging his knees. "And where is the parsonage where the holy man lives?"

"In town."

His voice was heavy with sarcasm. "Do you think you are like Santa Claus and can ride a flying deer to get there?"

His mocking tone sparked her anger. "I don't need to be like Santa Claus. I have two good feet and I know the way."

"Go then. You have a knife for protection."

"First light, that's what I intend to do," she hissed.

He sighed with exasperation. "You are so frightened now, you are almost on top of me."

"I am not," she snapped, moving away from him.

She was halted by an iron grip on her wrist. "Do not move."

She froze. "What is it?"

He reached for the dagger beside him and with a quick jerk of the wrist, speared the snake slithering inches away from her knee.

She jumped to her feet.

Proud Eagle grabbed the hem of her robe, and with a yank, pulled her down beside him. "You will listen to me, Golden Lady. A movement like that could signal the enemy. I do not intend to get my throat slit, *bigha*, because you are *zenogolache*."

She frowned annoyed. "What does that mean?"

"The crazy one," he interpreted.

She pushed him away. "I'm not crazy."

With a protective hand he pulled her closer. "Ah, but it is how you appear when you do not listen." He relaxed his grip. "From this point on, you will *ugashe*, go where I go, do exactly as I say, and not ask questions. Do you understand this?"

"Most of it," she quipped.

"And what do you not understand?"

"The part where you get to boss me around," she snapped.

"Well then let me make it clear. I am bigger and now stronger than you, thanks to your good care, so you will listen to me."

She stiffened as though she'd been slapped. "You ungrateful lout, I should have left you to die."

He tightened his arm around her waist. "And if you had, you would now either be dead or pleasing a Chiricahua warrior."

"No, I would have been far away from here and at the parsonage. I only stayed back to care for you."

He arched a brow. "Ah...then you would be pleasing the holy man."

Her cheeks heated. "You're disgusting." She pushed away from him. "Let me go."

"Not a chance, my *isdzan*, woman, we are going to warm each other until morning."

"I am not your woman!"

"You are now."

Fear knotted her stomach. He was no better than the Chiricahua. Why did she think he was?

The rich timbre of his voice cut through her thoughts. "I gave you my word I would not harm you. I only want to keep warm."

"In the knapsack I have a quilt." She squirmed out of his grasp to retrieve the blanket.

He wrapped it around her shoulders, again pulling her close, his voice softer when he spoke. "Lay your head on my shoulder, and rest. I will keep watch."

****

She woke to the smell of food cooking. Proud Eagle was roasting something over a small flame.

She sat up, rubbing the sleep from her eyes. "Is it safe now, for a fire?"

He nodded. "I have scouted the area. There is no sign of Chiricahua." He handed her a cooked piece of meat skewered on a stick.

Every bone in her body ached from sleeping on the ground, and her stomach gnawed with hunger. "What is it?"

"It is *zuzeca*."

She frowned confused.

He smiled and took a bite. "Our visitor from last night."

She widened her eyes in astonishment. "The snake?"

He grinned. "Now he is our morning meal."

She'd lost her appetite and handed him back the stick. "I'm not really hungry."

"*Yuta*, eat it, Golden Lady."

She swallowed hard. "I'll be sick if I do."

He leaned forward. "You will be sick if you do not."

She brought the tip of the stick to her mouth, reluctantly bit off a piece and chewed the tough meat, pretending it was beef or chicken, two of her favorite meals.

He smiled satisfied. "See how nice a meal together can be when you do as you are told?"

"It would be a lot nicer if you weren't a pig-head," she snapped.

His smile fell. "What is a pig-head?"

"Someone who is bossy, rude, and—"—she sniffed the air in his direction—"smells."

He spoke with light bitterness. "I cook for you and you say I smell?"

She threw her stick into the fire and folded her arms over her chest. "Well, it's true."

He nodded with a taut jerk of his head. "Then I ask you to forgive me for not being as clean as I would like." He motioned to his surroundings. "In case you have not noticed, we are not in a place where one can take a bath."

"I know the river isn't far," she challenged.

He inclined his head. "You speak the truth, but staying to the shadows has kept us alive. It is much wiser to be living and smell, than to be dead and clean."

"You have a point." Ashamed for her cruel retort, she apologized. "I'm sorry, Proud Eagle." A thoughtful smile curved her mouth. "I know you can't help that you smell."

He rewarded her with a larger smile of his own. "And you as well."

For a second she was taken aback by his candor, but then, she had started this conversation and now deserved what she got. She burst into uncontrollable laughter. "With the threat of the Chiricahua finding us, having little food and water; by comparison smelling is a silly thing to care about."

Proud Eagle's face brightened with merriment, and he joined in her mirth.

She couldn't help admiring the dark eyes, twinkling with humor that framed the inherent strength of his face. His teeth, even and white, contrasted against his skin; bronzed by the wind and sun. His masculinity exuded an air of command. Broad shoulders, bared, hard chest, and powerful arms were a disturbing attraction.

She stood and turned away from him, folding the quilt. "We should be on our way, don't you think?" She reached for the knapsack and busied herself with situating the comforter amongst the other items. After securing the buckles on her bag, she slung it across her back.

He looked up at the morning sun shining through the treetops. "Yes, there is much ground to cover before the *holos* burns too hot." He shook the canteen. "And soon we will need to find water." Throwing a handful of dirt on the fire, he stood.

"What do you think your people will say when you ride into your village with me?"

"I am not sure," he said with a significant lifting of his brows. "An *indah*, white man lived among us before. My mother's father. He came one day from the north to trade *ighaas*, furs, with the tribe. My grandmother caught his eye, and he stayed. He told *inju*, good, stories and I listened."

"Is that how you learned to speak English?"

He nodded. "Many in my tribe speak the *indah's* tongue."

She adjusted the knapsack to lie over her shoulders. "My mother came to these parts from a place called England."

He stirred the ashes with a stick. "Where is this England?"

"It is far, far away," she said.

"Across the big *guesas*?"

She nodded. "And she sailed on those big waters for many days to get here."

"Why did she leave her family?"

"She came to America to teach the children in the settlement of Willow Creek." Amanda sighed. "She was so beautiful, with her long golden curls. She loved to sing and dance, and bake pies that tasted so good they'd melt on your tongue." She paused, remembering her mother's face. "She had smiling eyes. That's what I see when I think about her, those smiling eyes."

For a moment, there was silence between them.

"What happened to her, Golden Lady?"

"She died of a fever when I was thirteen years old, and nothing was ever the same again."

He moved to stand before her. "I am sorry."

"And now my father is gone, too." She turned away from him in an attempt to stifle the sobs that rose from her heart.

He cupped her chin with his hand, turning her to face him. "Speak what troubles you."

She looked deep into his large dark eyes. They were filled with compassion and warmth. He waited for her to find her voice, standing so near she feared he could hear her pounding heart. The tears she fought to control slipped down her face. "Soon I will be among the very kind that killed him."

He searched her upturned face before wiping a tear with his thumb. "Chiricahua killed your father," he corrected. "Not the warriors of my tribe."

She took a deep, unsteady breath, and stepped back. "Does it make a difference?"

He reached out, catching her hand in his. "Yes, it makes a great difference." He pulled her to him. "I told you once. I am not at fault for what others do. Neither are my *nuhdee*." He pushed aside a wayward strand of her hair. "But I understand your concern, your fear, and sadness."

Confusing emotions tore at her heart, shaking her resolve. "Do you?"

"Yes." He gave her a sideways glance. "Why does that seem so strange to you?"

She wanted to hate this man, blame him and his tribe for all her sorrows. Yet, how could she hold him accountable for her pain? He had risked his own life to save her, and now he wanted to keep her safe by bringing her to his home.

Irascible patience flowed into his voice. "I believe my *nuhdee* will welcome you."

"Why should they?"

He gave her a smile that sent her pulses racing. "You have saved my life, for that they will be forever grateful."

She accepted his reasoning with a taut nod.

He reached for the violin, and studied the case before handing it to her. "What is this you carry?"

"It's a violin."

He fingered the case. "What is a violin?"

She took the instrument and placed it on the ground, snapping open the latches. She pulled out the violin and demonstrated the sound by plucking a string with the tip of a finger. "My father taught me how to play."

Proud Eagle bent to examine the instrument. "It is a singing wood."

She giggled. "A what?"

He smiled. "My *nuhdee* call this a singing wood."

Her face brightened. "Your people play the violin?"

"It does not look just like this, but is much the same, from a hollowed out piece of wood, rounded in shape. A string made of sinew is attached and played with a small bow made of *chelee*, horse hair."

She closed the case. "One day I will play you a song."

"I would like that." He stood and gazed up at the sky. "Come, it will soon grow warm."

A rustle in the trees halted them.

Proud Eagle reached for the spear and pushed her behind him.

She felt for the dagger in her pocket and wrapped her fingers around the handle. Her stomach knotted. Would she be capable of using it?

To both their relief, Duke came bursting through the underbrush. Old Todd came clopping along not far behind.

A mixture of joy and relief echoed in her chest as she threw her arms around the old dog, kissing the top of his head. "You're alive. You're both alive." She made her way to the horse, patting his nose. "I'm so glad to see you too, old boy." She turned to Proud Eagle. "What do you suppose happened to the cow?"

Proud Eagle bent to scratch the hound behind the ears. "I think she is why the Chiricahua did not follow us."

She frowned. "I don't understand?"

He chuckled. "It is hard for a man to leave the prospect of meat roasting over an open fire."

"Oh, no! My poor little Betsy."

"Wish her spirit a safe journey." He gathered the weapons and handed her the violin. "I would say she saved our lives."

****

Not quite noon and already the heat had reached scorching intensity. Their parched throats made the need for water evident. She was relieved at midday when they came upon a small creek. Proud Eagle rushed into the cool waters, slapping his face and chest, washing beneath his arms. She laughed at his exuberance and playful antics. He reminded her of a small boy having fun at the watering hole.

She quenched her own thirst, made sure Duke and Todd did as well, and then filled the canteen. While Proud Eagle went off to pick berries from a nearby bush for their lunch, she slipped off her robe and shoes to take her own bath.

She splashed the cool water over her shoulders and slid beneath the surface, luxuriating in the freedom her body enjoyed in the watery chill. She scrubbed her face and neck, and washed her hair.

Amanda floated on her back, making ripples in the water with her toes, refreshed and relaxed for the first time in days. Then she stood and stretched her arms over her head. Every muscle in her body breathed away the tension. She wrapped thick tresses around a hand to wring the golden curls, enjoying the moment. But her contentment was short lived. She sensed being watched and spun around to face the bank.

She froze in sight of the cold, beady eyes that stared back at her. His lips curled over uneven, yellowed teeth and large feathers adorned his headdress. A streak of red paint splashed from his sharp nose to his cheekbones.

She crossed her arms over her breasts and sank lower in the water before she screamed for Proud Eagle.

The Indian let out a yelp and leaped into the creek, the many beads and charms hanging around his neck clicking together.

She sank deeper, reaching down for a fistful of mud.

The Indian pulled a knife from his belt and held it over her head.

She stood and threw the mire in his face.

While he rid his eyes of the muck, she raced for shore and the dagger hidden in the robe's pocket.

But he overtook her, his fingers knotting a handful of her hair and yanking back her head. He placed the blade of the knife at her throat.

She clenched her eyes shut. She would not look another moment upon her killer's face. No, her last sight of life would not be the evil eyes of a Chiricahua.

Please Lord, let it be over quick.

It was true, life flashed before you previous to death. Heart filled memories of the love she had for her parents, thoughts of Josh's kindness, and the laughter of another Indian—the one who saved her life, swept through her mind's eye.

She took an audible breath, preparing to die

when the Chiricahua's hand relaxed the grip on her hair. The knife slipped down the front of her chest and splashed into the water.

Her eyes shot open, catching the last flicker of life leave his eyes before he fell face down into the creek, a large spear protruding from his back.

She glanced over to see another Indian standing on the bank.

****

Proud Eagle's heart pounded with fury as he offered up a silent thanks to the gods he had come back when he did. He berated himself now for ever leaving her side. Just a few moments later and he would have found her floating lifeless in the water.

She stood dazed, deep blue eyes wide with shock. Her long golden curls hung in wet snarls down a shoulder. The cotton nightdress clung to firm creamy mounds, their peaks noticeable.

His eyes eased down the length of her, taking in the flat belly and the soft curves of her hips. The saturated garment, transparent now, revealed all; even the triangular patch of hair between her thighs.

Beads of moisture sparkled on her honeyed flesh, making her appear a mythical princess warrior emerging from the water.

Proud Eagle's breath caught in his throat, his loins swelling beneath the buckskin breeches. He raised his gaze to her face and caught her lashes fluttering, eyes rolling, then she fell to her knees.

He rushed to her side and swept her into his arms, reaching for the spear and pulling it from the dead Chiricahua's back. He carried her to the bank and covered her with the robe, placing her upon his lap.

She wrapped her arms around him and buried her face in his neck, sobbing against his throat. "Thank goodness you came back."

His arms embraced her, rocked and soothed her like a little child. "I will never leave you again."

She pulled back to look at him, tears streaking her face. "Do you promise?"

He looked into her soft blue eyes, and he drowned in their depth. Never had the nearness of a woman brought him so much pleasure, undone him, as this one did, with just her presence. "When I give my word, I keep it."

"Yes. Yes, you do," she whispered.

Her mouth was very close and tempting, too tempting to resist covering her lips with his. His tongue parted her teeth and caressed the soft corners of her mouth.

She moved her hand to cup his neck, pressing her full breasts against him.

He groaned with pleasure, demanding more; tasting her, searching with fervor for the sweetness he had sampled before. When he woke to find her in his bed. He should have loved her then. He would love her now.

Mine. She is mine.

He moved his hands down her back to her hips, his passion mounting as he reached for the hem of her wet nightdress, lifting it higher upon her thighs and feeling the soft flesh. His senses reeled, his whole being filled with want—lost in burning desire.

Duke's barking over the top of them shattered the moment.

In one fluid motion, he pushed her behind him and reached for the spear, crouching like a mountain lion prepared to attack.

She scampered to her feet, standing shielded by his body.

But the woods were silent.

He cast an angry look Duke's way. "What was the barking for?"

"He was protecting me."

He stood, turning toward her. "From what?"

She slipped on the robe, securing the cloth belt around her waist. "From you, no doubt."

He frowned. "I would say he is a bit confused. Where was he when the Chiricahua had you?"

She glanced over at the dead Indian floating in the water and shivered. "Yes, that's a good question." She turned to Duke and frowned. "Knowing you as I do, I can almost bet you were eating clean the berry bush."

Duke barked.

Proud Eagle narrowed his eyes at the hound. "You owe me *woyute*, dog."

The animal owed him a lot more than a meal. With great effort, he pushed aside the dissatisfaction he now felt at the loss of her body beneath his. She had responded again, as she had done back at her home. This made the intrusion even harder to bear. He needed to busy himself, and be quick about it. Thinking of what could have been was becoming sheer torture, not to mention embarrassing.

He turned away to adjust himself in his breeches. Then he gathered their belongings, handing her the violin and canteen. He slipped the knapsack over one shoulder and looked down at Duke, arching a brow and advising the dog. "For the evening meal, it better be much more than berries."

****

She was proud of her old hound. He caught a large squirrel for dinner which they all enjoyed. Later, leaning against a tree and reading the Bible by the light of the fire, the tension lifted from her shoulders.

Proud Eagle had remained quiet throughout the day. The silence between them became even more awkward than the kiss at the creek. And riding in front of him on old Todd, her backside feeling every stir beneath his breeches, by far hadn't helped the situation. Her shifting with unease had angered him to the point of him placing a firm arm around her waist and demanding she sit still or walk. And with her shoes blistering her bare feet, walking was the last thing she wanted to do.

She watched him rest back on her knapsack, the firelight picking up the strong lines of his profile. From where she sat, she could observe him without notice. She admired the full, strong curves of his lips, remembering their touch as soft and warm on hers, arousing feelings she didn't know existed. If Duke hadn't barked, would she have let him—

His voice broke through her thoughts. "What is it you look at?"

She hesitated with an answer, surprised he decided now to speak to her.

Proud Eagle turned her way, propping his chin on a hand, waiting for her reply.

"I'm reading scripture from the Bible," she finally said.

He frowned. "What is scripture?"

"They are words written on a page. Each chapter is a different Gospel, which means good news."

Proud Eagle sat up. "And what is the good news?"

She fingered the book's worn cover and read to him about the beginning. "God created man first, but soon saw the man needed a helper. The woman was formed from the man's side, a place close to his heart. Not the soles of his feet. Woman was never meant for man to walk ahead of her, but beside her, as his equal." She sighed. "But some men think a woman is to be a servant and treat her as a slaves."

Proud Eagle frowned. "This is not the way of the men in my tribe. Women are listened to, even asked for their voice in many situations."

"That's how it should be. Women shouldn't be abused or disrespected, but should complete man."

He nodded in agreement. "A *isdzan*, woman, is given much respect by her man in my village. Tell me more from what you read."

His eagerness reminded her of a child excited to learn something new. She hesitated, calling upon her religious training before she went on to explain the mystery of her faith.

Proud Eagle blinked, baffled. "Your god is a man who walks the earth and has mated with a woman?"

She giggled at his expression. "I'm afraid I'm not explaining this very well. If Reverend Holmes were here, he'd know the words to say so you'd understand."

He shrugged. "What can the holy man say that you cannot?"

"Oh, lots. He's been taught how to preach."

He folded his arms across his chest. "I wish to hear how you tell it."

She sighed again. "I will try."

Further explanation confused him even more, since a few nights ago she'd told him about Santa Claus. She then had to separate the Santa aspect of Christmas from the Christian version of the holiday.

Proud Eagle listened, his eyes never wavering. "Knowing, believing in such a thing can change your life."

"Yes, it can. It has for many." She marveled over his quick grasp on what she said.

She moved on to tell him about the devil, and how he tricked people into sinning.

He nodded in agreement. "I know of *gode*, evil spirits, Apaches have many stories about such demons. When they are displeased they seek revenge."

She closed the Bible and several pieces of paper fell from the back. She scooped them up and replaced them, but one small piece remained on the ground. Upon retrieving it, she recognized her

75

mother's neat handwriting.

He stood, moving to sit cross-legged beside her. "More good news?"

"In a way, this paper lists the scripture to look up when feeling sad or afraid or worried."

"Is there one for forgiveness?"

She glanced up to look at him. "Yes, there is."

"Find it and read," he urged, moving closer.

His nearness made her heart race. Would he try to kiss her again? That thought made her hands tremble as she leafed through the Bible. When she came upon the scripture, she read it to herself first, and then explained the verse. "We are told not to be bitter, to put evil away from us and instead, forgive."

"So, you must forgive others what they do?"

She nodded. "Yes, that's what it says."

"Otherwise you are bound to the evil?" he questioned further.

"Something to that affect, yes, revenge keeps us a prisoner."

"And only forgiveness sets you free?"

She nodded, twirling the rings that hung from the chain around her neck.

Proud Eagle mused. "Then forgiving is to release a prisoner free, and then to realize the prisoner was you."

She stared at him in disbelief. "I never thought of it in that way, but yes."

He glanced at her fingers playing with the rings before searching her face. "When will you forgive, Golden Lady, and set yourself free?"

She closed the book and rested her head against the tree. "Believe me when I say I'm trying."

"It might be wise for you to try for a change of *biijii*, heart."

"You're probably right."

"Do not just try. Trust and do," he advised.

"And what do you trust, Proud Eagle?"

"My *nuhdee* trust the Great Spirit as well. In my village there are many holy places." He reached for a few sticks to throw on the fire. "They are piles of stone on which twigs and shingle rock are placed by each one who passes by, and cattail flag pollen is sprinkled about. We speak to the gods of the Zenith and Nadir, and to the gods of the four winds. We also speak to the Great Sprit when we gather herbs."

"Why do that?"

"It is done to ask the plant's permission to take a cutting. Never do we pluck the entire root, but instead cut the plant even with the surface of the earth, so another generation will be born in its place. At the holy places my *nuhdee* offer chants of thanks and it is a time of much respect. We also remember our dead."

"Are those that have died buried beneath the stones and shingle rock?"

"No, when an old Apache has gone to *O'zho*, his body, all he owns, and his home are burned to ashes. His family sets a part of their field aside for him, and will not touch it for many moons. All that is burned or left for him will follow his spirit's journey to *O'zho*."

She leaned forward with interest in his ways. "What happens when a young Apache dies?"

"The body is wrapped with many blankets and carried to the hills. Put between the rocks or a shallow grave that begins at the southwest corner, so the soul can safely enter *O'zho*. The grave is filled with *terte*, earth and stone, to keep *baya*, coyotes, out. When a baby dies, the body is wrapped in blankets and tied in a cradleboard that is hung from a tree. A jug filled with *guesa* is hung nearby so the child can drink at will."

"Even in death your people worry about the baby having water to drink?"

He nodded. "It is the custom."

77

She continued to fiddle with the gold rings hanging on the chain. Talking about death deepened the sorrow that already enveloped her heart.

Proud Eagle's gaze once more moved to the chain around her neck. He reached over and fingered a band. "What is that you wear close to your *biijii*?"

"My parent's wedding rings. It is a tradition for my people, after saying the marriage vow, to exchange rings." She looked down at the two circles of gold lying in the palm of his hand. "One day I will wear my mother's ring, and the man I choose to marry will wear my father's."

Proud Eagle released the rings. "The holy man you spoke of. He will wear your father's ring?"

He sat close enough for their hips to touch. The warmth of his body penetrating through hers. "I don't—No, he's more like family. Like a big brother perhaps."

"How is it then you speak of him with so much respect?"

"Well, because I do respect him. He is a good and kind man, who deserves my respect. But I do not feel here"—she placed her hand over her heart—"the way my mother felt for my father."

His gaze followed her hand, remaining fixed on her breasts.

Her cheeks heated "I want to feel toward my husband as my mother did for my father."

Proud Eagle smiled. "We learn much from our mothers."

Eager to change the subject, she asked, "What have you learned from yours?"

His smile broadened. "She has taught me many things, but most of all to be sensitive and gentle does not mean you are not strong. Backing away from danger does not mean you are not brave and being afraid does not mean you are a coward. Courage does not mean we do not fear, but the action we take in the face of fear. What we are not willing to do, but what we have to do even if we are doing it afraid."

She searched his face. "She is a wise woman."

Proud Eagle chuckled. "And patient. She has to be to live with my father."

She sat back against the tree again. "Tell me about your father."

He leaned back on his elbows. "He is called Cunning Eagle, and his name fits him well. Wise in a different way than my mother, he rules the tribe. My father, like the eagle, has powerful jaws. When he speaks he knows much and how strong the words must be."

"Then he is the Chief?"

He nodded, concern etched upon his face. "But he has been ill, and I fear his time is near to journey to *O'zho*."

"And when he is gone, then you will be the chief?"

Proud Eagle nodded again. "And even though I have been waiting all my years to wear his headdress, now that the time is near, I wish it to go away."

"We are so eager to want to be adults when we are young, then when we have grown, we long for the comforts of our youth," she reflected.

"You speak the truth," he agreed. "And we believe we know much more than we really do, not listening but only wanting to be heard."

"Our mistake is in growing up."

His lips curved into a mischievous smile. "Ah, but growing up has many good things between a man and woman the young know nothing about. Do you not agree?"

Her cheeks warmed with the heat stealing into her face. What power did he possess? He could turn her insides to jelly with just a smile or a look from his dark, brooding eyes, drawing from her any resolve she might have. Just sitting so near to him made her entire body tingle.

Not waiting for an answer he spoke again. "I, like you, admire the love my parents have for one another and want the same in my life."

A gust of wind made her pull the collar of her robe tighter around her neck.

Proud Eagle reached for the knapsack and removed the quilt, draping it around her shoulders. Along with the quilt came Amanda's mother's wedding dress. Before stuffing the garment back inside the pack, he fingered the delicate lace at the neckline. "This one is different than the ones I have seen you wear."

"That's because this one is worn for a wedding. It is part of our marriage custom for the woman to wear a white dress with a veil and pronounce words of love, vows, they are called, before a reverend."

"Apaches have a marriage custom as well. The courtship begins with the squaw choosing her brave by a look or a light slap at the mating ceremony."

A woman making such a move during courtship was alarming. "Isn't she ashamed to be so bold?"

He stifled a yawn. "No, it is how it is done."

"But what if the brave doesn't want to marry her?"

Proud Eagle shrugged. "Then he does not accept, but if he does accept, than he goes to a *yata*, place where he has seen her many times."

"What place would that be?"

He thought for a moment. "It would be the *yata* where she washes her clothes or carries her water from."

Her curiosity piqued. "Then what happens?"

"Then he places two rows of stones setting apart a space of five to fifteen warriors' feet, and hides himself where she cannot see him. If she passes the stones, then she has refused him. But if she walks down the path between the stones, then she has accepted his proposal."

She frowned. "But if she has chosen him at the mating ceremony, hasn't she already made her answer known?"

"She has let him know she wishes for him to court her, and upon his acceptance, the stone ceremony is his proposal." Proud Eagle's eyes twinkled. "Then he rushes out and takes her to his camp, where she stays for many nights, hanging out his bedding and catching his *chelee* for him to ride. He accepts her as his wife by eating what she has cooked and allowing all she does for him."

"While she's doing all these things, does he... do they—" She clipped her tongue.

He threw his head back and laughed. "Ah, that is most asked among the maidens." He arranged the knapsack behind his head and laid back. "A brave at this point is to have much control, or the honor of the ceremony is broken." Proud Eagle stretched his arms over his head. "It is a hard thing to do, but to start a marriage without honor is not wise."

"Then when does she become his wife?"

He rolled onto his side, so he could look at her. "First she is sent back to her family. Then in a day or so, the brave buys her from her parents or the ones who cared for her."

Her eyes narrowed "What do you mean, buys her? I thought you said your men respected their women."

"It is not that way, Golden Lady," he hurried to correct. "The brave brings blankets, ponies, and other goods as a token of honor to the family's *gowa* during the night."

"What is a *gowa*?"

"It is a wickiup, an Apache dwelling," he explained. "If the gifts are accepted, then she is sent the very next night to his wickiup as his wife."

"No vows are said in the eyes of God or the Great Spirit, as you believe he is called?"

He shook his head.

"Then how is it a binding commitment?"

"I have never seen a couple in my village who has married this way be anything but committed to one another."

"But they are doing it wrong."

"It is not wrong, Golden Lady, just different from your ways," he countered.

She looked down at him, the nights she had cared for him while he was sick coming to mind. She remembered how he saved her life, and the kisses that left her breathless. She longed now for just such a kiss. Never before had she felt this way about any man.

What am I doing? What am I thinking?

He reached up and caressed her cheek with the back of his hand. "It grows late, time to rest."

"When will we reach your village?"

He rolled onto his back, placing his hands beneath his head. "By noon, it really is a quick journey when there is no need to hide from the enemy and one can travel by *chelee*."

She scooted down to rest beside him. "But you didn't have a horse."

"I did when I started out from my village."

She sighed. "The Chiricahua take everything."

He yawned. "I am hoping my *chelee* somehow got away. If he did, he would return to my village." He turned his head her way and smiled. "Maybe he waits for me there."

What awaited her at his village? And how long did he expect her to stay? Josh would return soon to the farm and see it in ruins. When he didn't find her body amongst the ashes, what would he think? She couldn't let him worry over her when she was alive and well. She had to get to the parsonage somehow, and now with old Todd back, the journey would be easier. What wouldn't be easy was getting free from Proud Eagle. He'd never let her go, as long as he were awake.

Amanda listened to his even breathing.

I will just wait then, till he falls asleep.

****

The stirring of the old horse, the rustling in the trees, brought him to his feet. He reached for the spear, looking around for her. She was gone, along with her belongings.

His rage mounted. "*Zenogolache*, the crazy one, she will get herself killed yet," he grumbled.

It was not hard to find her trying her best to mount the horse and hang on to all her possessions as well.

He snuck up from behind, standing with hands on hips and feet apart. "Need some help?"

Startled, she screamed and fell off the horse, landing hard upon the ground.

He walked over to her and extended a hand.

She scowled and refused his help, standing on her own and grimacing with pain. She rubbed her backside. "I thought you were sleeping."

He arched a brow. "You thought wrong."

She turned upon him with rage. "And what on earth are you thinking, Proud Eagle?"

Besides needing sleep, his patience was wearing thin. "That we would get rest before we arrived home."

She squared her shoulders. "Well, you see, that's just the point. We are going to your home, not mine."

"Your home is no longer there," he reminded her.

"But I do have someplace else I can go," she said through grit teeth.

He knew she referred to the parsonage. "But there is no one to take you."

83

She placed her small hands on her hips. Hips that swayed when she walked. "That's why I was taking myself."

"Listen to my words. I cannot let you ride to your town alone." He reached out and grabbed her arm, pulling her close. "And I cannot go with you."

She pulled free from his grasp. "So what's the answer here?"

"You will come back to my village with me," he affirmed.

Her delicate chin rose in defiance. "That's only an answer for you."

"No, it is the only answer there is," he countered.

"Am I your prisoner?"

He frowned. "No. How could you believe such a thing?"

She waved her hand in the air. "Well, you're preventing me from leaving."

"I am preventing you from getting killed."

She turned away from him, picking up the violin and knapsack and headed for the horse. "I'll take my chances."

He blocked her way. "I am keeping you with me for your own safety."

Her pale brows arched above blue eyes glistening with determination. "Are you?"

"The thought of the Chiricahua, or any man, touching you is something I cannot allow."

Her voice rose an octave. "Allow? You have no say in anything I do."

"Ah, but I do," he countered.

"What are you saying?"

"No man can ever touch you, because you are mine, Golden Lady."

"I told you before. I am not your woman!"

He'd had enough. Taking her by the shoulders, he pulled her toward him. "I said, you are mine. You belong to me."

She ground the words out between her teeth. "I will not be treated like a piece of property."

He cupped her chin with his hands. "I am not in need of property."

"Oh, I can just imagine what you're in need of and I'm not the one who—"

He didn't wait for her to finish the sentence, claiming her lips and crushing her to him.

She fought in his embrace, struggled to push him away.

He held her firm but gentle, deepening the kiss, caressing her mouth with his tongue, drinking in her sweetness.

She relaxed in his arms, her body quivered against his.

He broke away long enough to stroke her cheek with a thumb. Then he kissed her eyelids and the tip of her nose, whispering, "I will never let you go. Never," he repeated, capturing her mouth again.

Amanda expected him to lay her upon the ground and have his way with her, but instead he took several deep breaths, gathered her things, and walked her back to camp. He spread out the quilt for her, threw more sticks on the fire, and sat down against a tree.

Now, he watched her.

"I promised I wouldn't try to leave again," she said.

"I heard you."

She sighed exasperated. "Then why aren't you lying down to rest?"

He folded his arms across his muscular chest. "I cannot sleep just yet, Golden Lady."

She frowned. "Why?"

Proud Eagle's lips thinned. "To explain it to you would not be wise." He arched a brow. "Especially for you."

She rolled onto her side, facing the opposite direction, but as tired as her body was, she couldn't sleep either. What happened tonight played over and over in her mind. His kisses left her weak and exhilarated all at once, and this frightened her more than anything else that lay ahead.

He was sharp and quick. Hadn't she seen for herself his ability to know his surroundings? Back at the farm, Proud Eagle knew the Chiricahua were there before she had the slightest inkling. His keen warrior training had alerted him. So, why, then, did she think she could escape him? She should have walked Todd away, mounted him far from camp. Did she want to get caught, hope he would stop her? She rubbed her hands over her eyes. Everything was so confusing, her emotions conflicted. She was falling in love with an Indian man. Yes, in love. How could this have happened? How could she allow this? And how could she be on her way to make a life with him and his people?

She groaned.

"What is wrong?"

She turned to look at him. "I'm afraid."

"I gave you my word I would not hurt you. I will never let anything hurt you from this day on."

"I'm not afraid of you. I'm afraid for us."

"*Hat'ugha*, why?"

She sat up. "Because we are from different worlds, we believe in different things, and our people are warring with one another."

"My *nuhdee* have not done your people wrong," he defended.

"But my people don't know that. All they see are Indians raiding their homes and killing their loved ones." She bit her bottom lip. "How can anything between us be good?"

There was a long silence before he spoke. "Golden Lady, when we kiss, is it not *nzhoo*, very good?"

"It is *nzhoo*," she repeated.

He smiled at her attempt to speak his language. "And when we speak to one another, do you enjoy it?"

"Yes, I do."

His smile deepened. "Then that is how things between us are good."

She curled her feet beneath her. "What about everything else? The differences in our lives, our ways, traditions, and all the fighting."

"Those are things around us, not between us."

"Don't you think they can come between us?"

He gave a taut nod. "If we let them."

Her frustration flowed into her voice. "How can we not?"

"By trusting in one another, sticking together, and standing strong." He moved closer, placing his hand over hers. "You said before, the reason you did not go to the parsonage with the holy man was because you stayed back to care for me."

"That's true. Had you not been lying wounded and sick in my barn, I would have packed up and moved to town, got a room at the boarding house, and found work at the general store for my keep."

"Why did you not let your lawmen take me?"

She cast her gaze away. "I just couldn't let them..." She choked on the thought of him hanging from a noose.

"Why did you care?" he probed deeper

"I can't explain the reason why. Maybe because of the sign."

"What sign?"

"The eagle I saw while at my father's grave. Your name." She shrugged. "I can't explain it. I just knew I had to stay back and help you." A chill ran down her spine, and she shivered. "No matter how afraid I was of my farm being attacked by

Chiricahua, I couldn't leave you to die, and I couldn't bear the thought of them taking you—and putting you to death."

He placed a finger beneath her chin, turning her face upward and locking eyes with hers. "We did not talk or kiss at that time, and still you could not let me go?"

"No," she admitted. "I couldn't let you go."

He traced her full lips with the tip of his finger. "Can you not see from the beginning there was a bond between us, in spite of what is going on around us?"

"But how do we ignore what's happening? How will we not let it crush us?"

"It will not be easy, but nothing good comes easy. And it is not shameful to do things afraid. What is shameful is if we walk away from something only because we are afraid." He pulled her closer. "I felt fear from the top of my head to the bottom of my feet when the Chiricahua burned your barn. But I knew I had to get you away. Did you think it was easy for me to end those warriors' lives in order to save ours?"

She was ashamed to admit she hadn't thought twice about what was going on inside of him when he fought the Chiricahua. "I'm sorry, Proud Eagle, for not realizing your feelings."

"It is over now. Behind us. We are alive and that is what truly matters." He smiled. "Now, we must look ahead. I believe what we have between us is worth every effort, Golden Lady. Just give us the *nkeez*, time, to find out. I promise you will not regret it."

That's what scared her the most. And the fact eagles mated for life.

****

When Proud Eagle announced his village was just over the ridge, a mixture of relief and anxiety coursed through Amanda. Relief the long, hot ride, sitting so close to Proud Eagle on horseback, was finally coming to an end. But anxious she would now be surrounded by Indians. She looked down at her soiled bedclothes. It wasn't a fitting outfit to wear when meeting new people.

She smoothed back the curls from her forehead and straightened her collar.

"You look fine," he whispered from behind.

She frowned. It wasn't the first time he read her thoughts.

Upon entering the village, she saw children playing in front of odd shaped dwellings, wickiups, Proud Eagle called them. They ran to surround Todd, staring at her and talking in their native tongue. Then, noticing Duke, they bent to pet and marvel over him, leaving her and Proud Eagle to ride farther into the village.

A few women watched them pass, their eyes glued on her. They wore moccasins similar to Proud Eagle's and buckskin dresses or skirts and tunics, with beads adorning their necks and wrists. Some women wore their hair loose around their shoulders, while others had their hair tied back.

"The *estunes*, matrons, that wear their hair free, are married," Proud Eagle explained. "*Nahlins*, maidens, wear their hair tied back in a *nah-leen*."

Several men ran to greet them, dressed in buckskin and moccasins. They gawked at her until Proud Eagle said something in his language to make them all laugh.

"What did you say to them?"

"That this time I caught a two-legged doe with golden hair," he boasted.

Her cheeks flushed with humiliation.

He took her to the far end of the village, stopping at a wickiup closest to the river. A smaller one sat beside it.

Proud Eagle swung down from old Todd and pointed to the larger dwelling. "That is my parents' *gowa*. You will stay with them and learn our women's ways from my mother. The smaller wickiup is where I live."

Her heart raced. "What if she hates me?"

He helped her down from old Todd. "My mother loves everyone. Especially someone who has saved her only son from *yunke-lo*, death." He rubbed her cheek with the back of his hand and smiled. "Trust me, Golden Lady, all will be fine."

"And what—what will you tell them?"

"I will tell them the truth."

"No. I mean, how will you explain me?"

He raked his eyes down the length of her. "It is plain to see you are a woman. What more is there to say?"

"I'm sure they will wonder why you've brought me home with you."

"Everyone who has seen us already knows why I have brought you home with me."

She folded her arms across her chest. "It is only right certain words are said."

He leaned toward her, bringing his mouth close to her ear. "We have already talked about what is *nzhoo* between us. I have already claimed you as mine. What more needs to be spoken?"

She sighed, exasperated. "A proposal is what I'm talking about."

He gave a taut nod and cleared his throat. "Golden Lady, I plan to take you as *shi'aad*, my wife."

"You didn't ask, you demanded."

Proud Eagle frowned annoyed. "You know what I mean, so why be troublesome?"

"It's tradition for the man to ask. You of all people should realize how important a tradition is."

He nodded, squaring his shoulders. "Will you let

me take you as my wife?"

She stifled a smile. It wasn't how she'd hoped to be proposed to, but it would have to do. "Yes, Proud Eagle, I will."

A broad smile spread across his face. "And after you claim me at the mating ceremony and walk through the stones, I will take you to my wickiup. Then you will build us a larger wickiup to live in. One we will share as husband and wife, and where our children will be born."

She gasped. "Build? I don't know how to build."

"Do not worry, Golden Lady, the other women in the village will help you. That is our way."

Her knees grew weak. Everything had happened too fast. She looked around the village. Would she ever fit in? Could these strangers really become her family?

With a finger beneath her chin, he turned her gaze his way. "There is much fear and doubt on your face."

She licked her lips. "Can you blame me?"

"No, I cannot, but I wish you would trust me."

She gave a curt nod and straightened her shoulders.

He smiled, taking her by the hand. "Come now, my woman, and meet my parents."

She bit her bottom lip to steel herself and followed him to the wickiup.

Two people from the tribe neared them as they walked on. One was a young boy, tall and slender with thick, dark hair to his chin. He gaped, his large black eyes taking in every inch of her. Her cheeks grew hot under his careful and slow scrutiny.

He turned to the young woman with him and spoke to her in Apache, his tone bragging.

Proud Eagle chuckled and translated. "He is proving I caught a two-legged doe with golden hair."

The young woman's gaze was more deliberate,

critical. Amanda, self-conscious of her appearance, was humiliated for traipsing around the countryside dressed in her bedclothes.

The girl approached Proud Eagle and cast him a demure look, speaking words Amanda understood. "I have missed you, my dear and trusted warrior, and feared daily for your life. I am glad to see my pleas to the gods for your safe return have been answered."

Proud Eagle gave the young woman a quick smile. "I thank you for those pleas, Running Doe."

She didn't appreciate Running Doe standing so near to Proud Eagle and did a bit of sizing herself. The other woman's features were large, her nose sharp, and her mouth consumed her face. She wore her black tresses tied up in the *nah-leen*, the hair-tie Proud Eagle explained earlier maidens wore. Upon a closer look it was dumb-bell shaped, covered in beaver fur and adorned with gilt buttons.

Running Doe glanced at her, contempt welling in her large brown eyes. "You have not one kill?" In a voice, heavy with sarcasm, she added. "Was the hunting so poor you could not bring back one good bounty worth your time?"

The Indian woman's attitude infuriated her. She was about to speak, when Proud Eagle's grasp tightened around her hand. She cast a look at him.

The muscles at his jaw throbbed. "I did not have a chance to hunt, Running Doe."

Running Doe's tone held a silky challenge. "Ah... I see. And why is that?"

"It is a long story." He turned to Amanda and smiled. "But one that has turned out well in spite of how it began."

Thankful for the tenderness and warmth he showed her, she came back with a smile of her own.

Proud Eagle returned his attention to Running Doe. "I wish now to tell my father what has happened."

Once again he led her toward his parents'
wickiup.

Running Doe followed. "Can I listen as well,
Proud Eagle?"

He hesitated, looking down at Amanda. She
could sense he weighed the question.

When he spoke, his tone was hard. "Yes, it is
wise for you to hear." He looked over at the boy and
smiled. "You too, Little Elk, it is wise for all to hear
what I have to say."

Her heart raced with a mixture of apprehension
and curiosity as she entered the wickiup with Proud
Eagle. The modest dwelling was made of a
framework of poles and limbs tied together, over
which a thatch of bear grass, brush, and yucca
leaves, were placed. A canvas material stretched
over the structure on the windward side and opened
at the top to allow the smoke to escape from the fire
pit, which sat in the center of the wickiup.

Two wooden-framed beds, one larger than the
other, sat in the corners. The small cot, about three
feet from the ground, was filled with dry grass and
covered with blankets.

An elder Indian man reclined on the bigger bed,
a blanket thrown over his legs. He smiled when he
saw Proud Eagle and spoke in their native tongue.

Again Proud Eagle translated. "My father is
happy to see me, says I have been gone this time for
too many nights."

It was easy for her to see Proud Eagle favored
his father's good looks. The elder man's jaw and nose
were similar to the son's, with eyes just as dark. And
now, those large, black eyes were set on her.

Cunning Eagle, hearing his son translating for
him, changed to speaking English. "I feared all was
not well with you."

Proud Eagle motioned for her to stay by the door

opening, and moved closer to the bed, sitting cross-legged on the ground. "All was not well, my father."

Cunning Eagle's eyes locked now with Proud Eagle's. "Why so?"

"I will tell you all, but first I want you to meet Golden Lady." He turned toward her and motioned for her to come near.

She made her way to him, taking hold of his outstretched hand, and knelt, joining him by his father's bed.

"This is my father, Cunning Eagle," Proud Eagle said.

She inclined her head. "I am pleased to meet you, sir."

The elder Indian stayed silent, his expression wooden, the black eyes examining her every feature.

She blushed beneath his harsh assessment.

Proud Eagle indicated with a wave of his hand the woman beside the fire pit. "And this is my mother, White Dove."

The elder woman sat amongst a pot, a skillet, a dishpan, a few knives, a pounding stone, and a pair of grinding slabs. Amanda summed up this area of the wickiup as the kitchen.

White Dove raised her eyes from her work to meet hers. Long, light brown hair fell to the woman's waist, framing a round and pleasant face—her complexion fairer than Proud Eagle's. White Dove smiled, revealing even white teeth, then returned her attention to the grinding.

"Soon she will be your mother as well," Proud Eagle whispered in her ear.

She watched him, catching the pride and admiration he had for the elder woman glowing in his eyes.

Cunning Eagle cleared his throat. "You have yet to tell me what happened." He glared at her, his voice low, composed. "And how she has come to be with you."

She glanced around the wickiup to find all eyes watched her. Her blood pounded, rushing to flush her face. And just when she thought things couldn't get any more awkward, Proud Eagle explained his story using the Apache dialect.

Proud Eagle noticed Golden Lady's cheeks turn scarlet. He took her hand and squeezed, hoping to ease her discomfort. "I was attacked near the river by a Chiricahua warrior. Before I sent his soul to *O'zho*, one of his poisoned tipped arrows pierced my shoulder. The poison left me weak and with fever. I feared for my life. I remember coming to a clearing, and then next I remember a big dog howling over the top of me."

From the corner of his eye, Proud Eagle saw Running Doe, who sat by the door flap, move closer. She hung on his every word, eager not to miss a thing.

"What then, my son," Cunning Eagle said.

"A white woman came out to silence the dog."

All eyes again were on the Golden Lady.

Proud Eagle felt her stiffen beside him. "I asked for her help, and at first she feared me. A Chiricahua killed her father, and she believed I was the one," he added. "But I gave her my word I would not harm her, that I was from another tribe. Then she did help me."

He looked over at her. Her deep blue eyes showed unease. Proud Eagle gave her an encouraging smile before he turned again to look at his father. "I do not remember what happened for many days after, but this I do know—every time I opened my eyes she was beside me. She tended to my wound, helped me drink and eat. Without her care I would be dead." He turned again to look her way. "She saved my life."

"Your mother and I will forever be grateful to

this white woman for what she did, but then, after you regained your strength, why did you not travel home alone?"

He let out a long, audible breath. "One night Chiricahua attacked her home, burnt the barn. Before they reached the house, I helped her escape. Together we ran into the woods. Hid for many days."

Cunning Eagle leaned forward in the bed. "Then, you saved her life as well."

Proud Eagle nodded.

"So now you owe her nothing. You have returned the goodness she showed you, a life for a life," Cunning Eagle reflected.

His voice hardened. "I did not bring her here to repay her kindness."

Cunning Eagle glanced over at Amanda. "Then why did you?"

"I plan on making her my wife."

Running Doe gasped.

Cunning Eagle arched a brow.

"In our travels here we had much time to talk. While we sat by the fire she told me of her god, and I told her of our traditions." He leaned forward, softening his tone. "She has much spirit, my father. And since the first I set eyes on her, I have not been able to rid her from my thoughts." Proud Eagle placed a hand over his chest. "Or from my heart."

Cunning Eagle cleared his throat. "Ah...it is that way for you?"

"Yes. I will never let her go," he concluded with strong conviction.

"But is it that way for her, my son?"

His voice rose with annoyance. "She would not be here if she did not agree."

Cunning Eagle stroked his chin. "Or could it be she had no where else to go. You did say her home was destroyed by Chiricahua."

"She does have somewhere else to go, but she

chose to stay with me."

"And her people...they will not miss her, want her back, or come looking for her?" Cunning Eagle challenged.

Proud Eagle ripped out the words. "There is only one she speaks of. A holy man. But he will not follow."

Cunning Eagle narrowed his eyes. "You are sure of this?"

"Ask her yourself."

Amanda didn't understand the words, but she could tell by the tone of their voices things had heated up between father and son.

She was surprised when Cunning Eagle turned to her and asked, "What do your people call you?"

For a second, she couldn't find her voice. She swallowed hard. "Amanda Gregory."

"Humph. Golden Lady fits you better."

She smiled. "That's what your son said."

"And what do you say about my son?"

She hesitated, wanting the words to be just right—truthful and heartfelt. They had to convey why she would consider leaving her world for Proud Eagle's.

Heaven help me, do I even have a clear grasp on the reasons myself?

How could she explain to the old man how his son turned her insides to molasses with just a look? How he sent shocks of pleasure through her entire being with a touch, gave her fever with his kiss? No, she'd never be able to put such intimate feelings into words and still remain a proper lady.

She glanced at Proud Eagle, waiting for her to talk. Then she returned her gaze to Cunning Eagle. "Your son is a brave warrior, gentle and kind. I will always be grateful for the way he protected me against the Chiricahua. And forever I will cherish the times we are together and the things that are good between us." She licked her dry lips. "This has not been an easy decision to make, yet, I know it's the right one because the eagle soared while I stood at my father's grave." She explained to Cunning Eagle the sign she prayed for and all she knew about the eagle.

"And you believe my son is the eagle that will set for you a new awakening?"

"He already has."

Cunning Eagle's voice softened. "You have given up much to be here because of your beliefs. That alone speaks of a true heart. But there are other things to consider."

"I know the things you mean. At first, they concerned me, as well," she admitted.

"What has overcome your concern?"

Her voice was shakier than she liked. "I'd have to say, the thought of not being with Proud Eagle."

"And what of the holy man my son speaks of—will he not worry? Will he not come looking for you, bring others to threaten our village?"

Her heart broke at the thought of Josh grieving over her. "He will worry, because he is a dear friend. No, he's more like family and the only one I have left. But he will not follow. No one will come to bother your tribe."

"Our ways are not your ways. The life of our women is a hard one," Cunning Eagle warned.

"I am the daughter of a farmer, whose wife died before she gave him a son." She raised her hands, turning the palms up. "These have been the only hands available to help my father plant and plow the field, chop the wood, repair the barn, milk the cow, as well as do the cooking, cleaning, and mending. Hard work is not new to me."

Cunning Eagle arched a brow. "There are many other hardships the tribe faces; seasons of hot and cold, of plenty and scarce."

She raised her chin. "I am familiar with the cycles of life. Your hardships are not so different from the ones I've known. My people have also seen suffering."

Cunning Eagle smirked. "My son is right, you do have much spirit." He narrowed his eyes. "But sometimes it can be *inju*, good, other *nkeezs*, times, it can be bad. You must learn when and how to use such determination." His voice held authority. "One day my son will be chief. If you are to stand by his side as his woman, you must earn the reverence of his people. Without their respect, you will not be able to help Proud Eagle in his duty to the tribe. Can you share what you have and all you know for the *inju*, good, of all?"

She squared her shoulders. "Yes, sir, I can, if you give me the chance to prove this to you, you will see I speak the truth. You won't be sorry, I promise."

Cunning Eagle nodded, satisfied. "Then I will take you at your word." He looked over at Proud Eagle, a twinkle in his eyes. "I can see why you cannot free her from your thoughts or your heart."

Proud Eagle pushed aside a wisp of hair curling at her temples, admiration twinkling in his eyes. "Does she not have the beautiful golden mane of a mystical horse?"

"And the bite of one, too," Cunning Eagle teased. Worn and tired, he lay back against a rolled blanket. "But my word is not the last say. You know I must gather *Ncpotonjc*, Bear Watcher, and Shaman *Lupan*, Gray Fox, and ask their council as well." His voice trembled with his weariness. "One day you will be chief, my son. Do you think the Elders will accept a white woman as their leader's wife?"

"They will if you will, my father."

Cunning Eagle nodded. "You have my agreement."

Proud Eagle smiled. "Then call a council

meeting, and let me have the chance to tell them of my Golden Lady, how I have chosen her to be my wife."

At Proud Eagle's words, Running Doe bolted to her feet. With tears streaming from her eyes, the young woman ran out of the wickiup in a hurry.

****

White Dove set out biscuit bread, dumplings, and a drink made from walnut meats. Already Amanda was shown how to boil and filter the liquid, which tasted much like milk. Getting involved in the evening's preparations had helped to take her mind off the fact she'd soon be put on display for the Elders. If it weren't for White Dove's hospitality, warm smiles, and words of encouragement, she would be far more anxious.

When Bear Watcher and Shaman Gray Fox arrived, Cunning Eagle welcomed them with a gesture to take a seat beside him. Proud Eagle stood with respect, remaining on his feet until the Elders took their places around the fire.

She took a seat beside White Dove, who whispered. "You have already met Bear Watcher's daughter, Running Doe."

She remembered the hostile glares the young woman cast her way and wondered if her father would do the same.

White Dove remained sitting behind her husband, weaving a basket, until Cunning Eagle motioned for his wife to take a seat beside him. Amanda remembered what Proud Eagle explained about Indian men valuing their wife's advice on many matters, and wasn't surprised over the Chief's actions. White Dove handed her the basket and moved forward, completing the circle.

Cunning Eagle took a sip of the milky liquid and then cleared his throat with authority. "I have called you here, my brothers, to tell you Proud Eagle has chosen a wife."

She was grateful the old chief decided to conduct the meeting in her language, but not so pleased when all eyes turned her way. She wished she could hide beneath a blanket, but since that option was not available, she smiled at each of the men instead.

There was a low murmur between the two Elders.

Cunning Eagle opened his mouth to speak again, but Proud Eagle held up his hand for him to wait. "My father, I wish to speak my heart to these good friends."

Cunning Eagle nodded in agreement.

Proud Eagle hesitated before speaking, gathering in his mind the right words to say. It was obvious the two men were much respected amongst the tribe, their approval essential for her and Proud Eagle to make a peaceful and happy life together in the village.

What would happen if they disagreed? Would she be cast out, forced to wander the countryside in search of the parsonage?

Although she couldn't believe Proud Eagle would abandon her, she didn't want his people to abandon him either. Cunning Eagle was a sick man, and Proud Eagle would be the next chief. She didn't want such an honor to be taken from him because of her.

Proud Eagle's words broke through her thoughts. "From the time I was a small boy, both of you have been close friends of my father. Each of you has watched me grow and has helped me to be the strong warrior I am today. You have taught me well, my friends." He paused, taking the time to look into the eyes of each Elder. "I respect you as much as I respect my father, which is why I speak to you now, with honor."

She smiled to herself. Her warrior was not only

clever, brave, and resourceful, but a diplomat as well.

Proud Eagle looked over at her. "You see the woman sitting outside the circle."

All eyes turned her way, again. This time she didn't smile, but raised her chin with pride, locking eyes with Proud Eagle. If he was brave enough to speak on her behalf, she needed to show they were united.

The slight nod he gave her indicated he understood her action. He continued with more confidence. "I call her Golden Lady. She saved me from death that would have been brought on by a Chiricahua's poisoned arrow." He looked again into their eyes. "But, know this, before she came upon me lying wounded by her home, a Chiricahua murdered her father." He held up his hand. "With only my word I was not the warrior that ended her father's life, she took care of me." Again his gaze met hers. "This beautiful and spirited woman showed me kindness beyond duty. Never have I felt so strong about anything, as I feel about making her my wife. I want her to move from outside the circle, to join it—as my mother has done."

She blinked back tears. His words melted her heart. Never had she felt so close to another person, as she did right now toward Proud Eagle.

He looked again around the circle. "I mean no disrespect when I say you have not been called here this night to offer advice, only to hear of my decision."

Bear Watcher's voice grated and she was taken aback by his harsh tone. "Well, we have heard, and since you have already made up your mind, what more do you wish from us?"

Proud Eagle arched a brow. "I wish for both of you to welcome her. If you show you accept her, it will encourage the others in the tribe to do the same."

Shaman Gray Fox turned toward Amanda and searched her face. "How do you feel living among us?"

Again, she was surprised to be spoken to and hesitated with an answer.

"Come," he offered. "Join the circle now and let your voice be heard."

Proud Eagle made room for her beside him.

Shaman Gray Fox smiled a toothless grin. "Now, speak your *biijii*, heart, Golden Lady."

Amanda clasped her hands in her lap, her heart pounding. *What if I say the wrong thing?*

Proud Eagle placed his hand over hers. "There is nothing to fear."

I beg to differ.

Looking around the circle, her gaze rested on White Dove. With a smile from the elder woman, and an encouraging nod, she found her voice.

"All right, I will speak from my heart, as you have asked." She sat cross-legged as the others. "I understand why you're all concerned. To be truthful with you, I had the same concerns myself. But along the way something else happened. I started to see, in spite of the many differences, there were many similarities." She looked over at Cunning Eagle. "You're much like my own father, a wise man and loyal to your family. The way you love your wife and want what is best for your son reminds me of how my father cared for my mother and me." She smiled. "I am sorry you will never have a chance to meet him, because I believe the two of you would have gotten along fine."

Cunning Eagle gave a taut nod. "I am sorry as well."

She turned to White Dove. "You are very much like my mother. She was a teacher who came to this land from across the ocean so she could help others learn how to read and write. Today, you taught me how to make the drink from the walnut meats, and I watched with interest while you weaved the basket. I know there is much more I can learn from you, and I'd like to have the opportunity."

White Dove's smile deepened, her entire face brightened.

She glanced at Bear Watcher and Shaman Gray Fox. "There is much you all can learn from me as well, that I will be glad to share." She looked over at Proud Eagle. "But what matters above all, is that Proud Eagle and I share each other's heart. How or why this has happened is not for us to say." She rested her eyes on each face. "There is a season, a time for every purpose." Her heart swelled with the hope her life's plan would be to bridge the gap between hers and Proud Eagle's people. That thought encouraged her to speak further. "We are all made the same, flesh is still flesh, no matter the color. Love is love, no matter who it is between."

There was a long silence, the crackling of the fire the only thing to be heard.

White Dove rose from her seat with grace, in spite of her stocky build, and served each man a biscuit. "My brothers, this is not the first time an Apache has taken a white mate. Have you forgotten my father?"

"I have not forgotten him, White Dove," Shaman Gray Fox said. "He was a good man and taught us many things."

"Give my son your good wishes, then, and let his woman teach us more." White Dove reached for the plate of dumplings, and served one to each guest. "Our land is becoming surrounded by the white man. How much wiser and safer it will be for us all if we are able to live in peace among them."

A time to keep silent and a time to speak. And when White Dove spoke, all listened.

Shaman Gray Fox nodded his head in agreement. "You speak wise words, White Dove." He looked at Amanda. "As do you, Golden Lady." Then he smiled at Proud Eagle. "I will welcome your woman, you have my good wishes."

Bear Watcher was more reluctant to concur.

Your daughter is just as unfriendly.

His tone was sharp when he finally agreed. "Mine as well."

Cunning Eagle reached out to pat his son on the shoulder. "You have the good wishes of the Council of Elders, my son. Along with them, I welcome your woman."

White Dove moved close and embraced her. "Welcome my daughter."

The tears welling in her eyes slid onto her cheeks. "Thank you all. You will not be sorry for your good wishes. I will teach your children many new things." She placed her hand on her chest. "My heart holds such joy. I don't think I'll be able to close my eyes in bed tonight long enough to fall asleep."

Proud Eagle lowered his voice for only her to hear. "Rest while you can, my woman, after we are married, sleep is the last thing you will be doing in bed."

****

Amanda was right, falling asleep was impossible. Whether her restlessness was contributed to the fact she was sleeping in a wickiup with Proud Eagle's parents—Cunning Eagle snored—or because the tiny bed was lumpy, she didn't know. All she was sure of was in spite of the adrenaline now rushing through her, she was exhausted. Not a good way to start the first day of a new life.

When dawn approached, she stepped out of the wickiup for a breath of air. Around her the village came to life. The men came out of their homes to

105

hunt and the women made their way to the river with the laundry.

Proud Eagle, coming up from behind, encompassed her waist with his hands. "Good morning." He placed a gentle kiss on the back of her neck. "Did you sleep well?"

She leaned back against the hardness of his chest. "Not a shred."

"Ah, it was the same for me."

She turned to face him. "Your father snores."

He arched a brow. "I do as well."

She sighed. "Perhaps its best I get used to it, then."

He chuckled. "That would be most wise."

She caressed his face. "What happens now, Proud Eagle?"

Before he could answer, White Dove's head peered out through the door opening. "Come." She motioned them inside. "Time now to eat."

Proud Eagle flashed a handsome smile, before he reached for her hand and led her into the wickiup.

She took her place around the fire pit and ate biscuit bread while Proud Eagle and his father talked in their native tongue. White Dove remained silent in a corner of the wickiup, her head bent over her weaving.

Proud Eagle turned to his mother and spoke something to her in Apache.

White Dove placed her work aside and rose from her seat. "Come," she said, motioning for Amanda to follow her. "We have much to do."

She cast a glance at Proud Eagle, and after receiving an encouraging nod, went with White Dove to the smaller wickiup.

It was much the same inside as the larger one, but without as many cooking utensils by the fire pit. A full sized bed was in one corner; a buckskin dress, moccasins, and a leather pouch were laid out in a neat row upon it. In another corner stood a small wooden stool, placed on top was a basin of water and a cloth.

"I have brought you here to help you wash and dress for the mating ceremony," White Dove explained.

Her heart raced. "I had no idea the ceremony was today."

White Dove gave a taut nod. "You have nothing to fear. You will be the most beautiful of all maidens." She helped remove the soiled robe and nightgown, wrapping her in a blanket before bending to remove the shoes. White Dove tossed everything into the fire.

Amanda pulled the blanket around her nakedness, watching the flames consume her clothes. For a fleeting moment, seeing the last shred of her world burn caused a flicker of doubt to cross her mind. Had she done the right thing?

White Dove gave her arm a reassuring pat. "It is always hard to end a way we have come to know." She pushed aside the dress and moccasins, motioning for Amanda to sit on the bed. "Things to come can be just as good and one day will be the things of old as time passes." White Dove brought the basin of water closer, wet the cloth, and wrung it out. "I will be here to teach you the ways of our women." She slid the blanket off Amanda's shoulders and washed her back. "Soon you will have a husband, who will love you beyond all things." She moved to wash her arms and neck. "You will not be sorry you came here." She pushed aside the rest of the blanket and washed her stomach and thighs. "You will see my words are true."

Her uneasiness increased under the elder woman's care. Not since she was a child of five had she had help bathing. White Dove rinsed the cloth and motioned for her to stand. Heat stole into her face as Proud Eagle's mother washed her backside and legs. Again, White Dove motioned for her to sit so she could wash her feet. The quick and skillful way she was bathed led her to believe the ritual was a custom performed before the mating ceremony. To complain or stop White Dove might cause to offend her. She decided not to protest, in spite of the humiliation, and allowed the Indian woman to finish the rite.

White Dove helped her slip into the buckskin dress. It felt soft and smooth as it clung to her clean flesh. But the garment only came to her knees, leaving the rest of her legs exposed. "Perhaps I need a larger size."

White Dove giggled. "It fits you perfect."

"But my legs are showing."

"It is how the dress is worn," White Dove explained.

She stretched the material. "It takes some getting used to."

White Dove smiled. "But in time you will."

She sighed. "I fear I'll make a fool of myself, do something wrong to embarrass Proud Eagle." She bit her bottom lip. "I couldn't bear bringing you all shame after you've opened your home to me and stuck by my side with the Elders of the tribe."

White Dove pulled from the pouch a bracelet and necklace made of coral and mother of pearl beads. She fastened the choker around Amanda's neck. "A fool is one who cannot see other ways, not one who tries to learn them." She slipped the bracelet around her wrist. "Now, I will do your hair."

A comb, fashioned out of a bunch of stiff grass tied in a bundle by a cord, served the purpose well. White Dove secured the golden tresses in the *nah-leen*, and stood back to admire her work. "You are a beautiful Indian Princess," she said in awe. "I am so proud my son has chosen you."

She fingered the delicate beadwork around the collar of the dress and believed she was an Indian Princess. While slipping her calloused feet into the moccasins, she admired the ornaments woven around the cuff. The soft buckskin allowed her to wiggle and stretch her toes. Never had she worn footwear that gave her feet so much freedom. In fact, to her surprise, all of what she now wore was comfortable.

"We must stay here until the women are called into the circle." White Dove sat upon the bed, legs crossed. "I will wait with you." She motioned for Amanda to sit beside her. "Come, sit, and I will tell you what to do when it is your time to choose Proud Eagle."

When she took a seat beside her future mother-in-law, the elder woman reached over and gave her a hug. Genuine warmth radiated from White Dove, and she was sure at least this member of the tribe would always make her feel welcome.

She listened to White Dove's directions and hoped she would do what was expected of her at the ceremony.

Her concern must have shown on her face, because White Dove patted her arm. "You will do just fine, not to worry."

"You have been so kind to me, so understanding." She placed a hand over White Dove's. "Is it because I helped your son?"

"At first, but now I see the love you and Proud Eagle have for each other. It shines from both of you, and I believe you will be *nzhoo* for each other."

"How do you know this?"

White Dove smiled. "When you are a mother you will understand."

She sat back on the bed, crossing her legs like White Dove's. "Proud Eagle told me your father was a white man."

White Dove nodded. "He came from the north to trade *ighaas*, furs, and fell in love with *shemaa*, my mother."

Amanda was eager to know more. "Was he from the north?"

"He came from the North Country but it was not his homeland. He came to this land from across the big *guesa* from a *yata* called Eng... Eng..." She frowned. "I cannot remember the name of his first *gowa*."

She leaned forward, keeping her excitement at bay. "Is it England?"

White Dove's plump face brightened. "Yes, England! Do you know of this *yata*?"

"Yes, that was my mother's homeland as well. She came to Arizona to teach the children in the settlement of Willow Creek."

White Dove smiled. "There, you see, we are not so different."

"Tell me more about your father, White Dove."

White Dove relaxed back against a pile of blankets. "My father was a small man, with eyes much the color of yours. His hair was as *dithith*, black, as a moonless night, with a streak of the *holos* sweeping across one side." She sighed. "I remember once asking *shemaa* about the splash of gold, and she told me he had been kissed by *ittindi*, lightning. His chin was covered with hair, like a bear," she added, "and so the tribe called him *Ittindi Maba*, Little Lightning Bear. But the other *indah* who came with him called him Silas."

"Did the other white man stay?"

"For a while, then he moved on. Little Lightning Bear stayed until he took his last breath. And I will never forget that day," she added, her face solemn. "It was the *nkeez* Proud Eagle was sent out on his first hunt. When my *ciye*, son, returned his *biijii* sorrowed." She shook her head sadly. "His grandfather would never see the bounty he was so proud to bring back."

A young Indian woman entered the wickiup. Her thick, black hair hung around her shoulders, her belly swollen with the growth of the child she carried.

"It is *nkeez* for the women to be called to the circle," she informed White Dove, then turned to introduce herself. "I am Rising Sun." She handed Amanda a rose with the thorns removed. "When you choose Proud Eagle, give him the rose as a symbol of your love." Large brown eyes twinkled when she smiled. "When I chose my *shikaa*, Falling Star, I did the same." She patted her belly. "Our marriage has been one of much happiness and love, as you can see."

After Rising Sun left the wickiup, White Dove explained, "She is my sister's daughter." Her eyes welled with tears. "Rising Sun's father lost his life in battle before she was born and my sister's *biijii* died along with her warrior *shikaa*. Her sorrow left her weak, too weak to bear childbirth. Her soul went to *O'zho* two nights after Rising Sun was born."

"I'm so sorry, White Dove."

"Proud Eagle was just learning to walk at that *nkeez*. I wanted to give life to another child, but could not nurture my *shikaa's* seed. So, I took Rising Sun into our *gowa* and raised her as my own."

"Then, in a sense, she is Proud Eagle's sister."

White Dove nodded. "That is how Cunning Eagle and I see her."

"I always wanted a sister," she reflected.

White Dove smiled. "Now, you will have one."

She returned the smile. "I will look forward to getting to know her."

White Dove fingered the rose's delicate petals. "I can tell Rising Sun has already found favor with you, as well." She stood and made her way to the opening of the wickiup. "It is *nkeez* for us to go, my child."

Amanda rose from the bed, her knees threatening to collapse, and took a deep breath. With the rose clutched to her racing heart, she followed White Dove to the mating ceremony.

All eyes turned her way. She felt awkward with their stares and sought out Proud Eagle. He sat on the side of the men, head held high, broad shoulders squared. An encouraging smile was sent her way before his eyes roamed the length of her with outward admiration. She blushed and joined the circle.

The drums beat, echoing in her ears, thundering in her chest.

A maiden from the women's side stood and danced in tiny circles closer and closer to a young brave seated beside Proud Eagle. She smiled at her chosen mate, feet keeping to the beat of the drums. Then, bending from the waist, she gave him a slight slap on the cheek.

The brave smiled in return and nodded his head in agreement.

The young girl then danced her way back to her seat, sitting a little outside of the circle.

When Amanda looked over at the brave, he too had moved back from the loop.

The drums continued to beat, and one by one, each maiden in the round chose a mate.

Soon it was Running Doe's turn. Dancing in a circle, her moccasin feet moved, inch by inch toward Proud Eagle. The maiden smiled down at him, swaying her hips in a seductive motion. Proud Eagle's lips thinned, his brow furrowed as he regarded the young woman with annoyance hovering in his eyes.

Amanda also grew annoyed and found it

impossible to steady her erratic pulse. Running Doe's intrusion upon Proud Eagle disturbed her.

In the next instant, she realized she was the intruder, stepping into Proud Eagle's life and upsetting more than tribal tradition. It was obvious to her why Running Doe glared with venom when she first arrived and ran from the wickiup in tears. And Bear Watcher is Running Doe's father. It made perfect sense to her now why he also held hostile eyes upon her throughout the council meeting.

Her sudden knowledge twisted inside of her, and a new anguish seared her heart.

Why didn't Proud Eagle tell me about Running Doe?

A bitter jealousy turned her demeanor grim as she watched Running Doe lean forward to tap Proud Eagle on the cheek.

Proud Eagle shook his head and pulled his face away.

Running Doe's hand froze in mid air.

Proud Eagle kept his face turned, his gaze cast to the ground.

The drums beat on, everyone waited.

Amanda was mortified—for herself, for Proud Eagle, and even for Running Doe, who bit her bottom lip and ran from the circle.

Still the drums beat on.

Proud Eagle turned now to look at her, his anger gone. A charming smile ruffled his mouth, disarming her uncertainties. He nodded, waiting for her to stand.

Good heavens, it's my turn!

All eyes were upon her as she stood. With knees trembling, she danced the way the other maidens had, in three tiny circles, stepping to the rhythm of the drums.

Proud Eagle watched her hips sway with each beat, her beautiful shaped legs moving with graceful steps nearer to him. The buckskin dress pulled taut across her full breasts as she stretched her arms above her head.

He glanced around the circle. Every brave was mesmerized by her performance, their mouths agape and eyes fixed on her hips.

Proud Eagle shifted in his seat, his loins swelling beneath the buckskin breeches.

Closer she came, dancing before him, the skirt of her dress rising higher, revealing the bare shapely legs moving in unison to the drums.

She bent forward, the V neck of the dress divulging the cleavage of her rounded mounds. Excitement stirred his blood, desire for her escalating.

Her face had a musk-rose flush on the cheekbones, the soft pinkish hue also tinting her sweet lips, which curled upward at the corners into a smile. There was both delicacy and strength in her blue eyes, as they searched his while reaching beneath the neckline of her dress and pulling from between her bosom a red rose.

She brought the flower to her lips and bestowed upon the bloom a gentle kiss, then knelt on one knee and brushed the rose down his cheek and across his mouth.

He took the rose from her and placed it in the opening of his shirt.

She smiled and gave his cheek a tender slap. Surprise widened her eyes when he stood, taking her with him. He pulled her close. So close he could feel the rapid beat of her heart. He looked deep into her azure eyes, their smoldering passion gleaming like glassy volcanic rock. They captivated his senses as he slipped his gaze down to her lips.

His head bent, his mouth coming upon hers, and he kissed her, the rush in his head drowning out the beat of the drums.

Then he released her and sat down outside the circle.

Amanda stumbled, catching her balance before she fell to the ground. After taking a moment to compose herself, she danced her way back to her seat.

When all had been chosen, the drums quieted, and the tribe's people mingled amongst one another, laughing and eating.

Proud Eagle brought her a bowl of pine nuts and willow beads. "Ah, my Golden Lady, the way you danced is beyond words."

"Then you were pleased?"

He spoke with light bitterness. "Very pleased, you dance the Apache mating dance better than the Apache women."

She narrowed her eyes. "Why is it then you don't sound so satisfied?"

He arched a brow. "I did not like that every man in the circle was also pleased."

Her lips trembled with the need to smile. She stroked the side of his face. "Then after this night, I will only please you with my dancing."

"Ah, my *isdzan*, you will please me in many ways." His eyes twinkled with mischief; a slow, lazy grin curved one side of his mouth. "After you are *shi'aad*, my wife, you will dance for me over and over, but different than you did today."

She frowned. "And how will I dance next time?"

He lowered his voice, his finger tracing the opening at her neckline. "Without the covering of the buckskin."

Chapter Four

The ruins of the Gregory farm brought Josh such acute misery—physical pain flowed through his bones. A maelstrom of grief assailed his heart, as he gazed upon the burnt homestead and barn. All that remained standing was the stone fireplace, where only days ago he sat beside the hearth, eating lunch with Amanda.

Regrets ripped through his thoughts like a hurricane. Why hadn't he laced her tea with Grace's sleeping herbs and taken her back to town? He knew the danger of her staying alone on the farm. Why hadn't he made her leave? Even if her anger had caused her to never speak to him again, she'd at least still be alive.

The heaviness of his guilt lodged in his heart. He climbed down from the wagon numbed with sorrow and made his way to the scorched structure of the house.

Will I find her remains there?

He shuddered, a dull ache of foreboding weakening his forced control. He searched endlessly for her body. Could he even bear to look upon her, bloodied and blackened, when her vibrancy was still so clear? He swallowed hard the memory of her voice, forever silenced, and continued to seek through the rumble.

His despair didn't matter now; she needed to be laid to rest.

Aye, my feelings cannot hinder the need for a proper burial.

When he dug Ethan Gregory's grave weeks

before, he had no idea Amanda would soon lie beside her father.

"Nay, you are too young, too beautiful for death," he shouted, fists clenched at his side. His bitter tone echoed throughout the desolation, overwhelming the wretched loneliness.

An even more terrifying realization seared his heart when her remains were nowhere to be found. He pressed a dirty hand over his face, the raw truth turning his torment into fear, then rage and repulsion.

Amanda has been kidnapped by the murdering heathens.

He had heard of the tortures and indecencies the savages inflicted upon their victims before death, especially to the women.

His stomach knotted, hot tears stained his cheeks, and he fell to his knees. Shoulders slumping, head bent in sorrow, he prayed she did not linger in their hands. Then he wept for the loss of life, for the loss of her, for the loss of love.

****

Amanda learned the Western Apaches were fun-loving, good-natured people who had a sense of humor and looked for every opportunity to have a celebration.

When Proud Eagle's horse found his way back to the village, everyone gathered to rejoice in the animal's homecoming. Drums sounded and there was much dancing and eating going on around the village.

With the help of White Dove and Rising Sun, there wasn't a day that went by without her learning something new. The two women had become her life-line into the tribe, their loyalty instrumental in how the other women accepted her. They also helped in honing her skills as an Apache wife, showing her how to make Proud Eagle's favorite dishes—biscuit bread, dumplings, and wheat flour dough bread, preparing them just as he liked.

White Dove was a good teacher, patient and diligent, showing her how to make pancakes, syrup, and sugar. "Syrup can only be made with the tender flower stock of the mescal." She handed Amanda a head of cabbage and showed her how to cut it.

She took great care not to over-shred the leafy vegetable with the large blade used for dicing. "Does Proud Eagle like syrup?"

White Dove nodded and brought the cabbage over to a pile of heated rocks, then covered it with bear grass and earth. "Now, we wait."

The next day, she was stunned to see the pulpy mass resembled the consistency much like molasses and just in time to pour over the pancakes made by mixing corn and water. The corn pone baked under ashes. She also learned how to gather a bean pod from the locust tree before it is fully matured to make sugar. Needless to say, Proud Eagle never left the wickiup a hungry man.

She learned many other chores, how the Apache wife did laundry and gathered water, but her favorite time was when she accompanied Rising Sun to the river to bathe. On one occasion, she spotted a woman splashing water in her son's face.

"Why is that woman so cruel to her son, Rising Sun?"

"She is not cruel, Golden Lady. She is *nzhoo* to her son and loves him very much. But he must have been naughty."

She must have looked perplexed for Rising Sun giggled. "Naughty children get cold water splashed in their face, or are sometimes ignored by their mother," she explained through her laughter. She found a rock to sit on and lowered herself upon it. "When a child is naughty a grandfather or a friend in the tribe will dress up as an evil ogre who will creep into the wickiup when the child is asleep."

Amanda sat on the ground beside the rock. "What happens then?"

"The ogre hovers over the child, saying he has come to take him away to the underground, because he has been so naughty." Rising Sun sighed. "I tell you, it is enough to make any child cry, and in return for not being taken away, there is a promise to be good."

"Does it work?"

"Oh yes." Rising Sun giggled again. "I remember when Proud Eagle had done something to anger his parents, and the ogre came. I heard him creep into the wickiup. I opened my eyes just in time to see him speaking his demands over Proud Eagle." Rising Sun threw her head back and laughed harder. "I think I was more frightened than Proud Eagle. I wet my bed."

She joined in on her friend's mirth. "You poor thing. What about Proud Eagle, was he good after that?"

"He was better, but not as *nzhoo* as I was. I wanted to make sure the ogre never visited me." Rising Sun stood with much effort. "Come," she said, "time for us to bathe."

She followed Rising Sun to a secluded pond, hidden by a copse of trees. A beautiful, tiny waterfall cascaded down smoothened rocks, adding tranquility to the sanctuary.

Rising Sun removed her clothes and waddled into the stream, her full belly descending beneath the clear water.

She was a bit more reluctant to undress.

Rising Sun giggled. "Do not worry, no one will bother us."

She disrobed and ran into the pond.

Rising Sun handed her roots of the aloe soap weed, pounded into pulp. "When rubbed together with the water, the weed makes soap for washing the hair."

The crispness of the water washed the heat from her body. She laughed and talked with Rising Sun, sharing secrets, traditions, and feelings but most of all friendship.

When Amanda and Rising Sun returned from their bath, a fire burned outside the Chief's wickiup. Proud Eagle, his parents, and Rising Sun's husband, Falling Star, were seated in a circle and telling stories.

Rising Sun whispered into her ear. "You will soon learn, telling a story is what we do most for fun."

Falling Star stood and helped his wife sit.

Proud Eagle made room for her. Duke, who loved sitting around the fire and catching everyone's food scraps, plopped down between them.

"You are a mangy old mutt," he said to the dog, draping an arm across her shoulders. "Will you tell a story this night, Golden Lady?"

Heat crept into her cheeks. "Goodness, I don't have a story entertaining enough for all to enjoy."

Proud Eagle grinned. "Tell the one about Santa Claus."

"Oh, Proud Eagle, I don't think…"

"It is a good tale. Let them hear it," he cut in.

All eyes were on her and stayed on her from the first words she spoke, "'Twas the night before Christmas and all through the house, not a creature was stirring, not even a mouse"—right through till the last—"and I heard him exclaim as he drove out of sight; Merry Christmas to all, and to all a goodnight."

Proud Eagle interjected remarks here and there, making them all laugh. And then she was bombarded with questions regarding Santa and his reindeers, how the fat, jolly man could fit down the chimney, and so on, until a drum was brought to the circle.

Falling Star played the instrument using a stick with a loop at one end. The drum, made from a pot partially filled with water and tightly covered with deer skin hide, when struck produced a steady, tranquil beat.

She gradually relaxed and scratched Duke behind the ears, comfortable with the company that surrounded her. She munched on the acorns and sunflower seeds, along with pine nuts, juniper berries and the wild turkey passed around. The whole evening was quite enjoyable, until Proud Eagle left the circle and returned with her violin.

He handed her the instrument. "Play for me, my Golden Lady."

She hadn't attempted to make music since her father's death. "I haven't played in many months, Proud Eagle."

He smiled and sat beside her. "Then it is time."

She opened the catch with trembling fingers and removed the violin from the case, placing it on her shoulder. She chose her father's favorite waltz, one he'd taught her first to play. The beautiful melody filled the village and brought others from their wickiups to listen.

The times she danced and laughed came to mind, not so long ago, when Papa played the same tune.

Her heart throbbed with a sick and fiery gnawing. She fought the tears that sprang to her eyes and finished the tune, but the grief was overwhelming. She clutched the violin to her heart and ran from the circle.

White Dove stood to follow, but Proud Eagle reached out to his mother with a restraining hand.

"I will go," he said, retrieving the case left behind.

He found her sitting on the bed, small hands covering her eyes.

The sobs stabbed his heart.

He paused a moment at the door opening, uncertain how to approach her. "Do not let the times of the past bring you sadness."

She raised her gaze to his, her voice shaky with emotion. "How can I not?"

He made his way over to the bed, sitting beside her. "Were they good times, filled with love and happiness?"

She nodded.

"Then remember them that way, not with sorrow."

She laid her head upon his shoulder. "I'm sorry if I've disappointed you in front of your family."

He arched a brow. "You have done nothing to disappoint me."

She lifted her gaze to look at him. "Truly?"

"I have no reason to speak with a false tongue." He wiped a tear from her eye. "Will you come back to the circle?"

She sighed. "I don't know if I can. I feel so foolish running off as I did."

He stood. "They will all be worried about you if you do not return."

"I wouldn't want them to worry."

He extended a hand to her. "Then, come."

She hesitated.

"We must hurry, Golden Lady," he urged.

She stood. "What's the rush?"

He took an audible breath. "I fear Falling Star and Duke will eat all the turkey."

****

Daily, Amanda accompanied Rising Sun to fetch water. Proud Eagle's sister was becoming the sister she never had.

On the way back to the wickiup, she spotted a

row of stones lined in a path. Each day she traveled down the same trail and never before noticed the rocks in such a pattern.

Rising Sun giggled beside her. "Proud Eagle has left the stones here."

She thought back to what Proud Eagle told her about this part of the courtship, and hoped she remembered what to do.

She looked to Rising Sun for guidance, but discovered she had been left on her own. Then, from the corner of her eye, she spied Proud Eagle standing behind a tree, a lopsided grin upon his face.

He waited for her decision.

Choosing to have some fun first, she sauntered up to the rocks, and then sidestepped passed them. When she looked over at Proud Eagle, the smile had faded from his face and replaced by an uncertain frown creasing his brow.

She giggled at his bewilderment and stepped down the stone path, waiting for him to seize her.

But now he pretended to be unconcerned by turning and walking away.

Her lips thinned with annoyance.

In one fluid motion he was by her side, catching her up into his arms, and carrying her to the little wickiup. There he dropped her upon the bed.

The unexpected plummet caused the buckskin skirt to rise to her thighs. She stood and covered herself. "You are a beast."

Proud Eagle arched a brow. "Ah, if that were true, my *isdzan*, your clothes would be in a pile on the floor."

She pushed aside a strand of hair that escaped the *nah-leen*. "What on earth has gotten into you? Are you such a poor sport that you cannot have fun?"

His eyes filled with hurt. "There is a place for fun and games, and a place for respect and honor."

Her cheeks grew hot. "You toyed with me, too."

"You were disrespecting the courtship. You needed to be taught a lesson."

Amanda was ashamed of herself for taking so light a tradition he was serious about. She hurt him by mocking his honor and beliefs.

She turned away and hung her head, hiding the tears that threatened to come. "I'm so sorry, Proud Eagle, I never meant any disrespect."

He went to her, lifting her chin with a finger. "Never hang your head in shame." He searched her face and softened his voice. "The wife of an Apache Chief will shed many tears. Some of pain and sorrow, others of love and joy, but never the ones of shame. You must always remember that, Golden Lady."

She straightened her shoulders and blinked back the tears. "I'll remember."

He smiled. "That is good, my woman. You will be an Apache yet," he whispered before sealing her lips with a kiss.

****

Proud Eagle made his way to the corner of the small wickiup, his tired bones resting upon the blanket that served as a bed. Only a few feet away, Golden Lady lay sprawled across the cot where he once took his rest.

He yawned, sure this night would be no different from the ones that passed. If he had to again endure looking from a distance at her pale hair fanning out around her beautiful face and her full breasts rising and falling as she breathed, he would go mad.

He groaned and sat up. "I cannot take this another night."

Golden Lady turned onto her side to look his way. "What can't you take?"

He took a deep breath. "I cannot take sleeping in this corner one more night or that we both go to bed

124

fully clothed." Annoyed with the whole situation, he stood and paced around the wickiup. "It is time for someone to accept my gifts."

She sat forward in the bed. "After that, we're married?"

He nodded. "And I can claim you and my bed."

"I see."

He made his way to the cot, sitting at the edge. "Who do you choose to have the gifts?"

She curled her knees to her chest. "I have a choice?"

He nodded.

"Anyone I want?" she inquired further.

"Yes," he said.

Her face brightened. "Josh. I want Josh to receive the gifts."

His eyes widened. "The holy man?"

She nodded.

"This you ask cannot be done. The danger is too great to make such a journey." Or was he really worried the danger might be in her seeing the holy man again, and choosing to stay with him?

She placed a hand upon his arm. "Please, Proud Eagle. It's only right I let him know I'm alive, and well, and marrying," she added.

"Danger aside, he will not accept the gifts. He wants you for his own." Jealousy rose to bite him like a hungry bear.

"But I never agreed to be his."

A sardonic laugh escaped his throat. "You are a foolish woman to believe he would stand aside and allow this marriage."

She lifted a defiant chin. "I'm not as foolish as you might think. I know Josh. He only wants my happiness."

"For some reason I do not think he would believe our marriage is a way for you to be happy."

She moved closer to him. "He would if I

explained this is what I want, as you've done with your people."

Proud Eagle stood, again pacing the small dwelling, his thoughts swirling like fallen leaves on a windy day. When he glanced in her direction, his heart was overwhelmed by the patient look upon her face. In silence, she waited for his decision.

He shook his head to clear his thoughts and ceased the pacing "It is better you choose Rising Sun to accept the gifts."

Her disappointment was evident. "But you said it was my choice."

He was crushed he failed her. "I am sorry, Golden Lady. This is how it has to be."

There was a long pause before she spoke. "Proud Eagle, daily I learn the ways of your people. For the rest of my life I will be eating and sleeping among them—as one of them." She paused for a moment. "And I do this with an open heart and mind, because this is what it takes to be your wife." She cast the blanket aside and stood, making her way to him. "You have the pleasure and blessings of your family. Their good wishes for a life we're embarking upon together. Don't I deserve the same?"

The truth of her words cut straight to his heart. "But what you ask is not easy to give."

She caressed his face. "But it isn't impossible."

Her touch melted him. "No, it is not impossible." He searched her face, seeing within her eyes a gleam of hope he would comply. "The holy man's blessing means that much to you?"

She nodded. "And the gifts would bring pleasure to the children he cares for. Please, Proud Eagle," she whispered. "Do this for me."

Her soft plea undid him. "Will you be ready by first light to ride with me back to your land and then from there, show me the way to the holy man's home?"

She nodded again, her full lips curving into a smile. "I will be ready."

"The tradition is I bring the gifts alone, so our journey together will only be so you can tell the holy man of your choice," he informed her. "Do you understand?"

Her happiness was evident in her voice. "Yes. Yes, I understand."

"Then, when I return the second time, after giving the gifts," he pulled her close, lowering his mouth to hers, "you will be my wife."

****

Amanda peered at Josh from behind the large oak tree. He sat in the shade of the porch smoking his pipe. She smiled to herself. He was probably thankful for the stillness that surrounded him. No doubt, Grace and the children were visiting her sister who lived at the edge of town. And Josh was basking in the silence, affording him the privacy to sit and ponder.

She focused on the sad, distant stare of his eyes and realized what he pondered over. *He's been to my farm and grieves over me.*

A rabbit scurried around the yard, made its way to the steps. Josh glanced at it, placing his pipe down on the nearby table, then leaned his head back and closed his eyes.

She moved from behind the tree and neared the porch. "Josh."

"Heaven help me, I can hear the soft, rich tone of her voice," he muttered, sitting forward and opening his eyes. He shook his head to clear it when he spotted her approaching.

She moved closer and once more spoke his name.

Josh stared at her, baffled. "Amanda?" His voice rose an octave with excitement. "Is it you? Is it really you?"

Excitement bubbled over in her own voice. "Yes, it's me, Josh."

He leaped from the chair and ran down the porch steps to embrace her.

"I'm all right. Everything's all right," she reassured him, her voice muffled against his neck.

He pushed her from him, devouring every feature of her face. "I'd lost hope in ever seeing... seeing..." His words caught, and he swallowed hard. "Losing you tore at my heart, and from the pain came a new found sympathy and understanding for the plight of the children dwelling beneath this roof."

"Then, there truly is a reason for all things," she said.

He smiled. "My own words back to haunt me. Do they sound as empty to others when I say them, as they do to me now?"

"Maybe you just can't realize another's sorrow until you've walked a mile in their shoes?"

"I've been plagued by the question whether or not you were alive." His smile deepened. "And thank the Lord, you are, but how did you escape from the Indians?"

"It's not what you think." She motioned toward the porch. "Please, can we sit?"

He pulled her into his arms again. "I'm sorry. So sorry, you must be exhausted and frightened and..." His eyes widened. "Are you hurt? Did they hurt you?"

She pulled free from his grasp. "Josh, I'm fine, but we need to talk."

He caressed her hair. "And we will, we will. No matter what happened, no matter what they did to you. It doesn't change a thing. I'm still here for you, my proposal stands."

She raised a hand to silence him. "I'm not hurt, my virtue was not compromised, and I haven't been with the Indians that attacked my farm."

He eyed her clothing. "But you're dressed like one of them." His brows furrowed. "I'm afraid I don't understand. Then where have you been?"

She gestured to the porch. "Please, can we sit? I have a lot to tell you."

He nodded. "I said I will stand by you."

She sat on the porch swing and patted the seat beside her. "Good, because what I am about to ask you—"

"Amanda, I'm here for you," he cut in, sitting close enough for their thighs to touch. "What ever it is you need, it's yours. Just ask me."

She bit her bottom lip and moved to leave a gap between them. "I need you to accept some gifts so I can be married."

He stared, the blood siphoning from his face. His voice was rough, cracking with anxiety. "Married? To whom?"

She cringed at the insensitive way she'd blurted out the situation after he had been in agony over her disappearance. Holding nothing back, she told him about the night she found Proud Eagle lying in her yard, wounded by a Chiricahua's poisoned arrow. She explained how he was able to speak English and her emotional turmoil while nursing him back to health. Then she concluded with the heroic way Proud Eagle saved her when the Chiricahua attacked the farm.

Josh's eyes darkened. "I knew the day I came to visit there was something in the barn." The muscles at his jaw throbbed. "I should have acted on my instincts and taken a look for myself."

Her neck and shoulders knotted with tension. "And then what would you have done?"

"Well, I would have—"

"You would have made Sara crazier than she already was," she interjected.

"He needed to be handed over to the

authorities."

"For what?" she snapped. "Being wounded?"

"Nay, for... for..." he stammered.

"He isn't responsible for any of the killings, nor are the warriors of his tribe," she added. "I've seen the Chiricahua for myself. I've been living among Proud Eagle's people all this time. The two are not the same." She took an audible breath. "You would have sent an innocent man to the noose."

Josh raked his fingers through his hair. "All right, Amanda, so you helped him, he helped you, for which I am grateful. But now you're back where you belong. Why is there a need to become his wife?"

How could she explain to him Proud Eagle's very presence stirred her passion? It would be like rubbing salt into a wound.

"I can understand you feeling obligated to him for his heroic actions, but not to the point of being wed," he pressed.

She glanced at the grove of trees where Proud Eagle hid. "I'm not marrying him out of duty. It's what I wish."

Josh followed her gaze. "He's here, isn't he?"

She nodded.

Josh stood and reached for the rifle propped up against the railing. "Show yourself!"

She jumped to her feet. "That isn't necessary."

"Oh, but it is, Amanda." Josh's lips thinned. "If you think I'm just going to roll over and allow this man—any man—to steal off into the night with you, you're wrong."

She clenched her fists to her side. "He isn't stealing away into the night with me. I'm willingly going."

He narrowed his eyes. "And that surprises me." His voice grated. "You of all people, after seeing the children here orphaned, after losing your own father." He shook his head with disdain. "You need to look at the hard question here and the differences between you, the fact his kind is fighting with ours."

His tone angered her. "But his kind isn't fighting with us. I've explained that to you already. He's an innocent man." She took a calming breath. "If we don't hold all white men accountable for the things the bad ones do, then we should exercise the same mindset for the Indians."

"And that's your answer for all this?"

"Maybe there will never be a way to arrive at an answer, Josh. Or perhaps it's just a case of us starting to understand and listen to what the other side is all about. To be less critical of their ways or what they have to say." She moved closer to him. "Believe me when I tell you I've gone all through this in my head, anguished over it and tormented myself to no end." She licked her dry lips. "But it all keeps coming around to the same fact."

"And what was your conclusion?"

"I'd rather live in his world with him, than in mine alone."

He glared at her, still aiming the gun at the trees. "Then why have you come back here?"

His steady gaze impaled her. "I knew you'd be worried about me. I wanted you to see I was all right."

He gritted his teeth, his tone cold and exact. "That wasn't your only intent, Amanda, and you know it."

She frowned, annoyed. "What are you saying?"

"Gifts. You mentioned gifts. What's that all about?"

She flinched at the nature of his voice. "For the courtship to be complete, gifts must be brought to the woman's parents or guardian. If these gifts are accepted, then the woman is his wife." She wrung her hands. "Since my parents have passed, I've chosen you as my next of kin."

He glared back in the direction of the trees. "And if I don't accept the gifts, does that mean you will stay, give up this foolish notion?"

Proud Eagle emerged from where he hid, his spear aimed for battle. "No, someone else she has grown close to in the tribe will then be chosen."

Josh's face turned crimson. He leveled the rifle, descending the steps two at a time. He met Proud Eagle head on. "She doesn't belong with you!"

Proud Eagle raised his chin, his voice deep, calm. "With me is the only place she belongs." He looked over at her, possessively eyeing the length of her. "She is my women now."

"Aye, and I see how much respect you have for her," Josh hissed. "Good heavens, you're leering at her like she was a ripe piece of fruit."

A vein at Proud Eagle's neck throbbed. "You are wrong, holy man. I hold much respect and honor for this woman."

Josh's brow was moist with sweat; an incandescent fury flowed in his voice. "I can bet my life you don't know the first thing about honor."

"Then you have not long to live," Proud Eagle challenged.

"Enough!" Amanda moved between the rifle and the spear. "Stop it, both of you. It doesn't have to be like this."

"Come, Golden Lady," Proud Eagle demanded. "We have no further business here."

Josh's lips turned upward into a sneer. "You have already changed her name?"

"Come," Proud Eagle insisted. "We must go."

"Don't go with him, Amanda," Josh implored.

She gripped the end of the rifle and the tip of the spear. "This is not the way this will be solved." She pushed each weapon aside, turning her attention to Josh. "Why are you being so stubborn?"

Josh's bitterness spilled over in his voice. "That's

rich coming from you, Amanda."

"I wanted you to have the gifts. They're blankets, a pony, and other items that can be sold to help care for and support the children."

"We're doing just fine as we are," Josh snapped.

She arched a brow. "You will not stop this marriage."

Josh's eyes locked with hers. "Perhaps, but I won't promote it either."

Her heart sank "Please, Josh, this is my choice."

Josh stepped back, turning away.

She reached out a restraining hand. "Please, do this for me."

Josh's gaze raked over Proud Eagle. "You're making a big mistake, Amanda." He pulled free from her grasp, making his way back up the steps and to the door.

"Josh, I must have your answer."

He reached for the knob and turned it.

"Will you accept the gifts?" she called out.

He glanced back at her, his anger replaced by an underlining defeat. For a long moment he searched her face.

His disappointment and loss tore at her heart, but she had to try one more time to change his mind. "Please," she pleaded. "I want you to have them."

With a taut jerk of his head he nodded in agreement, then shut the door with a bang behind him.

****

Proud Eagle was silent for most of the journey back to the village. She sat in front of him on his horse, feeling his warm breath upon her neck. His secure embrace protected her from slipping off, but held no other comfort. She didn't have to be a mind reader to know he was seething inside.

"I'm sorry. If I had any idea how this whole thing would turn out, I would have never asked for the gifts to be brought to the parsonage."

"How could you not know?" he countered.

She turned to look at him. "You think I wanted trouble?"

"I think you overlooked the truth," he quipped.

The whole episode had left her tired. "What truth?"

"The holy man is in love with you, any one with eyes can see that. How could you believe he would be happy to see you become another man's wife?"

She turned away. "I thought he'd be happy to know I was alive and well."

"He was, but he also wants you for himself."

"I told him before I didn't feel the same," she said, casting her eyes to the road ahead.

"And how did he take your refusal?"

She sighed. "I think he hoped in time I'd change my mind."

"Ah, I see, he still hoped, then, he would win you."

She bit her bottom lip. "I-I suppose so."

"I never set eyes on the holy man before this day, and yet I understand all he feels. How is it you do not?"

She swallowed hard to push back the tears that threatened to come.

"And still you wanted him to have the gifts, and were disrespectful to his feelings?"

The tears spilled down her cheeks. "I guess I didn't see it as disrespect, so much as including him in my happiness." She wiped the tears aside with the back of her hand. "Josh has been in my life since I was a little girl. He was there for me and Papa after Mama died, teaching me about the Bible and comforting my father. I saw him as a guardian, not as a suitor. And then when my father was killed, everything changed. He wanted to take care of me. The only respectful way, was if I became his wife."

She cleared her throat. "His proposal shocked me, because I still saw him through the eyes of a child."

"But you are no longer a child, Golden Lady." Proud Eagle kissed the back of her neck. "Any man can see that."

The warmth of his lips upon her flesh sent waves of excitement through her veins. She fought to keep her focus. "I don't expect you to understand."

"Ah, but I do. I felt the same toward Rising Sun."

Her voice rose in surprise. "How are the two situations the same?"

"You see Rising Sun as a married woman ready to give birth to her first child, but for a long time I still saw her as the little girl my mother fed and washed. To me she was the sister who would get into my things and break them," he explained. "I used to tease her, pull her hair, and pinch her arm, until one day Falling Star told me to keep my hands off his wife."

"What happened then?"

"Falling Star and I had a long talk, and he set me straight. I still saw Rising Sun as a child, because we had grown up together. But she is a woman, a wife, and her husband felt I was disrespecting her."

"So, what did you do?"

"I told Falling Star *wonunicun*, a mistake, has been made. I then asked for his forgiveness. From that time on I have done my best to treat Rising Sun as the woman she has become, instead of the little girl I once knew." He chuckled. "But when she gets me mad, I still pull her hair."

She smiled to herself, picturing the two acting like young siblings. "She'll always be your sister."

"But not my little sister, little girls grow up." Proud Eagle's thumb grazed her breast. "For that I am greatly pleased."

Her blood rushed to the spot he touched; her breast tingled against the soft fabric of the buckskin. "I am sorry for everything that happened today, Proud Eagle." She leaned her head back against his muscular chest. "I think it would be best if the gifts were given to your sister instead."

He lowered his mouth to her ear. "That is no longer possible."

"Why not?"

"For the sake of pride, his and my own, I must bring the gifts to the holy man."

She twisted in his arms and searched his face. "Is there nothing I can say to change your mind?"

He shook his head, bestowing a gentle kiss on the tip of her nose.

She turned, leaning back against him. "Are you sure?"

He tightened his embrace. "Very."

Every bone in her body cried out for rest. By the time she and Proud Eagle arrived at the village, it was a strain to keep her eyes open. He lifted her from the horse and carried her in his strong arms to his parent's wickiup, where she would stay until Josh accepted the gifts. Once that task was complete, she would return to Proud Eagle's wickiup, as his wife.

Proud Eagle placed her upon the small cot in the corner and covered her with a blanket.

"Please, let me go with you to bring the gifts," she whispered, not wanting to wake White Dove and Cunning Eagle.

"Your place is to stay here," he whispered in return.

She remembered the scene earlier between him and Josh. Both men were stubborn and temperamental. "But I fear, without me around to keep the peace between you, something might go wrong."

His warm lips kissed hers. "The custom is for me to go alone." He kissed her again, deeper and longer. Then his mouth moved to her earlobe, where he left another kiss. "No more talk, time to sleep," he whispered one last time before he left.

****

The noon-day sun was high in the sky when Proud Eagle arrived at the parsonage. He hid behind a thicket of trees, watching the children playing in the yard with a ball. It wasn't long before an elderly white woman, dressed in a flowered print dress, poked her head out the door and summoned the youngsters inside for lunch.

He waited several minutes before making his way across the yard. He tied the pony to a nearby tree, placed the other items on the porch, and knocked three times upon the door. Then he hid again in the brush to watch.

The holy man opened the door, glancing around for the one who knocked. When he spotted the blankets and baskets, his jaw clenched. His gaze searched the yard before he brought the gifts inside the house. A moment later he came back outside, walked over to the tree, and untied the pony; bringing him to the stable.

Proud Eagle nodded to himself, satisfied, and turned to leave.

"I know you're out there, hiding," the holy man's voice called. "I have done as you wish and accepted your gifts. Now, I want to speak with you." He raised his arms above his head. "I am not armed, so you have nothing to fear."

Proud Eagle stepped from the trees. With hands on hips, feet spread apart, he stood before the white man. "I do not fear you."

The holy man moved closer. "So now, I take it, she's your wife?"

He gave a taut nod.

"But her marriage ceremony is different. She will not feel your union is an honorable one, if she cannot say the wedding vows, exchange the rings, and wear the dress her mother wore."

"I know the traditions you speak of."

"If you really love her you'll want her happiness." The white man ran his hand through his hair. "Believe me when I tell you I've accepted the gifts for that reason alone." His eyes narrowed. "If you can't do right by her, then let her go. Send her back to me. I will be glad to take care of her and love her the way she deserves."

He thrust out his chin. "I will never let her go. I would sooner die first." His eyes locked with the other man's. In them he saw sadness. Proud Eagle's voice softened. "But you have my word I will share in her ways as well. Do not be troubled for her happiness again."

The holy man's fist clenched at his side. "I hope you speak the truth, because if I ever discover you've mistreated her in any way…" He turned and stalked back to the house, but before he opened the door, he turned again to face Proud Eagle, shaking a fist at the heavens. "So help me God, I'll come for you!"

****

It was nearing dawn of the next day when Proud Eagle rode into the village. In spite of his exhaustion, he made his way to his parent's wickiup. With quiet steps, he approached the bed where she slept and gathered her into his arms.

Cunning Eagle's voice broke through the stillness, halting him at the door. "The holy man has accepted the gifts?"

"Yes," Proud Eagle whispered.

"And you, my son, cannot wait just the few more hours till morning to take her?"

"No, my father, I cannot." He turned. "You will not try to stop me, will you?"

Cunning Eagle chuckled. "No, I will not try, but you disappoint me, my son."

His voice rose. "How so?"

"I would have found a way to take her much sooner," the elder said.

Proud Eagle smiled to himself as he imagined the mischievous expression his father must be wearing.

****

Amanda had fallen asleep many times yearning for the warmth of Proud Eagle's arms. Now the dream had become truly vivid. She could smell the scent of his flesh; feel the caress of his hands. She reveled in his touch and savored the realism, hoping to stay long into such a wonderful, deep slumber.

"*Shi'aad*, my wife," his voice whispered in her thoughts.

I can even hear his words.

"Wake, *shi'aad*."

She opened her eyes to find Proud Eagle lying naked beside her, his chin propped on one hand. The other hand stroked her breasts.

He smiled. "I will love you now as I have wished to do from the moment I saw you."

Her whole being filled with wanting him, yet she pulled away. "Proud Eagle, I've never—never been wi..."

"Shh," he whispered, his gaze soft as a caress. Gathering her into his arms, he held her. "There is nothing to fear."

His manner soothed her, unlocking her heart and soul. She buried her face against his neck, tenderly planting a kiss there, and stroked his smooth chest. "I'm not afraid."

"You never have to be, not of me."

She relaxed, sinking into his cushioning embrace. "I know."

Proud Eagle's hand, on the small of her back,

moved to her backside. "I want you, Golden Lady."

She moved a few inches from him, memorizing every handsome feature. "Then take me."

He crushed her to him and pressed his mouth to hers.

The touch of his lips, searing and sweet, sent a shock wave through her entire body. The feathery flicks of his tongue explored the soft crevices of her mouth, tasting her, consuming her.

He broke the kiss, his large black eyes searching her face, reaching into her thoughts. "From this night on we are bound as husband and wife. What we share in this bed is honorable."

She traced his lips with the tip of a finger, drinking in the comfort of his nearness. "I believe it to be no other way."

"I want you to be at peace with what is about to happen."

"I am. I want this as well."

He knelt beside her and slid the buckskin dress off her shoulders, kissing her down her neck. Farther he slipped the dress, exposing her breasts. With admiration he studied her naked body, his eyes feasting on every part. "Ah, more beautiful then I imagined."

Her cheeks heated under the intensity of his gaze. On impulse, she lifted her arms to cover her breasts.

His voice held a rasp of excitement. "They are for my eyes only." He gently placed her arms at her sides, then swept off the dress. He cast it to the ground, lowering his lips, touching a nipple with tantalizing possessiveness. With his tongue, he fondled the pink peak, making it hard, and then nibbled it with his teeth.

She moaned with the burst of heat that flashed through her loins.

He stopped to look up at her. "Have I hurt you?"

"No," she whispered, entwining her fingers in the long strands of hair that fell to his shoulders.

When he spoke again, his voice was tender, almost a murmur. "I want to touch, taste, and love every part of you, Golden Lady." His gaze melded into hers. "Will you let me?"

Her heart filled with a strange excitement. "Yes."

Again he lowered his mouth, his tongue tasting her belly, the tip swirling around the knot of her navel.

A warm glow wrapped her in a silky cocoon of euphoria.

He moved lower, to the triangular patch of golden hair covering her womanhood. There he kissed her; his warm breath stimulated a strange ache in her limbs. She parted them wider.

His tongue probed the soft flesh between her thighs, finding the core of her passion and teasing the soft bud with circular motions.

She delighted with her desire for him, senses whirling, swirling, tingling from head to toe. She arched her body toward him.

He moistened the soft folds with each flick of his tongue.

She wreathed with pleasure, waves of ecstasy crashed over her. In a voice thick with fervor, she cried out her release.

Her body quivered with passion's climax. The musky scent of her filled his nostrils. Proud Eagle swelled with the need—the want of her. Placing his hands beneath her rounded hips, he raised her to meet him. Long legs straddled him, melding the soft nubile curves of her body with his.

He revealed his throbbing shaft for her to see, her eyes widening as she took in the length. "I will be gentle," he promised, thrills of desire racing through him.

He penetrated the gate of her womanhood, moving back and forth, moistening the path. Then with a quick thrust, he broke through her maidenhood.

The fleshy membrane tore, her body jerked beneath him, and a sob escaped her throat.

Unspoken distress filled her eyes.

"The pain will not last. It will not always be this way," he said. "If you wish for me to stop, I will."

She spoke in a broken whisper. "No—don't stop."

He thrust forward, pushing all the way inside of her. She took his length, closing around him, hot and tight. His excitement climbed. She moved her hands down his back, pressing him closer. He rocked back and forth within her. She threw her head back, digging her nails into his shoulders.

His passion intensified, pressure mounted, and he breathed in short gasps. The rhythm of his thrusts increased. He groaned with pleasure from the deepest part of his being. Hot juices erupted from him like a volcano, spilling into her, filling her with the ultimate expression of being one.

He looked deep into her liquid eyes. "Do not move," he whispered, lowering his lips to kiss her nose, her chin, then capturing her mouth. He sucked and bit her lips until his exhausted member slipped from her, his body spent. Rolling onto his back, he pulled her close, his chest rising and falling with deep breaths.

She rested her head against his shoulder, splaying her fingers across his chest. "How do you say husband, in Apache?"

"*Shikaa*," he said.

"*Shikaa*," she repeated.

"And you are *shi'aad*, my wife, belonging to me now, forever," he whispered, falling asleep with her cradled in his arms.

Chapter Five

The days moved into autumn, the intense heat lessened, and the nights brought a deeper chill, leaving one to linger by the fire. The small wickiup Amanda shared with her husband was a cozy little love nest where Proud Eagle showed her new and wonderful expressions of physical desire, but it was also very cramped.

One morning, Proud Eagle brought her to a patch of ground he had cleared near the river. The sun hung like a big red ball in the sky, and a gentle breeze danced in the tree tops. Amanda was awed by the beauty that surrounded the tranquil bit of paradise.

"This is where I wish for you to build our wickiup. It is close to the river, and the ground is fertile for planting." He walked around the clearing, his anticipation mounting. "This is where the door opening should be." He pointed to a piece of land a few feet away. "And that portion is set aside for the garden." Proud Eagle gathered her into his arms and twirled her around. "*Shi'aad*, you have made me a happy man." His eyes beamed with his excitement. "Have I filled your life with as much joy as well?"

She smiled up at him. "In more ways then I can count." She wrapped her arms around his neck, pulling him close. "And soon there will be many children to fill the wickiup I will build for us."

His large, dark eyes filled with hope. "Has your woman's time been late? Could it be you nurture my seed deep within you as we speak?"

She giggled and shook her head. "Not yet, my

shikaa."

He smiled at her use of the Apache term for husband.

"Let me work on one thing at a time," she added. "First I must build a home to put them in."

The next day, White Dove gathered the Shaman's wife, Little Wolf, and a few other women from the tribe to help Amanda build the new wickiup.

She welcomed their help, offering each woman juniper nuts to munch on before the day's work began.

Little Wolf had a peaceful aura that surrounded her. She appreciated the elder woman's diligence and skill. Little Wolf smiled a lot and said little, not like the younger women, who giggled and talked more than they worked.

For days she labored and was quite pleased at how the dwelling took shape. At the end of the fifth day, she walked around the outside of the new wickiup to clear a pile of grasses left for thatch, and heard a scream. Fearing someone had gotten hurt, she ran through the door opening, stumbling over a pile of broken wood.

Her foot slammed against a pole, causing it to come loose from the ropes that held it in place. The large post fell. Amanda tried to move out of harm's way, but her ankle wouldn't hold her weight. She screamed for help as the huge dowel came down hard across her shoulders, pinning her to the ground. Intense pain shot through her body as she once more called out for help. Then the second beam came loose, hitting her hard in the back of the head—her world blurred and darkened.

****

Proud Eagle sat cross-legged by Cunning Eagle's bed, listening intently to the words his father spoke.

"It will be your responsibility to keep order and

peace among our people," Cunning Eagle said. "The tribe will look to you for guidance. You must be clever and wise when settling disputes and problems."

He nodded in agreement. Though he had been groomed for this time since he was a small boy, he doubted now if he would be able to fill his father's place as chief. Would the Elders respect his word, would they work alongside him for the good of all?

His sister's hysterical voice interrupted his thoughts.

"Proud Eagle, are you here?" Rising Sun shouted as she burst through the door flap.

He stood. "What is it?"

"As I walked by the building site I heard...I heard... " She gasped for breath.

Looking down into her fear-filled eyes, Proud Eagle's pulse raced. "Calm yourself first, then tell me what you heard."

Rising Sun nodded and took a moment to catch her breath before speaking again. "I heard a scream and found Golden Lady. She is at the new wickiup, and she has been hurt."

He did not stay to hear another word, running to the new dwelling as fast as his legs could carry him. He spotted her, lying still beneath the poles, and threw the wreckage aside. His heart raced with each pole he cleared from her body. He gathered her into his arms, carrying her to the small wickiup. Gently he placed her injured body upon the bed.

With his knife, he split apart the buckskin tunic and rolled her onto her side to examine the gash between her shoulders. There was some bleeding and already the wound was bruised and swollen. Somewhat to his relief, it was not as serious as he feared. But the gash at the back of her head worried him. It was much deeper and poured more blood.

With trembling hands, he mixed pulverized

herbs with water, cleaning both wounds and wrapping them to stop the bleeding.

White Dove entered the wickiup, surveyed the damage, and tended Golden Lady's ankle. "It is beginning to swell," she said, rolling a blanket and placing it beneath her daughter-in-law's foot.

He covered his wife and sat down beside the bed. His mother joined him; together they watched her still form.

"How is Rising Sun? She was full of fear when I saw her last."

"She will be fine," White Dove assured him. "I made her lie down to rest. She will come by later."

He took a deep breath. "Gather the women who helped with the building. I want to know how this happened."

White Dove answered with staid calmness. "Rising Sun said when she heard the scream she tried to enter the wickiup but was stopped by broken pieces of wood piled in front of the door opening. Golden Lady must have tripped herself on this wood when she entered the wickiup, hitting the two center poles and causing them to fall." Her brows puckered "But I cleaned the inside of the *gowa* this morning. When I left, there was nothing in front of the door. I do not understand how this has happened."

"What are you saying?"

Her gaze sent him a private message.

He arched a brow. "You are thinking someone put the wood there?"

White Dove nodded.

He stared at his mother with rounded eyes. "Who would do that? Who would want to hurt her?"

"I do not know, my son, but I will speak with your father." White Dove reached out and gave his arm a reassuring pat. "And we will find out."

****

Proud Eagle watched his wife weave in and out

146

of consciousness, throughout the night swabbing her flesh with cool water.

Shaman Gray Fox entered the wickiup and handed Proud Eagle a cup of pulverized herb and bark. "Make her drink this tea in great quantities the times she is awake," he instructed before he sat outside the wickiup, speaking and chanting to the gods.

Proud Eagle stayed by her side, caring for her as she had once done for him, not allowing anyone but the Shaman inside the wickiup. When she opened her eyes, he helped her drink the tea. When she shook, he covered her. When she tossed, he held her, speaking encouraging words, prompting her from unconsciousness.

"*Shi'aad*, open your eyes, come back to me." He pushed aside a pale lock of hair, trailing his finger down her temple. "I am to blame for all that has happened. I put upon you too much. Now, you lie before me, injured because you tried to build me a home." He traced the outline of her full lips—lips that never complained. "You try so hard to please me, want so much for me to be proud of you." He felt the tears burn the back of his throat. "And I am proud of you, *shi'aad*, beyond words. You have learned my ways and you..." He swallowed hard the grief rising to choke him. "You return my love with passion." Anguish overcame his control, hot tears slipping down his cheeks. "You are my *biijii*. Without you I will be like a wolf that has lost his mate, howling in agony for all to hear." He whispered against her mouth. "*Wo'ina*, I love you. Do not leave me."

****

Pain ripped through every fiber of Amanda's being. She must have entered hell, because a devil danced beside her, the menacing creature chanting over her words unbeknown to man.

Her head throbbed, her shoulders burned. She couldn't move her legs to run—couldn't cry out for help. She was at the demon's mercy as he hovered over her to cast his spell. She was trapped in the frightening and pain-filled limbo.

But then she heard his words, the rich timbre of his voice, smooth and comforting. It eased the hurt, quieted her fears, brought her through the darkness.

She opened her eyes to a ray of sunshine streaming through the top of the wickiup. Proud Eagle was on his knees beside the bed, his face buried in his hands.

She reached out and stroked his hair.

He lifted his head, tired black eyes locking with hers, and pressed her fingers to his lips.

The flood gates of his emotion reflected in his gaze. His face was vivid with liberation for her recovery, relief washing in volumes across his features. "My *biijii* is grateful," he whispered, then buried his face in the hollows of her neck and wept.

With what little strength she had, Amanda held him. His body shook with his sobs. When he raised his face to look at her, his cheeks glistened with tears.

"I feared you were to join me no longer."

She wiped his face with trembling fingers. "I'm not going anywhere, Proud Eagle. Ever," she added, before kissing his lips.

****

Amanda smiled when Rising Sun came through the door opening. "I hear drums."

Rising Sun helped her to sit forward, propping a blanket behind her shoulders. "They beat with thanks to the gods, who have been called upon to heal you."

She extended a hand to her new sister. "I've missed you."

Rising Sun sat at the edge of the bed. "Finally

Proud Eagle allowed me to visit you while he went to the Chief's wickiup on a tribal matter."

She sighed, her body sore, her spirit tired. "Is the new wickiup destroyed?"

Rising Sun forced a smile. "No, but there is much to fix." She squeezed Amanda's arm. "Do not worry. Several women in the tribe have gathered together to help."

She rubbed her hands over her eyes. "I'm so stupid, Rising Sun."

Rising Sun corrected her. "That is not true, my sister."

"It is true," she insisted. "I just ran into that wickiup without looking, but when I heard the scream I thought..."

"You heard a scream?" Rising Sun cut in.

She nodded. "I thought someone had gotten hurt, and I ran to help."

Rising Sun turned away and stared at the fire pit.

She moved up on her elbows. "What is it, Rising Sun."

The other women bit her bottom lip. "Something I saw." She glanced at her. "And something I overheard."

"What, Rising Sun, tell me."

Rising Sun changed the subject. "Did you know Proud Eagle would not let anyone enter this wickiup to help but the Shaman?"

"I know what you're trying to do, and it's not going to work."

Rising Sun took a deep breath. "I have said too much already, but it is just that all Proud Eagle suffered watching your pain has made me think he should be told."

"Told what?"

Rising Sun looked down at her large belly and gave it a loving rub.

Her voice softened. "Are you all right?"

"I am fine, Golden Lady."

"You're not fine. I can see it in your face," she said. "Please, tell me what troubles you."

Rising Sun shifted at the edge of the bed. Sitting in her condition had become uncomfortable. "I heard a scream as well. Your scream. Then I saw Running Doe run from the wickiup."

She arched a brow.

"At first," Rising Sun paused, taking a deep breath, "I thought she had heard you scream and was on her way to help. But then she ran the other way."

"Did she see you?" Amanda probed.

"I do not think so; her back was to me as she ran away."

"And what have you overheard," she queried further.

"You look tired, Golden Lady, as I am trying to sit when I should be lying down. We will talk more when you are better."

"Please, Rising Sun, I need to know," she begged.

Rising Sun gave a taut nod. "I heard my mother tell my father she cleaned the inside of the wickiup that morning. There should have been nothing in front of the door opening. And the poles," Rising Sun added, "had been secured. They should not have fallen as they did."

Her heart sunk to her toes. "You think Running Doe tampered with the poles and left the wood before the door?"

Rising Sun nodded. "And I should tell Proud Eagle."

"No, Rising Sun," she said, sitting forward. Pain shot through her shoulders and she grimaced, lying back against the rolled blanket. "Promise me you won't say a word."

"But why, my sister?"

"If I'm ever to fit in here, to be respected, I can't hide behind Proud Eagle."

"Your spirit was almost sent to *O'zho*," Rising Sun protested. "Proud Eagle has a right to know of her evil ways, as well as my father."

"But all you saw was her running from the wickiup. That's not proof she tried to harm me," she pointed out.

Rising Sun placed her hand over her heart. "Deep inside me I have the proof." Rising Sun paused, weighing her words. "There is something you should hear, Golden Lady. For many moons Running Doe's father, Bear Watcher, and the Chief talked of marriage between their children."

"I didn't think there was an agreement to marry her on Proud Eagle's part."

"That is true. There was not," Rising Sun agreed. "But Running Doe believed differently." She sighed. "Forgive me for saying this. If you had not come into Proud Eagle's life, he would have married Running Doe."

"I remember her choosing him at the mating ceremony," she reflected.

"Running Doe's actions were shameful. She knew why you sat in the circle and still she tried to win Proud Eagle, bringing dishonor upon her father."

"And I don't want to bring shame upon Proud Eagle's honor, if you are wrong with your conclusion."

"I am not wrong." Rising Sun insisted. "Running Doe is the only one in the tribe with a reason to hurt you." She searched Amanda's face. "She cannot be *zonta*, trusted."

"And it's for that reason I can't involve the tribe in this matter, not yet, anyway," she added.

Rising Sun looked perplexed. "I do not

understand."

"If I accuse her, Running Doe will act like she's been unjustly blamed. With her father the Chief's trusted Elder, she will gain sympathy among the tribe's people."

"Ah… I did not think of that, Golden Lady," Rising Sun countered. "Now, I fear for you even more."

She sighed. "I'm not feeling all that safe either, but the only way to beat her at her own game is if I try to first settle things on my own." She placed a hand on Rising Sun's arm. "And that's why it's important for you to keep this conversation between us."

"I do not think—"

"Please, Rising Sun," she broke in. "Give me your word you will say nothing about Running Doe to anyone."

Rising Sun hesitated with an answer.

"Give me your word," she insisted.

Rising Sun agreed with a heavy sigh. "If it is what you wish, Golden Lady…you have my word."

****

Amanda worked long hours to please Proud Eagle, weaving baskets, mats and doing the wash. At night the aroma of a delicious meal cooking welcomed him home after a day of hunting.

Though her daily life was quite wonderful, and Proud Eagle was devoted to her, the problem with Running Doe never left her thoughts. She'd never be at peace until she paid a visit to the troublesome woman, settling the problem between them.

If the problem could be settled. Was it possible for such anger and jealousy to ever be put to rest?

She walked in quiet contemplation through the village to Running Doe's wickiup. She hadn't a plan of any sort, didn't even have anything prepared to say, only needed to try and resolve things between them.

She stopped in front of the door flap and called into the wickiup. "Running Doe, it is Golden Lady. May I enter?" With her stomach churning, she waited for a response.

The flap lifted. Running Doe's large, round eyes, glazed with hate, glared at Amanda. "*Ha'andah*, come in."

She stepped through the opening.

Running Doe walked to the fire pit and gestured to a nearby mat. "Sit."

She gave a taut nod and made her way to the mat. "We need to talk, Running Doe."

Running Doe busied herself with her weaving. "I have nothing to say to you."

"Then, I will talk." She cleared her throat and squared her shoulders. "I'd like to start with what happened at my new wickiup."

Running Doe looked up from her weaving; her dark gaze bore into hers. "You must be more careful, Golden Lady."

She arched a brow. "I believed I was."

Running Doe's expression was a mask of stone. "You believed wrong, then." She flicked an imaginary piece of dirt from her skirt. "Accidents do happen."

The muscles at the back of her neck tensed. "That's true, if indeed, it was an accident."

Running Doe's eyes rounded, feigning innocence. "I do not know what you mean."

She leaned forward and lowered her voice. "You know exactly what I mean."

Running Doe's eyes narrowed. "If you think I had anything to do with—"

"You had everything to do with it," she interjected.

"Your words against mine," Running Doe snapped.

"But my words are the truth." She searched Running Doe's face. "You hoped Proud Eagle would make you his wife."

Running Doe ground out her words with gritted teeth. "He would have, if you had not tricked him."

Her eyes widened. "Tricked him? How have I tricked him?"

"You are witch. *Ihsta'nedleheh*, Changing Woman, a White Painted Lady. And you have put a spell on him," Running Doe spat.

She chuckled sardonically. "You don't really believe that."

Running Doe's lips twisted with hatred. "I speak the truth now. That is the only way Proud Eagle would have chosen you over me. When my *nuhdee* find out what you did, they will cut out your evil *biijii* from your chest and burn it."

She sprang to her feet. "Have you gone crazy?"

Running Doe stood in challenge. "*Zenogolache*, you are the crazy one." She waved her hand in a gesture of dismissal. "Leave. Leave my *gowa* and leave my village."

Amanda's fists bunched at her sides. "That's not going to happen, Running Doe. I'm Proud Eagle's wife now. This is my home as well."

Running Doe threw her weaving to the ground. "This will never be your *gowa*. You are an intruder. *Netdahe*, death, to all intruders!" she screamed. "And if the tribe must choose between us, you will be sorry."

To her surprise, her voice carried a unique force. "Wrong, Running Doe, it's you who will be sorry! One day my husband will be chief, and no one dares defy the chief. This much I've already learned."

"Then another chief will be chosen. My father is respected as well in this tribe."

"Not as much as Cunning Eagle, and no one but his son would be the tribe's choice for their next chief." She raised her chin. "There is nothing you could do or say to make a difference."

Running Doe shot her a twisted smile. "Ah...but there is much I can do, white woman." The words *white woman* slithered off her tongue like a curse. "And no one will know I did it."

"I'm not afraid of you, Running Doe," she said with a significant lifting of her brows. "Nor am I stupid. Our backgrounds may be different, but if I'm forced to defend myself, I will." She made her way to the door opening, hesitating before raising the flap. "Whatever it takes, mentally, physically, or emotionally, I will fight you," she warned. "And I will win."

In spite of her racing heart, she forced herself to remain calm as she walked through the village. When she reached her wickiup, she climbed into bed, throwing her mother's quilt over her head. She'd hid this way as a child whenever she was afraid. At this moment she was terrorized through and through. For a long time she sat beneath her own little tent, trying to still the trembling that shook her body.

What could I be thinking, challenging another woman to a fight?

She didn't know the first thing about fighting. Not like Running Doe. The little witch could use her hands in a savage way if she wanted, not to mention her probable skill with a knife.

She moved to sit before the pit and stared into the fire, picturing her heart being ripped from her chest and thrown into the flames.

Did Proud Eagle's people really do such things to those they believed were evil?

She shuddered at the thought and looked over at the door opening. There wasn't even a latch to lock. Anyone could walk right into her home at any time.

Was this what Running Doe meant when she said there was much she could do, and no one would know she did it?

The whole encounter with such a vile person made her insides cringe.

She agonized over Running Doe's words, until she realized rehashing the argument wasn't going to help her one little bit. What she really needed to do was take action—learn to fight.

Now, all she needed was to figure out a way to convince Proud Eagle to teach her, swearing him to secrecy as well. In this way, the element of surprise would be in her favor should she find herself coming up against Running Doe.

****

Amanda lay awake that night in bed and stared up at the peak of the wickiup. Running Doe could be plotting her revenge at this very moment.

She nudged Proud Eagle. "Are you asleep?"

He grunted. "If I say that I am, will it matter?"

"No," she said.

He turned to look at her, propping his chin upon one hand and pushing aside a wisp of hair from her forehead with the other. *"Aco'tndn'nil'gon'ye*, what is the trouble that now keeps me awake?"

She moved closer to him. "I want you to teach me how to fight."

He arched a brow. "Why do you wish to learn, *shi'aad*? No one dares harm you when I am here."

"What about the times when you are not here? How will I protect myself?"

"The tribe will protect you."

"And what if I am in a position where I have to be a protector?" There was a long silence while he mulled over the truth of her words. "If I am to pull my share around here, then I need to learn how to fight as well." She held up her hand and made a fist. "I want to learn how to use my hands, the knife, and the spear."

He glanced at her fisted hand and then searched

156

her face. "You truly wish to learn?"

She sat up in bed. "I've never been more serious about learning anything, as I am about this," she said. "But, it must remain our secret."

"Are you planning on a surprise attack?"

If you only knew. "I just would feel better if we kept it between us." She stroked his arm. "Will you teach me?"

"If it is what you want, then I will teach you how to fight like a warrior." He reached out and traced the curve of her lips with a finger. "And if you learn to fight as well as you learned to dance, I fear for your enemy."

I also hope to frighten the enemy, one in particular.

His face grew serious. "I will teach you all I know, but it will not be easy. I will show you no mercy," he warned. "If I do, I will be doing you great harm. An enemy shows no mercy in a fight."

I realize this already.

"If you are ready to accept all that comes with the learning, then I will teach you."

Proud Eagle's pride swelled for his young bride as he watched her eyes light with the spirit he admired.

"I'm ready to endure it all," she said, squaring her shoulders.

He threw back the blanket and jumped out of bed. "Stand up and face me."

"Now?"

"Now," he demanded.

She looked down at herself, and then at him. "But we are both naked."

Teaching you to fight is going to be more fun than teaching the tribe's braves. He stifled a smile and forced a frown. "I thought you wanted to learn to fight."

"I do," she said, scurrying off the bed.

Before she could get her feet on the ground, Proud Eagle picked up his foot and knocked her off balance.

She landed with a *thud* on the dirt floor. Stunned, she looked up at him with hurt in her eyes.

Her pride had been wounded, as well as her pretty little bared bottom, which by tomorrow would be sore and bruised. For a split second he contemplated offering her his hand...but for her sake he held his ground.

"First lesson—be ready for surprise. The enemy will not be so kind as to tell you when he will attack. Listen to the voice within you. And even if you are frightened beyond your flesh, never show it. You must, at all times, be in control of your emotions."

Now, leaning forward, he offered her his hand.

She started to reach for his help, but then pulled back.

He smiled. "That is *nzhoo, shi'aad*. Always remember, trust no one but yourself."

She stood. "I'll remember."

He scanned the length of her, legs spread apart, shoulders squared, full breasts heaving with her rapid breathing. *I wish to sweep you off your feet and place you right back into the bed, where I will satisfy my growing desire.*

She placed her hands on her hips. "What's the second lesson?"

He cleared his throat and fought to control his own emotions, focusing on her eyes instead of all the other wonderful parts in full view. "You really wish to go on?"

She thrust her chin out. "I do if you do."

He nodded in agreement. "Then, let us begin."

Chapter Six

"It will not be easy," Proud Eagle had said when Amanda asked him to teach her how to fight.

That was an understatement.

Not easy is trying to keep mice out of the wickiup or carrying her and Rising Sun's water jugs up the hill from the river. Learning the warrior's combat was much more than not easy, it was downright grueling.

Proud Eagle was an excellent teacher, leaving out no detail. She was grateful for his thoroughness, but after each lesson she ached for days in bones and muscles she was surprised existed.

She lay upon her stomach stretched out on the bed. "If you make me fall upon the hard ground and roll over the pebbles and stones one more time, my flesh will be forever battered."

He rubbed her shoulders with aloe from the yucca plant. "You are the one who asked for this."

She yawned; his strong, yet, gentle massage soothed her aching body. "I just didn't realize how much bruising went into the learning."

"Every inch of the body can be a useful weapon," he explained. "The knees, the heels, the elbows, even the head, when used right, can cause another much pain. Because of this, you must be in condition." He moved to rub down her back with the herbal salve. "You must learn to *doo*, spring back, onto your feet when you are down, crouch and stalk like the wild *gidi*, cat, hunting its prey," he coached further. "That is what the enemy is, *shi'aad*, your prey."

"And what's the reason for the tricky footwork

you've been teaching me?" she asked, her eyes unable to stay open.

"That is to confuse and catch the enemy off guard."

She groaned when he massaged the back of her thighs. "Oh, that feels so good."

His voice was as soothing as his administrations. "It is *nkeez*, for you to learn about complete awareness and concentration, *shi'aad*."

Her eyelids grew heavier. "How will concentration help my sore body?"

"A strong mind can conquer the pain—raise your level of acceptance." He pinched her thigh.

The pain pulled her from her relaxed state. "Ouch, what did you do that for?"

"Did that hurt?"

She snapped annoyed. "Yes, it hurt."

"Does it still hurt," he probed.

She turned to sit up. "Yes on that account as well, and I expect it will continue to hurt for quite a while."

"*Inju.*"

"Why would you think this pain is a good thing to suffer?" She narrowed her eyes. "Why are you being so mean?"

He pushed aside the strands of hair framing her face. "I am not being mean, *shi'aad*, I am about to teach you a lesson in managing your pain."

She rubbed her thigh. "I welcome this lesson above all."

He knelt down in front of her. "First, direct your thoughts to the *yata* that hurts."

She nodded, rubbing her thigh again.

"I will teach you now how to send relief to that sore place."

"Well, please do it quick."

"Set your eyes on something in the wickiup," he said.

She focused on the large center stone of the fire pit.

"Block out all things around you, seeing only the thing you have chosen," he tutored.

She concentrated on the large stone, shaped like a kidney bean and focused on the way it darkened in color on one side.

"I want you to breathe in deep through your nose and let the air out through your mouth," he continued.

She obeyed, her lungs filling and deflating.

"Now, set your mind free from your body, *shi'aad*, with each breath."

Again, she did as she was told, allowing her thoughts to escape along with the air she exhaled.

"Think of a *nkeez* you liked," he whispered.

Her fifth birthday came to mind, helping her mother frosted the cake they'd made together. After, she had been allowed to lick the bowl and spoon.

"How did that *nkeez* make you feel? How did it make you happy?" Proud Eagle prodded.

She targeted every sensation—the warmth of the room, the glow on her mother's face, the sweet taste of the icing—and how safe and loved she felt.

"Now, how is your pain?" he whispered.

She glanced at him, astounded. "Better, almost gone."

He smiled. "That is the power your mind has over the pain, but I have something else that will help." He tossed her the buckskin dress discarded beside the bed and donned his breeches.

She threw the dress aside. "I cannot move one muscle from this bed."

Again, he handed her the dress. "Come, I have been working on a surprise for you in a secluded area by the river. Now it is completed and ready for you to see."

She couldn't imagine when he found the time,

with all he did for the tribe and teaching her to fight, but her curiosity piqued. Tired or not, she rose from the bed, dressed, and followed him to a remote area, hidden by trees and concealed from the village or passers by.

He held the torch he carried high, allowing her to see the quiet piece of paradise.

She turned to look at him and smiled. The delight on his face added to her sudden burst of exhilaration. "I've never been to this part of the village before." She pointed to the tiny hut on the riverbank. "What is this place, Proud Eagle, and why are those stones being heated in the fire?"

"Watch and you will see, *shi'aad.*"

Proud Eagle stuck the torch into the ground and rolled the stones with a stick into the hut. He then went to the river and filled a jug with water, placing it by the hut's door opening.

"Take off your clothes," he said, removing his breeches.

She looked around. "Here? In the middle of nowhere?"

A playful twinkle shown in his eyes. "Do you need my help?"

She folded her arms across her chest. "No, I don't need your help. What I need is an answer to why you wish me to undress."

He cast a smile that set her pulse racing. "This is a sweat bath, *shi'aad.* After the stones are heated and rolled into the hut, we enter and pour the water from the jug on the stones. The hut will fill with steam and it will make your sore body feel good again. But we must hurry before the stones grow cold." His mouth curved into a seductive grin. "Or should I undress you myself?" he teased, moving closer, his bronzed, naked body revealing his growing desire.

She arched a brow at his swollen manhood. "You

start acting like that and your stones will really grow cold."

He motioned to the hut. "Not if we make love in there."

She shed her clothes and followed her husband into the tiny dwelling. When he poured the water over the hot stones, mist filled the hut.

"I can't see past my nose."

Proud Eagle swept her into his arms and lowered her to the ground. "You do not need to see a thing, *shi'aad*, only feel," he whispered against her mouth, the strong warmth of his lips caressing hers.

Transported on a soft and wispy cloud, she drank in the sweetness of his kiss. Pleasure radiated within as the mist surrounded her.

His voice broke with huskiness. "Now we will see what makes me sweat more, the steam of the stones or the fire of our love."

His kiss traveled down her neck, to her breasts, tantalizing a swollen bud with his tongue.

The tender massage sent currents of desire through her.

His tongue continued a path to her belly, ending at the juncture of her thighs.

She arched her body and opened her legs.

Proud Eagle's fingers parted the walls of her valley, stroking between the moist folds.

Her groan of fulfillment encouraged him to tease, harder and faster.

Amanda writhed with pleasure, fingers entwining in his thick, dark mane, soaring higher, until she reached the pinnacle of desire, shattering within. Her passion exploded.

Proud Eagle moved his body atop her, guiding her hand to his swollen shaft.

She encircled her fingers around him, teasing. He trembled with a downpour of fiery sensations she ignited within him. Faster she stroked, making his sweet agony grow to bursting proportions.

He removed her hand and slid himself inside her.

Her body melted around his, warm and moist, finding the tempo that rocked them in unison. Harder and faster they ascended together, his world careening with ecstasy.

He moaned in surrender and cried out his release, his love flowing into her like warm honey, filling her, joining their bodies in exquisite harmony.

His beautiful wife lay relaxed and content in the afterglow of their lovemaking, but he had other ideas.

He stood, taking her with him.

Before she could protest, he marched out of the hut with her in his arms and jumped into the river, submerging them both into the cold, crisp water.

His flesh tingled, every part of his body shocked and aware. She freed herself from his hold and popped to the surface with a loud gasp.

He emerged beside her, his spirit sparkling with elation. He reached out and pulled her close. "Are you *haua*, all right, *shi'aad*?"

She shook aside the strands of hair clinging to her face. "I didn't expect you to plunge us into the river."

Joy bubbled in his laugh. "How do you like the sweat bath?"

His merriment infected her and she giggled. Glee shone in her eyes. "Do you think everyone gets so carried away by the steam?"

"I do not know about others, but you can see how much fun it is for us." He lifted her into the cradle of his arms. "My flesh has never felt this much happiness at being clean."

She wrapped her arms around his neck. "Mine either," she whispered against his mouth. "And the pain has gone as well," she added, before devouring his lips with a searing kiss.

****

When her lessons using the knife and spear began, Amanda was apprehensive, but Proud Eagle's endless patience got her through it without losing a finger or toe or maiming him in any way.

"For a warrior to use a knife most effectively, it must feel comfortable and fit well in his *bigan,* hand. Because each person's hand is different, the only way to find what is best for you is by holding the knife and getting used to its weight."

She practiced holding the knife in the palm of her hand, to become accustomed to its heaviness

"Now the knife is a part of you and it will serve you well when you thrust it at your enemy."

"Won't my adversary be expecting me to throw it?"

"Not if you deceive him by throwing the knife from hand to hand," he explained. "Doing this confuses your foe as to which hand you will use to throw the knife."

It wasn't long before catching her off guard or surprising her during a lesson became harder and harder for Proud Eagle to do. She still had much ahead of her, but with the willingness to learn and devotion to constant practice, she became graceful and swift, her stamina increasing.

She wasn't just satisfied learning to fight. While cleaning Proud Eagle's arrows, she decided she wanted him to teach her how to shoot with the bow.

She caressed the four-foot-long weapon with a finger, playing with the sinew. The tanned skin of the mountain lion made up the quiver; the arrow's reed shaft and hardwood fore shaft was tipped with flint. She marveled over its precision. Proud Eagle was a true craftsman.

In her excitement, she woke her husband the next morning, not with the usual gentle kiss, but by standing over him with the bow and arrow in her hands. "Will you teach me how to shoot?"

He looked up at her in disbelief. "What for?" He rubbed the sleep from his eyes. "You already know how to fight with a knife and spear."

She pressed the issue. "I should learn how to hunt, as well."

He sat up, annoyed. "I am the one who hunts for this family." His tone was defensive. "You have not gone hungry yet, *shi'aad*."

"And I'm not questioning your ability or complaining, it's just, I love to hunt. It was something I did often with my father. No longer do I have a gun, but"—she held up the bow—"if I can learn to use this, it will be just as good." She reached for his breeches and dropped them in his lap. "Get dressed so we can begin."

Proud Eagle stood exasperated. "You hold a dangerous weapon, *shi'aad*." He slipped on his breeches and moccasins. "If not used right it can rip apart the flesh and bone of your arm."

"Then teach me how to use it properly," she persisted.

He made his way toward her, taking the bow and arrow from her grasp. "I am a much better teacher when my hunger is silenced." He reached for a pot, handing it to her. "*Woyute*, food, first, *shi'aad*."

****

Evenings once spent learning how to fight were now passed learning to shoot with the bow and arrow. The first few tries were disasters. Amanda's strength was not great enough to control the weapon. When she pulled the sinew back with the arrow, her arm would flail from side to side. Proud Eagle stood behind her and guided her aim with his strong arms until she was able to hold the form on her own.

Her shoulders throbbed and the thin blue veins

running down her arm bulged with the strain, but she persisted in spite of the pain. Using the mind control technique her husband had taught her, the pain became bearable, lessening as her arms became stronger.

She learned to shoot standing and kneeling, hitting both fixed and moving targets. It wasn't long before Proud Eagle asked her to join him on a few outings. They always had more than enough meat for their own dinner and even some to share with others in the tribe. Then they'd linger by the fire and tell stories. She liked the one Proud Eagle told about a coyote who was somewhat of a trickster, violating all the laws of society and responsible for all the foolish things people did. The moral of the story taught a good lesson.

She moved closer to Proud Eagle, resting her head on his shoulder. "You must tell that story to our children, so they will grow to be responsible adults."

"That is if I ever have children." He kissed the top of her head. "It seems my beautiful wife has her mind set on being a great warrior, instead of a mother."

"Don't worry, we will have a family." She pulled back to look at him and smiled. "All you taught me will be useful one day, you'll see. My father always told me knowledge of any sort is never wasted."

Proud Eagle cupped her chin with his hand. "You father was a wise man, but soon I want *ciyes*, sons, to carry my blood."

"Your sons will come when the time is right, but until they do, let me learn all I can."

He searched her face. "I have taught you all I know, *shi'aad*. What more can there be?"

She moistened her lips. "Well, there is one more thing I would like to learn."

"I am almost afraid to ask, but my curiosity gets

the best of me." He arched a brow. "What is it now?"

"Since I no longer have a saddle, and without you holding me upon the horse I would slide right off, I haven't been able to ride alone."

"If you have noticed the other women are not allowed to ride alone. With the Chiricahua roaming around, it is too dangerous for them to ride without their men."

"But when they do go riding with their men, they ride beside them, not on the same horse. Just think what fun it would be to ride with you, side by side."

He mused. "It would be nice, when the moon is full, to take a ride now and then together."

She jumped at the idea. "It would be more than nice. It would be wonderful."

He nodded in agreement.

"Then you will teach me how to ride bareback?"

He sighed, surrendering to her request. "Yes, *shi'aad*, I will teach you."

Chapter Seven

Proud Eagle burst through the door flap, his face beaming with excitement. "Come, I have a surprise for you." He took her by the hand. "But you must close your eyes."

Amanda allowed him to lead her out of the wickiup and a distance down a winding path before her footsteps came to a halt. "What is it, and where are we going?"

There was a trace of laughter in his voice. "You will see soon enough. Now, come," he urged. "We are almost there."

Another few yards, down a hill, and he stopped.

He released her hand and walked away. She waited. Then, she called out to him, "Proud Eagle, can I open my eyes?"

The answer came from a few feet ahead of her. "Yes, now look."

Her mouth flew open with delight upon spotting a beautiful little chestnut mare; its huge soft brown eyes stared at her. "Is she for me?"

Proud Eagle nodded, bringing the mare closer. "Do you like her, *shi'aad*?"

She squealed with delight. "Like her? I adore her. She's beautiful."

He smiled with satisfaction. "It is *nzhoo* you are pleased, Golden Lady."

She rushed forward, wrapping her arms around her husband's neck. "Oh, you sweet, darling man, you've made me so happy."

He looked deep into her eyes. "That is all I ever want to do." He kissed the tip of her nose. "I know you are used to your own *chelee*, but he is old, would not be able to keep up with my *chelee* on a ride."

She nodded in agreement. "It's time for Todd to retire, play with the children, and enjoy grazing."

He looked over at the mare. "What will you call her?"

She walked over to the mare and stroked her nose. "I'll name her Venus."

"What is Venus," he said, coming to stand beside her.

"She is the goddess of love and beauty."

"Is she one of your gods?"

She giggled. "Mercy, no. Only Jesus is my God."

"Then where is Venus from?"

"She's believed to be the god of love and beauty by the ancient Greeks. Her legend is only mythology, a story, made up around campfires, no doubt." She again stroked the mare's nose. "I just don't think any other name would fit this precious animal better."

Proud Eagle nodded in agreement. "Then from this day on she will be called Venus, *chelee* of the Golden Lady."

She turned to look up at him. "Thank you, my *shikaa*. I couldn't have dreamt of anything as grand."

"Come," he said, leading her by the hand to the side of the horse. "Let us begin the first lesson of bareback riding." He swept her off her feet, sitting her on the mare's back.

She grabbed for his hand. "I will fall and break my neck for sure."

"You wished to learn," he teased.

"But there is nothing to hold on to, I'll just bounce off," she protested.

"Sit tall, relax, and let your body move with hers. Now go. Ride her."

Her brows furrowed. "Ride her? Alone?"

He laughed at her worried expression "Do not

fear, *shi'aad*, I will not leave you." He took the end of the rope, leading the animal around in a circle. "We will go slowly, round and round and you will feel her move beneath you. Soon you will move with her, as one." He smiled up at her. "And only then will you ride her alone."

She did as Proud Eagle instructed, determined to master this skill as well as she had the fighting and shooting. Soon she was able to handle the mare with grace—a mysterious night rider beneath the light of the moon.

Riding beside her on Blazing Fire, Proud Eagle took pleasure in watching his wife ride Venus. Imagining her thighs, supple and warm, straddling the horse, he marveled as woman and beast were carried away to the horizon, swift and unencumbered. They appeared as one. A partnership so uniquely complete, the two looked ready to take flight.

She moved to block him, the side slit of her buckskin skirt revealing the splendor that so easily possessed him, and pulled Venus to a stop. She awakened his every desire, tempting him, teasing him.

With a slow, swipe of her tongue she moistened her lips, and rode off, daring him to take up the chase. Golden curls floating behind her in the wind lured him to follow. Proud Eagle yearned for her to straddle him, instead of the mare.

She led him to a secluded clearing behind the brush. He had once taken her here, to make love to her. He smiled to himself. *She remembered.*

She slid off the horse, skirt rising to the tops of her thighs, almost exposing the grandeur that waited for him. Her bold stance, hands on hips and head held high, piqued his desire. The golden mane cascaded over her shoulders, ripples of curls falling to her hips, tiny tendrils framing her face.

His princess warrior waited for him.

Proud Eagle's loins swelled, thick and hot. He sprang down from his horse and stood before her.

She parted her peach colored lips, driving him to taste their sweetness.

He shed his shirt and reached for her, unlacing the front of her tunic and pushing the sides apart. Her fullness spilled into his hands, and he caressed the rosy summits growing erect before his eyes. Proud Eagle crushed her to him, bare chest met bare chest.

She trembled and responded with fervor, wrapping her arms around his neck and offering her lips to him in complete surrender, whispering his name.

He lowered her to the ground, slid his hand across her silken belly and down to her inner thigh. He teased her there with circular motions, her passion writhing beneath his touch.

The tip of his finger drove her rhapsody to a shattering peak, and she groaned with pleasure. With a hungry gaze she reached for the front of his breeches, pulled apart the laces, and slipped her hand beneath the flap. He closed his eyes, desire washing over him with the touch of her fingers wrapped around his hardness. Satisfaction piqued with each stroke she bestowed upon his throbbing mass.

"Both torment and pleasure," he confessed. "With just a touch, you possess my body and strip me of all my will." He raised her skirt above her hips and penetrated her, the head of his sex wet and aroused.

She moved in unison with the rhythm of his thrust, tightening around him, drawing his body to its limit. He trembled with desire, filling her with his hot liquid.

"*Wo'ina*," he whispered in her ear. Never had he

uttered those words to another woman, and no other but her would ever hear them from his lips.

She cupped his chin, turning his face to look deep into his eyes. "I've heard you say this before, but when?"

"The time you lay injured," he reminded her. "I whispered it in your ear then, as I do now."

"And what does it mean?"

"It means"—he softened his voice—"I love you."

"Oh, my *shikaa*, I love you, too," she admitted, showering his face with kisses.

She rested satisfied in his arms, relaxed, and he smiled to himself. He was satisfied, as well.

She snuggled her face in the folds of his neck, her lips against the pulse that beat at his throat. "We've made love beneath the light of the moon."

He ran his hand down her back, across the concave hollow of her spine.

"I like the way you look in the moonlight. It makes the gold of your hair glow." He pulled her close. "You are the most beautiful woman in all the land, and you are all mine." He bestowed a tender kiss atop her head. "How is it I have been so favored as to be given such a treasure?"

She pulled back to look at him, smiling. "Perhaps you've pleased God in some way?"

"I cannot remember what I have done so well, but I am happy he does." He traced her nose with the tip of her finger. "*Shi'aad*, have I not taught you well the ways of my *nuhdee*?"

She nodded. "And I thank you from the bottom of my heart for all the time you've spent." She sighed. "I only regret there is nothing I can teach you."

"But there is something, Golden Lady."

"What?"

"I want to learn to read, write, and count like your people. Will you teach me?"

She smiled. "It would be my pleasure."

****

Amanda drew a capital A in the dirt with a stick. "This is the first letter of the alphabet. Its name is *Aaaa*," she explained. "You draw a line up, and then at the peak, draw a line back down, then connect with another line at the middle."

"The A looks like a mountain peak," he commented.

She giggled at his analysis. "It does, doesn't it?" She handed him the stick. "Now you draw the letter A."

Proud Eagle copied the way she printed the letter in the dirt, but his letter didn't quite look like hers. He sighed and scratched away the mark he'd made in the sand. "This is not going to be easy."

She caressed his cheek. "Learning something new never is my *shikaa*. But at least you have one advantage over me."

He frowned. "What is that?"

"Learning to read and write doesn't hurt."

She watched her husband struggle daily with his lessons. Reading proved much more difficult than writing or working with numbers. The only book she had to teach him from was the Bible, full of parables, not the easiest script for one just beginning. She worked long hours with him, explaining the meaning of the scripture, along with the words.

Proud Eagle was full of questions. "The men who wrote the words, where are they?"

"They are all in heaven. *O'zho*," she added, to help him understand.

"How long have they been gone?"

"Longer than the highest number you've learned to count." She took the Bible from his grasp. "The words written in this book are thousands of years old."

174

"Then they have passed through many tongues."

"Yes, they have," she agreed.

"If this is the way, then by the time the words have reached my ears, how can I believe they are truth?" he concluded.

"By faith. I believe the words because I have faith they are true."

"I do not understand what you mean by faith."

She took him by the hand and led him out of the wickiup. She pointed to the sky. "Do you see the wind, Proud Eagle?"

He chuckled. "No. No one can see the wind."

She raised her face to the heavens. A light breeze played with the tendrils that graced her forehead. "But you know it's there, because you can feel it."

"Yes," he agreed.

She turned toward him. "Well, that's what faith is, something you don't see, but can feel. Here," she said, placing a hand on her chest, "in your heart."

The expression on his face mingled eagerness and tenderness. "Then faith is much like love."

She gazed deep into his large, dark eyes. "I suppose in many ways it is."

He pulled her close, a mischievous twinkle gleaming in his eyes. "Come, *shi'aad*, back into the wickiup, where I can make you feel much love."

She smirked, arching a brow. "Oh, I'm sure you can, Proud Eagle. I'm sure you can."

****

While Amanda tutored Proud Eagle each day, the children often clustered around to watch and listen, drawing letters in the dirt and reading the words. Soon, a tiny school was established by the river, beneath the shade of a tree.

"They all love you, *shi'aad*."

She pushed aside a wayward strand of hair, looping it behind her ear. "And I love them." She

175

added. "They're teaching me as well."

Proud Eagle's face melted into a buttery smile. "And what have you learned?"

"I'm learning to sing songs and speak in Apache."

"Say something to me in my tongue," he urged.

She cleared her throat. "*Qha'n'tayl't'alu'ka?*" Then she translated. "What is going on around here?"

Proud Eagle threw his head back and laughed. "Something the children must hear a lot from their parents."

She giggled. "I'm sure you're right."

He pulled her close. "I am glad you enjoy my *nuhdee.*"

She rested her head upon his shoulder. "And I'm happy our marriage is making a difference in so many other lives."

****

It was rare for Cunning Eagle, frail and ailing, to leave his bed, and White Dove never left his side.

She lifted her in-law's spirits by bringing the meal she cooked each night to their wickiup. The time they spent together was enjoyed by all.

She loved the stories Cunning Eagle shared—legends, lessons, and even tales about Proud Eagle when he was a boy.

"*Shi'aad* does not need to know all the things I did," Proud Eagle complained, shifting in his seat, embarrassed over various accounts of the past.

"Sure I do," she teased. "In this way I will know what to expect from our children."

"It is unfair," he grumbled. "There is no one to tell me about you."

"I can tell you one thing about me. I love Thanksgiving almost as much as I love Christmas."

Cunning Eagle folded his hands together in his lap. "What is Thanksgiving, my daughter?"

"It's a tradition my people celebrate around this time of year," she explained. "A few years ago, President Abraham Lincoln declared a Thanksgiving Proclamation, making it a national holiday."

"Is he your people's chief?" White Dove queried.

"In a way, I guess he was," she agreed. "But not long ago, just last April on the fourteenth day, a man by the name of John Wilkes Booth shot President Lincoln in the head while he attended a performance at the Ford's Theater in Washington. He died a day later."

White Dove said, "How sad for his family."

She nodded. "And for us all, as well. He was loved by many and will be missed. A man named Andrew Johnson has now taken Lincoln's place as the President."

"Tell now about Thanksgiving," Cunning Eagle urged, lying back on a rolled blanket to get comfortable.

She relaxed in her seat. "Let's see." She paused to call upon all her mother had taught her about the Pilgrims and their journey to the new world. "About two-hundred and forty-five years ago, in the year 1620, a group of people called Pilgrims left England to find a new place to live."

White Dove's face brightened. "England is my father's homeland, as well as your mother's, Golden Lady."

She nodded in agreement. "That's true, my mother."

"*Hat'ugha*, why, *shi'aad*, did these Pilgrims leave their home?" Proud Eagle said.

"They didn't like the king—their chief," she added for their benefit, "because he wouldn't allow them to believe in God the way they chose."

"The whole village left?" White Dove asked.

"Not all, but many of those wanting their religious freedom. They sailed on a large boat, a ship named The Mayflower, traveling long weeks across the ocean."

Proud Eagle leaned forward. "*Heyii*, where did The Mayflower take them?"

"To a place called Massachusetts, where the Pilgrims soon built themselves homes. They called the colony or village, Plymouth Plantation."

His interest piqued. "What then?"

She stifled a smile. Her husband listened to her story with anticipation, much like the children in the tribe. "Well, since they didn't know how to live in their new surroundings, many became ill and died."

"They did not know how to plant or hunt?" Cunning Eagle asked astonished.

"There were a few who did, but they were up against many odds. Not being accustomed to the new land's weather, their crops failed."

Cunning Eagle sat up in the bed, looking as eager as his son to learn the story's conclusion. "What happened then, my daughter?"

"Chief Massasoit of the Pokanoket tribe and his people lived in a village not far from the Pilgrim's colony. When Pokanoket warriors explained what they saw, the white men dying, Chief Massasoit sent his people to lend a hand. With the tribe's help, the Pilgrim's crops grew."

Cunning Eagle nodded satisfied. "It is *nzhoo* Massasoit was an honorable man."

"The Pilgrims were so thankful, they shared the harvest. All of them clustered around outdoor fires, where deer, duck, and wild turkey turned on wooden spits. With their fingers and knives the people stripped the bones clean. The glorious aroma of simmering stews, made from a variety of meats and vegetables, called pottages, filled the colony, as well as the striped bass, bluefish, and cod."

Proud Eagle licked his lips. "Your story is making me hungry all over again."

She giggled. "It all does sound delicious at that."

"And so, your people remember this time each harvest?" Cunning Eagle said.

"Yes, in honor of the first Thanksgiving, we give thanks for all we have."

Cunning Eagle looked over at White Dove. "*Shi'aad*, our tribe has done well throughout each season, and we have a good harvest."

White Dove nodded in agreement. "Many male babies have been born, our daughter, Rising Sun is due to give birth." She cast a quick glance at Amanda, smiling. "And our son has taken a wife."

"We have many things to give thanks for," Proud Eagle chimed in.

"I wish for the tribe to celebrate your Thanksgiving, my daughter," Cunning Eagle decided. "You have honored our ways, now we will honor yours."

Her heart leapt with elation. She stood and moved closer to Cunning Eagle's bed, leaning over to give him a hug. "Thank you so much, my father."

Cunning Eagle cleared his throat at her display of affection, but his eyes softened. "You will go with White Dove to each wickiup, and she will help you explain about the feast. Every family is to bring something for the celebration." He lay back, looking satisfied with his decision. "In nine suns we will have our first Thanksgiving."

****

Amanda couldn't contain her happiness at the Chief's pronouncement. Her days were filled with preparations for the celebration. With her own chores still to do each day, coupled with helping Proud Eagle with his lessons and lending a hand to Rising Sun, she became exhausted. She found herself just sitting and staring into the fire most nights after the evening meal.

She watched the flames dance and her thoughts

turned back to another Thanksgiving first—Josh's experience. The celebration had been new to him, since he was from England. Void of his family on the special day, Amanda's mother had opened their home to the young reverend. It hadn't been declared a national holiday then, but folks still celebrated the tradition. How nice it would be to have Josh at the Apache's first Thanksgiving.

Proud Eagle stopped practicing his reading and moved closer to his wife, pushing aside a lock of hair that fell across her forehead. "What troubles you, *shi'aad?*"

She turned, her eyes blank, unseeing. "I'm sorry, Proud Eagle. What did you say?"

"I wish to know what has taken your thoughts so far away."

"Just," she paused. "Memories of another Thanksgiving."

"Tell them to me," he urged.

She faced him, her knees touching his. "I was just thinking of the first Thanksgiving Josh celebrated with my family."

"Josh? The holy man?"

She nodded. "How nice it would be if he could be our guest at the tribe's first Thanksgiving feast."

His heart hardened. "I do not think it would be so nice."

She reached for his hand. "He was kind enough to accept the gifts. Wouldn't it be good of us to do something for him in return?"

The muscles at his jaw tightened. "I do not think the holy man would feel *nzhoo* about sitting with my *nuhdee* and eating." He narrowed his eyes. "I would not like it much as well."

She caressed his lips with a gentle stroke of her finger. "I'm surrounded daily by your family and friends, my *shikaa*. I've grown to love them dearly, as I do you. But sometimes I wish to see one of my friends for a change. Do you understand, Proud Eagle?"

He nodded. "But it is an unwise wish."

She sighed. "Yes, I suppose you're right."

She stood, made her way to the bed and undressed in silence, slipping naked beneath the quilt.

Proud Eagle remained a moment longer by the fire, guilt filling his heart.

I have behaved like a fool. Does she not at all times live my way?

Frustration mounted, his thoughts disturbed.

Why does her way have to be so impossible?

The holy man's words came flooding back to him. So clear were they, he expected to see the white man sitting beside him. A chill ran down his spine and he shuddered; the words played over and over in his head.

"If you can't do right by her, send her back to me... to me... to me. I will treat her the way she deserves."

Proud Eagle blocked his ears with the palms of his hands, springing to his feet. He walked over to where she slept and knelt beside the bed. "*Shi'aad,* do you sleep?"

"No."

He placed a hand on her shoulder and turned her to face him. Her cheeks were moist with tears. The sadness in her eyes wrenched his heart. He wiped the tears away with his thumb.

"Do not cry... I spoke like a fool before." He traced the curve of her full lips. "Two days before the Thanksgiving feast I will ride, *alone,*" he emphasized, "to get the holy man. It will be much swifter and safer that way. If he agrees to come back with me, all will welcome him." He searched her face. "Does that please you, *shi'aad?*"

"Yes." She smiled, wrapping her arms around

181

his neck. "Thank you, Proud Eagle."

"*A he ya eh*, you are welcome."

"I love you beyond all things, forever," she said.

"As I do you, Golden Lady, for the rest of my days," he whispered, lowering his mouth to capture hers.

Chapter Eight

The yard was empty, except for the rabbit raiding the garden. Proud Eagle made his way to the parsonage porch and hesitated before knocking upon the door. He knew, from the previous visit, the holy man was not the only person living in the house. There could be trouble if he was seen by one of the children, or the stocky woman in the print flowered dress that he had seen when he brought the gifts.

But if I am to talk to the holy man, there is no other choice.

He rapped on one of the small, square panes of glass and held his breath, cringing when the plump woman swung open the door. Horror filled her eyes. Before he could explain she screamed, "Mother of God," and fell to the floor in a dead faint.

Proud Eagle knelt at her side, debating whether or not to revive her, when the holy man rushed into the room; no doubt he had heard the woman scream. Thankful no children followed, Proud Eagle stood and backed his way to the door, stating in his own defense, "I did nothing to harm her."

The holy man knelt beside the frightened woman. "Grace," he called, giving her a light slap on each cheek. "Can you hear me, Grace?"

When she regained consciousness, she glanced over at Proud Eagle and screamed again.

The holy man covered her mouth with a hand. "He's not going to harm you." He looked up at Proud Eagle, narrowing his eyes. "I assume you're not, anyway."

He squared his shoulders. "I come in peace."

The holy man helped the woman to stand, his tone disapproving. "It's all right, Grace, he's Amanda's Indian."

"Husband," he interjected. "I am Proud Eagle, her husband."

"Mercy me," the woman choked, her eyes wide with shock.

The holy man walked her over to a chair and helped her to sit.

The elder woman straightened the collar of her blouse, and smoothed aside a wisp of hair that had come loose from her bun. After she had collected her wits she faced Proud Eagle. "So yer the one who stole our little Amanda's heart?"

He did not understand why the white woman thought him a thief. "She gave it to me of her own will."

"I suppose she did." The woman stood and made her way toward him. "Well, well." Her gaze surveyed the length of him. "Yer a right big one at that."

His face warmed with her bold scrutiny.

Her eyes narrowed, her tone sharpened. "What in blue blazes are ya doin' sneakin' around white folk's back doors like that for? Ya darn near scared me half to death."

His voice came out shakier than he liked. "I have come to ask the holy man to a Thanksgiving feast."

"Ya Indians celebrate Thanksgivin'?" Grace asked, startled.

He arched a brow. "We do now."

The holy man threw his head back and laughed. "Well, I knew she had spunk, but to get an entire tribe to celebrate a white man's tradition is truly remarkable." He locked eyes with Proud Eagle. "I accept your invite, wouldn't miss it for the world."

The woman threw the holy man a horrified look. "Yer not serious, Reverend." She pulled the man

184

aside and lowered her voice, but not low enough. Proud Eagle could still hear what was being said. "Yer not really gonna sit with the bunch of 'em, are ya?"

"I can't see why not." He patted the woman's arm. "All will be fine, Grace. Obviously, Amanda has sent him for me. Don't you agree it would be impolite to refuse such a gracious invitation?"

"I'll agree yer crazy," she snapped.

"Besides," he added in a louder tone, looking over at Proud Eagle. "I'd never miss a chance to see *my* Amanda, again."

He flashed the holy man a look of disdain, swallowing the anger that rose to choke him. If he were not doing this for his Golden Lady, the fists he now held clenched at his sides would have no trouble finding a place on the white man's jaw.

Proud Eagle spoke with cool authority. "If you are coming, then we leave now."

The holy man nodded. "I'll just be a moment to gather a few things."

Awkward beneath the elder woman's stares, he busied himself with looking about the room. Bright colored cloth framed the windows and another was draped across the table. In the center, a fancy jar filled with water held a spray of flowers, and the worn wooden floors were scrubbed clean.

When the holy man returned, Proud Eagle let out a breath of relief and made his way out the door.

"Should anyone inquire on my whereabouts," the holy man instructed the woman, "just tell them I'm visiting a friend."

She followed him to the door. "I don't think this is such a good idea, Reverend."

"Not to worry," the holy man called back. "I'll be home in a few days."

"Ya've gone crazy, plumb crazy," she shouted, slamming shut the door.

Roberta C. M. DeCaprio

****

They rode most of the journey in silence. Proud Eagle could sense the holy man was paying strict attention to the direction they traveled so he could ride back to the parsonage on his own. He was the first to break the stillness between them. "I must have your word the way to my village will stay deep within your thoughts."

"Then you've seen the Cavalry soldiers patrolling the area?"

"Yes, on my way to get you. I do not want them knowing where to find my village. I have no reason to trust you, but my wife does, and I trust her."

"I understand your concerns, and I will keep the whereabouts of your village a secret." The holy man arched a brow. "With so many soldiers milling about, you too take a chance every time you roam these parts."

Proud Eagle's annoyance tinged his tone. "This is my land, why should I hide?"

"And so, for your stubborn pride, you'd risk execution?"

"Your white lawmen do not know the paths I take. I ride in the shadows. They will not find me. Besides, I have done nothing wrong." He raised a defiant chin. "Your lawmen should not be the judge of all. Does it not say in your holy book if they should condemn me, it will come back on them?"

The holy man's brows shot up in surprise. "You know scripture?"

He gave a taut nod. "My wife has taught me about your beliefs, how to read the words and understand the meanings."

"But the soldiers adhere to another law and judgment, that of their commanding officers in the military they serve," the holy man explained. "And since there have been more Indian raids on wagon trains, the victims brutally attacked, left mutilated

186

and the women stolen..." He hesitated before speaking further. "I shudder to think of the fate of those young women." The man sighed. "Anyway, my point being, because of all that's transpired, the soldiers are not going to give a notion for what scripture tells them to follow. Many now have hardened their hearts and no longer hear God's word."

"Then the lawmen should know there is good and bad of all kinds." He met the holy man's eyes. "Those warriors were not from my tribe. *Hat'ugha*, why blame all for what a few do."

"The soldiers don't care what tribe an Indian is from, and if you're captured, they won't stop to consider you're innocent of any crimes," he warned. "Emotions are high. You're an Indian, that's all they'll see. That's all they need to know."

"What do you care if I am captured?"

"It's Amanda I'm concerned about, and she would care if you were arrested. I only want her happiness. I told you that before. It's the only reason I accepted your gifts." The holy man arched a brow. "You risked a lot by coming for me."

"It was not my wish, but my wife's. I can enjoy my turkey with or without you sitting by the fire."

"I assure you, Proud Eagle, the feeling is mutual."

"I gave you my word I would share in her ways, and that is what I am doing," he added.

"I am glad for that," the holy man said. "And as much as it displeases us to admit, we are bound together."

"I have nothing that binds me..." His voice trailed off, the dawning of the holy man's inference. "Ah, Golden Lady."

"Aye, Amanda," the holy man agreed. "She is at the center of all of this, and her happiness is of the utmost importance to me."

"I know what you say, I feel the same," he admitted. "The woman has a power over me I cannot fight; whatever she wishes, I will do."

"You're not the only one she's rendered powerless," the holy man acknowledged, turning his focus once again to the road ahead.

****

They rode through the village; many came out from their homes to watch them pass. Josh followed Proud Eagle to a large tent-like dwelling at the end of the village.

"My father wishes first to see you," Proud Eagle explained, dismounting his horse and walking into the structure.

Josh slid off his horse and was greeted by Duke, wagging his tail and barking. "There you are, you good ol' boy." He scratched the dog behind the ears. "Have you been watching out for our girl?" Josh looked around. "Is Amanda near?"

"Later you will see Golden Lady," Proud Eagle said in a gruff tone. "Come, now, my father waits."

Josh nodded and followed Proud Eagle through the door opening.

A stern-faced, elderly man sitting cross-legged on a mat in front of a fire pit, motioned for him to sit.

Josh complied, taking a seat on a nearby mat.

"This is my father, Chief Cunning Eagle," Proud Eagle said, taking a seat on another mat.

Next to the Chief sat a pleasant looking woman with large round eyes and long dark hair falling around her shoulders

"And my mother, White Dove," Proud Eagle added, finishing the introductions.

He inclined his head. "I'm pleased to meet you both."

Cunning Eagle searched his face. "So, you are the holy man my new daughter speaks of."

Josh cleared his throat. "That I am, and I might add I'm honored you have asked me to join your celebration."

A smile quivered at one side of the old Indian's mouth. The elder's smirk turned into a fond smile. "She is a clever one, that Golden Lady, telling us her stories."

"My father has been taken with the one about Thanksgiving," Proud Eagle interjected. "When he learned of a tribe long ago living in peace with the *indah*, white man, it lifted his spirits."

"Such peace would lift my spirits as well," Josh commented.

Cunning Eagle's voice was shaky. "Golden Lady has captured all of our *biijiis,* heart. She has taught my *ciye,* son how to read and write the *indah's* words, as well as some of our children." He coughed and cleared his throat.

White Dove handed her husband something to drink.

The Chief took a sip from the cup before he continued. "With all she has done to learn our ways, we chose this *nkeez,* time to honor one of her traditions."

"You're here already," a voice came from behind.

He turned to find Amanda standing at the door opening. He was taken aback by her beauty, and the short skirt showing so much of her long, shapely legs. He swallowed hard and stood, making his way toward her.

"You're a vision of loveliness," he whispered, embracing her.

Amanda hugged him in return. "I'm so glad you agreed to join us for the Thanksgiving feast." She pulled back, looking up into his eyes. "I wasn't sure, since the last time I saw you..."

He hushed her with a raised hand. "All is well."

Relief sparkled in her eyes. "Then come." She

motioned to the floor mat. "Sit and tell me how things are with you."

He reclaimed his seat, and she circled around him to sit beside Proud Eagle, whose face at this point reminded Josh of a thunder cloud ready to wreak havoc.

Proud Eagle pulled Amanda close to his side, keeping his arm around her waist.

She cast him a reassuring smile.

The young Indian's face relaxed, but Josh noticed his other hand tightening around Amanda's.

She then turned her attention to Josh. "How are the children?"

He couldn't believe how beautiful she looked, skin bronzed, golden curls, pale and thick, cascading to her hips. And her legs, crossed in such a fashion, left her knees bared. He felt his mouth go dry.

"Are the children well?" she repeated, breaking through his thoughts.

He cleared his throat. "Aye. They are all well and have found homes with other families." He looked deep into her blue eyes. "So far, no more have come."

"That has to be a good sign, doesn't it?"

He shook his head. "As much as I'd love to tell you that were true, Amanda, I can't. The attackers have set their sights now on raiding wagon trains instead of homesteads. The young boys are killed and the girls are taken."

Her hand flew to her throat. "Oh no, the poor children, murdered and kidnapped."

There was a long, uneasy pause.

White Dove stood and with a warm smile, offered them all food and drink.

Cunning Eagle broke the silence. "Cochise is the Chief of the *Chokonen* band of Chiricahua, Apaches. A tall man with broad shoulders and a commanding way. His name means hardwood, because of his skill in carving wood." He paused. "I have heard Cochise prides himself with his skill of the spear as well. He has never met a man equal to him."

Cunning Eagle took several deep breaths.

"Do you wish to lay down, my *shikaa?*" White Dove searched her husband's face.

Cunning Eagle shook his head and continued. "Many years ago, Cochise was angered by the murder of his father-in-law, Mangas Coloradas, Red Sleeve, as he was called, who had been accused falsely of kidnapping a young white boy. Cochise knew nothing of the white boy's capture, but the white men did not believe Cochise and imprisoned him, his wife, and son until the white boy was found."

"I remember reading about the incident," Josh said.

White Dove handed the Chief his drink. He took a sip and placed the cup aside.

When Cunning Eagle spoke again, his voice shook. "When you hurt a man's family—"

"You strike at a raw nerve," Josh finished the sentence.

Cunning Eagle nodded in agreement. "Cochise escaped from the white men. His family did not, and war was declared. Now, the warriors are crazy with power, and they grow stronger with the spilt blood of others. But those who stain their hands," Cunning Eagle concluded, "act alone. They do not speak for all Apaches. They do not speak for me."

"Aye, it's true what you say," Josh agreed. "I have seen the hatred war brings to the hearts of men. On both sides things have gotten out of control."

"There is no honor in a victory won by unfairness," Amanda added. "And the sad part is the sufferings of the children."

Again a heavy silence filled the wickiup.

White Dove passed Josh a bowl of juniper nuts, changing the subject. "And what of you, holy man, do you have family?"

He smiled at the Indian woman. Her gentle manner and kind eyes won his instant admiration. He could tell she was the back-bone of her family, much as the white woman was. "Aye, in England, a sister and nephew, but here I only have the company of my housekeeper, Grace. She has been like family." He turned to Amanda. "And she was quite taken with Proud Eagle."

"Really?" Amanda turned to Proud Eagle. "So, you met Grace?"

Proud Eagle nodded.

"Not only did she meet him, but he took her breath away. And for Grace, that isn't an easy thing to do," Josh said.

Proud Eagle started to laugh.

Amanda looked from side to side at each man. "What's so funny?"

"Well," he went on to explain. "He surprised her by coming and knocking at the back door."

Proud Eagle laughed harder.

"Proud Eagle, standing at the door in all his glory was a trifle too much for poor old Grace," he continued, laughing himself at this point. "She took one look at him and passed out cold."

They all laughed now, even the Chief.

"Poor Grace," Amanda said. "Is she all right?"

"She's fine," Josh said, wiping tears of amusement from his eyes. "Don't worry about Grace, Amanda. She's a tough old biddy. Why, as I was leaving," he added, "she was yelling after me, I was plumb crazy."

Amanda nodded in agreement. "Now, that sounds more like Grace."

****

Amanda walked Josh to the tiny wickiup, the

one she shared with Proud Eagle during the first weeks they were married. A small bed, heaped with blankets, sat in one corner and a fire burned in the pit, warming the small dwelling from the autumn night's chill.

"I hope you'll feel at home here," she said.

Josh looked around the cozy hut. "I am at home in any dwelling, my safekeeping and comfort lies in God, not in the place where I'm staying."

How she had missed him, his wisdom and spirituality. "Thank you so much for coming, and for giving me the opportunity to show you my hospitality. I wanted so much to open my home to you, and in turn give you a chance to know my new family."

Josh inclined his head. "It's my pleasure, Amanda." Their eyes met. "I've missed you so much," he whispered, taking her hand and turning it over. He placed a kiss in the center of her palm.

His display of affection surprised her, leaving her at a loss for words. Her face warmed at his close scrutiny.

Proud Eagle stepped through the door flap with an arm full of wood, arching a brow at the display of affection he interrupted.

After dropping the wood by the pit, Proud Eagle turned to Josh. "Sleep well, holy man. The nights grow cold here. I hope the fire will be enough to keep you warm." He reached for her hand, taking her with him through the door opening.

Once outside, she had to run to keep up with her husband's quick, stiff steps. With eyes straight ahead and the muscles at his jaw throbbing, Proud Eagle led the way to their wickiup.

He remained quiet while throwing wood on the fire.

"I know what angers you."

"Do you?" He undressed and slipped beneath the

blanket.

She looked at her husband in bed, hands locked behind his head, eyes closed. "What you saw meant nothing. It's the custom of his people, Proud Eagle."

Still he ignored her.

"In England, where he's from, a man kissing a woman's hand is just a form of being polite. It means nothing," she repeated.

His eyes snapped open, glaring up into hers. "It does mean something to him, *shi'aad*."

She knelt beside the bed. "But it means nothing to me, Proud Eagle, and to believe otherwise is foolish."

He arched a brow. "Now you call me foolish?"

She nodded, tickling him under the arm. "Like a troublesome coyote."

He pulled her on top of him. "Ah, that unwise?"

She lowered her mouth to his. "Yes, as bad as that," she teased before capturing his lips with a kiss.

****

Amanda couldn't believe what a beautiful day they were blessed with for the Thanksgiving celebration. She donned a white deerskin dress and ankle-high moccasins to match; turquoise beads adorned her neck and wrists.

Arm in arm, she and Proud Eagle walked to the Chief's wickiup, where everyone gathered out front.

Josh sat beside Cunning Eagle, engaged in conversation. She smiled to herself, happy the two men got along.

Josh stood when he saw her arrive, bowing and taking her hand. "You are a lovely sight, Amanda." He kissed her hand as he'd done the night before. When she politely pulled away, he glanced over at Proud Eagle. "I envy your husband and wonder if he realizes what a fortunate man he is."

Proud Eagle's glare shot Josh daggers. "I do,

every time I love her."

She stiffened. *Was this how it was to be throughout the celebration?*

Cunning Eagle came to her rescue, clearing his throat and waving his hand commanding everyone to sit. "Let the festivities begin."

The drums beat, and Amanda felt the vibration deep within her. Warriors with blue painted faces, garbed in bright colored outfits and head dresses, stepped to the rhythm.

Proud Eagle explained to her and Josh the story the dance told.

Then the maidens appeared, serving bowls filled with sunflower seeds, acorns, pine nuts, willow bead, juniper berries, and walnuts.

Proud Eagle leaned toward Josh. "The main course of turkey, deer, and boiled corn smut, along with biscuit bread, dumplings, and wheat flour dough bread, will be served later in the day."

Josh nodded his head and licked his lips.

They have at least one thing in common—a hearty appetite. Amanda stifled a smile and started to rise, intending to help the women serve.

Cunning Eagle placed a restraining hand on her arm. "Today you will not serve. You are the guest of honor."

Out of respect for Cunning Eagle's position, she stayed seated, but grew uncomfortable. "It's unfair for them to be doing all the work," she confided to Proud Eagle.

He squeezed her hand to reassure her. "All these women are honored to serve you. Can you not see in their eyes how much they care for and respect you? You have taught their children and become their friend. They are happy to give you something in return."

"But I started this whole celebration," she protested. "The least I can do is to lend a hand."

Cunning Eagle leaned toward her. "My daughter, if you feel you need to do something, after the children sing their song, I have a special favor to ask of you." He smiled, pointing at the dish of berries set before her. "For now, sit and eat."

An unwelcome heat crept into her cheeks; her new father-in-law had just politely told her to shut her mouth.

She was so proud of the children. They didn't make one mistake while singing the song about a turkey who didn't want to be dinner.

Josh was delighted and praised the children. "You are all so wonderful." He then turned to her. "The fruits of your labor are abundant."

Cunning Eagle then raised his hands above his head, and all went silent. "I now have a special favor to ask of my new daughter."

The Chief turned his attention to her, his eyes twinkling. She saw the traces of a once handsome man. It wasn't hard to see where Proud Eagle got his charm.

"Golden Lady, will you please an old man with your dancing," Cunning Eagle said.

His request took her by surprise. She looked over at Proud Eagle. Other than the familiar throbbing at his jaw, a clear indicator he was not pleased with his father's wish, his face remained impassive. In spite of the stricken look she knew was upon her own face, her husband nodded for her to comply.

With leaden legs she stood and made her way to the center of the circle. The drums beat louder, their hum resounding through her feet. She picked up the rhythm, toe first, then heel, toe and heel, knees bending higher and higher. She closed her eyes, blocking out her surroundings and freeing her body to move in sync with the tempo. Her arms, in graceful swirls, lifted high above her head, and she let the dance carry her away.

Proud Eagle glanced at the holy man's face, color rose to his cheeks. Disturbed, he turned back to watch his wife dance, her dress pulling tight across her full breasts. She twirled, and the deerskin skirt crept higher, revealing the bare splendor of her thighs. Again Proud Eagle looked the holy man's way. Their guest swallowed hard, watching Golden Lady's hips sway back and forth, in and out, the dress clinging to every sensuous curve. He cast another glance at his wife, his mood veering sharply to anger, and clenched his teeth as he seethed. Golden Lady, lost in the dance, closed her eyes, oblivious to the stares and the emotion she stirred from all the men who watched. With a swish of her tongue she moistened her lips and Proud Eagle's blood boiled. He imagined the holy man wishing to caress the softness of her flesh, the full breasts. His insides shook with impotent rage, face growing hotter with dazzling fury, and he fought for control.

The holy man whispered, "She isn't wearing anything underneath,"

It was Cunning Eagle who answered, his tone calm, matter-of-fact, "Animal skin can be warm to wear."

"Mercy, it just—it just clings to her," the holy man stammered.

Hearing this banter and scanning the faces of the other men, the excited pleasure in their eyes, Proud Eagle's fury piqued. A heated rage soared from the depths of his stomach to the top if his head. With his fists clenched, he began to rise, but his father's hand came down hard upon his shoulder.

"Do not be a fool, like the coyote, my son," Cunning Eagle warned.

His lips thinned. Just the night before his wife also compared him to the troublesome critter.

"If you want her to fall at her own will into your

arms and not the arms of another, you must be clever, like the fox," Cunning Eagle advised.

Amanda was absorbed in the dance, her heart beating in unison to the drums. Around and around she twirled, until a strong pair of arms encircled her waist.

His dark eyes searched her face. "Dance now with me, *shi'aad*."

She smiled, falling into his possessive arms.

The drums quieted, and the singing wood played. Others danced, filling the circle with merriment.

Proud Eagle tightened his embrace and kissed her temple. "Do you love me, *shi'aad*?"

Her voice echoed her longing. "You know I do, with all my heart."

He spoke in a low, seductive tone. "Come, show me."

"What about dinner?" She looked around the circle. "We can't be gone while everyone is eating."

"There is time yet before the main meal is to be served." His eyes grew tender. "Come, *shi'aad*, before I can wait no longer and take you here."

"What, and shock your poor father?" she teased.

"That one is beyond being shocked. Was it not he who asked you to dance?" Proud Eagle shook his head amused. "The old fox still has an eye for beauty, but after this day he will have to be happy with his dreams. No longer will you dance for all eyes to see."

"But I love to dance, my *shikaa*."

A smile trembled over his lips. "Then come with me." He took her by the hand and pulled her through the crowd.

Together they ran to their wickiup.

She giggled. "Where's the fire?"

"Burning within me," he said, rushing through the door opening. With a devilish twinkle in his eyes, he brought her to stand in front of the bed and reclined on the rolled blankets.

She looked down at him with amused wonder. "Now what?"

The smile in his eyes contained a sensuous flame. "Now, dance. But first take off the dress."

Chapter Nine

The morning of Josh's departure, Amanda made her way to the small wickiup he occupied and called through the door opening. "Josh, may I come in?"

A moment later the flap rose, his mouth curved into a broad smile. "Good morning to you, sweet lady."

She returned the smile and entered the wickiup, noticing his satchel upon the bed. "I see you're packed and ready to leave."

He nodded. "As much as I hate to, Amanda, I must get back to my duties at the parsonage. But these last four days I've had such a wonderful time here; everyone is just—just—"

"Like normal folks," she finished his sentence.

"Touché. I had that one coming."

She handed him a folded piece of paper. "I found this in the back of my mother's Bible, and I want you to have it."

He opened the document and scanned it. "This is the deed to your property."

"Your property," she corrected. "There isn't much there but a burned down house and barn, but someday, should you want a home of your own, you will now have land to build on."

"But why?" he asked bewildered.

She shrugged. "I have no need for it."

His gaze searched hers. "I must admit to you, I held the small hope perhaps this trip would find you returning to the parsonage with me."

"My place is here, with Proud Eagle."

He nodded and folded the deed, placing it in his

vest pocket. "You do seem quite happy and content."

She smiled, thinking of her wonderful husband, "I am."

"And I owe you an apology."

"How so?"

"I had no right to be so judgmental, to condemn Proud Eagle and his people." He smirked. "I must admit he's done right by you in every way, caring for your needs, honoring your wishes, treating you with respect."

"And loving me with all his heart," she added.

He nodded. "Aye, and loving you as well. There was no more I could have given you, had you been my wife." His smile broadened. "Enjoy your happiness, Golden Lady."

Her heart beamed with joy at hearing him call her by her Apache name. "Come back soon, *shills aash*."

Josh's eyes twinkled with amusement. "What does that mean?"

She giggled. "It's Apache for my friend."

"Then, *shills aash*," he repeated. "I will return, and know always I am here for you."

****

Amanda sat cross-legged by the fire, weaving, when Falling Star's panicked voice called to her from the door opening.

Proud Eagle raised the flap. "Come in, *skee'kizzen*, welcome brother." He motioned for Falling Star to enter. "What brings you to our wickiup so late?"

Falling Star looked over at her, his brown eyes widening with concern. "It is Rising Sun. Her *nkeez* has come."

She placed her weaving aside and stood. "Is the midwife with her?"

Falling Star nodded. "As well as White Dove, but she calls for you." He threaded his fingers through his long hair. "Will you come?"

Falling Star's complexion looked pale. "Of course I'll come." She motioned to the door. "Lead on and I'll follow."

"I will come as well," Proud Eagle offered. He leaned down and whispered in her ear. "Falling Star looks as though he will pass out."

She stifled a smile. "Don't be too harsh on him, my *shi'kaa*. Your time has yet to come."

Proud Eagle walked beside her in thoughtful silence the rest of the way to Rising Sun's wickiup.

White Dove waited at the door opening and summoned her inside.

She made her way to the bed, where Rising Sun writhed in pain. Beads of perspiration moistened her forehead, long strands of hair clung to her neck.

"It will be better for her without the clothes, and then we will help her to stand," White Dove instructed.

She nodded in agreement and helped White Dove pull Rising Sun's tunic over her head, freeing the large breasts filled with mother's milk. They hung low and heavy, blue veins surrounding swollen nipples that would soon nourish the baby.

Rising Sun lay naked, except for the animal skin belt she wore around her waist. Amanda hadn't seen the belt before, but refrained from questioning the tradition.

White Dove moved to one side of her daughter, taking her beneath the arm. "We must help her to her feet, and then we will be the ones to keep her standing."

She moved to the other side of Rising Sun, her own legs trembling, and helped to hold her friend, using all the strength she could muster.

The night passed, Rising Sun laboring hard and long to give her child life. When the light of dawn filtered through the smoke hole, Rising Sun's baby dropped from her womb, into the midwife's waiting hands.

There were no words to explain the complete, yet wonderful, exhaustion that wearied Amanda. She made her way out of the wickiup, and down a path to where Proud Eagle and Falling Star waited a few feet away.

Falling Star paced like a caged animal, his appearance disheveled and worn. Proud Eagle sat on a nearby rock watching with sympathy.

When Falling Star spotted her, he hurried over. "Rising Sun, she is *haua*, all right?"

She gave him a weary smile. "She is fine, as well as your son."

Falling Star let out a victorious yelp and raised his hands to the heavens, giving thanks.

"She waits for you now, Falling Star," she said.

He nodded and left to join his wife and new baby.

Amanda made her way to where Proud Eagle sat.

He slid over to give her room.

She lowered her body next to his.

For a moment they sat in silence, feeling the breeze on their faces, listening to the quiet of the approaching dawn.

She raised her arms and stretched. Every muscle in her body ached. "It's been a long night."

Proud Eagle pushed aside a wisp of hair that clung to her temple. "You need rest."

"I'm so tired; I fear if I close my eyes, I might never wake up."

Proud Eagle nodded. "Rising Sun's baby has tired us all."

She stifled a yawn. "Why are you so tired?"

He sighed with exasperation. "If you were here to see the time I had with Falling Star, you would not have to ask."

"What happened?" She laid her head on his shoulder.

He put his arm around her and pulled her close. "When Falling Star heard Rising Sun scream, he went crazy. I had to jump on him and hold him down to keep him from entering the wickiup."

She snuggled closer. "What would it have hurt to let him go?"

"Tribal law forbids a man to watch his wife give birth," he explained.

She forced her eyes to stay open. "If I were the one screaming, would you want anyone to keep you from me?"

"No, there would be no one who could." He stood, with her in his arms. "I would come to be by your side, no matter what the tribal law allowed."

She wrapped her arms around his neck. "I'm glad to hear you say that."

"Is it what you wish, for me to be with you when it is your time?"

"Yes," she said, stifling another yawn.

Proud Eagle kissed the top of her head. "Then I will not leave your side, you have my word," he whispered, carrying her back to their wickiup.

****

Amanda spent most of the morning watching Rising Sun feed her son, Rising Star. The babe was rightly named, a combination of both his parents.

Rising Sun looked down at her infant as he suckled. "All he wants to do is eat."

She giggled. "Don't most men?"

Rising Sun laughed too. "It does seem to be that way."

She caressed the child's soft head. "He's just storing up food so he'll grow to be a strong warrior."

Rising Sun's eyes glistened with joy. "Ah, just like his father."

Her tone turned somber. "You and Falling Star

204

have been very blessed."

Rising Sun looked over, her smile encouraging. "And next it will be your time, Golden Lady."

"I hope so." She forced a smile. "But for now I am happy to hold your son."

After visiting Rising Sun, she went to the river for water. There, she spotted Running Doe doing laundry. Not wanting an unpleasant confrontation, she filled the jugs in a hurry and turned to leave.

Most days Running Doe was just as content to uphold the silence between them, but today she called out, "Golden Lady, how are Rising Sun and the baby?"

Suspicious of the other woman's pleasant inquiry, she hesitated a moment before answering. "Both are doing well."

Running Doe smiled. "That is *inju* to hear. I will visit her soon."

She nodded and again turned to leave.

Running Doe spoke again, moving closer. "Did Proud Eagle ever find you?"

She hadn't seen her husband since early that morning. "Why do you ask?"

Running Doe shrugged. "Some time ago he came by looking for you." She bent to retrieve a piece of clothing and dipped it into the water. "He asked if I had seen you, and I told him I had not." She beat the material against a rock. "But I told him if I did, I would be happy to give you his words."

"What were his words," she probed.

"He wishes to go riding with you." Running Doe squeezed the moisture from the garment.

Why would Proud Eagle ask Running Doe to relay anything to me?

But upon further scrutiny, she realized her husband wasn't aware of the rift between her and Running Doe. He could have very well spoken to her in such a way.

She bit her bottom lip, still undecided the other woman spoke the truth. If Running Doe was being clever, she could be clever too. "Did he say where to meet him?"

Running Doe arched a brow. "Do you not have a favored spot?"

Not satisfied with the response, she forced a smile and picked up the jugs. "Thank you for the message." Proud Eagle cautioned her many times about the dangers of riding in broad daylight. He would never ask for her to meet him for a ride before sundown.

She spent the next hour cleaning the wickiup and thinking about Running Doe's message from Proud Eagle. What if he did expect her to meet him riding? Confused, she wandered around the wickiup until she heard Little Elk's voice from the door opening. She raised the flap in welcome to Proud Eagle's new student. "What a pleasure, Little Elk... but Proud Eagle isn't here right now."

Little Elk's lopsided grin filled his face. "I have not come for a lesson, Golden Lady... I have a message for you." The young Indian locked his gangly arms behind him. "Proud Eagle wishes for you to meet him riding."

She took a deep breath. "Now, I am truly confused."

Little Elk frowned. "Why so?"

"Proud Eagle never rides with me during the day. He says the danger is greater when the sun is up."

Little Elk nodded in agreement. "I understand, but it is a beautiful day. Could it be Proud Eagle decided it would be foolish to waste?"

Frustrated, she pondered the situation further. "I'm just not sure if I should—"

"I have never known Proud Eagle to be unwise," Little Elk interjected.

She sighed. "That's true."

"I must go now," Little Elk said, turning to leave. "Enjoy your day."

"Thank you, Little Elk," she called after him.

Amanda pinched the bridge of her nose with a thumb and forefinger. Now, she had received word from Proud Eagle through two messengers. She had decided not to heed the one from Running Doe, but Little Elk had no reason to lie. He was right about one thing, Proud Eagle never made an unwise decision. He had taught her to ride low, and she did know the area well. If she stuck to the shadows, what harm would it do to meet him?

She ran to Venus, mounted her, and gave the little mare a nudge. The crisp wind blew through her hair as she galloped out of the village. The sleek easy strides of the mare, combined with the sun beating down upon her face, made for a most enjoyable ride. She smiled, feeling happy and free.

The autumn countryside was alive with the last traces of gold and red for the season. Perhaps this was why Proud Eagle wanted them to ride during daylight; at night the colors could not be as appreciated.

The little mare knew the way to their secret place by heart. She let Venus take her down the familiar path. Her anticipation grew, their hideaway wasn't far.

Venus jerked as her hoof stepped onto a ground hornet's nest. Insects as big and round as her large toe swarmed, frightening the horse. Venus tossed her head and ran with fury.

Her arms flailed like a weather vane on a windy day. Her attempt to grasp a piece of the horse's mane became impossible. She tightened her knees to stay seated.

Venus bucked and kicked, twisted her head, pin-wheeled in circles, and stood on hind legs.

Her limbs, locked around the mare's barrel, could no longer keep her astride. She was thrown backwards, falling into the brush. The cracking of the brittle branches serenaded her on the way down. She met the ground with a *thud*, scattering a bed of dried leaves, her senses reeling into darkness.

****

When Amanda opened her eyes, the blurred figure of a man stood over her. She blinked several times to focus, but the pain in her head made her wince. She swallowed hard, closing her eyes again.

A raspy voice broke the silence. "*Mira*, Pedro, what have we found here? *Muy bonita*, an Injun Princess."

The man standing knelt beside her. "She's no Injun, Chico. She's a *gringa*... see," he said, grabbing a fistful of her hair, "*mira*, all the yellow curls."

She opened her eyes again, looking straight into a pair of beady black eyes.

He smiled down at her, revealing a mouthful of huge, yellow teeth. "Ya runnin' from somethin', lady?"

The other man's wicked laugh made her cringe, and a shiver of panic raced down her spine.

"I bet she ain't no lady no more, Pedro. No doubt them Injuns she ran from already had their fill."

"Whatcha think, *amigo*? Could be a reward for this one, *si*?"

"*Si*, Pedro. Could be some rich *gringo* got his bitch taken by them savages and will pay plenty for her return." He laughed again, his voice cracking. "Let's get her back to camp before the redskin she got loose from comes lookin' for her."

The man kneeling lifted her from the ground.

She fisted her hand and hit him in the head.

He was stunned for a moment, but was quick to regain his wits. He slapped her hard across the face and straddled her.

In spite of her cheeks burning from the blow, she clawed at his face with her nails.

The other man grabbed her arms, pulling them above her head and pinning them to the ground. Again he cackled. "She even fights like a stinkin' savage."

The one straddling her brought his face inches from hers. The sour stench of his breath made her gag. She swallowed hard to keep from retching.

He toyed with the laces on her tunic. "We know many ways to make a woman obey, ain't that right, Chico?"

She spat in his face.

He wiped his cheek and glared down at her.

The one holding her arms tightened his grip. "This one is *loco*, like a wild animal."

The one sitting on her legs entwined his fingers in her hair and brought her face up to meet his. He sneered. "It's time she was tamed."

The one above her cackled a crazy laugh. "First, we tie her."

"*Si*, Chico. But there is only one way to get her back to camp," he said, doubling his fist and slamming it hard against her chin.

They both laughed, and she lost consciousness again.

****

Proud Eagle scouted the area all morning, spotting several Pima, Maricopas, and Nakai'ye, Mexicans. These bands were helping the white lawmen track Indians. In his surveillance, he discovered how brutal the trackers could be, more unmerciful than the militia, if that were possible. He shook his head to clear the irony. In a strange way the *silaada*, soldiers, had turned out to be the lesser of two evils. No matter how you looked at the situation, the Indian still lost.

Tired and hungry, he headed back to the village.

The thought of Golden Lady waiting for him with a good meal and a sensuous body made him speed his pace.

He was stopped short as the chestnut colored mare galloped by him. Recognizing Venus, Proud Eagle wasted no time in catching up with the horse, and pulling her to a stop.

After making sure Venus was not hurt, he pointed her in the direction of the village and gave her backside a sharp slap, sending her on her way. Then he backtracked her hoofprints, hoping in his heart what he feared would not be true.

****

Amanda's senses returned in a rush of pain. The rope binding her hands was knotted so tight, her fingers went numb. Her feet were tied, her head throbbed, and one side of her face burned. She was placed beneath a tree, far from the warmth of the campfire. A chill ran down her spine, and she shivered. Whether from the coldness of the night or from the fear that consumed her, she didn't know.

The one she heard called Chico moved closer, squinting down at her with pig-like eyes; his laugh an eerie screech. "*Como esta, gringa*? Are you cold?" He came down on one knee beside her. "If you're a nice *la nina*, Chico will untie you and bring you over to the fire."

"Keep her hands tied, Chico," the one by the fire shouted. "She claws like a mountain lion," he grumbled, rubbing his face with the memory.

Chico freed her feet and pulled her to a stand. A wave of dizziness washed over her and she stumbled. He steadied her and pushed her toward the campfire.

The one called Pedro smiled, motioning for her to sit beside him.

She hesitated, panic welling in her throat.

Chico pushed her to the ground and sat beside

her. His lopsided grin exposed huge, rotted teeth. "Is this not cozy, *senorita*?"

She remained silent, keeping her eyes on the fire.

Chico laughed. "Could it be she is not a *senorita, mi amigo*?"

Pedro shrugged "Could be, Chico."

Chico leaned closer. "Are ya married, *gringa*?"

Again she held her tongue.

Chico knotted a lock of her hair around his hand and pulled her head back. "Are ya married?"

"Yes," she choked out, another wave of dizziness threatening to make her sick.

Pedro smiled. "There, see, we only want to be *amigos*. Now we know you are a *senora*." He stuffed a piece of beef jerky in his mouth, chewed, and swallowed it. "*Como se llama su esposa*?" He held up a finger. "*Excusa por favor*, what is your husband's name," he repeated for her to understand.

She fought the tears stinging the back of her throat. "His name..." she hesitated with a quick and disturbing thought. If she told the truth these derelicts might gather their companions to search out Proud Eagle and the village. "His name is Chief Cochise of the Chiricahua, Apaches," she lied.

Chico's face turned white. "Holy shit, she's *la esposa* to an Apache Chief, Pedro. And one I know better than to deal with. The Chiricahua warriors are ruthless." He ran a hand through his dirty hair. "What if he comes lookin' for her with the whole damned tribe?"

She glared at Chico. "He will, you can count on that."

"Shit, Pedro, what are we gonna do?"

"*Callate*!" Pedro snapped, raising his hand to silence Chico. "Let me think, *amigo*."

Icy fear twisted her heart while she waited her fate from the man sitting next to her. At least Proud

Eagle and his people would be safe.

Pedro stood, grabbed her by the hair, and pulled her to her feet, dragging her to the tree where she had been before.

"Whatcha gonna do, Pedro?" Chico followed close behind.

Pedro forced her to her knees. "I have often heard, *mi amigo*, Injuns only attack the homesteads at *la noche*, but not the enemy hiding in the wilds. For such a battle they wait for the light of day, where they have the advantage. If we're outta here by sun-up, we ain't got a problem." He stared at her like a hungry wolf. "But for now, I'm gonna have me some fun with this here *gringa* squaw." He removed his vest and shirt. "I haven't had me a woman in a long time—too long. Scoutin' for redskins has left no time for enjoyin' such pleasures. Might as well have fun while we can, is that not so, *amigo*?"

They both laughed and her heart thudded in her head. The thought of them touching her made her flesh crawl.

Pedro knelt beside her, shoving her onto her back. He straddled her legs and ripped apart the laces, cupping her breasts. The overriding excitement glared in his eyes. "Never thought I'd see teats bigger than Rosie's, Chico."

Chico licked his lips, his gaze riveted on her full, bared bosom. "*Si*, I remember Rosie."

"Who don't," Pedro commented.

They both laughed, high pitched and hysterical.

The crazed look of lust in their eyes sent sheer black fright coursing through her body.

"You gotta tame her first, Pedro," Chico suggested, rubbing his hands together in delight. "She weren't all that thankful for our hospitality."

"You're right, *amigo*, scratchin' and spittin' like she done," Pedro said, again rubbing his hand across the gashes her nails left on his face. "She's gonna have to answer for her wild ways." He ground out the words between his teeth. "Know what we do back home when our women are bad?" He lowered his face. "We spank their bare bottoms so they can't sit for a week."

Chico's sinister laughter echoed in her head as Pedro turned her face down, raising the skirt to her hips.

Tears of rage and humiliation stung her eyes.

Pedro slapped her across the backside. "This is for spittin'." Another firm wallop smarted her flesh. "And that one's for the scratchin'."

"My turn now, Pedro," Chico hooted.

Pedro's menacing laugh shocked the stillness of the night. Then the evil bellowing caught in his throat.

He fell with a *thud* beside her.

Chico screamed, "Holy shit," before he fell to the ground alongside Pedro.

She turned her head to look.

Pedro lay with an arrow in his back. Chico, an arrow in his chest.

She turned away from the horrible sight, her lungs bursting with silent screams of fear. Were they Chiricahua arrows? It was too dark to tell. Tears slipped down her cheeks, panic consuming her as the blade of a knife slipped between her hands and cut the rope.

Her arms fell limply to her sides.

A pair of hands rolled her onto her back.

Blind fury swept over her. *I will not let them take me without a fight.*

With her eyes clenched, she screamed and growled like an animal, kicking with her feet and clawing at the hands that forced her arms to her chest. Tears flooded from the tightly shut lids, her feet fighting, trying with her last ounce of strength to free herself from the enemy.

"Golden Lady, you are safe now. They cannot hurt you any longer, *shi'aad*."

The familiar voice, the tender words took a moment to filter through her terror. She ceased her fight when they took on meaning. Opening her eyes, she looked deep into those of her husband's. He released her arms and gathered her into his protective embrace.

She sobbed against his neck as he stroked her hair. "Shh, it is *haua* now, *shi'aad*." He kissed her forehead, tightening his hold. "I thought I lost you," he whispered.

She locked her arms around him and buried her face beneath his chin. Never did she want his arms to release her.

He retied the laces of her tunic and carried her into the brush, where Blazing Fire waited. After placing her upon the horse's back, he mounted behind her and pulled her close.

She rested back against him and closed her eyes.

His voice was soft, yet stern. "Why did you go riding without me, Golden Lady? Have I not warned you of the danger of riding in the full light of day?"

She spun her head to look at him, bewildered. "I was coming to meet you. You left word for me to ride with you."

He shook his head. "I would never leave word for you to do such a thing."

She sank back into his arms, rage rushing through her body.

"Who told you these words?" he demanded, his arms tensing around her.

She could just visualize the jaw muscles throbbing, something he often did when trying to control his anger.

His voice was cold and exact. "Tell me who gave you these words?"

214

She took a deep breath to calm the anger that consumed her. She had no choice now but to tell him the entire situation with Running Doe.

When she had finished her explanation, she expected him to fly into a rage, but instead he remained quite calm and asked her, "Why did you not come to me with this before?"

She sighed. "Because of the way you are."

"And what way is that, *shi'aad*?"

"Proud."

His tone remained patient. "What does my pride have to do with you not coming to me about the trouble with Running Doe?"

"I remember once you telling me you could accept anything but to be shamed." She licked her dry lips. "I would shame you in front of the others in the tribe if I couldn't handle this myself."

He threw his head back and let out a great peal of laughter.

She twisted to look at him, puzzled and annoyed by his reaction. "I'm glad you find this so amusing."

"Forgive me, *shi'aad*, I am not laughing at you or this trouble," he said, a trace of wit in his voice. "I was just thinking back at a few things." He looked down at her, a humorous twinkle in his eyes. "Could any of this be why you wanted to learn to fight?"

She sighed. "Why, yes, don't you see?"

"Ah, I see only too well," he said with his brows high and rounded. "It seems you have chosen from the start to take care of Running Doe."

"I didn't want you to think you married a coward."

One brow arched higher. "Then what has taken you so long? She almost sent your spirit to *O'zho* two times. Why did you not take care of her after the first time?"

She was astonished. "You know of the first time?"

He narrowed his eyes. "I would say it is more of a feeling than really knowing."

"And how did you come by the feeling?"

"Through *shemaa*. The day of your accident White Dove told me she had cleared the wickiup of the wood and the poles were secure." He tightened his hold around her. "We both went to my father with the problem, and he agreed someone in the tribe was responsible for your injuries."

"But how did you know it was Running Doe?"

"I did not put that together until just now. It is clear to see whoever tried the first time would be the one who tried now."

"The day of my accident, Rising Sun saw Running Doe leaving the area of our wickiup," she explained. "Rising Sun believed Running Doe was the culprit."

Proud Eagle's lips thinned. "Why did you and my sister not seek council with me and my father?"

"There was no real proof, and I didn't want to make problems within the tribe." She searched his face. "You need to remember, Proud Eagle, I'm the intruder here. I was not sure the Elders, with so little proof, would choose my side over Running Doe's, especially since one of the Elders is her father. I didn't want to be banished from the tribe."

He kissed the tip of her nose. "I would not have allowed that to happen, and my father would have stood with me."

She looked ahead. "Well, I wasn't quite sure."

Proud Eagle lowered his mouth to her ear and whispered. "No woman will ever be as you are to me. My father and the tribe know this."

She sighed, his hot breath racing her heart. "Well, I did make an attempt to solve the problem. I went to her wickiup to confront her. I even thought, perhaps, we could call a truce. But she denied being involved, became furious, and told me I had to leave

216

because the village was her home and the tribe, her people."

"And yet you believed her when she gave you the words to meet me riding?"

"No, I didn't believe her. Instead, I went back to our wickiup and did my chores, but shortly after, Little Elk came calling with the same message. I had no reason to mistrust him." She leaned back against her husband. "When Little Elk visits our wickiup to learn from you the fighting lessons, he always smiles and talks to me. I believed he liked me, but now I see I'm wrong."

"You are not wrong, *shi'aad*. Little Elk thinks only good things about you. I am sure he would never be a part of something that would bring you harm."

"Then how do you explain his involvement?"

"Little Elk, since his father was killed, has looked up to Bear Watcher, who is his father's brother and responsible for Little Elk. He admires Running Doe as well, and would believe anything she told him. I am sure what happened was she asked Little Elk to give you a message, and that is what he did."

Her eyes narrowed. "And if he had no idea Running Doe was trying to harm me, he wouldn't think twice about relaying that message to me."

"I am sure he thought he was doing us both a favor, and when he learns what really happened he will be shamed and sorrowed. As well as my sister for not telling me she saw Running Doe the day of you got hurt."

"No, Proud Eagle, please," she begged. "Say nothing to Rising Sun. It was my fault she didn't come to you. I made her promise to let me handle things on my own first. You wouldn't expect her to break her word once she gave it, would you?"

"No, I would not," he agreed.

"Then you will leave her out of this?"

"Yes. You have my word I will say nothing to Rising Sun," he agreed again, reluctant this time.

She turned to look at him. "What happens now, my *shikaa*?"

His eyes blazed with sudden anger. "If you stay silent, the little witch will think you fear her and will harm you again."

Her heart sunk to her toes. "Are you saying I should fight her?"

Proud Eagle arched a brow. "Have I not taught you well?"

"Yes, you have taught me very well, but—"

"There is no other way, Golden Lady," he broke in. "I will go to my father and Bear Watcher when we return to the village. I will tell them all that has happened. Then together you and I will go to see Running Doe. But," he added, "the fight is yours."

****

Amanda waited in the wickiup while Proud Eagle sought council with the Chief and Bear Watcher. Back and forth she paced, like a trapped animal, her stomach clenched tight.

When her husband returned he carried a weapon, a large knife, which he handed her. "You will use this." The emotionless tone of his voice chilled her.

She looked down at the knife and gulped. *Will I really be able to use it against another?*

He read her thoughts. "You must do what you have to do to win."

She raised her eyes to his, the silence looming between them like a heavy mist.

He took her by the arm. "Come, it is time."

She fought to control the spasmodic trembling within, walking with quick steps to keep up with Proud Eagle's long strides. "Your father has agreed?"

He gave her a taut nod.

218

"And he's on my side?"

Proud Eagle kept his eyes ahead. "I told you he would stand with me."

"What about Bear Watcher?"

"He is shamed by his daughter's evil ways and has agreed, as well."

"And Little Elk, what's his story?"

"Just as I thought," Proud Eagle said. "Little Elk only believed he was delivering an important message."

She halted her steps. Icy fear twisted around her heart. "I'm frightened, Proud Eagle."

He stopped and faced her, the intensity of his gaze washed over every feature of her face. "Every warrior is, before a battle, *shi'aad*. There is no shame in feeling fear, only in not doing something about it." He turned her head sideways, and touched the bruise on her cheek.

She flinched with the pain.

"Did they not get what they deserved for doing this?"

"Yes," she replied in a small, anxious voice.

He kissed the bruise. "Now it is time for Running Doe to get hers."

A flicker of apprehension coursed through her. "What if I am the one to lose?"

Proud Eagle again took her by the hand and continued walking, his tone confident. "You will not lose."

She halted a second time, pulling her hand free from his. "What makes you so sure I won't?"

He arched a brow. "I remember who taught you to fight."

She searched his face; the dark, powerful presence of his strength and wisdom glimmered in his dark eyes. The private message they conveyed was a reminder of the endless hours of training and pain she had endured with each fighting lesson.

She squared her shoulders and took a deep breath. "I remember too."

****

They were all there, waiting in front of the Chief's tent.

She glanced around at each face, trying to keep her emotions under control. White Dove and Rising Sun wore expressions etched with concern, the Chief's, a mask of stone, Little Elk's, horrified, and Bear Watcher's, grave.

"My daughter has caused you much trouble, Golden Lady. For this I am sorry." Bear Watcher inclined his head. "Do what you have to do." He turned to look at Running Doe, then back at her, his tone solemn. "She is ready."

She looked over at Running Doe; she held a knife similar to hers. Amanda glanced at Proud Eagle. With a stern face he nodded for her to begin.

Everyone stepped back, and her breath solidified in her throat.

Running Doe's cold black eyes impaled her.

A chill ran down her spine, the hairs on the back of her neck standing straight. The silence lengthened between them.

Running Doe arched her back, resembling a feline ready to pounce on its prey.

She took a cleansing breath to still her nerves, spread her legs apart and crouched, preparing herself for the attack, gripping the knife the way she had been taught was most effective.

Running Doe raised the knife she held above her head and lunged at her.

But Amanda was quick and jumped out of harm's way.

Running Doe landed on her knees, but sprang to her feet.

Around in a circle they walked, watching the other's every move in anticipation of another attack.

She shifted her knife from hand to hand, confusing her opponent, then leapt at Running Doe, knocking her to the ground.

Running Doe rolled away, again springing to her feet. But this time, she kicked forward, knocking the knife from Amanda's hand. She grabbed a handful of her hair and dragged her to the ground. Placing the knife between her teeth, Running Doe straddled her hips, then fisted her hand and punched her in the face.

Her head spun, pain rioting through her skull. *Don't faint... I can't faint!*

She shook her head to clear her focus and caught Running Doe's doubled fist about to strike another blow. With not a second to spare, she swung her own punch, clipping Running Doe hard at the base of her throat.

Running Doe's eyes widened, dropping the knife she held in her teeth.

She reached for the knife and slashed Running Doe in the arm.

Shocked, Running Doe watched blood flow from the wound, down to her hand and between her fingers.

Amanda took that opportunity to punch Running Doe in the stomach.

The other woman, writhing in pain, rolled off.

She hurried to her feet and kicked Running Doe in the face.

Her opponent rolled away and struggled to her knees. Blood trickled from her mouth. She spit. "*Shiwoo*, my teeth," she cried, looking horrified at the two teeth lying on the ground. She pushed her finger through the gaping hole at the front of her mouth, then turned on Amanda with a double vengeance. "You *zuzeca*, snake in the grass, look what you have done." She dove for her knife and came back with it held high over her head. "*Yunke-*

221

lo, death to you," she cursed.

Amanda circled around Running Doe, looking for her knife. Her heart lurched to her throat. It lay too far away to reach.

Running Doe slithered closer, aiming the knife at her heart.

She ducked, picked up a fistful of dirt, and shot to her feet, throwing the sand at Running Doe's face.

The women turned away for only a second, to wipe the muck and tears from her eyes. Amanda circled behind and jumped onto her back, knocking her challenger to the ground. She clouted her in the head and pushed her face into the dirt.

Running Doe swung backward with the knife, but seeing the flash of the blade from the corner of her eye, she pounded at the wrist wielding the knife, knocking the blade from her grasp. She yanked Running Doe's arms to her side and pinned them to the ground with her knees, then she grabbed a chunk of Running Doe's hair, which had now fallen free of the *nah-leen*, and reached for the knife. Pulling Running Doe's head way back, she placed the blade at her throat.

"Stop her, Proud Eagle," Running Doe choked out.

"The fight is hers."

"She will end my life," Running Doe screeched. "Have you no mercy for me?"

"No more than you had for her," Proud Eagle snapped.

Amanda locked eyes with her husband. His face remained emotionless. He wouldn't interfere, the decision was hers. She then glanced over at Bear Watcher. He, too, stood like he was made of stone, the fear in his eyes the only indication he held any feeling.

She raised the knife above Running Doe's head, the blade catching the moon's light. One plunge into

Running Doe's back and it would be over.

The silence surrounding her was deafening. Everyone watching held their breath. Her heart pounded.

Running Doe sobbed.

The humiliation and degradation she endured by the Mexican men came back to her in clarity. Her face grew hot with the memory of them touching her bosom, raising her skirt, and abusing her naked flesh—no doubt resulting in her death if Proud Eagle hadn't come along. All that was Running Doe's fault, yet, she still couldn't end her life. Instead, she twisted Running Doe's hair around her hand and lopped it off with the knife. When she threw the long strands to the ground for Running Doe to see, the maiden wailed at the top of her lungs. She shoved Running Doe's face into the shorn tresses and in one fluid motion leapt off her back.

With feet spread apart, she stood over Running Doe. "Get up!" she demanded.

Running Doe sat up, sputtering dirt, blood, and hair from her mouth.

She squared her shoulders and commanded, "I said, get up!"

Running Doe, tears streaking the dirt down her face, sought with a hand her sheared head. "I cannot."

"Then this between us is over!" Amanda shouted.

She walked over to her husband and handed him the knife. He looked at her with respect gleaming in his eyes. She raised her chin. "Come, my *shikaa*, let's go home."

Chapter Ten

Amanda was overjoyed to see Josh riding into the village. He hadn't visited since Christmas, when he brought the children candy and helped to decorate a tree with beads. With a smile, she ran to greet him. "This is such a delightful surprise."

His swung down from the wagon and gave her a hug. "I've brought books, writing slates, and chalk for the children."

She watched him rummage through his satchel for the items. "What a wonderful thought, but to come all this way—"

"I've also brought a letter for you,' he interjected.

She arched a brow. "For me? From whom?"

He removed the envelope from his vest pocket and handed it to her. "Open it and see."

She fingered the fine paper, acknowledging the return post. "It's from Brighton, England, my mother's folks." Her hands trembled breaking the seal. After reading the letter she raised her gaze to Josh.

His face was etched with concern. "Is anything wrong, Amanda?"

"The letter's from my mother's sister, Kaylena Bentley. She writes, my grandfather, Wilson Bentley has passed away."

Josh moved closer, laying a hand on her arm. "I'm so sorry."

"His entire estate of Bentwood Manor is willed to his eldest daughter, Amelia Bentley Gregory, my mother. In the event of her death, all of it becomes mine. My Aunt Kaylena is traveling to America to see me. She has documents for me to sign, and plans on taking me back to England with her."

He motioned to the letter. "When is she scheduled to arrive?"

She glanced at the date. "This was dated December 15th, 1864, almost two months ago." Her eyes widened. "Aunt Kaylena should be arriving any day now."

Josh frowned. "What are you planning to do?"

She took an audible breath. "Well, there's no doubt I must meet with her."

"In view of the Chiricahua attacks, it would be unwise for Kaylena to meet with you here. You'd have to come to town."

She rolled her eyes heavenward. "Proud Eagle's not going to like this."

"What am I not going to like?" a voice came from behind, startling them both.

"You've got the uncanny knack for creeping up on a person," Josh said, annoyed. "For the sake of keeping everyone from jumping out of their skin, perhaps you might consider wearing a bell."

Proud Eagle walked over to her, putting an arm around her shoulders. "Why have you come, holy man?"

"I have come to bring Amanda a letter from her aunt in England." Josh turned to her. "It might be best if you talked in private with him on the matter," he advised, taking a seat upon a nearby rock.

She took hold of Proud Eagle's hand. "Come. Let's sit by the river while I explain."

Proud Eagle gazed out over the water, his jaw clenched, as she read him her aunt's letter.

"You do not need your grandfather's home. You have a home here."

"And this is the only place I want to live, and belong," she reassured him. "But my aunt has traveled a very long way to see me. It's only right I meet with her." She moved closer to Proud Eagle. "I will sign the documents she has brought and give up my right to what's been left to me." She caressed his arm. "Since it wouldn't be wise for Kaylena to come here, I'll have to meet with her at the parsonage."

He nodded in agreement. "We will leave first thing come morning."

She moved her hand over his and squeezed. "I'm afraid you don't understand my *shikaa*."

Proud Eagle protested. "You cannot mean—"

She silenced his lips with a finger. "It is too dangerous for you to be seen in town. Besides," she added, "Cunning Eagle is very ill, you need to stay here, just in case he should—"

It was his turn to interrupt her. "I understand." Proud Eagle pulled her close. "The thought of being apart from you fills my *biijii* with sadness." He kissed the top of her head. "What do I do, *shi'aad*, if you should decide to go with your aunt to England?"

She wrapped her arms around his waist and laid her head against his hard chest. "That will never, ever happen, because I love you beyond my own life." She raised her eyes to his. "I would sooner die than live without you."

He lowered his head, whispering against her mouth. "Do not talk of your death."

"But that's how I feel. To live without you would be worse than death."

"Come back to me, alive, *shi'aad*."

"I will. You have my word as an Apache woman, I will return," she said, before his lips stifled any further words with a kiss.

****

It was late when the wagon stopped at the parsonage. Amanda was exhausted clear through to her bones. Neither she nor Proud Eagle had gotten much sleep the night before, knowing she'd leave in

226

the morning. Her lack of rest, coupled with wearing the cumbersome clothes Grace provided, made the journey hard and long. It was only when she spotted Grace's round, familiar face beaming at the door, did her spirits lift.

"Ya poor child," Grace crooned, putting a motherly arm around her shoulders. "Ya look plumb tuckered out." She peered at her through watery gray eyes. "Could I interest ya in a nice hot bath, with scented oil and all?"

She sighed. "Oh, Grace, you sure could."

She hurried up the stairs and to the room at the end of the hall. Fresh linens made up the bed and a small spray of yellow oleanders stood tall in a vase on the dressing table. It was almost hard to believe such beautiful, fragrant blooms of yellow and orange were poison.

Grace pointed to the tub in the corner of the room, waiting to be filled. "The Reverend will be bringin' up the buckets of hot water, so ya can enjoy a nice soak."

She took the elder woman's hands in hers. "Thank you so much, Grace, but I don't want to be a bother."

Grace's eyes twinkled. "Ya ain't no bother, child." A slow smile spread across her face. "Have ya a hankerin' for a plate of fried chicken and dumplins, topped with homemade apple cobbler for dessert?"

Her mouth watered. "You bet I have."

Grace nodded. "Then after ya soak a spell, some will be waitin' for ya downstairs." She made her way to the door, and then halted, turning to face her again. "Reverend tells me the Indian takes right good care of ya." She eyed her up and down. "I have to admit, ya look fit as a fiddle and right happy to boot."

She smiled, the mere thought of Proud Eagle

making her body tingle. "I am Grace, extremely happy. My husband is loving and kind, respectful and thoughtful. I don't regret for one moment marrying him. And right now I'm missing him something fierce."

Grace nodded. "I know the feelin', child. It's the same for me, even after all these years, when I think of my Clyde." Her eyes grew misty, her voice softened. "Then ya really love him, Amanda?"

"Oh, yes, Grace, with all my heart."

"That's all that matters then, I reckon," Grace mumbled before she left the room.

Enveloped in a blanket of warm water, every tense and achy muscle in Amanda's body relaxed. She groaned with pleasure and closed her eyes, resting her head back against the ridge of the tub. The soft scent of lilac filled her senses, transporting her back to the times she brought flowers to her mother.

She smiled, almost hearing again her mother's velvety smooth voice. Amelia's cheery, English accent lilted upon her tongue, her laughter rising light with joy.

Her memories took on a life of their own, and she could almost feel her mother's gentle touch, braiding her hair, wiping her tears, tending to the many scraped knees and bee stings she acquired.

"Look what a mess you are, my little miss," Amelia had scolded. "Pretty young ladies don't play in the mud."

She sighed. The memories were prominent because she anticipated her aunt's visit. Would Kaylena look like Amelia? Would she be as kind and loving?

After Grace's delicious meal, Amanda excused herself and climbed the stairs to her room. She crawled between the fresh linens, settling down for the night. Though numb with exhaustion, slumber would not come.

She sat up, looking around the room. From the window the moonlight danced across the bed, an empty bed, a bed without Proud Eagle. In spite of her fatigue, she couldn't fall asleep. She missed her husband's warm body entwined with hers—needed his protective arms wrapped around her.

Frustrated, she rose and walked to the window, gazing up at the moon. Was Proud Eagle, at this very moment, looking at the same moon and thinking of her? She grabbed the robe Grace lent her, and with quiet steps made her way downstairs to the sitting room. A fire still blazed in the fireplace. She sat cross-legged on the floor in front of it watching the flames dance. Her heart grew heavy with sadness. She sensed all was not well with Proud Eagle. Could it just be he missed her, too, or was it something more?

"Having trouble sleeping, Amanda?" The voice in the darkness startled her.

She turned to find Josh seated in a corner armchair, smoking his pipe. She tucked her bare legs beneath the robe. "I have a feeling something isn't right with Proud Eagle."

He set his pipe aside and came to sit on the floor beside her. "It's just the strain of the day catching up with you. Right now you have a lot on your mind, and are no doubt even a little nervous about meeting your aunt."

She fidgeted with the lace collar of her nightgown, adjusting the large robe to stay on her shoulders. "You're right, I'm sure."

"It seems your nightwear is bothering you as well."

"I'm just not used to sleeping with so much—" She clipped her tongue.

He raised a brow. "Indeed."

Her cheeks burned. Her blunder no doubt

painted him a vivid picture of her slipping into bed each night clad only in her flesh.

They sat for a long time in silence watching the fire.

"I'm still in lo—"

She glared at him, cutting his words off. "Don't. Don't say it." She licked her dry lips. "You need to remember I'm a married woman now."

He faced her, his eyes alone betraying his ardor. "Only by Indian law, not by our law. Not in the eyes of God."

She jumped to her feet. "We are married in my eyes." She fisted her hands by her side, digging her nails into the palms. "It doesn't matter to me what the law says. Proud Eagle is my husband in every sense of the word," she emphasized. "Make no mistake about that." She turned on her heels and strode toward the archway.

Josh stood, reaching for her with a restraining hand. "Listen to me, Amanda, you live in perpetual danger."

She pulled her arm free. "How can you still believe such nonsense?" She searched his face. "You've sat with Proud Eagle's people, eaten with them, and listened to their stories. You know as well as I do no harm will come to me by their hands."

"Please, Amanda, hear me out. It's not by their hands I fear for your welfare."

She questioned annoyed. "Then by whose?"

He raked his fingers through his hair. "In the time you've been living at the village there have been more raids, on wagon trains, homesteads, even miners were killed at their work. Entire families are murdered, buildings and hay fields are burned, and the raiders make off with the horses, mules, cattle and sheep."

"Then, according to what you say, I'm much safer living in an Indian village than on a ranch or farm."

Josh shook his head to the contrary. "Perhaps that was the case before, but not now."

He motioned for her to come back into the sitting room.

Reluctantly she followed.

Josh lit a lantern and reached for a stack of papers on a shelf, bringing them to a nearby table. He gestured to a chair adjacent to his. "Please, sit."

She obeyed, hands clasped together in her lap to stop them from trembling.

"If I had been given the opportunity to talk with you more during my Christmas visit, I would have told you then what I'm about to tell you now." He let out a long, audible breath. "I'd be signing your death warrant if I didn't make you aware of the heightened emotions and state of mind most white folks are in over these attacks."

Her pulse raced with his unwelcome frankness. "Go on."

"Let me read to you a letter General Carleton wrote to Governor Goodwin." He picked up one of the newspapers from the table. "Let us work earnestly and hard, and before next Christmas your Apaches are whipped. Unless troops, citizens, and friendly Indian mercenaries combine forces against the Apache, you will have a twenty years' war."

I know all about Indian mercenaries She shivered from memories of Chico and Pablo. *They were not an answer to solving any problem, especially a war.*

Josh looked up from his reading. "The first Territorial Legislature gave full support to Carleton's extermination policy. The words leave a bitter taste in my mouth," he added with a scowl upon his face.

She was almost afraid to ask. "And what does the policy declare?"

He placed the newspaper aside. "That the only sure way to remove the red menace, as Indians are now being called, was for military commanders to kill every male Indian encountered and to take prisoner the women and children." Josh paused. "And sadly enough, the entire white population virtually hailed Carleton's orders."

"No, this cannot happen."

Josh's square jaw tensed. "But it is happening, Amanda."

"Then we must go to the governor and tell him the truth. Not all tribes are involved in the attacks."

He shook his head. "Your pleas will fall on deaf ears."

Her heart raced. "There must be some folks who believe this is not the way to solve the problem?"

"Aye, there are those religious societies and various other types of humanitarians opposing Carleton's ruthlessness, but most of Arizona wants the Apache gone."

"Even the peaceful tribes?"

"Aye, every last one," he said.

"But why?"

He sat back in the chair. "Greed, my dear lady. All of it is a matter of greed. They want all the good land, by right of conquest, which the Apache occupy."

She frowned. "But the land is theirs; they have a right to stay."

"That's not how the military sees it, I'm afraid."

"Then they aren't interested in making peace, are they?"

"Nay, Amanda... I believe peace is the last priority right now on the list. What they want is Apache annihilation, women, children, and every last man. The Arizona white folk agree. They want all the Indians gone."

"Why do you fear for me? I'm a white woman;

my own people wouldn't harm me."

His laugh was sarcastic. "Oh, I wouldn't be too sure about that."

"I don't understand."

He leaned forward in his seat. "Then let me put it this way. Emotions are high. People are acting crazy, riding into villages in a blaze of gunfire. It's not likely a time would be taken to weed you out from the rest. Not until it was too late, anyway." His agitation escalated with the tone of his voice. "Besides, I've read things about these Indian hunters. None of them are practicing moral conduct."

She forced down the hard lump growing in her throat. "What do you mean?"

The sudden anguish that pierced his cobalt eyes made her heart quicken.

Josh took a deep breath. "What I am about to tell you will upset you, Amanda, but I can't sugarcoat the facts. You need to be aware of the truth."

Her voice was shakier than she liked. "Go on."

"There was an incident at Weaver's diggings. Two Indian boys, who just wandered in to see the sights, were shot to death."

"But they were just children."

For an instant his glance sharpened. "They were Indians, Amanda. That's all that matters."

"No, what matters is they are human beings— children," she protested.

"You aren't hearing me, Amanda. There is no ethics, no decency among any of them when it comes to the Indians."

She shuddered with the foreboding chill that ran down her spine.

He continued. "King Woolsey, a rancher and an aide to Governor Goodwin, while on a trip to the Bradshaw Mountains, left some Pinole where he knew Apache would find it."

The blood drained from her face and she struggled for composure. "Pinole contains strychnine, doesn't it?"

"Aye, it does. A dozen more of these Apaches died in horrible agony." He searched for another newspaper. "Daniel Ellis Conner is a prospector from Kentucky and a writer who's written about some shocking goings on." Upon finding the correct article, he held it up for a moment. "According to his reports in this publication, when the men in settlements or diggings had nothing else to do, they'd go Indian hunting. If an Indian was found he was shot, stripped, scalped, and left to rot."

She bit back the tears threatening to come, frightened Proud Eagle and his people could be slain by these ruthless men.

Josh's lips thinned. "There is a man they call Sugarfoot Jack, who was an escaped convict from Tasmania, Australia. By some means, this devil's spawn reached San Diego and enlisted in the army. He didn't last long in Arizona's Walker Company, and was dishonorably discharged for thievery and striking an officer. But he joined a group of civilians who had been organized to hunt Apache on the Verde River."

Her stomach lurched. "I don't think I want to hear anymore."

"And I wish I didn't have to tell you, Amanda, but you need to know what's going on, every tragic uprising."

"Very well, continue," she agreed in a weak, reluctant tone.

"This Sugarfoot Jack found a deserted Apache village, and went about burning all the dwellings. In the course of his destruction, he came upon an Apache baby."

She met his eyes disparagingly. "Impossible. A

mother would never leave her baby behind."

Josh's response held a note of impatience. "In all the chaos, in the mad rush to escape, anything's possible. Connor reports Sugarfoot Jack threw the babe into the fire, sat down, and watched the child burn."

She pictured Rising Star and the other babies in the tribe she held upon her lap and loved, being murdered.

"On another raid he found another small child left behind. He sat down on a stone and jiggled the child on his knees, tickling the youngster under the chin. When he tired of playing with the child he drew a heavy dragoon six shooter, placed the muzzle to the babe's head and fired."

She sprang to her feet, covering her ears with the palms of her hands. "Stop! I will listen to no more!"

He stood, grasped her wrists, and pulled her hands from her head. "You will listen, you must listen."

She pulled free from his hold, hot tears slipping down her cheeks. "I cannot stand to hear another word."

Josh's tone was stern. "If you choose to continue living in an Indian village, you've got to be aware of all the risks and the danger you place yourself in with each passing day."

She walked to the fireplace, covered her face with her hands and wept.

"I hate inflicting such agony on you." He placed a comforting arm around her shoulders. "But you need to understand the seriousness of the situation."

She wiped her eyes with the backs of her hands. "I need to go to my room now."

"Not just yet, Amanda. I need to read you one more testimony, from Sylvester Mowry, an Arizona pioneer booster, mine promoter, newspaper owner, and writer." He walked back to the table beside his chair. Again rummaging through the pile of newspapers, he chose one and read. "There is only one way to wage war against the Apaches. They must be surrounded, starved into coming in, surprised or inveigled, by white flags, or any other method, human or divine, and then put to death. If these ideas shock any weak-minded individual who thinks himself a philanthropist, I can only say, I pity without respecting his mistaken sympathy."

"And I pity all of them," she spat through clenched teeth. "General Carleton's extermination policy," she stressed with venom, "will be an unwise move on the part of the white man and will not be successful. The horrible murders of a few Apache will only result in driving all other Indians to increase their fury and the number of attacks on soldiers and settlers."

"The situation is already out of control, Amanda."

She pointed a finger at him. "You listen now to me, Josh. From living among them, I've learned for survival they can be elusive. It's not often they are unwise enough to be trapped, and a direct confrontation will not be possible." She cleared her throat. "Why, I've heard of the Chiricahua trailing a party for days, just waiting for the opportunity to catch their victim off guard. They seldom attack, unless they believe they hold the advantage. They would wait until their enemies were in a position where defense was difficult. Then they would strike and scatter"—she splayed her fingers wide for emphasis—"making pursuit all but impossible. General Carleton's bloody campaign will only be an exercise in futility."

"The futility will be on the part of the Indians," he countered.

"No. For the white man," she challenged.

He stepped forward and shook her by the shoulders. "What will it take to get you to understand, the military is at a point of no return?"

"It is the Indians who will be angered to the point of no return, if they aren't already. And Arizona will be washed in the blood of all men!"

"And women, yours included!" Josh screamed.

"Enough!" a sharp retort came from behind.

They both turned to find Grace standing in the archway.

"Mercy, ya two are gonna wake my sister, Eunice and her daughter, Sylvie, and they live at the edge of town," she snapped, walking toward Amanda.

"I'm sorry, Grace, if we woke you," Josh apologized.

"It's Amanda ya should be apologizin' to. She's a guest in yer home, or have ya forgotten?" Grace scolded.

"Nay, I haven't forgotten."

Grace placed a hand on her arm. "Why, yer shakin' to yer very core, child." She turned an accusing eye on Josh. "Yer cruelty has tarnished yer intentions, Reverend."

His eyes clouded with emotion, a mixture of unprecedented anxiety, concern, and fear washing over his face. "My intent was never to be cruel."

"I know," Amanda reassured him.

Grace again turned her attention to Amanda, forcing a smile. "If my memory serves me right, ya always enjoyed a cup of hot milk before bed."

She smiled in return. "Yes, I still do."

Grace gave her arm another pat. "I've got a cup waitin' for ya on the table beside the bed."

She followed the elder woman out of the sitting room. "I thank you kindly, Grace."

"Not a problem, child," Grace said, making her way up the stairs.

She hesitated at the bottom, turning to look at Josh still standing in the archway of the sitting room.

"I worry for you, Amanda. I'm sure by now you know the reason why."

She lifted her voice above a whisper. "Don't worry. I'll be fine."

He opened his mouth, ready to protest when Grace called down from the landing.

"Hurry on up, child, before your milk grows cold."

"Coming, Grace," she called, and without looking back, ran up the stairs to her room.

****

The night was still. Proud Eagle lay restless on the bed, missing the warmth and comfort of lying beside his wife. He sat up, slipped on his breeches and moccasins, and made his way outside. Gazing up at the moon he wondered if she slept in peace or shared his pain of separation. Her being with the holy man tormented him. Would he ever see his Golden Lady again, or had the white man won? He paced back and forth beneath the tree, his buckskin-clad feet crunching the leaves with each step, a rude affront to the stillness that surrounded him.

"Proud Eagle," a voice came from behind.

He turned to see Bear Watcher, his face troubled. "What is wrong my friend?"

Bear Watcher's voice was solemn. "It is your father, he calls for you." He motioned for Proud Eagle to follow. "Come, there is not much time."

His heart raced on his way to his parents' wickiup. This time had been long in coming, and in spite of all Cunning Eagle had done to prepare his son, Proud Eagle still wasn't ready. How fruitless to believe a person is ever ready to lose someone he loves.

He rushed through the door opening and found

his mother kneeling beside the bed, head bowed, hands folded in her lap. White Dove was the ever dutiful, ever loving, loyal wife to the end. He swallowed hard the lump growing in his throat. His wife's voice, her smile, her arms around him, all came to mind. He needed his Golden Lady beside him now, more than ever.

Shaman Gray Fox hunched over Cunning Eagle in the bed, chanting to the gods for the chief's soul to safely enter *O'zho*. Rising Sun, with her husband's consoling arms around her, stood in the corner weeping with her baby in her arms. Bear Watcher, Elder, confidant, stood at the foot of the bed, kneeling beside him was his daughter, Running Doe.

When his eyes met Running Doe's, a tear slipped down her cheek. Resentment welled deep within him. It was Golden Lady's place to be here, not Running Doe's.

He turned his gaze from hers and fixed his eyes on his father's pallid face. Like a frightened child, he went to his mother's side. She gripped his hand, fear gripped his heart. Closing his eyes for a moment, he wished to wake from the horrible nightmare.

Cunning Eagle spoke, his weak voice barely audible over the Shaman's chanting. Proud Eagle motioned Gray Fox to be silent and bent his ear to his father's mouth.

"Fear not, my son. It is time for me to join my ancestors. I have suffered many moons in pain. It is the mercy of the gods my peace finally comes. Remember all I have taught you." Cunning Eagle's frail hand reached for his. "It is a true love you have with your Golden Lady. She is a good woman, one you can trust. She will give you many children and bring you much happiness—if you remember, my son, happiness is not a destination, but a journey you must walk day-by-day."

Tears fell from his eyes. "An old tree is strong,

my father. You are needed here."

Cunning Eagle's intake of breath rattled in his chest. "An old man is tired, my son. It is time to make room for the young ones to come. You are needed now." His father's eyes grew dim. "You will take care of your mother, as well," Cunning Eagle whispered.

He nodded. "You have my word."

The life flickered from Cunning Eagle's eyes, and he stared ahead. Proud Eagle reached over to close his father's lids.

White Dove and Rising Sun wept while the shaman chanted.

The walls of the wickiup closed in on him, sorrow strangled each breath he took. He stood and left the wickiup, running to the riverbank and gulping the night air. There he sat upon a rock, teary eyes gazing out over the water.

"I loved him as well, Proud Eagle," Running Doe said. She came to kneel beside him, caressing the top of his hand. "I know you are sad the white woman has left with the holy man, but it is best she is gone. She would have not understood the sorrow we all feel this night. She is not one of us."

He sprang to his feet, his grief momentarily replaced by rage. "The white woman has a name. She is Golden Lady, and she is my wife," he spat with a snarl. "Now she is wife of the chief. It would be wise for you to remember that."

Running Doe stood, hands on hips. "It would be wise for you to forget her."

He glared at her. "She is my love, my life. Never will I forget." Disgust filled him, and he stepped back. "Never has she spoken a mean word of another to gain honor for herself. She puts you to shame, Running Doe."

"What is shameful is that you made her your wife," Running Doe snapped.

The corner of his mouth twisted with disdain. "She should have sent your evil spirit to *O'zho* when she held the knife to your throat."

Her lower lip trembled. "I am glad she is gone!"

He grabbed her by the arm. "She will not be gone for long. As soon as I can, I am going for her, to bring her back where she belongs. She loved my father as well, and must be told of his death."

Running Doe reached up and wrapped her arms around his neck. "No, Proud Eagle, it is too dangerous for you to follow her."

He unlocked her hands and pushed her from him. "I would face all the white lawmen in the land, just to see her face again, rather than stay here without her."

Running Doe threw her arms around his chest. "No, Proud Eagle, you are the chief now, your place is here." She looked up into his eyes. "You would break your word to Cunning Eagle?"

He released her grip again, stepping away. "I will be chief, but with Golden Lady by my side."

"Let her go, Proud Eagle," Running Doe begged. "She is not one of us. All she will do is bring us trouble."

"She has brought nothing but happiness to me, as well as many in the tribe."

Running Doe moved closer to him, grabbing his arm. "Listen to me, Proud Eagle, she does not belong here. Let the holy man have her."

He pulled free from her grasp. "No, I will never let him have her! She belongs to me. She is mine, and I will listen no longer to your forked tongue." His jaw tensed with his deep annoyance. "You are an evil woman, Running Doe. Your heart is filled with hate and jealousy. You are like a troublesome coyote and I only see sorrow for your life."

He left her standing alone in the darkness.

Chapter Eleven

Amanda was pinning up her hair in front of the dressing table mirror when Grace barged into the room. "Yer aunt! The wagon train is here!"

She took a deep breath, followed Grace down the stairs and to Miller's General store, where they stood to watch the band of six wagons roll into town.

Two young Cavalry soldiers took up the lead. The older one politely tipped his hat at her as he passed. She gave him a taut nod, and cast her glance at the approaching wagons. After what she'd learned from Josh about the military's ruthless actions on innocent Indians, she found it hard to face one of their militia without disdain.

Two more wagons went by, both she and Grace stretched their necks with the hope they'd spot Kaylena Bentley.

The last covered coach came to a halt directly in front of her. An elegantly dressed woman sat beside Abe, the wagon train master. She'd seen Abe about town before, when he brought other wagon train travelers through Willow Creek. She moved farther to her right to catch the woman's gaze, but because of the large bonnet that covered most of her face, the woman didn't see Amanda.

She waited for Abe to help the woman down from the wagon before approaching. "Are you Kaylena Bentley?"

The woman turned around, her blue eyes sparkling. "Aye, I'm Kaylena Bentley." A sweet smile spread across her face. "I don't need to ask who you are. You're the image of my dear sister, Amelia."

242

Her eyes filled with tears. "You are, too."

The two women embraced, and then Amanda introduced Grace.

"Ya could be sisters," Grace commented, wiping tears from her own eyes.

Amanda took her aunt's arm, and the three women made their way toward the parsonage.

"How was your journey?" she asked.

Kaylena sighed. "Difficult, long and tiring, I never expected the events that happened." She gave Amanda's arm an affectionate pat. "But I've put that all behind me now." Kaylena smiled. "I'm feeling blessed to finally be here with you."

The Cavalry Officer came up beside them, carrying Kaylena's luggage. "Where would you like your bags brought, Miss Kaylena?"

His presence made Amanda anxious. She kept her eyes ahead and pointed to the parsonage. "To that white house yonder, Sir."

He supplied a name for her. "Lieutenant Duffy, ma'am. Ryan Duffy, at your service."

"Where are my manners?" Kaylena turned to Ryan. "Lieutenant Duffy, this is my niece, Amanda Gregory."

He inclined his head and followed them to the parsonage.

At the door, Kaylena thanked the Lieutenant. "I appreciate your dedication in getting me safely to my destination."

Ryan's eyes twinkled. "I assure you, Miss Bentley, the pleasure was all mine." He turned his attention to Amanda and tipped his hat. "It was nice meeting you, Miss Gregory."

She definitely didn't share his sentiment, but forced a polite smile before she closed the door behind her.

****

Amanda wasn't the least bit surprised Josh and

Kaylena got along. After dinner the two struck up quite a conversation.

"I grew up in London, before coming to America to study for the clergy," he said, offering Kaylena another of Grace's homemade apple cookies.

Kaylena accepted with a gracious smile. "Then you must know the Chambers, Tilly and Hamilton."

"Aye, quite well, in fact, "Josh admitted. "I was taken with their daughter Veronica when I was all but twelve."

Kaylena's laughter reminded Amanda of Amelia's. "Ah, dear, Veronica, a cheeky miss if I ever met one." She took a sip of her tea. "I heard she married well. I believe someone with a title."

"Oh, I'm not surprised, she was adamant, even as a child, she'd win the heart of a man with means and wear elegant gowns at court," Josh reflected.

The discussion continued, along with talk about the books they'd both read, their favorite performances at the theater and their scope of the Bible.

Amanda found her attention straying from their exchange, wishing she had excused herself earlier, like Grace had done. But that wouldn't have been very polite. After all, Kaylena had come to see her.

Her thoughts wandered to Proud Eagle. She missed him so, longing for the warmth of his arms at night, aching for his love. She yearned to hear his voice murmuring low and husky the words that sent her senses burning, to gaze into the sultry depths of his dark eyes, the tickle of his thick hair against her face, and inhale the familiar scent of leather and musk so much a part of him. In her mind's eye, she could see him standing strong and proud. Her vision so real she could almost reach out and touch his hard, muscular body.

The astonished, high-pitched tone of Kaylena's voice interrupted her thoughts. "Oh, Amanda, how dreadful."

She blinked, pulling herself from her daydream. "Dreadful? Pardon?"

"Josh just told me your father was killed by Indians and the farm burned to the ground," Kaylena said.

She shifted in her seat. "Yes, by the Chiricahua."

Kaylena took an audible breath "You mean there is more than one group of them?"

"Not group...tribe," she corrected. "And, yes, there are a few tribes that have villages scattered around. Most are peaceful," she emphasized, "not wanting any trouble. They mind their own business and just want to hunt and fish to feed their families. And then there are the Chiricahua, whose warriors are hostile."

Kaylena's intense gaze locked with hers. "My goodness, Amanda, you know a lot about Indians."

"One in particular," Josh mumbled with a mischievous twinkle in his eyes.

She threw him a warning look.

Kaylena didn't seem to pay attention to his remark and took another sip of her tea. "I suppose you have to be aware of your surroundings, especially if they can get you killed."

She shifted in her chair and changed the subject. "I read in the family Bible you were only ten when my mother left England."

Kaylena nodded in agreement. "And I must say, recalling her has become rather foggy with the passing years. But I do remember she had hair and eyes like yours, and she loved to ride horses, dance, and sing. Amelia's smile was soft, if memory serves me right her eyes smiled along with her mouth when she was amused."

Amanda laughed. "Yes, I know what you mean. Papa would say she twinkled when she was happy."

"The family never met Ethan Gregory. Was he a good man, did he treat Amelia well?"

"Oh, yes, Aunt Kaylena, Papa loved Mama, so much so, he never got over her death."

"My poor sister, dying so young." She reached over to pat her arm. "And my poor little Amanda, you've been through so much, losing both parents and your home. It's no wonder you're not out of your senses, living in this heathen country."

"I love Arizona territory, it's my home.

"Home is with family, isn't that right, Reverend?" Kaylena said.

Josh cleared his throat. "Grace and I feel like we're Amanda's family."

Kaylena smiled. "And thank heaven the two of you were here when she needed you, but now I've arrived and will see to my niece's welfare. Her place is in England, with me."

Her heart sunk to her toes. "Aunt Kaylena I can't thank you enough for making this trip, for coming to see me, but—"

"No need to thank me, dear," Kaylena interjected. "With your parents gone, I am now responsible for you. It's my duty to you and to Amelia's memory I see to your coming out, get you properly suited." She rolled her eyes heavenward. "And that isn't going to happen in a town like this with the threat of Indian attacks hanging over your head." She gave her arm another maternal pat. "But we'll discuss the matter further in the morning, right now I'm growing weary." She stood, ending a chance for Amanda to protest. "I think I'm going to say my farewells for the evening."

Josh rose from his seat. "How thoughtless of me, Kaylena, here I've kept you talking when you must be exhausted after such a journey."

"Nonsense, Josh, I've enjoyed every minute of it."

"We have no servants about the place," he said, moving to take Kaylena by the arm. "But if you'll allow me, I'll show you to your room."

Kaylena inclined her head. "Thank you, Josh, I should like that very much."

****

Amanda lay awake in the dark, her thoughts jumbled and troubled. She'd have to explain to her aunt in the morning why she wouldn't be returning to England with her.

It wouldn't be an easy conversation, or an appreciated one, that was obvious. Kaylena Bentley already had Amanda's life planned out for her. Or could it be her aunt was more concerned she would boot her from her home, now that she was the rightful heir? Kaylena's position of staying on at the mansion would be secure if she took Amanda under her wing, became her guardian.

Well, Kaylena didn't have to worry; she didn't want Bentwood Manor. Her plain and simple wickiup was home, and where she planned on staying. She understood now how her mother could leave such grandeur to live in a small farmhouse with Ethan Gregory. Home is where the heart is, and her heart is with Proud Eagle.

She rose from the bed and made her way to the window, gazing down at the empty street below. Since Josh told her of General Carleton's policy and the other ruthless behavior, she'd been living in a fog.

She lifted her eyes to the stars, thoughts returning to Proud Eagle. The separation from him had become physically painful. The anxiety to warn him of the atrocities sat heavy on her mind. And each moment ticking by only made her wish harder and stronger she could ride to the village to sleep the rest of the night cradled in his arms.

****

The smoke from the burning wickiup curled to the sky, looming over the village like gray clouds. Proud Eagle sat on a nearby rock and watched his parents' home, his father's body inside, being consumed by the flames.

The women in the tribe moaned and cried with their grief while Shaman Gray Fox danced and chanted to the gods before the fiery structure. For a period of thirty days, a fog of gloom would hover over the village in honor of the old chief's passing. The women would continue to mourn, each woman taking a turn of a few hours, completing the night and into the early morning as required by tradition.

Proud Eagle was bothered by the fact Golden Lady would not see him made chief. Come sunup, the ceremony would take place at the center of the village for all to witness. Shaman Gray Fox would bestow upon him the rights of a chosen one, and then he would be acknowledged and welcomed with much respect from all in the tribe. Drums would beat, warriors with blue painted faces would dance, and much food would be served. And when the ceremony was over he would be Chief Proud Eagle. Such a milestone, if only he could have achieved it another way.

Once the ritual was complete, he planned to retrieve Golden Lady. He had done without her long enough. She must take on her duties as the chief's wife and be a part of Cunning Eagle's mourning rites.

His mother approached, her shoulders slumped and head bowed in sorrow. He helped her that morning move her things to the small wickiup, the one he'd occupied before his Golden Lady, before the women in the tribe built the larger dwelling, now too large without his wife. Everything was empty without her presence—his home—his life—his heart.

White Dove knelt on the ground beside him, her

solemn eyes gazing into his. "You look so tired and worn. Do you think of your Golden Lady?"

He nodded, turning to watch the wickiup burn. "I could never hide much from you."

"You never should feel you have to." She also turned to stare into the flames.

"My heart is full of grief. From losing my father and being separated from my wife."

"I am lonely for my love as well, my son. I cannot bear the fact I will never hear his voice again."

"It is a crazy thing. So wrong to never hear him speak again," he reflected.

White Dove stood, giving him a hug. "Your love will return soon."

He watched his mother walk away, into the arms of the sympathetic women sharing her grief.

He stayed sitting on the rock until the last ember flickered and died. Now his father's spirit had been safely sent to *O'zho*, where he would rest in peace with his ancestors.

"Till we meet again, father," he whispered. "And know always, I love you."

****

Bear Watcher sat cross-legged in front of the fire pit, his dark eyes etched with concern. "I do not think this is wise, Proud Eagle."

"I must go for her, Bear Watcher, she is my wife. She belongs with me."

Bear Watcher's lips thinned. "You are chief now, your place is here, with your people. What will a tribe do with their chief gone?"

"That is why I have called this council meeting." Proud Eagle turned to Gray Fox, sitting to his left. "I wish for you to bestow upon Bear Watcher your blessing to act in my place until I return."

Gray Fox nodded. "If it is your wish, but I agree with Bear Watcher."

He sighed. "I thank you both for your concern and advice, but I must go for my wife—as Cochise did."

Bear Watcher frowned. "But your wife has not been captured. If that had happened, we would all ride to her defense. Golden Lady has left of her own will and said she would return." He arched a brow. "Do you doubt her word?"

"No," he snapped. "She has never spoken with a false tongue. It has just been too long a time without her."

"I know how it can be, my friend," Bear Watcher said. "I have loved a woman, and now have lost her. No day passes without her coming to my mind or the want of her in my bed. But there is a time when a man must remain strong and in control of his actions and emotions."

He took a calming breath. "I understand your wise words, but I must follow my heart. In the end, that is always best." He searched Bear Watcher's face. "I know all here will be in good hands with you taking my place. I ask you to please do this for me."

Bear Watcher nodded. "Then I wish you a safe journey, and an even safer return."

****

Proud Eagle rode in the shadows throughout the night. Come dawn he would be at the holy man's house. By now he knew the way well.

He could not wait to see her face, to feel her body next to his and bathe in the sweet taste of her. His nostrils would fill with the scent of her flesh, the same clean, pure aroma that clung to the quilt and blankets he slept on, driving him even crazier for her passion. He missed her lips kissing, caressing every part of his body, taking him soaring to heights of pleasure and fulfillment.

His loins swelled and chafed. He shifted on his horse and rode faster to the town of Willow Creek.

Chapter Twelve

Proud Eagle dismounted his horse, and tied him to a tree. He walked down the path and hid behind the brush, peering out at the back of the holy man's home. He spotted the gold of her hair, and a surge of happiness filled him. He came forward, surprising her from behind and gathered her into his arms. Playfully, he swung her around in circles. "I have you now and will never let you go," he teased. When she stiffened with fear, he realized the woman was not his wife and released her.

She spun around to look at him, the expression on her face one of complete horror, before she screamed.

He held up his hand to silence her, but she mistook the gesture and stepped back in panic, screaming even louder and longer.

****

Amanda was talking with Josh and Grace over tea when she heard her aunt's hysterics. She ran to the garden, the others following close behind.

Her heart lurched with a mixture of happiness and dread when she saw her husband standing in the garden.

"And all I did when I saw him was faint," Grace mumbled.

"We need to get him inside, before—" Ryan Duffy jumped over the fence, aiming his gun at Proud Eagle's head.

Her heart rose to her throat. This is what she feared. She started for the stairs, but Josh stopped her with a restraining hand. "Wait, let me handle

251

this."

She pulled away from him, but he reached for her again and tightened his grip.

"Do you want to get him killed?" he snapped.

She stopped struggling, her heart pounding with fright. "No."

"Then stay put," he warned in a low, firm voice.

Grace moved closer to her. "The Reverend knows what he's doin', child."

"Oh, I hope so, Grace," she whispered.

With long, purposeful strides, Josh walked toward the lieutenant. "See here, sir, not in the presence of these ladies. Surely you have enough respect for the house of God not to shoot a man in the garden of a parsonage?"

Ryan Duffy removed Proud Eagle's knife from around his waist and tucked it in his own belt loop. "He's an Indian, Reverend," he drawled. "He attacked this defenseless woman, and now I must do my job." He cocked the trigger.

"I did not attack this woman," Proud Eagle said in his defense.

She blinked back the tears welling in her eyes. Her husband stood tall, his bravery never faltering in the face of danger.

"There, you see," Josh said. "He speaks our language, appears to be educated. He may not be from the same tribe as those you hunt."

"I hunt them all, Reverend," Ryan snapped.

Josh moved closer to Proud Eagle. "Are you a Chiricahua?"

Proud Eagle took a deep breath and raised his chin. "No, I hold no honor to the Chiricahua." His eyes went to Amanda's. "I am Chief Proud Eagle."

She caught the meaning of his words and lowered her head with the grief of losing her father-in-law, saying a silent prayer for Cunning Eagle's soul.

"You see, Lieutenant, he's not from that hostile tribe," Josh said.

Ryan's eyes squinted with suspicion. "An Indian is an Indian. I've learned not to trust any of them."

Josh frowned. "But this man is a chief, wouldn't it be more profitable to spare his life and inquire about him instead?"

"My orders are to kill all males," Ryan said again.

Her stomach tightened when Josh's words didn't change the lieutenant's decision.

"Well, that's an absurd policy," Josh snapped. "If both sides came together it would be a beginning for peace. When peace is established, it makes way for progress and success. Isn't that a much better plan than running around killing everyone and getting killed?"

"Except for that's not General Carleton's plan, and I take my orders from him," Ryan said, his eyes narrowed and his tone annoyed. "Look, Reverend, I understand, being a man in your position and all, why you've gotta go around and preach all that brotherly love crap. But I've seen the other side of the situation. What the red menaces have done to the white folks just aren't fitting to rehash here with you in front of the women." He frowned. "Let's just say, what I've witnessed"—he paused—"well, saying it was horrific is a drastic understatement." He arched a brow. "But I have regarded the fact this Indian is a chief, and it might be profitable to General Carleton's cause if I do a bit of interrogating first." Ryan took his finger off the trigger and motioned for Proud Eagle to walk ahead of him.

Proud Eagle's eyes caught hers.

"Keep your eyes to yourself, savage," Ryan snapped, jabbing the gun between Proud Eagle's shoulder blades.

Proud Eagle's gaze never wavered. "I was only

admiring her beauty."

Her gaze melted into his. "I thank you."

"The last thing you wanna do is thank him, ma'am," Ryan retorted. "I'd say, truth be told, he's admiring those long golden curls of yours and thinking they'd look right nice hanging from his belt."

Kaylena gasped. "Good Lord."

For a moment Ryan turned his attention to Kaylena. "Not to fear, Miss Kaylena, this one isn't gonna bother anyone again."

"What are you going to do with him, Lieutenant?" Josh said.

Ryan pushed Proud Eagle forward with the tip of the gun. "I'm gonna get some information from him, Reverend."

Amanda followed them out to the street. "And how do you plan on doing that?"

"With a whip lashing."

"No, please don't beat him, Lieutenant." Her stomach knotted further with the horrid fact her husband's smooth, brown flesh was soon to be ripped apart by a whip.

Ryan motioned with his hand toward the house. "Now, you just go back inside, Miss Amanda, and let me handle this the way I've been trained to." The lieutenant spotted the younger soldier standing confused in front of Miller's General Store. "Well, just don't stand there like an idiot, Thomas, go get some rope."

She ran back to the garden. "Joshua," she screamed, falling into his arms and sobbing. "He's going to beat him with a whip."

He held her close, whispering in her ear. "Get a grip, Amanda. Calling attention to yourself or the attachment you have to Proud Eagle will only make things worse."

She buried her face in his collar. "What can we

do?"

He caressed her hair. "I don't know yet, but I'll think of something."

She pulled back, looking up at him with tears blurring her eyes. "We don't have much time, Josh."

Kaylena moved to stand beside her, "I'm a bit confused over what's happened here." She frowned bewildered. "Why are you upset, Amanda, and carrying on so over the fate of that savage?"

"He's not a savage," she snapped.

"Why don't we get inside, where it's a bit more private," Grace suggested, wringing her hands in front of her.

"I agree," Josh added, taking Amanda and Kaylena by the arm. "Shall we, ladies?"

Kaylena stood fast, her frown deepening. "How on earth would you know anything about the creature, Amanda?"

"I think its best we get on inside," Grace persisted.

She shot her aunt a penetrating look. "The *creature* happens to be my husband."

Kaylena clutched her throat with her hands. "Good Lord."

Grace threw her hands up in despair. "Well, there ya have it."

Kaylena hyperventilated. "I can't breathe."

Josh assisted Kaylena over to the steps, helping her to sit down. "Take deep breaths."

"I'll fetch ya a glass of water," Grace offered, making her way into the house.

"I think I'm going to faint," Kaylena whispered.

"Well, be quick about it," she quipped, annoyed. "There is no time to play nursemaid to you when my husband needs our help."

"Amanda, where's your sense?" Josh admonished. "She had no idea who Proud Eagle was." He arched a brow. "And lower your voice, before the whole town hears you."

Kaylena's voice shook. "It's true, Amanda, I had no idea he was…he was…"

Her eyes narrowed. "The word just sticks in your throat, doesn't it?"

Grace returned with the glass of water, and handed it to Kaylena. "This is not a time for us all to be fightin' with each other."

Josh agreed. "Grace is right. We need to stick together if we're going to help Proud Eagle."

Kaylena brought a trembling hand to her forehead. "As I think of it now, no doubt he mistook me for you, Amanda. But when he grabbed me, all I could remember were those horrible stories that crude Lieutenant Duffy told me about what the Indians did to women."

Her heart went out to her aunt. "I'm sorry. Of course you wouldn't have reacted different." She walked over to Kaylena, placing a hand on her shoulder. "If you had the chance to really get to know Proud Eagle, you'd like him." She sat down on a step beside Kaylena, her voice softening. "He's wise and brave, treats me with much love and respect, as do the rest of his people."

Kaylena's eyes widened. "You live with him and his people?"

She nodded. "Isn't that what husband and wife do, live together?"

Kaylena turned her attention to Josh. "You've allowed this?"

Josh was abashed by her chastisement. "Now, see here, Kaylena—"

"It wasn't up to him," Amanda interrupted.

"Kaylena, please listen," Josh said.

"Nay, you listen," Kaylena countered. "My niece is just a young girl who is too naive to understand the consequences such a lethal mistake as this can have on the rest of her life." She stood, eyes blazing with her vexation. "But you do. You know how tongues wag. And for you to allow her to run off, destroy her reputation, her social standing in the community... Well, it's just unforgivable."

She sprung to her feet. "You know nothing of what you speak, and right now I don't have the time to explain it to you." She ran down the path, back to the street.

Josh ran after her, catching up to her, and grabbing her arm. "Where are you going?"

"To stop this beating, my husband has done nothing to deserve such treatment."

He retorted with a sarcastic tone. "And what are you going to do, tap the good lieutenant on the shoulder and say, 'Excuse me, sir, but that's my husband you're planning on whipping, and I'll be taking him home for dinner now'? Do you believe that will suffice?"

She didn't appreciate his mockery. "Well, no. But I have to do something."

Josh walked her back to the garden. "You stay with Grace and Kaylena, and let me handle this."

She halted her steps. "I want to go with you."

He spoke in a low tone. "Amanda, I'm this close," he held up his hand and measured out the span of an inch with his thumb and forefinger, "to turning you over my knee and giving you the spanking you should have gotten at least twenty times from your father."

An unwelcome blush colored her cheeks. "You dare to speak to me that way? Do you even know? Do you even care what I'm going through inside right now?"

He gritted his teeth. "I can only imagine, but I warned you of this day when you first came to me asking for my blessing. I told you then you were making the biggest mistake of your life. Let's hope it hasn't cost Proud Eagle his."

Fear exploded in her heart. "Please, Josh, you've got to help him."

He combed his fingers through his hair. "I'm going to try, Amanda, I'm really going to try."

****

The white lawman tied Proud Eagle to a tree, and with a knife, ripped his tunic up the back, leaving him naked to the waist.

"Let's see how long it's gonna take to get some answers out of you, renegade. I'll find your tribe and wipe out another bunch of bothersome snakes." The soldier's wicked laugh grated on his nerves. "Another star, it all looks good on my record."

He tightened his back muscles and spread his legs wide to brace himself for the blows to come.

"Let's see how brave you are now, when alone and helpless, like the women and children you've slain," the lieutenant mocked.

The whip came down with a piercing sting across his back. He caught the exclamation in his throat and bit his bottom lip. *I will not cry out. If it be part of the white lawman's glory to hear me scream, I will not let him have it.*

The white lawman raised the whip again and again, coming down hard across his neck, shoulder, lower back. His head flew back with the burning agony his flesh endured. The lashes came faster, leaving no time in between to cope with the pain.

He separated his mind from his body, detaching himself from his hurting flesh, and focused on a time he held his wife close, kissed her lips. But his legs grew weak, trembling beneath him. The whip tore at his skin, ripped away his resolve, and his senses clouded.

****

Josh winced with every crack of the whip, horrified at Proud Eagle's back ripped to a bloody pulp. Filled with admiration for the Indian, who took each blow without so much as a whimper, he cleared the emotion from his own throat.

With every strike of the whip, the lieutenant's amber eyes flashed with a blood-thirsty pleasure. The satisfaction Duffy received doling out the punishment infuriated Josh.

He moved closer to the soldier, keeping his rage under control. "Pray God, Lieutenant, hasn't the man had enough?"

Ryan Duffy sneered, raising the whip again. "I don't tell you how to write your sermons, Preacher, don't tell me how to uphold the law."

"But the man won't be able to answer a thing, if you continue to beat him," he said. "You've whipped him to near unconsciousness now."

The lieutenant beat Proud Eagle's lower back, but slowed the blows, taking into consideration Josh's advice.

"Go back to the ladies," Ryan spat, perspiration trickling down his face. "And let me do my job."

****

She paced in torment, hearing the crack of the whip from the garden. "The lieutenant's still thrashing Proud Eagle. Josh hasn't been able to stop him."

"I'm sure the reverend's doin' all he can, child," Grace comforted.

"Well, his best is not good enough," she sobbed.

"Come with me now, Amanda. Let's both join yer aunt inside," Grace urged.

She put her hands over her ears to block out the sound of the lashes. "Oh, I can't stand another moment of this." She started for the street.

"Amanda wait," Grace called after her.

"I just can't stand by and do nothing, Grace," she hollered over her shoulder.

"Ya'll make matters worse," Grace warned.

"I won't leave Proud Eagle to suffer this alone."

She ran with fists clenched to where Proud Eagle was tied.

She had to squeeze through the small crowd gathered to near her husband. When she caught sight of his back, bloody, raw and swollen, she shrieked, "My God!"

Lieutenant Duffy spun around, his face flushed and wet with perspiration. "Go back to the house, ma'am. This is not a sight a lady should see."

Josh grabbed her by the arm and pulled her away from the scene. "Amanda, go back to the parsonage."

The blood drained from her face, her knees trembled. "Please, Lieutenant, I beg of you to stop," she cried, her voice broken and torn, her body trembled.

She'd never seen Josh in such a rage. He flew at Ryan Duffy and grabbed the whip from his hands. "Cut the man down, Lieutenant!" he demanded.

Ryan's hair fell in disarray around his face, amber eyes glazed with hate. "This is no concern of yours, Preacher! You are interfering with an officer upholding the law." He reached for the whip.

Josh threw the strap to the ground and stepped on it. "If that's true, Lieutenant, then torture and inhuman treatment is against the principles you are sworn to uphold." His eyes bulged. "Your conduct here today has been just as ruthless and barbaric as you condemn the Indians of being. If this is your idea of justice, then I hold little, if no respect, for the United States Cavalry." He glared into Duffy's eyes. "Maybe your superiors would like to hear how you've handled your authority in this situation." He motioned to the onlookers who had gathered. "Look around you at all the horrified faces; you've managed to upset the entire town."

Ryan wiped his brow with his arm, his tone sarcastic. "Then, what do you suggest, Reverend?"

Josh turned to Jonas Miller, one of the spectators. "Can we use the storage room and billing office behind the store as a makeshift jail, Jonas?"

Jonas nodded. "Be my guest, Reverend."

He turned his attention to Ryan. "Behind Miller's General store there is a storage room with barred windows and a door that locks from the outside. Because Willow Creek is such a small town we haven't a sheriff or jail. The nearest law enforcer is ten miles away, in the next county. But when we have any kind of a disturbance, we lock up the troublemaker in the building behind the store until someone goes for the authorities."

"There's an old cot and some blankets back there, too," Jonas Miller added.

"Please, Lieutenant, let the reverend take the Indian there to revive him," she pleaded.

Ryan hesitated. "I'm not so sure that would be smart, ma'am."

Josh's tone grated harshly. "It's a better plan then subjecting us all to this violence."

She wanted to fly at Ryan Duffy and claw the insolent expression from his face.

Ryan narrowed his eyes. "You're not qualified to handle the savage when he comes around. Besides, I can't put civilians' lives in jeopardy like that."

Josh motioned to the younger soldier, who looked like he was ready to be sick at any moment. "Then let the private here stand guard by the door."

Ryan Duffy nodded and threw a knife to Private Thomas. "Cut the Indian down and help the Reverend here, get him to the room he spoke of." He pointed a finger at the young soldier. "Don't let the prisoner out of your sight for a moment. If you need me, send the wagon train master, Abe, to fetch me, but don't leave your post."

Private Thomas saluted. "Yes, sir! And where will ya be, sir?"

Ryan looked down at his naked, sweaty chest. "I'm gonna get cleaned up, put on a shirt and see if I can rustle up some grub in this town." He wiped a hand over his mouth. "On second thought, Private, I'll be in the hotel saloon. I could use a drink."

****

Amanda ran to the parsonage for salve, a basin of water, and some cloths while Josh and Private Thomas carried Proud Eagle's battered body to the storage room.

Grace found a bottle of whiskey in Josh's study and handed it to her. "I'd say he's gonna need this."

"Thanks Grace," she said. "We might all benefit from a swig."

The men had just laid Proud Eagle face down on the cot when she arrived at the makeshift jail. "I've brought some medicinal things."

"Just leave 'em on the floor by the cot," Private Thomas instructed.

"I might need her help, Private," Josh said.

Private Thomas scratched his head. "I don't recall the lieutenant sayin' the lady could be here. If ya need help, I'd be right pleased to lend a hand."

She batted her lashes. "Why Private, how will you stand guard and help, too?" She cast him a demure smile. "I'm sure I'll be just fine in here helping the reverend, with you right outside the door."

Private Thomas's chest swelled with her attention. "Well, I am pretty quick with a gun."

She spoke with the thickness of honey edging her voice. "I feel right confident, sir, knowing such a qualified soldier and a gentleman stands ready to defend me."

Private Thomas stood taller. "One holler, ma'am, and I'll be beside ya in a flash."

She edged her way farther into the storage room. "Thank you, kindly."

The moment the private had gone, she rushed to Proud Eagle. With a shaking hand she pushed aside the hair that clung to his neck and face, moistened a cloth and put it to his forehead. "My sweet, dear husband, why did you come for me? You, above all, know the danger," she whispered.

Proud Eagle opened his eyes; the agony in his gaze matched the strain in his voice. "I could not bear the sorrow of my father passing from this life without you, *shi'aad*."

She cleaned his wounds. With each stroke of the cloth he cringed. "You've been more foolish than the coyote this time, my husband." While applying the salve, her fingers sunk into the raw slits.

His teeth ground together with his pain. "As foolish as it was, I would do it again." His trembling hand reached for hers. "I have seen your beautiful face and felt the love of your tender touch."

Josh offered Proud Eagle the whiskey. "Here, take a sip of this."

He raised his head for a sip, swallowed, coughed, and laid his head back down. "My *chelee* is tied behind the path to the holy man's house."

"We'll see to Blazing Fire," she reassured him with a kiss to his forehead. "You've stepped into a lion's den, my love."

Josh knit his brows together. "Keep your voice low, Amanda. It wouldn't do him any good if the lieutenant found out about you two."

She stroked Proud Eagle's cheek. "We've got to figure out how to get him out of here."

Josh lowered his own voice. "That's not going to be an easy task. Remember the reports I read you?"

She nodded, her gaze resting on her husband's anguished face.

"Well, we're lucky we've bought him this much time," Josh concluded. "But I do have a plan."

Her heart filled with hope for the first time in

hours. "Tell us."

Josh looked around the tiny room. "See those boards stacked against the wall? Behind them is a door. I know this for fact, because I helped Jonas install it. When we leave here, Amanda, you go first; distract Private Thomas a few moments while I find the door and unlock it. Then, late tonight we can sneak in here through that door and get Proud Eagle out of town."

She kissed Proud Eagle on the temple. "Not to worry, we'll get you out of here soon."

Proud Eagle nodded and closed his eyes.

****

Private Thomas bolted the door behind Amanda, his copper colored curls hung in disarray across a freckled brow. She smiled, dropping her eyes in a coy manner. "It was pure comfort knowing you were close by, Private."

"Call me Alexander, ma'am."

"Alexander is it?" she drawled.

He nodded.

She moved closer. "Such a nice, strong name, and it fits you well."

He blushed. "Thank ya, ma'am."

"Oh, please, call me Amanda." She batted her lashes. "I do hate formalities between friends...and I do hope we can be friends?"

Alexander swallowed hard. "Oh, yes, ma'am, I mean Amanda. I'd like that very much."

She laid a slight hand upon his arm. "Good, then when I return to bring the prisoner something to eat, we can chat a bit more."

Alexander smiled. "I'd like that a lot." He shot a glance at the cell door and frowned. "Why hasn't the reverend come out with ya?"

"He asked me to give him a moment of privacy while he prayed for the Indian's soul."

The young private nodded in agreement. "I

reckon it's his Christian duty."

Josh was out of breath, his face flushed when he came through the cell door. He took her by the arm and led her away.

She sensed Alexander's eyes watching her from behind. Turning one last time to look at him, she cast him an overly-sweet smile and hurried out the door.

Once on the street, Josh let out a breath. "The door's locked, and I have the horrible suspicion the key's in the desk."

"I'll do whatever it takes to get Proud Eagle away from here. Even if that means standing on the parsonage roof and playing the violin while you sneak in to steal the key."

Josh stroked his chin. "There's no doubt we need something to buy us more time."

They spotted the swaying figure of Ryan Duffy, standing against the hotel post, trying to light his pipe.

Josh shook his head in disgust. "I'd say our gallant soldier had a bit too much to drink."

Her face brightened. "His condition could work to our advantage."

He narrowed his eyes. "How so?"

"If he's drunker than a skunk, he won't be able to conduct his interrogations until tomorrow. And if I can get him to pass out, he won't be fit enough to do a thing until much later tomorrow. In the meanwhile, I can lure Private Thomas away from the desk long enough for you to find the key."

"And how do you propose getting the lieutenant unconscious?"

She held up the whiskey bottle in her hand. "By filling him with enough spirits to sink a ship."

Josh's lips thinned. "That plan is out of the question."

"Josh listen to me, please," she pleaded.

"Nay, Amanda, it's time you started listening to me." He raked a hand through his hair. "Your aunt was right to admonish me as she did. I knew better than to let you run off and marry an Indian, and I should have done more to stop it."

She raised her chin. "There was nothing you could have done."

He arched a brow. "I could have had him imprisoned and sent for the authorities, which would have put a damper on things."

She gasped. "You could never have carried that out."

"For your sake, I should have, Amanda." He gestured to the inebriated lieutenant. "And if you think I'm going to let you anywhere near that scoundrel, you're mistaken."

"Look at him, Josh. He can't even stand to light his pipe."

"I feel that man could take advantage of a woman while he was sound asleep."

"Well, then, that's where you come in, just in case I've misjudged his stamina," she said.

Josh frowned. "What do you mean? Where I come in?"

"It's simple. Come looking for me, and if he's acting up instead of passing out, then your interruption will give me a way to escape."

He let out an audible breath. "I've heard quite enough of this foolery, Amanda, and must insist upon your immediate return with me to the parsonage."

"Josh, I can do this. Really I can. And it will buy Proud Eagle more time, to gain his strength, and for us to get the key." She placed a hand on his arm. "Please, go take care of my husband's horse, and then come to the lieutenant's room in twenty minutes. That's all I ask…just twenty minutes."

Josh finally agreed and left her to approach the

soldier.

She came upon Ryan with a warm smile. "Good evening, lieutenant."

Ryan's speech was slurred. "Well, howdy, ma'am, but call me Ryan."

"Ryan," she said, holding up the whiskey bottle. "I remember you saying you could use a drink, but it appears you've had a bit too much already."

"Nah, you can never have too much to drink." A crooked smile curved his lips. "I've got a couple of glasses up in my room. Care to join me?"

She gave him the same coy look she used on Private Thomas. "I'll be glad to help you to your room, and pour you a glass. But beyond that..."

He scanned the length of her with vulture-like eyes. "You're sure a pretty little thing."

Amanda moved closer. "Let's get you to your room before you topple into the street." She handed him the whiskey bottle and braced him with her shoulder. She steadied herself with the other hand upon the banister to keep from collapsing beneath his weight.

When they reached the top of the stairway she was out of breath. "Which is your room?"

He paused confused, then pointed to a door marked with the number four.

She leaned him against the wall and turned the knob. "It's locked, do you have the key?"

Ryan smiled. "Yup."

She fought to keep annoyance from her tone. "May I have it?"

His eyes roamed over her breasts in a shameless manner. "Search for it."

Her cheeks warmed at the way his amber eyes leered into hers while she hunted for the key. She found it in the front pants pocket.

Before she could pull it free, he pressed his hand over hers. "Move down a little deeper, love, and you'll find something a lot better than a key."

Her stomach lurched, but she had too much at stake to allow him to intimidate her. It was important she put Ryan Duffy out of commission for a while. Forcing a smile, she sweetened her tone. "Let's get you into the room."

He nodded and released her hand.

She turned the key in the lock.

Ryan stumbled to the bed and plopped down. "Come here, love."

She walked toward the bed and to her doom.

With one hand, he pulled her close, bending her head to meet his. His clumsy search for her mouth made her fall forward, into his arms. He thrust his tongue down her throat, and she had all to do to keep from gagging, her flesh crawling at his touch. Wiggling free, she reached for the bottle.

He smiled. "You can do the honors."

She scanned the room. "Where are the glasses?"

He motioned to a table at the foot of the bed. She poured him a large amount and handed him the glass. He threw the drink down his throat in one gulp.

Without the least bit of conscious, she poured him a refill.

Again he downed the whiskey and reached for a breast.

"Perhaps you'd be more comfortable if I removed your boots?" she said, removing his hand from her chest and kneeling down before him.

Ryan entwined his fingers in her hair. "You look like an angel with all these golden curls."

She stood with a smile and refilled his glass for a third time.

He downed the contents again with one swig and threw the glass across the room. It shattered against the wall. "What man wouldn't wanna make love to an angel?"

268

Grabbing her around the waist, he pulled her close.

Nausea rose to gag her, as she smelled the spirits on his breath, but she forced herself to continue the charade by unbuttoning his shirt. "You've had quite a day, Ryan." She slipped the shirt off his shoulders and down his arms. "Lay down and I'll give you a massage."

He rid himself of his shirt and rolled onto his stomach.

With one knee upon the bed, she rubbed his neck and shoulders, then moved down to his lower back. His hot flesh made every fiber in her body recoil.

A low, sensuous groan escaped his throat, and he relaxed, snorted, and passed out.

She backed away, lifted his arm, and dropped the limp hand back onto the bed.

It was at that point a knock came at the door. She let Josh into the room with a triumphant smile. "Perfect timing."

He looked over at the bed, arching a brow. "I'd say you achieved your goal."

"He's out cold. Let's hope he'll stay that way for a long time." She slipped off her petticoat and threw it to the floor.

Josh folded his arms across his chest. "What on earth are you doing?"

"Just a little added assurance, so the lieutenant doesn't think he dreamt it all. And if you strip him naked," she said, going to the door, "hopefully, he won't remember the truth." She saluted the limp figure snoring. "Thank you for passing out, sir. You really know how to charm a woman."

"He's not going to feel so charming tomorrow," she heard Josh grumble before she shut the door.

Chapter Thirteen

Amanda hadn't slept a wink all night, concocting a plan to get Private Thomas away from the desk long enough for Josh to search for the key. She decided, as long as she was awake, she'd fix Proud Eagle breakfast, and for good measure, the private something to eat as well, before the lieutenant awakened.

She found Kaylena sitting alone at the kitchen table, sipping tea. Pouring herself a cup, she sat beside her aunt. "I'm truly sorry your visit has fallen in the middle of such a tragic situation."

"Aye, it's tragic at that."

She forced a smile. "Josh has a plan, and if it works..."

"And if it doesn't?" Kaylena countered.

She couldn't think of life without Proud Eagle. "It has to. It just has to."

Kaylena covered Amanda's hand with hers. "You might have to walk away from this, Amanda."

Her eyes filled with tears. "I will never walk away. I love my husband with all my heart."

Kaylena searched her face. "Marriage isn't easy under normal conditions, with each partner coming into the relationship with a different upbringing. Though I can't speak for myself, I have seen many of my married women friends deal with just such obstacles. Love suffers long with the faults and habits of a spouse." She cleared her throat. "What I'm trying to say, Amanda, is with the best of circumstances loving someone is hard...especially if he's supposed to be your enemy."

"But Proud Eagle's not my enemy, never has been, and it doesn't matter to me what color his skin is, what his beliefs are, or where he lives. We've adjusted to all that, and we share our cultures."

"Your cultural differences aren't the only things involved here. The bitterness each side holds for one another is the result of far more unforgivable reasons then one's beliefs. Men, women, even small children, on both sides, have been murdered in the process. How are you able to live with that, Amanda?"

"My own father was one of those victims, but my husband and his people aren't the ones responsible." She took a calming breath, collecting her thoughts. "I hated all Indians at one time, Aunt Kaylena, because of what happened to Papa. But it was Proud Eagle who showed me hating an entire race for the actions of a few is wrong. When I realized this, I was also able to forgive and move on with my life. I can't hate someone for something he didn't do." She swallowed the lump growing in her throat. "And the hostiles, though I don't condone their measures, are not entirely to blame either. Our authorities have been just as brutal. Their greed in acquiring Indian land has kept them from wanting to solve the conflict, preventing any hope of peace. The Indians are only defending what has always been theirs, as I'm sure the men in your country have done. It's a sad and unfortunate fact lives are lost when there is a war."

"And no one knows better than I."

"How do you know?" she probed.

"When I was your age, I fell in love with a Royal Navy Officer. His name was Wesley Hughes, and he was tall, strong, and very handsome. We became engaged to be wed before he shipped out on a voyage. But the nuptials never took place, because Wesley didn't return. He was killed at sea."

She squeezed her aunt's hand. "I'm so sorry, Aunt Kaylena."

Kaylena dropped her gaze. "I've read the reverend's newspaper reports, and quite frankly, I don't see your husband standing much of a chance to survive this. I'm surprised Lieutenant Duffy hasn't already—"

"Don't say it," she raised a hand to silence her aunt's next words.

"If you can't free him, Amanda, where does that leave you?"

She bit her bottom lip. "He will be freed. Josh has a plan."

"Do you think for one minute, should your wedded status become a public matter, you'll have any peace or freedom?" Kaylena continued. "You'll be hounded day and night as a traitor. No man will ever take you for his wife."

"I would never marry another man."

"I said the same, when Wesley died, and so I never gave myself a chance to love someone else. Take it from me, Amanda, life is long. Too long to live it alone."

She stood. "I won't listen to anymore."

"Come back to England with me. You're the rightful heiress to Bentwood Manor, and that's where you belong. No one ever has to know your past predicament, and you can start fresh."

She thrust her chin out. "Is that what you think my marriage to Proud Eagle is—a predicament?"

Kaylena stood, challenging her. "Aye, Amanda, I do. In Brighton you will be a lady of society. Have a chance to meet a proper English gentleman."

"I've met a proper American gentleman," she argued. "And I'd sooner die than leave him." She made her way to the pantry for cornmeal.

"Amanda wait," Kaylena called after her.

"No, Aunt Kaylena, we've both said enough. I'm

signing Bentwood Manor over to you. I don't want any part of it. Now if you'll excuse me, I must make breakfast for my husband."

****

She set the tray upon the desk. "I brought you breakfast as well, Alexander."

The young private's red-rimmed eyes peered out from beneath fair lashes. "I can't thank ya enough, Amanda." He cast a glance at the other plate. "I reckon that's for the Indian?"

She nodded.

Alexander's brows knit together in a concerned frown. "I can't have ya in there alone, Amanda, since I'd have to untie his hands to eat."

She inhaled sharply. "He's tied up?"

"Oh, sure, can't take the chance of him jumpin' me, so when Abe stopped in late last night, he held the Indian at gunpoint while I tied his hands and feet."

She hid the dread squeezing her heart. "Well, then, I'll leave his food here with you."

Alexander nodded. "When the lieutenant relieves me, he can stand watch while I untie the Indian's hands."

She was sure Ryan wouldn't care one way or another if Proud Eagle ate breakfast, and instead, would eat the food himself.

Her mind raced. If Proud Eagle went too long without water or a meal he'd be too weak for Josh's escape plan. And if Ryan Duffy came back before Josh could get access to the desk, they'd never get the key.

Her thoughts were interrupted by Grace Thomas coming through the door.

"Howdy, there, Private Thomas," her tone light and cheery. "I had to meander over when I heard that Thomas was yer last name, and take a gander at ya."

Alexander ran a hand over his tired eyes. "And why is that, ma'am?"

Grace made her way closer to the desk. "Because I'm a Thomas too—by marriage that is."

Alexander's face brightened. "Really, ma'am?"

Grace nodded. "Wouldn't spoof ya on that, boy." She looked deep into the young man's eyes. "Where ya from?"

"Cold Falls, West Virginia, ma'am," Alexander said.

"My late husband, Clyde, has a mess of kinfolk livin' in that neck of the woods."

Alexander's smile broadened. "I'm Isabelle and Henry's son."

"Well, now, ya don't say. If my memory serves me right, I believe yer pa, and my Clyde was cousins."

Alexander slapped a hand across his thigh. "Well, if that doesn't beat all. Findin' kin so far from home." His eyes grew moist. "Can't tell ya how much it means to me, to make yer acquaintance, ma'am."

"Reckon ya'll have to call me Aunty Grace," Grace suggested.

"I'd be right proud to," Alexander boasted.

"And could I interest ya in a dish of my homemade apple cobbler when ya get off duty here?" Grace said.

"Boy, could ya," Alexander beamed.

"Well, first I've gotta ask ya a small favor. Seems I need a set of keys in that there drawer," Grace said, pointing to the desk. "I help Jonas a few days a week at the store, and he sent me to fetch 'em."

Alexander nodded. "Sure, Aunty Grace, take what ya need."

Grace opened the drawer. "I'll just be wantin' the keys." She reached for the set of keys hanging from a leather cord. "Got 'em," she said, holding them up and slipping them in her apron pocket. "And I thank ya kindly."

Alexander licked his lips. "Where can I find ya? I mean, so I can taste that cobbler."

"Over yonder, at the parsonage," Grace said. "Come a knockin' at the back door, and I'll have it ready for ya."

Alexander smiled. "I'll be there."

Grace turned her attention to Amanda. "Comin' back with me to the parsonage, child?"

She nodded. "I'm right behind you, Grace."

Once they were outside, she thanked Grace with a hug. "I can't believe you just walked in and took the keys."

"My ma always said, if ya do somethin' in plain sight, no one's the wiser."

"Grace, you're an absolute genius."

"Ain't had much schoolin', had to help out on the farm. But my pa made sure me and my sister, Eunice, could read so we could learn the Bible."

"And who would have thought Alexander was related to your late husband," she mused.

Grace giggled like a school girl. "That boy in there ain't no kin to Clyde. My husband didn't have family, besides he came to these here parts from Montana."

"Then why did you let Alexander believe otherwise?"

"I could see he was missin' his folks, the look of a homesick pup was as plain as day on that freckled face, and winnin' his confidence allowed me to get ya the key." She shrugged. "I just made everybody a little happier." She smiled. "He gets apple cobbler from Aunty Grace, and ya"—she pulled the key from her pocket and handed it to Amanda—"get to save yer husband." She pointed her finger at Amanda. "But in the future, there's just one thing ya gotta keep in mind."

"What's that, Grace?"

"Never send a man to do a woman's job."

****

Proud Eagle lay on his stomach, watching an army of ants run through the cracks of the wall, busy, organized, and free. If only he could become as small, just long enough to escape through the uneven boards. Then he would find his Golden Lady and together they would go home.

He longed to kiss her, touch her, have her warmth beneath him. With the memory of their lovemaking, he closed his eyes, his heart yearning for her passion, to sit again by the fire and hear her read from the holy book. He remembered the prayer, and mentally recited it, not for himself, but for Golden Lady. He feared she would step into a trap the white lawman planned.

The walls were thin between his makeshift cell and the outer room. Words spoken could easily be overheard. The young soldier listened to Golden Lady's wifely endearment on the first day of Proud Eagle's capture and relayed his findings to the one called Duffy. Now he feared for Golden Lady. What would the lieutenant do to her, knowing she was an Indian's woman?

His thoughts were interrupted when the door opened and the white lawman, his face twisted into a cruel sneer, stood beside the cot with his gun drawn.

"Get up, you mangy filth," was his demand.

He swung his tied feet off the cot, and stood. With hands bound in front of him, he raised a proud chin in the face of his enemy.

"Your insolence annoys me, savage," Ryan spat, waving the gun in his face. "And when I'm annoyed, I lose my patience." He cocked the trigger. "Where's your tribe?"

He kept his silence, his gaze locking with the

lieutenant's.

The lieutenant smirked. "Maybe your wife can tell me, then."

His heart raced, and he denied the accusation. "I know not what you speak."

The white soldier pressed the tip of the gun against Proud Eagle's chest. "Oh, come on, Chief. We both know you understand my words quite well. The advantage, no doubt, of living with a white woman."

He remained silent, jaw muscles throbbing. Even if it meant his death, here and now, he would not tell the lieutenant what he wanted to hear. He would protect his wife to the end.

Duffy's wicked laughter filled the room. "Well, if I can't get the information I want from you, I'll just have to persuade Amanda over dinner." He stepped back, unbuttoning his jacket. "I'm sure she'll tell me. You see, we've grown quite friendly since I've seen you last. She has, you might say, grown lonesome for the love of a real man." He pulled the petticoat from beneath his jacket. "She's quite the woman—satisfying, passionate." He brought the white material to his nose and inhaled. "Even her scent excites me, but you already know all that. Enjoyed the splendor for a time yourself." The lawman moved closer. "Too bad all good things must come to an end."

Rage rushed through Proud Eagle's body. "You speak with a forked tongue."

"Oh, really?" Duffy opened the petticoat and dangled it in front of Proud Eagle's nose. "How do you think I got this?"

He clenched his teeth. He could not believe—would not believe—the bastard's words.

The lieutenant threw the petticoat at him. "Smell it, savage. It's her scent, isn't it?"

He swallowed the anger, the regret, and the sorrow rising to choke him. *Ah, my wife, what have you done for my sake?*

He moved closer. "How does it feel to know I've had my way with her? Your woman. Your wife!"

Proud Eagle flew at the lieutenant in a blind fury.

Ryan Duffy brought the butt of his gun across his face.

The impact of the blow coupled with his feet tied, threw him off balance. He fell hard to the wooden floor.

"You just answered my question," Ryan shouted, bringing the gun down across the back of Proud Eagle's head.

****

Amanda paced her room. Just a half hour till midnight, and Josh would be able to make his way to the back of the storage room, unlock the rear door, and free Proud Eagle.

She had readied Blazing Fire about twenty minutes ago. When she had thrown the blanket over his back, he swished his golden tail and mane, stamping a foot in his excitement.

She had spoken softly to him, "I'm happy too, boy. We're finally going home."

The plan was for her to meet them a ways down the path with Blazing Fire for Proud Eagle to ride back to the village. She would follow in a few days, not to alert suspicion.

She wrung her hands, worried for her husband's condition. If he hadn't been given the food she brought, or water, it would be difficult for Josh to help him escape. Proud Eagle would also be too weak to ride to the village on his own.

She checked the grandfather clock for the hundredth time when a knock came at the door. She descended the stairs to see Josh talking to a stranger, a young man with pale blonde hair and large aqua eyes. He spoke with a strange accent and looked tired.

She went to stand beside Josh, and he introduced the young man to her as Benjamin Newcomb.

"And this is Amanda Gregory, Kaylena's niece." Josh said, turning his attention back to Benjamin.

Benjamin smiled. "Pleased to meet you, miss. I met your aunt on the ship. She said if things didn't vork out vhere I was headed, to look for her in Villow Creek."

Benjamin is from Sweden, Amanda," Josh added. "He was on his way to California to set up a church there for the folks panning for gold."

"Then you're a minister?" she inquired.

"Yaw, Miss, a minister vithout a church."

"It seems Benjamin was not received well by some of the folks there. He decided the wisest thing would be to move on and hitched a ride with a homesick miner returning to these parts," Josh explained further.

"Miss Kaylena talked about Villow Creek, and vell, here I am," Benjamin said, sporting a larger smile.

"How did you know where to find my aunt?"

"I asked the lieutenant leading the vagon train just pulling out of town," Benjamin said.

Panic constricted her chest. "The wagons are leaving?"

Benjamin nodded. "And the lieutenant said I could find Miss Kaylena here." Benjamin pulled a piece of paper from his jacket pocket. "He also asked if I'd bring this letter to you, Miss Amanda."

Her body tensed. She took the letter from the young reverend and scanned the words, her eyes filling with tears. Clutching the letter to her chest she looked up at Josh and blinked the tears from her eyes. "It's too late," she choked out in a suffocated whisper before she collapsed.

Josh caught her, excusing himself from a very worried looking Benjamin Newcomb, and helped her to her room.

"Oh, merciful heavens," Kaylena shrieked, when they passed the doorway of her room. "What's happened?"

"I haven't a clue," Josh said, helping her sit upon the bed. He wet a cloth from the wash table basin and handed it to her.

"Whatever is in that letter from Lieutenant Duffy, caused her to collapse."

She was too numb to speak and just handed Kaylena the letter.

Her aunt read aloud. "Dearest Amanda, I regret, due to important military matters, I have been instructed by my superiors to leave immediately." Kaylena paused. "Why did Lieutenant Duffy need to explain his departure to you?"

She remained silent, her throat closed with her grief.

Josh answered for her. "It's a long story, Kaylena, which I'll explain later. Just read on."

Kaylena continued. "The matter of the Indian Chief who attacked Miss Bentley has been handled in a manner suitable for the situation and will cause no further upset to the good citizens of Willow Creek. The hostile was taken earlier this evening to the ridge and executed by hanging." Kaylena looked up from the letter. "Oh, sweet Lord."

"A manner suitable for the situation," Josh ground out through clenched teeth. "Filthy bastard."

"I feared this would happen," Kaylena whispered, coming to sit beside her.

Josh sat down on the other side of her and swallowed hard. "We all did."

Kaylena put her arm around her shoulder, looking genuinely upset for her. Maybe she'd been too quick to judge her aunt. She'd lost a love, too.

"I am so sorry, my dear," Kaylena whispered. "What can I do right now to make things better…to be useful in someway?"

Josh combed his fingers through his hair. "You could take yourself downstairs and greet the guest you've invited here."

Kaylena blinked bewildered. "I beg your pardon?"

"There's a young minister standing in the foyer by the name of Benjamin Newcomb. He claims you invited him here."

"I never thought he'd really come." Kaylena said.

"Well, he has, and I think the man deserves an explanation as to why Amanda dropped to her knees in front of him," Josh said.

"Aye, you're right, Josh. I'll go downstairs and take care of the situation." Kaylena hesitated a moment. "Perhaps I should stay with Amanda and let you explain things to Benjamin."

"You go take care of your guest." Josh reached over to take her hand. "Amanda and I are old friends. It's best if I stay."

"Very well, if you're sure," she said, making her way to the door.

"Aye, Kaylena, I'm sure."

Kaylena held up the letter. "What should I do with the letter?"

"Burn it," Amanda choked.

She searched Josh's face; her sorrow was mirrored in his large, blue eyes. "I'm so very sorry, Amanda."

She turned away from him and buried her face in the pillow, her body rocking with her sobs.

He put a tender hand on her shoulder. "When times are good, we are happy. When times are bad, we must also consider God has made one as well as the other."

"Lately, I don't understand good or bad, or the

whole *there is a reason for all things* theory," she cried, tears wetting the linen pillow cover, her heart breaking in two.

Josh stayed beside her in silence. She knew he shared her pain and agony. He was a good man, there once again to comfort her, stroking her hair and rubbing her shoulder while she sobbed.

She woke to find herself alone. Had she cried herself to sleep?

She eased off the bed and walked to the dressing table. She lit the lantern and caught her reflection in the mirror. Her hair fell in a tangled mass to her waist, her eyes red and swollen. She reached for the hair brush and pulled it through the snarled curls.

I'm his Golden Lady, with hair the gold of the sun, he would say.

She brought a pale lock forward, rubbing it against her cheek. *How am I supposed to live on without you, Proud Eagle?*

For hours she sat staring at her reflection, the times she had with Proud Eagle circling her thoughts. It was the knock at the door that brought her from the fond memories.

"Amanda, may I come in?"

"Yes," she said

Josh peeked into the room. "I saw the light through the crack under the door."

He moved to sit on the bed, watching her pull the brush through each curl.

She kept her eyes on her reflection in the mirror. "He loved the golden color of my hair, did you know that?"

"Aye, he loved you very much."

"And I loved him...love him," she corrected.

"I know you do, Amanda. He was a good, brave man, and I know he'd want you to be brave as well."

She placed the brush aside, turning toward him. "Why has this happened?"

He sighed. "There is a reason for—"

"No, don't!" She stood and pointed a finger at him. "Don't you dare tell me there is a reason for all things, because there isn't one good damn reason for what's happened." She made her way over to the window and gazed down at the street below.

"Duffy, the blood thirsty son of a culprit that he is, cared nothing for the fact Proud Eagle is an innocent man. He never did anything to hurt anyone. But this lawless land doesn't want justice... not really. Judging a man on how he looks, his differences, associating him with all others, isn't justice." Tears stung her eyes. "All Proud Eagle and I want is to live in peace, to love each other, to have a family." She turned and rested her back against the wall, staring up at the rafters. "He is my only hope, the sign, my eagle soaring and giving me a new awakening, a new plan for my life."

"Amanda..."

She looked over at Josh. "And I don't think he's dead." She put a hand over her heart. "I'd feel it, if he were."

He stood and made his way to her. "Deep inside you will always feel him with you." He led her to a chair, and then knelt in front of her. "But he's gone. Lieutenant Duffy wouldn't have spared his life on any account."

She bit her bottom lip. "I won't believe he's dead till I ride out to the ridge and see for myself. And if he is there," she swallowed hard. "Then I'm going to take him home, let his people grieve for him in their tradition. He deserves that much."

Josh pushed aside a pale curl from her face. "We'll talk more in the morning, work something out. For now, you try to get some sleep."

She grabbed for his hand. "I'm going to stay with his people, Josh."

He nodded. "We both will, till the mourning time

283

is over."

"No, you don't understand. I intend to make the village my home."

"There's no reason to remain there without Proud Eagle, Amanda."

"Yes there is, Josh." She placed a hand over her belly. "I'm with child."

He stared at her, for a moment speechless, then he whispered, "Are you sure?"

She nodded.

"How far along are you?"

"Only two months," she said.

"Does anyone else know?"

"No, I didn't even have the chance to tell Proud Eagle." She stood, went to the window again, and looked out. "I was sure the morning he was captured, but didn't want to tell him, give him an added worry."

Josh stood. "Then none of his people know you're carrying his child?"

"No, I left to come here before I knew myself."

He neared her, taking her hands and bringing them to his lips to kiss. "Marry me, Amanda, and let me take care of you and the baby."

"I have no right asking you to do that."

"You didn't ask, I offered."

She pulled free from his grasp and made her way to bed, sitting at the edge. "Josh, I—"

"I've never stopped loving you, never will," he interjected. "We'll go to London; you can meet my family. I have a sister named Marietta you'd get along famously with. She and her husband, Jerome Cavandish, have one son. Simon. He's going on four and I've never seen him. We can all be a family and no one will ever have to know—"

"That I fell in love with an Indian," she finished his sentence.

"I didn't mean it to sound derogatory."

She clasped her hands together in her lap. "I'm sorry, but my place is with Proud Eagle's people."

Again he knelt down in front of her. "Nay, Amanda, your place is with me, where it's safe. Come away from this untamed land."

Her tone was sharp. "And there is no crime in England?"

"There is crime everywhere, but not like here. The threat of being murdered in your bed isn't as likely where I'm from." He searched her face. "Have you forgotten all I've read to you? If you haven't a care for yourself, then think of your child."

She gazed deep into his eyes. "I am thinking of my child. This baby needs to know Proud Eagle's heritage. It's the least I can do in my husband's..." she almost said, memory. But she had no proof Proud Eagle was dead. Until she did, she had to believe he still lived.

"I come from a well-to-do family, Amanda. You will be safe, looked after and cared for in the manner you deserve."

She covered her eyes with her hands. "Please, leave me alone now. I need to think, I need to be alone."

"Of course you do." He stood and kissed the top of her head. "If you need anything, come for me, no matter the hour."

****

Amanda sat for a long time, staring into space before going to the writing table and scribbling a letter to her aunt, relinquishing her right to Bentwood Manor. The second letter was to Josh. Propping both scripts against the pillow, she stripped off all her clothes. Naked, she washed at the basin, then pulled from the armoire a pair of britches and a shirt once belonging to an orphan boy who had stayed at the parsonage. She dressed, braided her hair, and tip-toed barefoot downstairs to the kitchen. Removing one of the boy's hats from a peg by the door, she stuffed her hair beneath it and pulled the rim down over her ears. Then she slipped her feet into a pair of Grace's boots and ran out the back door.

Blazing Fire stood waiting.

She gave the horse a loving pat. "Come, boy, it's time to go home."

Chapter Fourteen

He came out of nowhere, riding beside her, cutting her off, and reaching out, grabbing her arm. Amanda lifted a booted foot and kicked Ryan Duffy in the thigh. He winced and pulled away, cursing at her. But then he gained speed again, catching her the second time and lifting her from the horse in one sweep. With sheer black terror coursing through every fiber of her being, she dug at his knuckles and wrists with her nails and thrashed around to throw him off balance. But he was a good horseman, his grip around her waist strong. He halted the chestnut Morgan, managed to dismount the horse while holding her like a folded bedroll beneath an arm, and pinned her to the ground. Sitting on her legs, he held her hands above her head.

She glared into his cold, amber eyes. "Get off me!"

He laughed low and wicked, his gaze dropping to her heaving breasts. "Not a chance. This time I'll have my way," he sneered. "But first, don't you wanna hear what's gonna happen to your Indian man?"

Relief washed over her in spite of her predicament. "Then, he's still alive?"

"Oh, yeah, he's still alive," Ryan drawled. "But when I get done with him, he'll wish he wasn't."

She stiffened. "Where is he, where have you taken him?"

Ryan brought his face within an inch from hers. "I reckon there isn't any harm in telling you, since there isn't anything you can do." He pressed his weight down upon her. "He's at Fort Bayard. He'll be arriving there tomorrow night, in fact. And after I wipe out the rest of his people, and have my way with you, I'll return to the fort and give him the news. Then, at my command, he'll be hanged; after I let my boys have some fun with him first."

Panic welled in her throat. "Why are you doing this? What has he ever done to you?"

Raw hate was etched on the lieutenant's face. "His kind butchered my wife and child." He swallowed hard. "Do you know what it's like to find the remains of a loved one?"

His weight upon her made her gasp for breath. "As a matter of fact, I do, and I'm sorry for your loss, as well as for the pain and fear they endured before death, but Proud Eagle's people are not responsible."

"Indians are Indians, and I'm gonna wipe out all the savage bastards from the face of the earth."

"Please, listen to me, Ryan," she begged.

"No, you listen." He tightened his knees against her hips. "Do you know how shabbily the men in Washington treat the Cavalry?" He didn't wait for an answer. "Hell, we're fighting a war, and Congress still hasn't recognized it as one. Poor support, poor rations and quarters, not to mention lousy hospital conditions. And then, to add insult to injury, General Carleton's volunteers—the Mexicans, Pimas, and Maricopas, are many times more effective in Indian warfare then two or three times the number of regular troops, so they get the glory." His sardonic laugh echoed through the trees. "But the credit for exterminating your Indian's tribe will go to me and my men."

She flinched at the tone of his voice. "War is good for absolutely nothing. It's much more profitable to try and make peace, but General Carleton is greedy. He wants the Indian's land and doesn't care how many innocent lives get snuffed out in the process, including his own men," she argued.

"Beauty and brains... a dangerous combination," Ryan snapped.

"This is a peaceful tribe," she said. "If you attack them you'll only create more trouble, can't you see that?"

His amber eyes darkening locked with hers. "You know what the Cavalry call Indians? *Mr. Low,* because they're vermin, the lowest form of life around. Peaceful or not, they're beneath all creatures and I'm gonna wipe them all out with pleasure."

She reacted to the challenge of his words. "You're wrong. They're wise, loving people. The white man could gain a lot learning their ways."

"And who would know better than you—his wife?"

Her teeth clenched.

He raked a look of distain over her. "Oh, yeah, I know about you, and it disgusts me. How could you submit yourself to such disgrace?"

Her eyes narrowed. "I would feel more disgrace having you touch me, than I ever would my husband."

Ryan's eyes went wild. He pulled her to her feet, twisting her arms behind her back. "Well, I'm gonna touch you. And then I'm gonna kill you."

"You're insane!" she screamed.

"You're right, bitch! A man's got to be insane to risk his life, day in and day out, to protect all you white folks from the savages."

"You're just asking for more trouble. I'm warning you. Leave Proud Eagle's people alone!"

"You're in no position to warn me about anything, you little traitor." He took the gun from his hip and cocked the trigger. Then he released her and threw her to the ground. "I've wasted enough time with you."

She scurried to her feet, facing Ryan Duffy and the point of a gun.

"Strip," he demanded. He shrugged off his jacket and shirt, throwing them to the ground. "Letting you die now would be too easy. No one makes a fool out of Ryan Duffy. You're gonna finish what you started in the hotel room."

An arrow whooshed past Amanda, burying itself in Ryan's chest.

Her heart sank further. *Chiricahua.*

Blood gushed from the wound. He dropped the gun and fell to his knees.

"Bastard Indians," were his last words.

She spun around on her heels to fight again for her life, but instead found Little Elk standing behind her.

"I was out on my first hunt, when I heard your voice, Golden Lady."

She ran to the young brave and threw her arms around his neck. "Thank God, it's you," she sobbed, holding him tight.

An owl's scream echoed in the distance and Little Elk stiffened.

She pulled back to look at him. "What is it, Little Elk?"

Little Elk swallowed hard. "Did you hear the *bu*, owl, screech?"

She nodded.

"You have heard my *nuhdee* tell many stories about many animals, but never the *bu*."

"No, I have never heard the owl mentioned," she agreed.

"It is because the *bu* is bad luck. The spirits of the dead rise from their graves and enter the body of the *dhoo*, bird. The hooting is the voices of their spirits speaking to us and threatening the living."

She placed a consoling hand on the young boy's arm. "It's all right. I'm sure the bad luck was meant for him," she said, gesturing to Ryan's body. "Not us. You have done nothing wrong. You saved my life."

"Then, you will forgive me for what happened with Running Doe?"

A smile trembled over her lips. "I never blamed you, Little Elk."

He looked around. "I see Proud Eagle's *chelee* but not him."

Crestfallen for her husband's plight, her smile faded. "He's on his way to the white lawman's fort, Little Elk, and if I don't go to him they will..." Her voice trailed off, the words too horrible to say.

"What can I do to help," Little Elk offered.

She paused. Her gaze wandered over Ryan Duffy's body. Then her face brightened. "I think I have a plan that might work. But first I need you to help me remove his breeches, boots, and gun belt."

Once Ryan Duffy was stripped, she gathered up the trousers, boots, holster, and gun, as well as the discarded shirt and jacket, and stuffed them into his horse's saddle bag.

Little Elk looked down at the half naked man. "I will drag his body into the bush. The *baya*, coyotes, will have a feast tonight."

She shuddered, even though Ryan Duffy got what he deserved.

"Take Blazing Fire back to the village, and tell Bear Watcher and White Dove what happened," she said.

Little Elk nodded in agreement. "And what about you, Golden Lady? What will you do?"

She grabbed for the reins and mounted the lieutenant's horse. "Now, I will go to find my husband."

****

Amanda rode at a steady pace back to the parsonage, not stopping for a moment in spite of her body crying out for rest. The sound of a horse's hoofs hitting the dirt brought her rigid in the saddle. She reached for the gun.

The figure of Josh Holmes sitting tall on his horse appeared from around a cluster of trees.

Her face broke into a smile. "I'm sure glad to see you!" She replaced the gun back into the holster.

He arched a brow, his voice deep and stern. "You frightened all of us to death. Your aunt and Grace are beside themselves with worry."

"Didn't you get the letter I left you?"

He waived a hand in the air, his voice cracking. "Aye, I got your letter. Did you believe it would suffice?" He brought his horse beside hers. "I've laid my feelings before you so many times, Amanda. Did you really think I would let you go?"

"Josh, listen—"

"Nay, you listen," he cut in. "You could have gotten yourself, and your baby, killed out here alone."

"Proud Eagle isn't dead," she blurted out.

His eyes widened. "What? What do you mean?" He noticed the horse she was riding. "Whose horse is this?"

"He's the lieutenant's."

"The lieutenant's?" he echoed, bewildered. "But how... where..."

"He's the one who is dead," she said. "Little Elk killed him just before Ryan tried to compromise and murder me."

Josh held up a hand. "Hold on a moment—you've lost me. Suppose you start from the beginning."

She explained how Ryan Duffy had followed her. That Proud Eagle had been taken to Fort Bayard, the execution on hold until the lieutenant arrived and her plan on how to save her husband's life.

Josh's voice rose an octave. "Do you realize the enormous risk you're asking us to take? Interfering in military procedure could get us hanged."

"I am in full understanding of the consequences, but it's the only way to save Proud Eagle." She searched his face. "Please, Josh, will you help me?"

"You must think me insane to consider—"

"He's the father of my baby," she broke in.

He arched a brow. "All right, Amanda, I'll help you." He folded his arms across his chest. "Explain to me again what I have to do."

She nodded. "But we ride while we talk. I can't afford to let any more time pass; it could mean the difference between life and death for Proud Eagle."

****

Josh knew a cut off to Fort Bayard, saving them time. They rode until dark. Amanda forced her body to stay upright in the saddle. When they stopped for the night, she dismounted the horse in blind exhaustion.

Josh made a fire and opened the lieutenant's bedroll, then handed her pieces of dried meat and bread, sitting with his share beside her.

Mesmerized by the flames, she ate, not really tasting the food.

"Why don't you lie down on the blanket, Amanda," he advised. "You look worn out, and we have a long way to ride tomorrow. In your present condition, you'll never make it if you don't rest now."

She nodded and complied in silence, the glorious state of sleep overtaking her soon after she closed her eyes. Throughout the night, she dreamt of her husband's warm embrace, keeping out the cold. When she opened her eyes she was enfolded in the comforting arms of Joshua Holmes. She sat up, rubbing the sleep from her eyes.

"I was just keeping you warm. You were shivering in your sleep."

She stood and searched the saddlebag for food. "I'd like to reach the fort by early tomorrow morning.

Do you think we can do that?"

He took a bite of the beef jerky she handed him. "It will take some tall riding. Are you up to so many hours in a saddle?"

"For pity sake, Josh, I'm expecting a baby not the plague." She reached for the saddle to hoist upon the horse.

"Here, let me do that," he demanded, assisting her. "The last thing we need is for you to miscarry. I'm not knowledgeable about such things, nor do I relish finding out, or having to sit by while you hemorrhage to death."

She nodded, standing aside and busying herself with raking a stick through the fire, making sure no hot cinders remained. *He is right. I haven't given much concern about taking care of myself.*

"Josh?"

He looked up from his task.

"I'll be more careful, I promise."

He nodded. "That's all I ask, Amanda." He offered her his hand and helped her up onto the horse. Then he mounted and turned his horse toward the path. "Shall we go?"

****

By noon of the second day, the fort loomed ahead of them.

"There it is, Amanda, Fort Bayard."

Her heart raced with a mixture of anxiety and anticipation. "You must change into the lieutenant's clothes and switch horses with me before we get any closer."

He motioned to a clump of trees. "Over there."

She followed, handing him the clothes, and moved to wait by the horses while he changed. When he reappeared, he was dressed as a soldier in the United States Cavalry.

She was astonished. "It fits you perfect; you look like a real lieutenant."

Josh mounted the lieutenant's horse. "Now, we can only hope the soldiers believe that as well."

She secured her hair atop her head, pulled the hat down over her ears, and then rubbed dirt all over her face and hands.

"Here," Josh said, handing her his vest. "This will cover your womanly endowments a bit better than just the shirt."

She buttoned the shirt to her neck, donned the vest, and mounted Josh's horse. "Are you ready Lieutenant Ryan Duffy?"

Josh straightened his shoulders. "Aye, I'm ready, boy."

The rode in silence to the fort's gate, halting in front of two soldiers on sentry duty. They saluted and opened the gate.

Josh returned their salute. "At ease, men."

One soldier teased her. "Hey, boy...when was the last time you had a bath?"

"We have been on the road for several days, private," Josh snapped. "Duty before all else, remember that."

"Yes, sir, sorry, sir," the private mumbled.

She waited until they were through the gate and out of ear shot to speak. "You play the part well. Let's hope I don't falter in mine."

"Just keep quiet and let me do all the talking. Oh, and one more thing, boy."

"What's that Lieutenant Duffy?"

"Try to remember not to sway so when you walk," he teased. "Though I've enjoyed it on other occasions, I can do without it this time. It would be a dead giveaway."

She saluted him like a soldier and disguised her voice in a deeper tone. "Yes, sir, I'll remember, sir. And here's a bit of advice for you, easy with the British accent."

Other military men saluted Josh as they rode

through the compound. They dismounted their horses and tied them to a hitching post in front of a small building marked *The Brig*. The words were painted in bold white letters and hung over the door on a cracked shingle.

Her nerves tensed upon entering the building. She pulled the brim of her hat farther over her brow and lowered her face.

The soldier sitting at a desk stood and saluted Josh. "Private Timothy Williams, sir."

"At ease, Private Williams," Josh said with authority. He cleared his throat and moved closer to the desk. "I'm Lieutenant Ryan Duffy." He reached into his jacket and threw the credentials he found in the pocket onto the desk.

Private Williams scanned the documents, nodded with satisfaction and handed the papers back to Josh. "What can I do for you, sir?"

"I had a prisoner—an Indian Chief sent here for execution. I captured him at Willow Creek. Have my orders been carried out?"

"No, sir, not yet, sir," the private said.

She let out the breath she'd been holding.

The private motioned to a barred door in the corner of the room. "He's being kept in that cell over there, sir." The young soldier cleared his throat. "Private Thomas, when he brought him in, said your orders were to stay execution until you arrived, or midnight tonight, whichever came first."

Josh nodded. "Well, it's good to know my men are listening to me." He crossed his arms over his chest. "But the fact is the orders have been changed."

"Changed, sir?" Private Williams rummaged through a stack of official looking papers. "I haven't received a notification of order change, sir."

Josh scowled. "Are you calling me a liar, Private Williams?"

The young officer swallowed hard, his face turning a deep shade of red. "Oh, no, sir. Never, sir."

"It's not my problem the papers got detained. I've got a job to do, and I'm trying to do it," Josh bellowed.

She thought he performed the military authority act quite well. Private Williams looked ready to cry at any moment.

"Yes, sir. Of course, sir." Private Williams combed a trembling hand through his sandy colored hair. "Pardon, sir, but maybe you'd be so kind as to bring me up to date?"

Josh scowled. "I have received orders from General Carleton himself to bring the Indian to Fort Lowell in Tucson."

Private Williams's brows furrowed. "Why at Lowell, sir?"

"My job's not to question orders, private," Josh snapped. "I just follow them. Something you might take a lesson in doing."

"Yes, sir. Sorry, sir." Private Williams cleared his throat again. "But to be honest, sir, I don't know if the prisoner is fit for travel."

"And why is that, Williams?"

The private shifted on his feet. "Well, when Private Thomas brought him in here, he was in pretty rough shape. And the army can't waste rations on a condemned man, so the Indian's only been allowed water...just to give him enough strength to walk to the gallows."

Her knees grew weak, and she gripped the edge of the desk to steady herself.

"But Private Thomas could better inform you as to what's what, sir. He's set to replace me in about an hour," Private Williams added.

Her heart sank to her toes. If Alexander Thomas saw them, all would be lost.

Josh got right up into the young private's face.

"If you ever want to be respected in the military, private, you can't be passing a situation off onto another soldier."

"Yes, sir, I understand, sir," Private Williams choked out.

Josh waved a disgusted hand in the air. "You're dismissed, Williams. I'll take over here until Thomas comes on duty. It'll give me time to look the situation over and construct a plan on how to best carry out my duties."

"Yes, sir. Thank you, sir," Private Williams saluted. "Good day to you, sir."

Josh returned the salute and Private Williams all but ran out the door.

She bit her bottom lip. "We've got to get Proud Eagle out of here before Alexander Thomas arrives."

"I know, but you heard what the private said, Amanda. Proud Eagle might not be fit to move."

"If he stays here, he'll be hanged." She walked over to the barred door. "We'll just have to take the chance he survives the journey. Right now that's the lesser of two evils."

"Aye," he agreed, unlocking the cell.

She gasped at the sight of her husband, bound and gagged. A gash across the back of his head matted his hair with dried blood. His back, bruised from the whipping in Willow Creek, was left bare to endure the dampness of the cell's dirt floor. The buckskin breeches were stained, the stench enough to make the strongest stomach retch.

She ran to Proud Eagle, falling to her knees beside him. She turned his head and caressed his face. "He's unconscious." She looked up at Josh. "You'll have to carry him to the horses." She stood. "I saw a knife on the desk; I'll get it to cut the ropes."

He reached out with a restraining hand. "Nay, leave him bound."

"But his hands are blue."

"It will look better to the guards at the gate if he's still tied up," Josh explained.

She nodded in agreement and stood aside while he lifted Proud Eagle onto his shoulder and carried him to the waiting horses.

Josh put Proud Eagle on his horse, and then mounted the lieutenant's, holding a hand out to her. She climbed up behind him, heart racing as they rode to the gate.

The soldier gave Josh a parting salute. "Good day, sir. Have a safe journey."

He returned the salute. "At ease, private, I'm sure from here on out it will be all down hill."

They waited until the fort was out of sight to pick up speed, cutting off the path through the wilderness, to Proud Eagle's village. A few yards farther they stopped to cut the ropes binding Proud Eagle's wrists and ankles.

Josh brought the horses by a small spring that ran through a secluded clump of trees. "We'll camp here until morning. Proud Eagle is in need of some care before we dare take him farther."

He lifted Proud Eagle from the horse and placed him on the bank.

She rubbed the circulation back into her husband's hands, biting back the tears threatening to come. She couldn't fall apart now, her husband needed her.

Josh slipped off Proud Eagle's moccasins and removed the breeches.

She scooped up a handful of mud, and applied it to Proud Eagle's naked body, cleansing every part of him with the mire.

Josh watched. "I am in admiration of your love for him, the way you gently scrub the dried blood, filth, and stench from his body." He sighed. "I'm realizing you'd never look at me the way you look at him, Amanda."

She remained silent to his words, continuing to care for her husband. When she had finished with the scrubbing, Josh lifted Proud Eagle into the water, where the two of them rinsed his mud smeared, battered and bruised body clean, dunking his head to wash his hair.

Proud Eagle regained consciousness. His eyes flew open in terror. Hot, strangled lungs struggled for breath. He choked on the air he gulped and with every ounce of strength he could muster, swung with a fisted hand. His blow caught the boy standing to his right across the face and knocked him into the water.

He shook his head to clear it, leveling his focus on the white lawman holding his hands up in surrender and coming toward him. Proud Eagle wondered where the others were. Had they gathered to drown him in the creek? His heart pounded, his nerves raw, he had to fight for his life. He crouched, ready to attack.

The white lawman was speaking to him, but the pounding in his head blocked out the words. He didn't care anyway what words the enemy spoke. If he could rid himself of this one, he might have a chance to escape. He lunged forward and knocked the soldier on his back. Not giving the lieutenant time to react, he went for his throat, wrapping his hands around his neck and squeezing.

"No," the young boy screamed, running to pry his fingers from around the soldier's throat. "Stop, Proud Eagle!"

He turned his gaze to the boy, shocked to hear his name.

The boy shook him by the shoulders. "Proud Eagle, please stop! It's Josh, the holy man you're strangling. The holy man, not the lieutenant!"

Confused, he focused his eyes on the boy's face, straining to acknowledge the words.

The boy ripped the hat from his head, liberating the hair stuffed beneath the brim. Golden curls fell in disarray past the shoulders. "It's me! Golden Lady!"

He released his hold on the holy man's throat and stumbled back.

The reverend stood, coughing and sputtering.

Golden Lady ran to the holy man. "Are you all right?"

He nodded, holding up his hand. "I'm fine—fine," he choked out.

She moved closer to Proud Eagle, her eyes brimming with tears. "You're safe now, my *shikaa*."

He fell to his knees, tears trickling down his face, and raised his arms, holding them out to her.

His wife walked into his embrace.

He wrapped his arms around her legs and buried his face in her belly.

She stroked his hair, their bodies rocking with the intensity of his sobs. Her soft voice soothed him. "All is well now, my *shikaa*. I am with you, and you're safe."

****

Proud Eagle, wearing Josh's black breeches and a blanket draped over his shoulders, sat against a tree and consumed a piece of dried meat.

Amanda sat beside him. "Take it slow," she warned. "You have not eaten much in days."

Her own clothes, wet and clinging to her body, chilled her. She shivered.

Proud Eagle noticed. "You are cold *shi'aad*?" He leaned forward and removed the blanket from his shoulders. "Here, take this."

"I'm fine, Proud Eagle. You keep the blanket; it will protect your wounds from the dirt."

"Here, Amanda," Josh broke in, handing her another blanket. "Remove those wet garments before you catch your death." He turned to leave. "I'll

301

gather kindling so we'll have the warmth of a fire, and give you privacy."

When she was sure Josh was out of sight, she stripped off the wet clothes and hung them on a tree branch.

Proud Eagle watched her from where he sat, smiling. "I had almost forgotten what a pleasure it is to watch you undress, standing naked before my eyes." Squinting, he turned his head sideways to study her. "Is it that I have been away too long, or is there something different about you, *shi'aad?*"

She wrapped the blanket around her cold flesh and sat beside him. "What seems different?"

He drew her close, and opened the blanket, studying her further. "There is more here," he said, caressing her breast.

Her flesh warmed where he touched, nipples growing erect with the tender brush of his hand.

He moved down to touch her belly. "And it is rounder here." He lifted his gaze, searching her face. "Do my eyes play tricks on me, *shi'aad?*"

"No, you still hold the keen eye of an eagle and the sharp instincts of a warrior."

He sighed exasperated. "What good is any of it if it leads me halfway?"

She nuzzled close to him. "Think, my *shikaa.*" She reached for his hand and placed it over one breast. "What would make a woman's breast's grow heavier?" She moved his hand to rest upon her abdomen. "Or swell her belly?"

He studied her again. Then his eyes brightened with recognition, a broad smile curving his lips. "If she were growing her husband's seed beneath her *biijii?*"

She nodded. "And I am."

His eyes grew moist, and he gathered her into his arms. "At last we will have a family."

"I'm so glad I've finally pleased you."

He pulled back to look at her. "You have always pleased me, *shi'aad*, from the first time I woke and found you beside me in your father's bed. I knew then I would make you mine." He traced her lips with the tip of a finger. "*Wo'ina.*"

****

Proud Eagle held her in his arms while she slept, the fire warming them against the night's chill. He glanced over at the holy man resting on his saddlebag, looking up at the star-filled sky.

"Why did you help me?" he said in a low voice, not to wake his wife.

The holy man turned to face him. "I promised her I'd always be there for her, no matter what the circumstance. I just kept my word."

"Did you not think with me gone, she could be yours?"

"Aye, many times."

"And still you helped. Why?"

The white man rolled onto his side, propping his chin upon a hand. "Because I love her, and when you love someone you want their happiness. You make her happy."

He arched a brow. "It angers me at times when the love for her shows on your face."

The holy man sat, staring into the flames. "You have nothing to be angry over. Amanda loves only you and has been true to you right along."

"What of the night she spent with the white lawman?"

He lifted his gaze. "Ryan Duffy thought far too much of himself. The truth is Amanda filled him with liquor then left him in a drunken sleep before the swine could even get his breeches down. I stripped him naked so he'd believe just what he did."

"He showed me the lacy piece of clothing white women wear beneath the dress. It was hers, smelled of her scent. How did he get this?"

"Your wife is a very smart woman. She left the petticoat on purpose so there'd be no doubt in the lieutenant's mind something happened between them."

"But why?" Proud Eagle probed.

"She planned the whole charade to gain his favor, so she could bargain for your release."

"He would never have set me free."

"She was grasping at anything that appeared hopeful, Proud Eagle, desperate to save you anyway she could," the holy man explained. "There's more you should know." He went on to tell of the danger his tribe faced and what he had read in the newspapers.

In silence he listened, his heart sickening. The holy man recounted the lieutenant's letter and his wife's refusal to believe he was dead. Proud Eagle's heart burst with pride, hearing she traveled alone to find out the truth and that Little Elk came to Golden Lady's rescue.

The holy man leaned forward to put more wood on the fire. "When we all thought the lieutenant had executed you, I begged her to marry me. I wanted to take care of her and the child. But she insisted your baby had the right to your heritage and decided she'd continue to live with your people. She made it clear she considered them her family."

He smiled with pride. "She is a true Apache woman."

"That might be true for many things, but she still holds sacred the traditions of her own people." He met Proud Eagle's gaze. "In our laws you are not married to her, and after she bears your child this will bother her."

His voice hardened. "Have I not done right by her all this time?"

"Aye, so far, you have. I must admit you've done an amazing job at making her happy and content,

304

caring for her needs and providing her a home. But there is a lifetime ahead and at times there is more than love shared by two people. If you cannot honor her ways, as she's done yours, she will grow resentful. If that day should come, and she leaves you, my door will be open. By my law she has never been married."

His set his jaw in a stubborn line. "I respect you for all you have done, holy man. You are a wise and good man, and I owe you my life. But Golden Lady is very much married, and now carries my baby deep inside her. I almost lost my life just to be near her, do you truly believe I would be so foolish as to make her want to leave me?" He looked down at his wife sleeping in his arms and drew the blanket up around her shoulders. "But I will remember all that you have spoken. You have my word."

****

The next day's ride brought them to the fork in the road where they'd part. In spite of being anxious to get home, a pang of sorrow pierced Amanda's heart at saying good-bye to Josh. Tears of gratitude filled her eyes. "I never can repay you for all you've done, nor can I find the words to express my heartfelt thanks."

Josh smiled. "There is no need for any words. The happiness I've seen in your eyes has been my reward." He tipped his hat. "God be with you both."

She inclined her head. "And also with you."

"*Ka Dish Day*, farewell," Proud Eagle said. "And may we live to meet again."

She smiled to herself. Her husband meant it.

Chapter Fifteen

The rest of spring and into summer Amanda found herself busy with preparations for the baby. Rising Sun showed her how to make a cradleboard using split wood. She scraped the wood until it was smooth, and then bent long willow switches or limbs to make the frame. She secured the ends of the flexible branches to form the bed of the cradle and covered it with buckskin. At the head, another elongated loop was secured at a right angle to form a canopy, which was also covered with buckskin to protect the infant from the rain and sun. Another cloth or blanket could be laid over this for additional protection. Laces of buckskin strips or cloth bands would keep the child from falling out, and a carrying strap was attached. This was so she could carry the baby on her back, leaving her hands free for daily chores.

Proud Eagle didn't leave her side, and as the end of summer approached, she found sitting on the floor impossible to achieve alone. Standing up was even worse.

"I'm so tired, and yet, sleeping is so difficult. The wickiup is hot and stuffy, and either you've gotten bigger or the bed's smaller," she complained while he helped her off with her clothes.

"It is you who have gotten bigger, *shi'aad*," he teased.

She was eased onto the bed by his strong, gentle hands. "I'm as big as an overstuffed bear."

He laughed, rubbing her swollen belly. "Soon the baby will come, and you will be a slender doe again."

She yawned. "That can't happen soon enough."

He knelt beside the bed and stroked her cheek. "I have spoken with the midwife, and she has said your time is near. Tomorrow I will take you to Shaman Gray Fox's wickiup."

"Why must I go to see him?"

"There is a ceremony traditional before the birth. Sacred pollen will be sprinkled around you, and the shaman will chant to the gods," he explained. "Then I will place a belt made of the skins from the white-tailed and black-tailed deer, the mountain lion, and the antelope around your hips."

She made a face, remembering the belt around Rising Sun's swollen belly when she gave birth. "And I suppose I'm going to have to wear this belt till the baby is born?"

He tweaked the tip of her nose. "It is for your own good. These animals are believed to give birth to their young without great pain. Wearing the belt till after the birth will help you do the same."

She arched a brow. "Rising Sun wore the belt, and she still had pain."

He helped her onto her side, placing a rolled blanket between her knees and one beneath her head. "You must wear it day and night, only removing it to bathe." He shrugged. "It could be my sister did not do this."

She agreed. "Very well...but I'm not holding much hope it will help."

❦❦❦❦

Amanda didn't need to wear the belt long. Two nights later she woke to the walls of the wickiup closing in on her. She struggled for air, awakening Proud Eagle. He helped her to stand, rubbing her back to help her catch her breath.

He pulled on his breeches and draped a blanket around her naked form. "I will help you outside, for air."

She nodded and waddled out of the wickiup, thankful there was a slight breeze. She raised her face to let it cool her cheeks. He helped her lean back against a tree, and soon she was breathing easier.

"Do you wish to sit?" he offered.

She shook her head. "Standing is better."

He sat on a nearby rock, facing her.

She drew an audible breath, the night sounds bringing her peace. Her gaze wandered across the sky, lit with stars that twinkled like small, bright lights.

"Such a beautiful ni—" the words caught in her throat with the pressure that built at the bottom of her belly. There was a snap deep inside and then a *whoosh*, and a gush of water poured from her.

He watched the puddle form between her legs. "If you had to go—" He clipped his words, his eyes widening. "You did not—"

"No, I didn't...that's a sign the baby's coming," she interjected.

He jumped to his feet, picked her up in his strong arms, and carried her back to the wickiup.

He laid her on the bed and knelt beside her. "I will go for the midwife."

A sharp pain ripped through her. "Oh, Proud Eagle, I don't think this belt is working. It hurts."

He rubbed her hand. "Try to call upon the warrior's way. Think of something other than the pain, while I get the midwife."

She reached for his hand. "No, don't leave me." Another pain shot through her, and she clenched her jaw.

His voice trembled. "Just long enough to get the midwife, and then I will be with you. You have my word."

She released his hand. "Hurry, then."

He nodded, making his way to the door opening.

Another pain assailed her. "Oh, hurry...please,

Proud Eagle," she called after him.

****

Proud Eagle did not know when his feet carried him so fast, but they did not stop until they took him through the door opening of the midwife's wickiup. "Come," he shouted, scaring the poor woman from her bed. "It is time for my wife to give birth."

She rose, slipping a buckskin dress over her naked, wrinkled form.

He turned away to give her privacy. "Please, hurry."

The midwife took her time slipping on her moccasins. "There is time, Proud Eagle. The first one always takes long in coming."

They walked back to his wickiup, the midwife's steps slow.

He grew annoyed. "Can you not go faster?"

The woman sighed. "I am an old woman, Proud Eagle. If I fall, and strike my head upon a rock, who will help your wife then?"

He reached for her. "Let me just pick you up and carry you."

She halted and turned to him, pointing a bony finger. "You keep your hands to yourself." Again she walked on, slow and steady. "If you really want to save time, go get White Dove and Rising Sun to help."

"I will help."

"It is not allowed," she shot back, her fragile body blocking the entrance to the wickiup. "You must go somewhere and speak to the gods for the baby to come safely."

The muscles at his jaw throbbed. "I will speak to them beside my wife."

The midwife folded her arms across her chest. "It is not allowed. Now go."

He ground the words out between his teeth. "I am the chief, I say it is allowed."

The old woman threw her hands up in frustration and walked into the wickiup.

His wife lay in intense pain on the bed.

He ran to her, pushing aside the golden curls that clung to her neck. "What can I do?"

"Help her to stand," the midwife demanded.

He helped Golden Lady to her feet, whispering in her ear. "I will not leave you."

The midwife knelt in front of her and felt between her thighs.

She groaned and laid her head back against his chest.

"You have hurt her doing that, old woman," he snapped.

The midwife stood, again admonishing him with a pointed finger. "You keep your tongue silent, or I will find a few warriors to help you pass this night the way you should." Her eyes gleamed with wisdom. "You forget I helped you fall from your mother." She sighed. "You must trust me. I will not hurt your woman or your child."

Golden Lady's body stiffened, another pain consumed her.

His voice was rough with anxiety. "Do something for her pain, old woman."

The midwife shook her head. "There is nothing I can do." She pointed to the belt around Golden Lady's waist. "The belt will help."

"But it is not," he said.

The midwife shrugged. "It is the way of things, Proud Eagle. If you cannot take her pain, then I will get White Dove to help."

"No, I will stay to help," he insisted.

The midwife made her way to the jug and wet a cloth. "But I see much anguish in your face."

"Never mind what you see in my face, just help my wife."

The midwife swabbed Golden Lady's face, neck

and breasts. "All will be fine, child."

She trembled in his arms. "My legs. They are so weak, I think my bones have turned to dust."

His voice cracked with emotion. "I have you, *shi'aad*, you will not fall."

The midwife grunted. "Ah, the brave warrior—he can hunt a wild beast but is sick at the sight of his wife's pain." The old woman locked her gaze with his. "Watch her well, Chief. She will suffer much on this night to give your child life." Narrowing her eyes she spoke in a softer tone. "It is wise, after all, for you to see how your seed will so painfully come out." She clicked her tongue. "You are young. Know nothing of life."

He arched a brow. "I know I want my wife's pain to stop."

The midwife placed her hands on her hips. "And who do you think you are?"

Golden Lady released a hoarse laugh through her pain. "Santa Claus."

The confused expression on the midwife's face made him laugh too.

But in the next breath his wife choked out. "Please, can I have a sip of water?"

The midwife helped Golden Lady to take a drink.

Again her head fell back against his strength, and he held her close.

The midwife knelt and probed between Golden Lady's thighs. "She has time yet. Lay her down to rest."

He placed her on the bed, wiping her face and neck with a wet cloth. She reached for his hand and squeezed, another pain sliced through her. Then she lay limp with exhaustion, breathing hard from the intense agony she endured.

"Set your sight on my spear that stands in the corner, *shi'aad*, and let everything else go away," he coaxed. "Center your thoughts on its color and shape, and then move away from the pain."

"With this pain it's not that easy," she said in a choked voice.

Throughout the night the pain worsened, coming faster and harder. He watched, helpless to do anything but cool her flesh with a damp cloth and soothe her with his voice.

Hours later, he woke to find himself in a half-sitting, half-lying position beside the bed. He blinked his eyes into focus.

"You fell asleep," the midwife said. She had moved Golden Lady onto her side and was rubbing her back.

He stood and stretched. "Why did you not wake me?"

The old woman's hands moved to massage Golden Lady's lower back and thighs. "Your wife would not let me. She said it was best you slept." The midwife grunted. "She is worried for you while she is in so much pain."

Guilt burned his cheeks. He stilled the midwife's hands. "I will rub her."

She nodded in agreement and backed away, sitting beside the bed. "It will not be long now."

While his wife slept, he went outside for a breath of air, and watched the pinks and oranges of a new day light the sky. His own body was engulfed in tides of weariness, crying out for rest. But nothing measured her exhaustion. Fatigue settled in the pockets under her eyes.

Her scream was an affront to the quiet village, shaking his moment of silence. He ran back into the wickiup.

"Get her on her feet," the midwife demanded.

He obeyed.

The midwife felt between Golden Lady's legs. "I feel the head."

She stiffened and gripped Proud Eagle's arm. "Oh, please, let this be over."

"Crouch and push, Golden Lady," the midwife instructed.

"I'm tired," she moaned.

"You can do this, *shi'aad*," he whispered. "You have done well, and it will soon be over, then you will hold our baby close to your breast."

"If you do as I say, all will be fine," the midwife said. "Now, open your legs wider and when you get the pain, push."

She nodded, spread her legs and crouched.

His arms trembled holding her. His every nerve throbbed.

She pushed, her face turning red, purple veins bulging on her neck and temple. He worried the blue lines would burst with her torment.

The midwife went down on her knees, arms outstretched to catch the baby. "Push again."

Blood and water poured from his wife's loins, causing his own heart to thump like wild horses in his chest.

Golden Lady took a deep breath and pushed harder, her groan rising to a scream, so shrill it pierced his ears.

His voice shook with compassion, his heart aching for all she endured. "Soon, *shi'aad*, it will be over."

A flame of pain ran up Amanda's back and down her legs. The agony penetrated her body and tore her apart. Wider and wider she stretched, pushing her child from her womb. The sobs that rose from her throat made her husband's arms shiver around her.

One last hurt flashed through her, and she strained to give her child life.

The midwife gripped the child's head, pulling the babe from her.

She was drained, hollowed, falling limp against her husband's chest.

Proud Eagle breathed a sigh of relief, gathered her up and laid her upon the bed. "*Hidisho*, it is finished."

In spite of the weariness that enveloped her, she fought to stay alert, concentrating on the sound of her baby's cry. She took a cleansing breath. "What is my child?"

"A boy," the midwife announced. "He is strong, *inju*. Good color is in his face."

She turned her tired eyes to Proud Eagle. Tears streamed down his face. She reached for his hand, pulling him down on his knees beside the bed. "You have your son, my *shikaa*."

"*Ashoge*, thank you," he whispered, bestowing a tender kiss upon her lips. "*Wo'ina*."

The midwife washed the baby by squirting him with water she had warmed in her mouth, and then rubbed the child dry with grass, soft moss, and a cloth. The old woman blew on the child's body, sprinkled him with cattail-pollen, and wrapped him in a blanket, placing him in the cradleboard padded with moss and cloth.

Proud Eagle went for the shaman, who sprinkled more pollen on Amanda and the baby while chanting a song of thanks to the gods for a safe delivery.

"You rest now," the midwife advised.

"Thank you," she said, taking the old woman's hand and squeezing it. "Thank you for everything."

Well-wishers came by throughout the day, bringing food and marveling over the baby. At nightfall drums could be heard beating in the distance, announcing the birth of the Chief's son.

Proud Eagle lay beside her, watching in awe his tiny boy taking his meal from her breast. "We have the greatest baby."

She laughed. "I'm sure all parents think as you do."

He laid his head back on a rolled blanket. "He took long enough to come."

She sighed. "He's worth all the pain."

He yawned and closed his eyes. "I am sorry the belt did not help."

She heard him snore and smiled to herself, snuggling beside him. "Sleep, my *shikaa*," she whispered. "You've had a hard day."

****

The medicine sing ceremony was held to name the baby. The shaman rattled gourds and chanted prayers while sprinkling pollen and herbs about for good fortune.

"He will be called Golden Eagle," Proud Eagle announced, pride swelling his heart for the babe. Everything about his tiny son was perfect, and his name—a combination of both his parents, fit him well. The deep blue of his huge, round eyes and full lips were like his mother's. His nose and chin came from Proud Eagle. And his hair was dark, with a sweep of gold at his right temple.

"He has been kissed by lightning, like my father, Little Lightning Bear," White Dove commented, touching the baby's tiny foot. "He even has the same half moon mark on his ankle. Proud Eagle has one like his grandfather on a thigh."

Pride swelled his heart as he held Golden Eagle, telling him stories each night. He put a large finger into the baby's tiny palm. "He has a strong grip. I will enjoy teaching him the ways of an Apache warrior." He kissed his son's soft head. "The golden eagle is the symbol for masculinity, heroism, and spirit of the sun. He will be the best of the tribe."

"No one could be as good as you, my *shikaa*," Golden Lady said, taking the baby from his arms and bringing him to her breast.

"But one day I will grow old, like my father, and Golden Eagle will take over, as I have done. He must be the best." He watched Golden Eagle's mouth work upon his mother's nipple. "Someday he will be chief."

Golden Lady looked down at her son and caressed the soft flesh of his cheek while he took his nourishment. "Right now all he's concerned with is filling his belly." She tightened her hold on the baby. "Besides, I don't want him to learn to fight before it's necessary."

He chuckled, raising his gaze to hers. "Ah, already the mother lion protects her cub."

She said nothing in response to his remark and cast her gaze to the fire pit, mesmerized by the flames.

He knew that far away look all too well. "What troubles you, *shi'aad?*"

She sighed. "Oh, I was just thinking of my parents and your father. How they won't have the chance to know our son—to watch him grow."

His voice saddened. "I have thought of my father many times since the baby's birth."

She glanced over at him. "Our son has an Apache name to carry on your heritage, but not a Christian name to represent mine."

The holy man's words replayed in his mind. *One day she will resent you for never sharing her traditions.* He touched her face with a soft caress. "I have read in your holy book of a naming ceremony."

She nodded. "It's called Baptism, whereby water is sprinkled on the child's head to bless him, and he's given a name from the Bible, or of someone we once loved that has passed on."

"The Apache believe it is bad luck to name a child after one who has gone from this earth."

"Yes, we must not do anything to bring us bad luck." Her voice held a note of sarcasm.

Her tone upset him. He took her hand and

316

searched her face. "If the Baptism ceremony means as much to you as the medicine sing meant to me, it is only right it be done."

"But we need Josh to perform the ceremony," she said.

"I will go for the holy man and bring him back to the village so he can sprinkle the water and do the blessing."

She bit her bottom lip. "I'm not sure that's a good idea, my *shikaa*. Remember the last time you went to Willow Creek and Lieutenant Duffy."

His body stiffened with anger hearing the name. "I will never forget Duffy." He was silent for a moment, to compose the raw emotions that now consumed him. "But it is the only way to get the holy man." He forced a reassuring smile. "I will use my head this time, stick to the heavy brush, and then there is nothing for you to fear." He moved his hand to caress her hip, giving it a playful pinch. "Only that I might lose my will power and forget I cannot touch you just yet."

Her eyes twinkled. "Would a kiss make it worse or better?"

"It will not keep my flesh from wanting you, but never would I turn away one of your kisses." He brought his mouth to hers, her response making his desire mount.

She broke the kiss. "I don't know who is tormented more, you or me."

He laughed and motioned to the mats by the fire. "Then let us sit and fill our heads with other thoughts." He took the sleeping baby from her arms and placed him in the cradleboard.

She moved to take a place by the fire. "How about we decide on a Christian name for our son?"

He plopped down beside her. "I would want one to bring him respect."

"My father knew about eagle symbols as well.

317

The golden eagle is also called a heavenly messenger. In the Bible, Gabriel, the messenger angel, brought the news to Mary she'd give birth to a special child."

He spoke aloud the name. "Gabriel Golden Eagle." Smiling, satisfied he added, "That is the name we will choose for our *ciye*, that of the messenger, the divine spirit."

"I like it too," she agreed, resting her head on his shoulder. "It's a special name for a special child, who has the heritage of both our familys' blood running through his body. Perhaps, as a man, he will be the messenger of peace to both of our people."

"He is born of proud blood. He will be proud of both his parents' ways. And come dawn, I will go for the holy man."

****

Proud Eagle rode with caution, not only the white lawmen roamed the land, but the Chiricahua were troublesome as well. Some of the hostile warriors challenged those of his tribe, coming too near the village. He set up his men to watch at night, and some of the women stood guard during the day.

He took the familiar path to the holy man's home and knocked on the back door. It was Grace who welcomed him inside. This time she did not faint.

"I figured ya'd be a comin' this way sooner or later." She cast him a sideways glance. "What'd she have?"

"We have a *ciye*, a son." He couldn't contain his pride.

Grace slapped him on the shoulder. "Well, congratulations, Chief. And the babe is healthy?"

He nodded. "Already, he is strong."

"And Amanda?" Josh's voice came from behind. "How is she?"

He turned to face the holy man. "She is well. I was with her through the birth." He frowned with the memory of what his wife endured. "There was much pain."

Grace took an audible breath. "Ya watched her give birth?"

He nodded. "It is what we wanted, to bring our child into this life together." His voice dropped in volume. "Watching her pain drove me sick, but I held her, and my words comforted her. She was pleased I stayed with her."

"Well, I'll be, if that doesn't beat all," Grace declared. "Were ya pleased ya stayed with her?"

"Yes, I learned of the pain women bear to give their husband's seed life." He sighed. "I will never forget it."

Grace chuckled. "My ma always said if the woman had the first baby, and the husband could have the second, there would never be a third."

He cringed with the thought of his body trying to give birth. "Your mother was a wise woman."

The holy man moved closer, giving Proud Eagle a pat on the back. "Your love for her is honest and true, and you've proven to me you are a good man, a man of your word."

"That is why I have come. I have given her my word I would bring you back to the village to do the baptism ceremony."

"Whatcha gonna name him?" Grace asked.

"Gabriel Golden Eagle," he said.

"My, my," Grace murmured. "A mighty big name for such a tiny fella."

He smiled. "Ah, that might be true now, but one day he will be a powerful chief. His name must match his wisdom and courage."

"Do you know who Gabriel is?" the holy man questioned.

He nodded. "He is your god's heavenly

messenger."

"I'm quite impressed."

"I gave you my word I would share in her ways," he said.

"Aye, you did at that." The holy man smiled. "Then let's waste no more time here. I'll fetch my Bible and a few other things I'll need, and we can be on our way." He hesitated. "Would you mind if I brought along my friend Benjamin, another holy man?"

He shrugged. "If he is a friend of yours, he will be welcomed."

"While the reverend gets his gear packed, ya come with me," Grace ordered, pulling him by the sleeve of his tunic into the kitchen. "Sit," she said, pointing to a chair.

He obeyed and watched her pour them each a drink from a tin pot with a spout.

"Here," she said, handing him a cup of the steaming brew. "It's hot, so sip it slow."

He nodded and tasted the drink, making a face at its sour flavor.

Grace stifled a smile at his expression. "I like to put lots of lemon in my tea." She took a seat facing him. "Now, Chief, suppose ya tell me all about that there son of yers."

Chapter Sixteen

Amanda smiled at White Dove, holding her grandson in her arms. "Go, my daughter, and prepare a corner of your wickiup for the holy man." She kissed the baby. "And let an old woman enjoy her grandson for a while."

"He's already been fed, so he should sleep," she said.

White Dove rocked the baby. "I still remember how to comfort a crying child." She gestured to the door opening. "Go, and do not worry. Finish your work in peace."

Amanda left and went to her wickiup, clearing a corner for Josh to sleep. She padded the ground with many layers of blankets, and then fastened more blankets around poles, shielding his area from their bed to ensure everyone's privacy. She shook out the mats, arranged the pots and jugs in an orderly fashion next to the grinding slab, and brought in the wood for the evening fire. While stacking the wood beside the pit, she knocked over Proud Eagle's hunting weapons that stood in the corner. Arrows fell from the deerskin pouch. She replaced them, but they didn't fit properly. Something at the bottom of the pouch obstructed her from stacking them in a row. Growing annoyed, she removed the arrows and turned the quiver upside down. An object fell to the ground. There, between her feet, lay her father's knife with the abalone chips inlaid in the handle.

She retrieved the knife and turned it over in her hand, shocked to see the heirloom again, and of all places, in her husband's arrow pouch. How did

Proud Eagle have the knife? Her father was carrying the small blade the day the Chiricahua—"Oh, God, please, no," she whispered. "Don't let my husband be the one."

Her mind swam in confusion. She dropped the knife and ran from the wickiup, not stopping till she reached the river. Falling to her knees, she splashed cold water on her face. River water, mixed with the uncontrollable tears, moistened her cheeks. She hung her head and sobbed, her heart breaking in two. Had Proud Eagle lied to her? And if so... God help her, she married the man who murdered her father.

"Golden Lady," a voice came from behind.

She sprang to her feet, turning around to find Running Doe standing by a tree. She wiped her tears with the backs of her hands.

"Your dog is wounded," Running Doe said, pointing to a coppice of trees. "He lies over there, beyond the brush."

"Duke. Here boy," she called.

Running Doe stepped closer and took her by the hand. "He is unable to come to you, he has lost much blood and cannot walk, and I cannot lift him alone."

She pulled her hand free. "I'll find Falling Star to help."

"That would take too much time, he guards the village to the north, and if you do not hurry your dog will die." Running Doe reached for her arm. "Come, I will show you."

She allowed the woman to lead her into the thicket. She searched for Duke. "I don't see him, Running Doe."

A Chiricahua warrior leaped out in front of her, wearing the traditional red war paint across his face, beads of coral and turquoise adorning his wrists and neck. He aimed an arrow, no doubt tipped with poison, at her chest.

"At last we meet, golden one," he scoffed.

She was shocked he spoke her language.

"Go, Running Doe! Run!" she said, backing away.

The Chiricahua lunged at her, grabbing a fistful of her hair, pulling her to the ground.

"Warn the others!" she screamed.

Running Doe didn't move. "There is no need, Golden Lady, to warn anyone. It is you the Chricahua want. It is why they bother us and have come so near."

"You little fool, don't you see what you've done allowing them to actually come into our village?"

"My village!" Running Doe shrieked. "You are the intruder and have never belonged here. With you gone, I will be the next wife of the chief."

Her anger flared. "How could you be so stupid? Don't you realize Proud Eagle will come looking for me?"

The Chiricahua warrior wrenched her neck back. "He will not find you, white woman. You belong to me. I will *zas'tee*, kill your chief."

"No," Running Doe said. "You gave me your word no one in my tribe would be harmed if I brought you her."

"And you believed him?" Amanda shot back. "Do you think the Chiricahua will care about the village after they've captured me? And when Proud Eagle comes looking for me, he could get killed too."

Running Doe walked over to her, reached down and yanked from her throat the chain that held her parents' wedding bands. "I will tell Proud Eagle I found this by the river." Running Doe's black eyes blazed with revenge. "The last remains of one who drowned. In believing you are dead, he will have no reason to search for you." She threw her head back and laughed like a crazy woman. "I hope you suffer much the tortures they give, and all through your pain, hold this in your thoughts. I will be comforting Proud Eagle and taking care of his son."

Running Doe turned to leave, but another Chiricahua walked from the trees. He raised his weapon and shot an arrow through her back. The buckskin tunic soaked with blood, and Running Doe fell to the ground.

The warrior holding Amanda yanked her to her feet by the hair. She kicked him in the shins and scratched him down the left side of his face. Blood oozed from the wound.

His eyes flashed with his rage, and he slammed his fist against the side of her head.

The pain from the blow brought tears to her eyes. She choked for air, her arms and legs numb, and limp as a rag doll's, fell to her side. And a veil of darkness consumed her.

****

It was nearing nightfall when Proud Eagle rode into the village with the two holy men. He sprang down from his horse and hurried ahead of the others to meet his mother.

She rushed from her small wickiup, her face tight with worry. "Oh, my *ciye*, thank the gods you have finally returned."

He took his mother's hands in his. "What troubles you, *shemaa*?"

White Dove's eyes welled with tears. "Golden Lady is nowhere to be found."

His stomach clenched. "Tell me all that has happened."

White Dove took a moment to collect herself. "I took the baby to give Golden Lady time to get ready for the holy man's visit."

"And where is my son now?"

"Rising Sun has him. He hungered, and when his mother couldn't be found Rising Sun offered to feed him."

He nodded. "This is good. Rising Sun will take care of him till we find my wife."

"When and where was the last time anyone saw her," the holy man broke in.

White Dove pulled her shaking hands free from his grasp and wrung them. "The midwife saw her at mid-day, by the river. She said Golden Lady was crying."

The holy man's eyes darkened. "Did the midwife bother to find out why Amanda was crying?"

White Dove's voice trembled. "She had no time to stop and ask. She was on her way to Wind Hawk's wickiup. It was his wife's time to give birth."

Proud Eagle's nerves tensed. "And no one has seen her since?"

White Dove swallowed hard. "No. No one, my son."

The holy man ran a hand through his hair. "I don't like the sound of this, Proud Eagle."

"Ah, I know what you feel. Golden Lady would never miss our son's feeding time or leave the village alone, unless..." He paused, a disturbing thought raced through his mind.

"Unless what?" the holy man interjected.

He turned back to his mother. "Has anyone seen Running Doe?"

White Dove clutched her heart. "No. Bear Watcher was looking for her just before you arrived." Her eyes widened. "You do not think..." Her voice trailed off.

His voice hardened. "I hope I am wrong, *shemaa*."

White Dove's voice rose an octave. "What now, Proud Eagle?"

"Find Falling Star and Bear Watcher. Send them to my wickiup," he instructed. He turned to the holy man. "It is best if you and the young holy man go with my mother, there could be much danger."

The holy man countered icily. "Well, that never stopped me before. If Amanda's in trouble, I'm going to help you find her."

He looked over at the other white man. "The young holy man is not wise to the ways of this land. If he cannot keep up with us, he will make us lose time."

"Yaw, he is right, Josh," the younger man agreed. He turned to Proud Eagle. "I vill stay vith your mother. She is very upset, and perhaps I can help vith the baby."

Proud Eagle nodded and motioned to the other man. "Come, holy man, to my wickiup."

He looked around his home, hawk-like eyes taking inventory, hoping somehow to find a clue to his wife's strange departure. A shiny object on the ground near his arrows caught his eye. He picked up the tiny knife, rolling it in the palm of his hand. "Nothing here seems out of place, except for my knife being on the ground. It must have fallen from the deerskin pouch."

The holy man extended a hand. "May I see it?"

Proud Eagle nodded and handed him the small blade.

The other man's eyes widened. "Where did you find this knife?"

He motioned to the corner. "On the ground, by my arrows. It must have fallen out of the sack."

"Then this belongs to you?"

He nodded.

The holy man's accusing voice stabbed the air. "How did you come by this knife, Proud Eagle?"

Proud Eagle cast him a black layered look and ripped the knife from his hand, putting it in the pouch he wore at his waist. "There is no time to worry over this knife."

"Oh, I beg to differ. This knife once belonged to—" His sharp retort was interrupted by a voice at the door opening.

"Proud Eagle, can we enter?" Falling Star called.

He raised the flap, gesturing for Falling Star to come in. "*Skee'kizzen*, welcome, brother."

Bear Watcher followed close behind. "White Dove said she has not seen Golden Lady since midday."

He nodded. "We are all worried. This is not like my wife to be gone from the village alone."

Bear Watcher's brows furrowed. "I know what is in all of your thoughts. Running Doe has something to do with Golden Lady's disappearance." He took an audible breath. "Last I looked for my daughter, she was standing guard to the east of the village. But now I cannot find her as well."

"We all know how Running Doe feels about Golden Lady," Proud Eagle interjected. "Do you fault me for thinking she might try to harm her again?"

"No, I do not fault you," Bear Watcher said.

His tone was abrupt. "We waste time with this talk." He strapped two daggers to his waist belt and gathered his bow and arrows, slinging the quiver across his shoulders. "The midwife said she last saw my wife by the river. Let us begin our search there."

****

Amanda groaned and moved to touch her head. But her hands and feet were restrained. She lifted her head, the bruise on her temple throbbing, and gazed through blurred vision at her extremities— bound to pegs driven in the dirt, legs spread wide, no doubt for the Chiricahua's pleasure. With a shiver, she recollected the painful degradation and prolonged torture they inflicted on women before ending their life. How long would it be before her golden curls hung from a belt?

She laid her head back down with a thud and winced. How could she have been so foolish to believe Running Doe when she said Duke was injured? And why didn't she just wait for Proud Eagle to return and ask him herself how he had come by her father's knife?

The truth will slice my heart. I assume the worst, and fear what his answer will be.

Tears fell from her eyes and slid into her ears. It didn't matter now how he got the knife, she'd never see him again, or watch their son grow. Her mind burned with the memory of every touch, every word, and every glance passed between them. She recalled the ecstasy of being held against his hard body, the smoldering passion, the burning imprint his kisses left upon her lips. Her thoughts flickered back to the day she met Proud Eagle, how she spared his life, the times he saved hers.

It is too late to save me now.

All she had were the memories. They would be her life preserver during whatever loomed ahead at the hands of the Chricahuas. And while she breathed her last, it would be his image she'd focus on. Her final and silent farewell to the love of her life.

Her bittersweet musings were interrupted by a male voice. "You are mine, golden one."

A Chiricahua stood over her, his small, pig-like eyes surveying her body. Waves of nausea tugged at the back of her throat. She swallowed hard to keep from choking.

The warrior knelt beside her and pulled out a knife, ripping apart the buckskin dress, grazing her skin with the blade.

She squeezed her eyes shut and prayed.

****

Proud Eagle and the holy man, along with Falling Star and Bear Watcher, searched the area by the river to no avail.

The holy man sighed, frustrated. "How could they just disappear without a trace?"

Little Elk came running from the thicket. "Come! Come!"

Proud Eagle took the young brave by the shoulders. "Where do you wish us to go?"

Little Elk spoke out of breath. "I know of a path from the river to Running Doe's wickiup. It is not used much because of an outcropping of rocks, but it is a place where Running Doe likes to hide." Little Elk bit his bottom lip. "If we find her, we might find Golden Lady as well."

Together the men followed Little Elk to the big rocks.

The holy man stumbled entering the grove. "I've tripped over something." He knelt and probed the darkness with his hands. "It's a body—a woman's body."

Proud Eagle came beside him, his voice shaken with emotion. "Is it Golden Lady?"

"I don't know. It's too dark to tell. Help me get her into the clearing, where we'll be able to see more."

He helped the holy man move the body, and the moon's ray cast a silver streak of light across the woman's black hair.

They sighed, relieved.

Proud Eagle knelt and pulled the arrow from Running Doe's back, felt the feathers and brought the tip to his nose. "It belongs to Chiricahua, I remember the smell of the poison."

Bear Watcher stood silent, looking down at his daughter.

He rose to his feet. "I am sorry, my friend."

Bear Watcher gave a taut nod, his eyes dismayed. "Little Elk, help me get her home."

Little Elk wiped a tear from his eye and lifted Running Doe's arm. "She has something in her hand." He pried apart the clasped fingers, freeing the object. "Look what I found." Little Elk dangled the gold bands from Golden Lady's chain.

Proud Eagle's eyes locked with the holy man's, and a silent moment of understanding flashed between them. His heart raced with dread and anguish.

"The Chiricahua have Amanda," the holy man whispered.

Proud Eagle ripped the chain from Little Elk's hand and put it in his waist pouch. He squared his shoulders and gazed northward. "I think I know where we will find the Chiricahua's *go-tah*, camp."

"How many do you think there are?" Falling Star asked.

He narrowed his eyes. "Not less than three, not more than six." He slapped Falling Star on the shoulder. "We can do this, my brother. The eagle, once he sets his sights on his prey, will die rather than let it go."

"But if there are six, should we not wait for first morning light and bring with us more warriors to attack?"

"No, it will be too late then to save my wife. And by dawn the warriors might come to attack our village. Now is better, the Chiricahua will not be expecting us," he said.

Falling Star gave a taut nod. "Then I will get my weapons."

"Meet me by the *chelees*." With quick strides, he made his way to Blazing Fire.

The holy man followed. "I'm coming with you."

He raised a hand to stop the holy man. "No, you stay here and wait."

"Like hell I will."

"Have you ever taken a life, holy man?"

The white man took a deep breath. "Nay, the Christian commandments of my faith state *thy shalt not kill*."

He moved closer, his pulse throbbing in his

head. "Do you know what the Chiricahua will do to her?"

The holy man swallowed hard. "Aye, I know."

His voice carried the force of his own fear. "After they have their way with her, they will peel back the pink flesh of her breasts and shove knives up into her, tearing apart her insides. Then"—his voice cracked with emotion—"they will disembowel her." He grabbed the other man by the lapel of his jacket, crumpling the material in his fist. "I have seen the hacked remains of women they have tortured. If you do not stand with me, if you are unable to *zas'tee,* kill that will be how my wife's life will end."

The holy man spoke through gritted teeth. "I will do whatever it takes to save her."

He pulled a dagger from his belt and slapped it into the white man's hand. "Can you slit a man's throat while he sleeps? Sneak up behind him and plunge a knife into his back?"

The holy man looked down at the knife, then back at Proud Eagle. "Aye, for her, I can. I will."

He gave a taut nod. "Then come, we have wasted enough time."

****

They left their horses tied two hundred feet away from the Chiricahua's campfire, and moved through the shadows. Proud Eagle pushed aside the brush and spotted his wife, tied to stakes, naked and ready for their evil torture. He bit the inside of his mouth to still his rage. If he lost control of the situation, it could mean all of their lives. He offered up a silent prayer to the gods, even to her god. *Guide me to victory.*

Dragging his gaze from her, he counted the warriors. There were five.

He whispered to Falling Star. "They are sleeping scattered."

"This is good," Falling Star responded. "We can

slit the throats of the sleeping ones first."

He nodded in agreement. "Then there will be only two left, the one sitting by the fire and the one kneeling beside my wife." He pointed to his left. "You take the Chiricahua closer to the fire." He turned to the holy man. "You go for the one in the middle, and I will take the one on the end. Then, we meet back here."

Proud Eagle led the way, crouching and stalking his prey like a wild beast. Josh followed, his own silent steps taking him closer to the warrior he'd slay. He watched Proud Eagle and Falling Star. With one quick slash of their knife they slit the throats of the enemy.

On shaking legs, Josh darted to the third one, his knuckles white, gripping the dagger with a sweaty hand. His heart pounded in his ears as he raised the knife and prayed for forgiveness for what he was about to do. Then he slashed the Chiricahua's gullet. Blood poured from the wound, staining his hand. His throat tightened, his stomach churned. He snuck back to the safety of the trees and retched.

Proud Eagle came beside him, placing a sympathetic hand on his shoulder. "I did the same after the first killing. It was to save a friend, as you are doing now," he consoled. "Keep that first in your thoughts."

He nodded. "What happens now?"

Proud Eagle's lips thinned. "Two still remain. The one by the fire can be taken easily. He has his back to us, one shot with an arrow through him, and he will be no more of a problem." He frowned, glancing at the second warrior. "But the other—the one by Golden Lady troubles me. He will see his friend fall and know there is danger. I fear he will drive his knife through her *biijii,* heart before I can reach him."

"What if I circle around and get behind him." He pushed aside his jacket lapel to reveal the pistol he had hidden in a shoulder holster. "I took the gun from my saddlebag. As you shoot the arrow, I will pull the trigger."

Proud Eagle shook his head. "It would make too much noise."

"But he is the last man, what's the difference?" he said.

"There could be more of them," Proud Eagle explained.

"There are always more hiding somewhere. The Chiricahua are cunning," Falling Star added.

"A sound from a *petiltow* is like asking them all to join us," Proud Eagle said. "But part of your plan was a wise one, holy man." He turned to Falling Star. "You circle around behind the warrior near Golden Lady. Give me the call of the coyote when you are ready to shoot, and I will do the same." Proud Eagle turned his attention back to him. "You go with Falling Star. When the Chiricahua beside her falls, you cut her loose. Take her to your *chelee* and ride to the village. Do not look back no matter what you hear. If there are more Chiricahua hiding, I want Golden Lady away from the danger."

He nodded again, wiping his bloody hand down the side of his breeches. He followed Falling Star to the opposite area of the camp, watching the Indian ready his bow and arrow. He aimed, made a coyote sound and fired, slaying the Chiricahua beside Amanda.

Across the way the other Chiricahua fell.

He ran to Amanda, cutting the binds around her ankle, and then freed her hands.

She opened her eyes, shocked to see him. "Josh?"

From the brush came two more Chiricahua warriors. Falling Star took aim, wounding one warrior, but not enough to stop him from charging forward with a dagger, burying it into Falling Star's shoulder.

Falling Star dropped to his knees, but was able to reach for the knife hanging from his belt and with whatever remaining strength he possessed, sprang up and drove the blade through the Chiricahua's stomach.

The second Chiricahua let out a scream that curdled Josh's blood and lunged at Proud Eagle, engaging him in hand to hand combat.

"Amanda, we've got to move now," he advised, helping her to sit. He removed his jacket, guided each of her arms into a sleeve and wrapped it around her. "Do you think you can walk?"

Amanda took the hand he offered and stood. "My legs are so weak, I don't know if I can." The words caught in her throat when she saw Proud Eagle fighting the Chiricahua. She squared her shoulders, drawing strength from the love they shared.

Josh took her by the arm. "We've got to go, Amanda."

She pulled away from him. "I can't just leave him. He might need help."

"He can handle that one," Josh said.

"I won't leave without Proud Eagle," she said, watching every move the two men made.

She listened to what surrounded her. Like a deer sensing a presence, she cocked her head sideways. "There's someone coming."

Josh reached for her arm again. "I hate to do this, Amanda, but—"

"Shh," she snapped, pulling away again and listening harder.

Her nostrils flared with the smell of danger, her eyes searched the night until she spotted him, another Chiricahua creeping from the brush about sixty feet from Proud Eagle.

The campfire cast a dim light across the

warrior's face. He snuck closer, his eyes boring into Proud Eagle's back, his hand gripping a spear.

Amanda rushed to where Falling Star lay, grabbed his bow and an arrow, and aimed it at the Chiricahua.

Just as the warrior raised his arm to throw the spear, she pulled back on the string.

She held the weapon steady, releasing the arrow with ease. It flew the distance and hit the Chiricahua through the chest. He fell to the ground.

She glanced over at her husband in time to see he had his opponent on the ground, driving a knife through the enemy's heart. He stood, chest heaving, then turned to look at her. Realizing she held a bow in her hand, Proud Eagle whirled around to see the dead man behind him. He faced her and smiled. "You were right, *shi'aad*. Teaching you to shoot was a wise thing to do."

She dropped the bow and fell to her knees.

Proud Eagle reached her in a few quick strides.

"She's fainting." Josh's muffled voice made her shake her head to clear it.

Proud Eagle gathered her into his arms.

Falling Star struggled to stand.

Josh rushed to Falling Star's aid and helped him to his feet.

Proud Eagle addressed his friend with genuine concern. "Are you able to walk, my brother?"

Falling Star gave a taut nod, draping an arm over Josh's shoulder. "You lead, we will follow."

"Come then...it is time to go home." Proud Eagle adjusted his hold on her. She buried her face in his neck and drew comfort from his strength and love.

Chapter Seventeen

When they arrived at the village, the holy man helped Falling Star to his wickiup. Proud Eagle brought Golden Lady to theirs, placing her upon the bed. He removed the holy man's jacket and wet a cloth from a bowl of clean water, washing her face.

She opened her eyes. "Where is our son?"

"He is with Rising Sun. He is safe." He forced an encouraging smile, holding raw emotion in check for her sake. Inside, his stomach twisted with anxiety. Silently he washed the knife gashes and dried blood from her bruised body. How had they touched her, hurt her?

In spite of her outward reserve her voice shook with uncertainty. "And Falling Star, he is all right?"

That is always her way, to be concerned for everyone else.

"He will be fine," he assured her, studying her face. Fear and torment were carved upon each delicate feature. "Your wounds are not deep; they will not leave much of a scar."

A mix of shame and terror filled her eyes. "The biggest scar will forever be etched in my mind."

His tone was gentle, though every part of him screamed with the rage coursing through his veins for what she suffered. If Running Doe were still alive, he would kill her. "That only time can wash away and heal." He wet a clean cloth and washed the blood from between her thighs, his voice solemn. "In what way did they touch you?"

"With their eyes, their knives." Her eyes welled with tears. "And with their dirty hands."

He continued to wash her, the muscles at his jaw throbbing, his heart aching for her humiliation. His voice cracked with emotion. "There is much blood between your legs. Did they..." the words stuck in his throat. *Can I even bear to know if her womanhood has been plundered?*

She swallowed with difficulty before finding her voice, and then the words trembled from her lips. "No, you came in time, my *shikaa*. The blood still comes from giving birth."

He felt the muscles in his face relax, thankful she had not been shamed.

She choked out the next words, her face an unbearable mask of sorrow. "They killed Running Doe. They just shot her where she stood."

"We have found her."

"Without as much as a bat of an eye her life was snuffed out. I watched it all, unable to do a thing. Not one..."

"There was nothing you could do." When he interrupted her, his own voice wavered.

"Poor Bear Watcher. She was his only child. I cannot fathom the thought of losing a child." Tears fell from her eyes, trickling down her face like a waterfall. "Maybe you should help with the burial."

He dried her body. "The woman was evil. I will have no part in wishing her spirit to *O'zho*."

She reached for his hand, bringing it to rest upon her heart. "She only hated me because she loved you."

He caressed the soft flesh of a bared breast. "*Shi'aad*, when you truly love someone, you want their happiness." He moved his hand to cup her chin. "Like the holy man. It was for you he helped free me from the white lawman. For you, he took the chance. Your happiness means everything to him." He pushed a wayward tendril from her forehead. "Running Doe placed no value on my feelings. If she truly loved me, she would not have been so quick to take from me the one thing I lived for—your love."

"Bear Watcher has been your father's friend for many years, and when you were away he stood in as chief for you. Surely, my *shikaa*, you can swallow your own feelings for his sake."

"For his sake, I will try," he agreed, seeing she was becoming too upset. "The holy man and the young holy man are with Bear Watcher now. They will stay with him tonight, I am not needed. My place is here, caring for you."

"You mean Benjamin? Reverend Newcomb?"

He shrugged. "He talks stranger than the holy man."

She nodded. "Yes, that's my Aunt Kaylena's friend from Sweden." She frowned. "I wonder why he's still here."

He shrugged again. "He came with the holy man for the Baptism." He covered her with the quilt and kissed her lips. "I will go for our son now; he needs to be with his mother."

****

Amanda held her child close to her heart, his tiny mouth working to drain her swollen breasts. She glanced deep into her husband's eyes. He gazed in awe at their beautiful son taking nourishment. She tightened her grip on the baby. "This little boy seems much heavier tonight. I can't support his weight."

Proud Eagle caressed her cheek with the back of his hand. "You have been through much today." His eyes were compassionate searching her face. "If only I could feed him."

She giggled. "There isn't much hope in that."

He looked down at his flat breasts and joined her mirth. Then his face brightened. "But I might know of another way I can help." He slid behind her and straddled her with his long legs. "Lean back."

She reclined, relaxing her head and shoulders against his muscular chest.

Proud Eagle wrapped his strong arms around her, supporting the baby. "I cannot feed him, but I can hold him while he feeds from you."

She released her grasp, arms dropping to her sides.

Golden Eagle suckled until he was satisfied, and then fell into a baby's sleep.

Proud Eagle took the infant from her and placed him in the cradleboard. When he returned to the bed, he drew her close. "Why were you at the river crying, *shi'aad*?"

Her whole body was engulfed in tides of weariness and despair. "I was stacking wood by the fire pit and knocked over your quiver bag. All the arrows spilled out. When I replaced them, they didn't fit. Something at the bottom of the bag prevented them from standing in a row. So, I turned the bag upside down and out fell the pocket knife."

He pulled back, staring at her baffled. "And this would make you run crying to the river?"

"Yes, don't you see?" she choked out.

"No, *shi'aad*, I do not see." he countered. He rose from the bed and went to his waist pouch, pulling from it the small blade. He sat at the edge of the bed and handed it to her. "I do not understand the worry over that knife. The holy man questioned me about it as well. He wanted to know how I got it."

She bit her lip to steal herself. "And what was your answer?"

"I never had the chance to tell him. Falling Star and Bear Watcher came to the wickiup at that time to help look for you." He gave her a curious glance. "I have a question for you now. Why did you go with Running Doe?"

"She told me Duke was wounded. I followed her to where she said he was lying. But instead of Duke, there was a Chiricahua warrior waiting for me. She had allowed him into the village and made a deal to hand me over if they didn't attack."

Proud Eagle's eyebrows rose in amazement. "After the last trick she played on you, how could you believe her word?"

She sat up in bed and looped a strand of hair behind her ear. "I wasn't thinking clearly. I had just found the knife."

He threw up his hands exasperated. "Again the knife. What is so important about it?"

She looked at the tiny blade sitting in the palm of her hand. "This knife once belonged to my father. He had it on him the day he was murdered." Tears burned her tired eyes. She raised her gaze to meet his. "When Josh buried him, it was gone."

Raw hurt glittered in his dark eyes. "And you believe I took it from him?"

"At first, the shock of seeing it robbed me of all rationality. So I ran, crying to the river to think. That's when Running Doe arrived with the news about Duke."

Proud Eagle's gaze clung to hers. "And now that you have had time to think?"

She closed her eyes, the tears slipping down her face. "In my heart I know you didn't murder my father."

He reached out and cupped her chin. "What of your mind, *shi'aad*."

She opened her eyes, searching his face. "My mind wants to know how you could have gotten the knife."

There was a long silence.

"I gave you my word before, and it holds true to this night. I did not *zas'tee* your father." He traced her lips with the tip of his finger. "Before I go on to tell how I got the knife, I need to hear you trust me." He whispered. "I must know."

The stillness was deafening.

Her throat ached with grief for her father, seeing still his bludgeoned body. A terrible sense of bitterness rose to choke her, and she swallowed hard her despair. "Yes," she blurted out with a sob. "I trust you."

Proud Eagle pulled her to him.

She wrapped her arms around his neck and wept against his throat.

He kissed the top of her head. "I got the knife from the Chiricahua warrior who injured me while I hunted near your home. After I sent his spirit to *O'zho*, I took it from his body."

She pulled back to look at him. "But I never saw it on you when I cared for you."

He stood and reached for his spear, twisting off the blade from the pole. He turned the pole so she could see the hollowed out area near the tip. "I placed it in here so I would not lose it." He replaced the blade and set the spear aside. "I had never seen such a knife, and I wanted to keep it safe."

She sprang from the bed and hugged him. "My *shikaa*, you've avenged my father's death."

"It looks that way," he said.

She pulled back to search his face. "I'm sorry, Proud Eagle, for having the slightest doubts. Can you ever forgive me?"

His dark eyes flashed with his desire for her, his hands roaming down to settle on the naked roundness of her hips. "There is nothing to forgive, *shi'aad*. You acted out of love for your father. It is that fierce loyalty and undying respect for family that makes me love you the most."

She rested her head on his shoulder. "I think we should wait another day for the Baptism. I'd like to have the chance to explain to Josh about the knife, and give Bear Watcher time to bury Running Doe. Falling Star could also use more time to heal."

"You are wise, *shi'aad*," he said. "I will take care of it all in the morning. Which will come too soon if we do not get some rest."

She placed her father's knife into his hand. "I'm glad you have it now. Since Papa had no sons, I'm sure he would have given it to my husband."

Proud Eagle nodded. "I will cherish it always, and pass it on to our son."

She yawned and got into bed.

Proud Eagle replaced the knife into the pouch and checked on the baby before joining her. He pulled her close and kissed the top of her head. "Sleep well, *shi'aad*."

She snuggled into his arms and whispered against his throat. "I love you, Proud Eagle."

"And I love you, beyond my own life," she heard him add as she drifted off to sleep.

****

Amanda couldn't think of two people she trusted more then Rising Sun and Falling Star to guide her son down the right path, should anything happen to her and Proud Eagle.

The proud godparents stood beside her and Proud Eagle. Josh knelt at the riverbank with the baby in his arms. They all watched Josh bless the child with water, christening him Gabriel Golden Eagle.

Later in the day the women of the tribe brought out food, setting it before the chief with respect. She smiled to herself watching Proud Eagle eat, cradling in one arm his tiny son.

Mid-way through the meal he leaned toward White Dove and whispered something in her ear. She wondered why her mother-in-law's plump, pleasant face broke into a smile, like a schoolgirl with a secret.

White Dove stood and made her way to her. "My daughter, I wish to speak with you alone. Come with me to my wickiup."

She obeyed, dismayed when she discovered her mother's wedding dress laid out on White Dove's bed. "Why is my mother's dress here?"

"Proud Eagle wishes for you to wear it." White Dove went over to the dress and fingered the delicate lace. "It is so beautiful."

"I don't understand why he'd want me to wear it?"

White Dove handed the dress to her. "When a woman has found the right man, one who is good and honest, there is no need to question his wishes. He has asked to see you in the dress that belonged to your mother." She shrugged. "If it pleases him how can it be wrong?"

She squeezed her mother-in-law's hand. "You're a good and wise woman." She sighed. "Will I ever have such wisdom?"

White Dove helped her slip off the buckskin dress. "You will get a turn to look wise, and one day your sons and daughters will say the same about you."

She put her arms through the dress's fragile sleeves. "I hope I'll have the right words for them."

"You will," White Dove said with confidence. She handed Amanda a pair of delicate, white buckskin slippers. "I made these many years ago for my own mating ceremony." She looked at the moccasins already on Amanda's feet. "Those do not seem to fit the dress."

She slipped off her everyday footwear and glided her feet into the new pair. "They're so soft and light." She bestowed a kiss upon White Dove's cheek. "Thank you so much. Today I have something to wear from both my mothers."

White Dove arranged her curls around her shoulders, placing a halo of wildflowers upon her head, then stood back to admire her handiwork. "So this is what the white women wear for the mating ceremony."

She nodded, and smoothed the skirt's full material.

White Dove smiled with approval. "I like your tradition."

Rising Sun rushed through the door opening, face flushed with excitement. She took a quick breath when she saw her. "Oh, Golden Lady, you are so beautiful." She handed her a rose, thorns removed.

Amanda smiled. "Is this for me to give Proud Eagle again?"

"No, my sister, this one he has sent to you." Rising Sun held out her hand. "Come, he wishes for you to join him now."

Eager to learn what surprise her husband planned, she followed Rising Sun down the path and behind the trees to one of the village's tiny sacred alters.

Josh stood behind the stone structure, dressed in his black minister's garb, holding a Bible. On the right of him stood Benjamin, also dressed in traditional black, and on the left stood Falling Star

When she spotted Proud Eagle, her breath caught. He looked so handsome and regal standing in front of the altar, wearing a tunic, breeches and moccasins of white buckskin. Upon his head sat the Chief's headdress, feathers cascading down his back.

She held the rose close to her heart, walking toward him while a warrior played a melody on the singing wood.

Proud Eagle reached out and took her hand, leaning to whisper in her ear. "In my thoughts I have seen the angels from the holy book looking as you do now."

Josh cleared his throat and read from his book. "We are gathered here today, in the eyes of God, to join together this man and this woman in the bonds of holy matrimony."

Her eyes grew misty when Proud Eagle recited the marriage vows. Her own voice shook when it was time to declare her love and devotion to him.

"The rings, please," Josh said, turning to Falling Star.

To her amazement, Falling Star handed Josh her parent's rings. After Running Doe had ripped the chain from her neck, she thought the rings were lost forever.

Proud Eagle placed her mother's ring on her finger, then extended his hand so she could place her father's ring on his.

He brought her hand to his heart, and while looking deep into her eyes, he recited his own prayer.

The rich baritone of his voice was warm and mellow. "O' Great Spirit, I cannot see the wind, but I know it is there, as I know you are *bigha,* because of faith. And I have faith you can hear me. You give breath to all things that roam the *terte,* earth, and I am grateful for all you have given to me. I *ashoge,* thank you, for the eyes I use to see *shi'aad's* face. I *ashoge* for the hands I use to touch her flesh. And I *ashoge* for the *biijii* that will love her forever."

The meaning of his words made her eyes blur with tears of joy.

Proud Eagle's prayer and soft gaze reached straight to her heart. "I come humbly to you now, Lord Jesus, asking for your strength and wisdom." He squeezed her hand, his voice trembling. "Let me learn the lessons You have hidden in every leaf and rock and pass them to my children." His eyes grew misty with the conclusion. "If one is true to God, he cannot be false to others. Make me always ready to come to You with clean hands, a true tongue, and straight eyes, so when I take my last breath, my spirit may come to You without shame."

"Amen," she whispered.

Josh choked out the remaining words of the ceremony. "What God has joined together, let no man put asunder. And so, by the power invested in me, I now pronounce you man and wife." He turned to Proud Eagle and arched a brow. "You may kiss the bride, Chief."

Proud Eagle pulled her to him and moved his mouth over hers.

Her body arched toward him.

He lifted her off her feet, let out a triumphant yelp, and swung her in a circle. "We are married in tribal law and white man's law. You can never leave me now, *shi'aad*."

Her heart sang with delight, her voice tinged with laughter. "No. Never."

He gathered her up into his strong arms and carried her to their wickiup, placing her upon the bed. He knelt down in front of her. "Do you think you are healed from giving birth?"

She smiled. "I think I've healed all I'm going to."

He removed his headdress and shirt, then took the flowers from her hair and placed them aside.

She stood, slipped off the dress and shoes, and reclined on the bed. With open admiration, she watched him shed his breeches. His gaze sent a thrill of arousal through her body and she opened her arms to him.

His body covered hers and together they soared in the pleasures of their love.

Chapter Eighteen

Amanda inhaled the morning air and glanced up at the soft, rosy pink sky, clouds delicate puffs of white. "You've got a nice day to ride."

"Aye, looks that way," Josh agreed, helping Benjamin saddle the horses, their few belongings packed and ready to go. He turned to Proud Eagle, a teasing smile curving his mouth. "May I borrow your wife for one last farewell?"

Proud Eagle nodded, making his way over to help Benjamin secure his satchel.

Josh took her by the arm and walked with her to the river.

"What do you mean, one last farewell," she teased, plopping down on a nearby rock. "We'll see each other soon."

"Not unless you plan to come to England."

She sprang to her feet. "You're going to England?"

"Aye."

She took a quick, sharp breath "But why?"

He motioned for her to reclaim her seat upon the rock, and then sat beside her. "When I returned to the parsonage after our Fort Bayard adventure, your aunt asked if she could stay on a few weeks. I agreed, and we spent many nights talking about England."

"Did she make you homesick?"

"Aye, in a way," he admitted, standing and leaning against a tree. "I haven't seen my sister, Marietta in years. And it would be nice to finally meet my nephew, Simon." He smiled. "I believe I mentioned them to you before."

She nodded, swallowing the lump growing in her throat. "When will you be back?"

"I won't be, Amanda. The chaplain at Kaylena's church has decided to retire, and she offered me the position. The only reason I've waited this long was to see your baby born. I wanted to be sure everything went well."

"Is that why Benjamin Newcomb stayed on, so you could get him ready to take over for you?"

"Aye, and he is ready now…eager to be a good minister." He smiled. "Benjamin has become quite taken with Grace's niece, Sylvie, so this has helped the cause. But all in all, I think he'll step in for me just fine, so have no fear. Reverend Newcomb has promised me he'll look in on you and Proud Eagle from time to time."

She stood and made her way to him. "Then, Kaylena waits for you?"

"I won't see her until after the first of the year. When Kaylena left America last March, she planned to visit friends living in France. She said she needed to get away from everything for a while. And this suits me fine. I'll be able to spend the coming holidays with my family in London before taking on my duties in Brighton."

"It won't be the same without you. You've been in my life since I was a little girl."

He chuckled. "Aye, and a scrawny little thing you were, with pigtails and scabby knees. But you have bloomed into a beautiful woman, a wife, and mother. Your husband will look out for you now."

"Can you really say goodbye to Willow Creek… to me?"

He pushed aside a curl from her forehead. "Before you and Proud Eagle were married by our law, I still hoped…entertained the thought one day you would come to me." He looked deep into her eyes. "I've fallen in love with you, Amanda, and I don't believe that's ever going to change. But now, you are married through and through, by your husband's laws and by ours. For me to continue coveting another man's wife is a sin."

"Josh, I..."

"Nay, don't say a word." He placed the tip of a finger over her mouth. "It's not necessary any longer. You're Proud Eagle's wife, and if I'm to respect that, I must leave, remove myself from the equation so both of us can get on with our lives." He lifted her chin. "I never did get to kiss the bride." He brushed his lips against hers. "Farewell my love."

She watched him walk up the path to his horse. His broad shoulders filling out the black coat, the wide brimmed hat atop his head completed the proper Englishman's look. He had done so much for her, risked all he had to make her happy. She couldn't allow him to just walk away without letting him know she didn't want this to be the last time she'd set eyes upon his face.

"Joshua... wait," she called after him.

He turned to look at her, his blue eyes melting the distance between them.

She bit her bottom lip, searching for the right words but all that came out was, "Have a safe journey."

He tipped his hat. "God bless, Amanda."

Tears filled her eyes. "God bless you, too." That wasn't enough, she needed to say more. Her throat closed, the tears slipping down her face. Then the right words came to her. "And may we live to meet again."

****

Proud Eagle sat on the bank of the river, his back resting against a tree. Amanda snuggled in his arms, looking out at the water. The night was quiet and peaceful, with old Duke lying at her feet and her son sleeping beside her in the cradleboard.

She gazed up at the stars, her mind revisiting the scenes of the past year. Incredible events had taken place, and if she hadn't lived them, she would have never believed they happened.

She looked up at her Apache husband, his strong, handsome profile outlined against the night sky.

He turned and smiled down at her. "I love you, my Golden Lady."

Before she could respond, the eagle's call echoed through the heavens.

She caught sight of the majestic bird, soaring to the moon.

Thank you, my friend, for a new beginning.

Proud Eagle cupped her chin and lowered his head, enveloping her mouth with his.

She wrapped her arms around his neck, the passion rousing deep inside of her, confident they would overcome the heartbreaks and trials of their turbulent times. Once again she became lost in the ecstasy of his kiss. She knew now nothing, not even war, can break the vow of eternal love.

Epilogue

Josh gazed out at the distant shore. The ship had sailed far enough from land to see above the trees. Overhead the gulls screeched; below the waves crashed against the side of the large vessel, shattering it with white foam. He walked to the opposite end of the deck and looked out at the vast expanse of water, appearing to meet the sky.

What will lie beyond those waters for me?

He laughed to himself. How would his new congregation react if they learned they trusted their pulpit to someone who was in love with another man's wife, impersonated a Cavalry officer, and even murdered a man while he slept?

He inhaled the salty air and squared his shoulders. It had taken more courage and strength to walk away from Amanda then it did for anything he endured, or would undergo in the future.

He continued to worry for her safety, with the white man and Indian conflict still raging. But Amanda would never leave with him, and he could no longer stay with her, watching from the sidelines while she loved another man.

Nay, it is time to move on, in spite of the fact I will never forget you and will always love you. Just thinking of you has brought a smile to my face.

He recalled her last words to him. "May we live to meet again."

"God willing, Golden Lady," he whispered. "God willing."

A word about the author...

Roberta C. M. DeCaprio has been writing for over twenty-five years, winning awards for her poetry. She is a member of Romance Writers of America, holding the position of Newsletter Editor of her local group from 2002 to 2004.

She is a former Assistant Editor for *Independence Today* newspaper (a national publication dedicated to the needs and rights of the disabled). Having a walking impairment since birth, Roberta knows first hand the challenges of living with a disability.

Roberta is a mother and grandmother of two who shares her upstate New York home with her artist husband and many beloved pets.

She has authored three books to date: *Coma Coast*, a paranormal romantic suspense, and its sequel *The Vanity*, a paranormal romantic thriller, both published by Wings Press. *A River of Orange*, a historical romantic fantasy published by The Wild Rose Press.

You can visit her site at:
www.robertadecaprio.com

Thank you for purchasing
this Wild Rose Press publication.
For other wonderful stories of romance,
please visit
our on-line bookstore at
www.thewildrosepress.com

For questions or more information
contact us at
info@thewildrosepress.com

The Wild Rose Press
www.TheWildRosePress.com

Other Cactus Rose titles to enjoy:

OUTLAW IN PETTICOATS
by Paty Jager

Maeve Loman has had her heart crushed before; she isn't about to have it happen again. Zeke Halsey has wanted Maeve Loman since he first set eyes on the prickly schoolteacher. Offering to help her find her father, he hopes to prove he's not going anywhere. Neither one knows the extent to which they will stoop to get the answers they crave.

SECRETS IN THE SHADOWS
by Sheridon Smythe

The lovely widow Lacy had taken in two young children—and the rambunctious little angels wasted no time getting her into trouble with Shadow City's new sheriff...

STANDOFF AT THE WATERIN' HORSE SALOON
(Rosette) by Stacy Dawn

Bridget Schneider has a few things to say to the cowboy who stole her heart over a year ago and never came back—but she's not about to let her anger be hog-tied by sudden...distractions. Jonas might've stolen her heart, but she's sure as shootin' gonna get her pride back.

A LAW OF HER OWN
(Miniature Rose) by Linda LaRoque

When Charity Dawson resigns her father's corporate law firm to pursue a career as a trial lawyer, she gets more of a change than she wanted. She finds herself transported to 1888 Texas in the middle of a murder trial.